FIERCE *Storm*

FIERCE STORM

Cover image by J. Ashley Converse Photography / Cover model - Christopher David

Cover design by © Books and Moods

Editing by Happily Editing Anns

Contents

Author's Note

This book contains subject matter that some people may find triggering. A list of the main potential triggers can be found on Katherine's website:

http://www.katherinejayauthor.com

Please note, triggers are not listed here to avoid spoilers for the book.

STORM PRODUCTIONS PRESENTS

FIERCE STORM'S SOUNDTRACK

Storm - Ruelle
Run - OneRepublic
Bones - Imagine Dragons
I'm Good (Blue) - David Guetta, Bebe Rexha
Never Til Now - Ashley Cooke
Need You Tonight- INXS
Summer Of '69 - Bryan Adams
I Want You - Savage Garden
End Game - Taylor Swift, Ed Sheeran, Future
Daylight - Taylor Swift
Love Me Like You Do - Ellie Goulding
I Get To Love You - Ruelle
One Call Away - Charlie Puth
Baker Street - Gerry Rafferty
Toxic - Britney Spears

AVAILABLE NOW ON SPOTIFY

Special Note

While Fierce Storm *can* be read as a standalone, it takes place after the events of book four, Careless Storm, and contains spoilers for that book.

If you haven't read Zane and Blair's story, and don't like spoilers, then I recommend you begin with Careless Storm, as the beginning of this book focuses on parts of Zane's story.

If you're okay with spoilers, please proceed.

Careless Storm, and the rest of the San Francisco End Game books are available now on eBook and paperback.

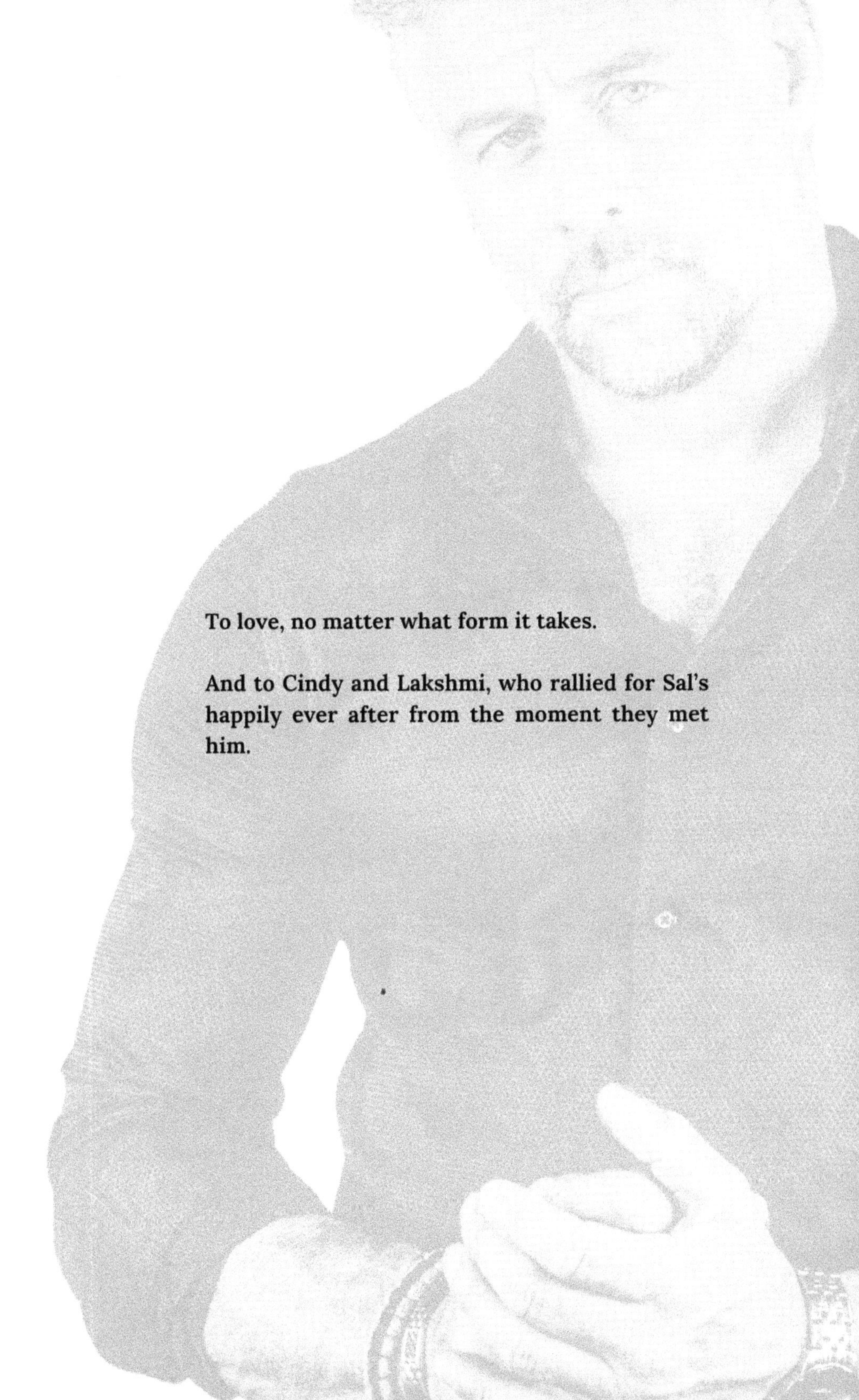

To love, no matter what form it takes.

And to Cindy and Lakshmi, who rallied for Sal's happily ever after from the moment they met him.

Prologue

SALVATORE

D*'Angelo. D'Angelo. Where is fucking D'Angelo?*

I can't remember another time when I heard my surname said so much. Even as a CEO. Dad, yes. Salvatore, yes. Even Sal. But Mr. D'Angelo and *sir*? I'm not my fucking father. Sure, I have a dusting of salt in my previously pepper hair, but that doesn't warrant the grandeur. Most of the *salt* came from the stress surrounding my divorce. I'm only fifty and I've been graying for years.

Why does it feel like my new role as team owner for the San Francisco Storm is going to speed up the process?

My mind runs rampant with the million things I have to get done, and I internally groan.

Book a meeting with the coaching staff.

Organize dinner with the board.

Meet the players.

Check in on Paige.

Paige.

Fuck. I can't let work take over again. I only just got her back. She left her mother and moved here to be with me. It's a big deal.

It's all a big deal. *Everything*. Not one thing on my goddamn mind is small and God, my head hurts.

I hold my breath as I stride through the halls of Lightning Stadium, breathing a sigh of relief when I make it to my office without anyone stopping me. The door clicks shut behind me, and I jolt. Even that's too loud for the hammering pain pulsing through my head.

What am I doing?

"Fuck. Fuuck!" I toss my phone across the room, but it lands softly on the couch, giving me no satisfaction. I wanted to see it shatter. Better the phone than my confident composure, because God knows, that's wavering.

After kicking off my shoes, I lie back on the couch like it's a psychiatrist's office and cover my face with my hands.

Five minutes. That's all I need. Five minutes, and I'll be Mr. D'Angelo again. San Francisco Storm's team owner. Business titan. New York billionaire. I just need a moment to be Sal. Father. Son. The man that built his empire from the ground up while still remembering where he came from.

I only manage a few deep breaths before knuckles softly rap against my door. *And there goes that.* With a huff under my breath, I stretch my toes and reluctantly sit up, pulling on my shoes before standing. *I've been found.*

"Yes?" I call out, keeping my tone as even as possible.

"Sorry to interrupt," Tabitha, my new assistant, speaks quietly through the closed door, and it's nearly impossible to hear her. "Keeley's needed for a media call."

Did she say Keeley? "What?"

"Keeley's—"

"You can come in, Tabitha. I'm not naked in here."

The door opens and my assistant pops her head in, her messy brown hair escaping from her ponytail, as though she's been frantically rushing around, her flushed cheeks suggesting the same. She smiles shyly and fuck my life. This isn't going to work if she feels the need to tiptoe around me all the time. "Thank you. What were you saying?"

"Oh. Ah..." She frowns, her eyes darting around the room. "I thought Keeley was in here."

"Who's Keeley?" I tilt my head to the side, lips pursed as I follow her gaze. Other than me, my office is empty.

I was advised to bring my own assistant, but no, I left her in New York to keep an eye on my new general manager, while I gallivanted to the other side of America to follow a childhood dream. *Just because one has enough money to buy a football franchise doesn't mean they should.*

Tabitha rubs her forehead in confusion, which in turn confuses me. "Keeley's our media liaison. You haven't met her?"

"Tabitha, I've met a hell of a lot of people today, but I'm ninety-nine percent sure I would remember that name."

"Okay. Well, she's great. You'll love her. Now I have to try and track her down because I said she was here. Do you need anything before I do that?"

"Why would you— Never mind. No. I'm good. Thank you."

"Good." Tabitha turns to leave, and my pounding head makes me stop her. "Actually, can I have fifteen minutes to myself? Uninterrupted."

"Yes, of course. I'm sorry." Tabitha's pink cheeks darken, and I internally curse myself.

"You don't have to be sorry, Tabitha. You're doing your job."

"Thank you, sir."

"Please don't call me sir."

"Okay, sir."

For fuck's sake. I force a smile and wave her away before I fall back onto the couch, my fingers immediately moving to rub my throbbing temples. This is a goddamn shit show. Financial issues, management power struggles, a fucking TV show. It's a mess. And I'm the idiot who volunteered to pick up the pieces. Actually, I didn't volunteer; I paid a shit ton of money to do it. All because of a fucking dream.

"Fuuck." This day needs to end and it's only eleven thirty.

"Can I help?"

"Jesus Christ." I stiffen at the honeyed voice coming from above my head, dropping my hands to reveal a beautiful woman with thick auburn hair cascading down her shoulders. She stares down at me, her expression confident as she pops her hip. *Where the hell did she come from?*

I push up from the couch, preparing to greet her, thankful that I'd left my shoes on this time. As I stand, my gaze sweeps along her fitted navy suit, following the line of her dress pants until it stops at her pointed-toe stiletto heel. The kind that tells me she means business.

Though, the fact that she's standing in my office *unannounced* should have given that away.

When I'm at full height, she straightens, standing taller, but still has to lift her gaze to meet mine, and her striking blue eyes catch my attention.

"Can I help *you?*" I counter, my lips curling into a forced grin. "I'm Salvatore, and you are..."

"Keeley. *Sir.*"

"Keeley?" She winks and my brows raise so fast, I guarantee it looks comical. "Right. So you *were* in my office?" As the question leaves my mouth, it occurs to me that she could have just walked in, until I remember the way she said "sir." *She was here.* But where?

"I was," she confirms, and while her confidence never wavers, the hint of guilt flashes in her eyes.

"I just told my assistant you *weren't*."

"I heard." She cringes adorably before a smile lights up her face, telling me she doesn't actually care about my mistake. "You also asked for fifteen minutes of *uninterrupted* alone time." Her smile widens as she stares at me pointedly, and when I understand her meaning, I actually laugh. My first since I got here. *What a fucking day.*

"How can I help you, Keeley?"

"You're not going to ask why I was hiding?"

"Nope. I've had a pretty surreal morning. What's one more bizarre occurrence? Though I am curious as to *where* you were hiding. In case I need to disappear one day."

Keeley snorts, her gaze falling to my hands, alerting me to the fact that my fists are clenched. "I was under your desk." She gestures toward the grand mahogany structure in the middle of my office, and I chuckle again, flexing my fingers.

"Okay. Good to know." Though I won't be hiding there anytime soon, considering there's a full wall of windows behind that desk. Windows that look directly onto the Storm practice field. If anyone had been on that turf, they would have seen Keeley.

A visual of this beautiful woman on her knees under my desk threatens to further complicate my already complicated day, and I change the subject to push it from my mind.

"Anyway, back to why—"

"Ugh. Fine. I was patiently waiting for you to finish your meeting, and that painting caught my eye." She points to the original work I had commissioned during the build of my first luxury apartment complex, after making it to the big leagues. I still smile when I pass by that building in New York, thankful that it's not the project that ended my marriage. That one came with proud smiles from my now ex-wife.

"I didn't mean to hide," Keeley continues, bringing my mind back to the present, "but when you walked in and tossed your phone against the cushions, yelling 'fuck' several times, I deduced that you might need a minute to yourself. My brother owns the title for the world's grumpiest human, so I can tell when it's better to stay out of the way."

Wow, okay. "Thanks for that." *She's a talker.* "I was actually asking why you wanted to see me."

"Oh." Keeley throws her head back and laughs out loud, the light sound pulling another genuine response from within me. This time a smile. "I wanted to introduce myself. I'm Storm's media liaison. I'm here to help make this as easy and painless as possible. At least when it comes to the public's perception of what's going on."

"Great. Any idea who's here to help with the *players'* perception of what's going on? Or management?" I chuckle so she'll think I'm joking, but if she has an answer, I want to hear it. I couldn't give a fuck about what the media thinks. It's the people within these stadium walls that concern me the most, and it's not looking good.

Keeley smiles sympathetically. "There lies your first problem. No one knows what's happening. There are rumors, of course. That's always going to be the case. But with so many conflicting stories, no one knows what to believe. And you're the man they're expecting to set it all straight. The man we're *all* expecting to set it straight."

She stares at me in question and I wince.

"Fuck." Spinning away from her, I run my hand through my hair and inhale slowly. I prepared for this. I knew it wasn't going to be easy. "It—"

"Sucks to be you?"

A throaty chuckle rumbles out of me as I turn back around, and Keeley shrugs, a mischievous grin lighting up her face. That's exactly what I've been thinking, and yet, hearing it aloud feels wrong.

My eyeline shifts to the field out my window, and a moment of calm washes over me. I chose this. I'm here because I want to be here and I've never shied away from a challenge.

Closing my eyes, I let the moment consume me, vowing to fight my battles head-on from here on out. I'm Salvatore *Fucking* D'Angelo. I've got this.

"I take it back." Keeley cuts into my thoughts, drawing my attention, and I catch her gaze morphing from amusement to curiosity, then to something that looks a hell of a lot like respect and understanding. "It doesn't suck to be you at all. You're not just the man we expect to set it straight; you're the man we *need* to fix the problem. And something tells me you're going to do a hell of a job."

My stomach clenches, and for the first time since making the decision to buy this team, I think I have an ally.

So, instead of puffing my chest out and confidently accepting the compliment, I offer her a rare moment of truth.

"I'm not so sure you're right. I guess we're going to find out."

CHAPTER ONE

KEELEY

SIXTEEN MONTHS LATER

The dark clouds hover ominously over San Francisco Storm's practice field, but no one pays them any mind. Not the players crowding around their fearless leader, as he fills them in on the team's upcoming fundraiser, or the spectators waiting outside, lining up for their chance to watch their favorite team in action.

Mondays are usually reserved for recovery and video review, but once a season, we open practice up for our fans and they never disappoint. There must have been thousands lined up when I arrived this morning, and that was hours before we were due to let them in.

Murmurs start up around the field when Sal pauses, but his deep voice cuts through the chatter, commanding attention as the players fall silent, all eyes in his direction, everyone hooked on his words.

Including me.

"On top of the open practice today, we have a huge week ahead of us, leading into the biggest game of the season. Not only is Chicago one of our toughest rivals this year, they're also sitting pretty with an extra notch on their belt. But we're a much sexier team."

Laughter rings out and I subtly roll my eyes. Sal is the last person here that would ever make a record of his sexual encounters, but the guys seem to enjoy his humor.

"You all played like champions yesterday, and I'm going to need you to bring that A game again this weekend. We need to show them we're the team walking away with a trophy this year."

The respect he garners now, after so much uncertainty when he first arrived, is amazing to watch, and I'm in awe of the time and energy he's invested into gaining everyone's trust.

His eyes briefly flit to mine as he takes a quick breath, and I don't miss the thanks reflected back at me.

Sal's a confident man, and he knows how to keep a room quiet, but when it comes to matters dear to his heart, that confidence wavers. This year, Storm's raising money for Motor Neuron Disease, a matter that affects *me* more than it does him, with my mom suffering from ALS. Sal and his daughter, Paige—one of my closest friends and future sister-in-law—run the D'Angelo Foundation that organizes the Storm events. This year they suggested MND for their fundraising charity, and my family will forever be grateful for that.

Sal and my mom became friends after my brother, Easton, one of Storm's players, started dating Sal's daughter, Paige. He cares just as much about my mom's health as we do, and standing up there to talk about it just now hit him hard. Not that anyone really noticed. He's a pro when it comes to hiding his feelings.

I wink, and the smallest of smiles tugs at his lips before he continues on.

I'm not exactly sure when it happened, but sometime over the last almost year and a half, Sal became my confidant, and I, his.

We clicked from the very first meeting in his office, getting along like we'd been friends for years, despite the twenty-year difference in age between us, and along the way, it became more than that. Our relationship blossomed into something much deeper, and now, I don't know what I'd do without him. Which is not exactly something I need to worry about considering Sal's daughter is engaged to my grumpy-ass baby brother, and they're raising my beautiful nephew together.

Not only do I see Sal every day at work, he also lives in the same building as Easton and my mom. Not to mention he pops up occasionally at our family functions, like my mom's birthday and Christmas last year.

Despite all that, we've managed to keep our close friendship mostly to ourselves, convincing everyone we're nothing more than colleagues. The only person I've told is my oldest friend, Callum. But since he lives in Scotland, he's not about to give the game away.

In this chaotic and sometimes messed-up world, it's been nice having this little secret between us. Something away from the headlines constantly surrounding our team, and away from our family and friends. Something just for us.

Here, he's Salvatore D'Angelo, team owner and boss man, while I'm Keeley Reynolds, Storm media liaison, sometimes known as Easton's sister. And that's the way I plan to keep it, for as long as we can get away with it. Inside these walls we're brief, courteous, and always professional, but once we're alone, shoes come off, hair comes out of its tight hold—for me anyway—and we can both be ourselves, calming each other in this otherwise hectic world.

"Last," Sal finishes up, and I wave to our security officer, signaling that it's almost time to open the gates for the general public. "Please send all your good vibes Coach Pierce's way as he recovers from food poisoning, and be prepared to show him you care by proving you don't actually need him in order to succeed."

Sal steps away from the mic and immediately joins my side, walking with me back to our offices. "How'd I do?" he asks when we're away from the masses, raising an eyebrow.

"You nailed it." I can't help but laugh. "The perfect mix of dad humor and the famous Salvatore D'Angelo charm."

"Dad humor and charm?" Sal draws his lips into a frown and my laughter increases.

"Yep."

"I was going for serious but cool."

"Oh. Well, you did that too. Good job." I jokingly pat him on the back, and he scoffs under his breath.

"*Keel-ley.*"

"I'm kidding. It was perfect. The guys were all listening intently. Especially for your 'we're going to win' speech. They're as determined as you are. Can't you feel the energy in the air? They want this. It's going to be our year."

"Fuck, I hope so."

"I know so. We have Wes at the helm. Coach Pierce is happy, when he's not sick. You might even be able to relax those shoulders a little after this weekend."

Sal makes a show of lowering his shoulders, and I suck my lips into my mouth, suppressing my reaction. "You noticed?"

"I did." I grin through a wince. "No one faults you for being stressed lately. There has been a lot going on. Especially with Zane. But he played incredibly last weekend, and he's all smiles now that he has Blair in his life. Even if they won't admit they're together."

"I'm not interested in my player's love life, Keels. Just his well-being."

"You're a good guy, Sal. Better than most. Coach is ready to write him off because he keeps disappearing, and you're worried about him."

"Yeah, well, I hate that he's still in limbo. Hell, the entire team is in limbo. It's going to be a media circus if and when anything changes with Landon. No matter what happens."

Landon. *Fucking Landon.* I don't usually speak ill of anyone that can't stand up for themselves, but I made an exception for our rookie last season, Landon McKenna. He may be in a coma right now, and that in itself is devastating, but he pulled a knife on my friend Hayley and stabbed one of our players—her boyfriend, Reed—after stalking both of them for almost a year. If it wasn't for Zane's heroics, God knows what else he would have done.

Now, Zane's suffering because of it. He's been hounded by the media and forced to face the dark truths of his past.

He doesn't deserve it, and like Sal, I hate that it's still affecting him months later, and likely to continue messing with him until something happens with Landon, one way or the other.

"I'm ready for whatever we have to face. Zane won't have to deal with it alone. And you know I'll make sure the team doesn't suffer."

"I have no doubt. Thanks, Keels. Do you need anything from me for the media meeting tomorrow?"

"Nope. I'm good. You're free to take the rest of the day off."

"How very kind of you." Sal smirks and as always, it's delicious.

"Someone has to tell you what to do. You're far too powerful."

"If I'm going to listen to anyone, it's you. Only, I have a mountain of paperwork to get through and I want to catch the end of practice."

"No rest for the wicked."

"Never." He winks. "Enjoy your day."

"Thanks. You too."

Headphones on, I'm listening to music that's been specifically curated for deep concentration when a notification pops up on my screen, immediately pulling my attention from work.

Mom's neurology appointment – 9 a.m.

My heart pounds in my chest as all my other priorities instantly drift away. I set this notification months ago, after her last appointment, and pushed it from my mind. Mom's been doing well. She stutters occasionally, and has had a few falls over the past couple of months, but she's happy and she's living her life to the fullest.

This reminder is like a kick in the gut, because while she's good now, no one can tell us how quickly her muscles will deteriorate. MND is so variable there's no way to give it a timeline and it sucks.

I clear the notification and try to keep working, but it's pointless. I am well and truly distracted, and I need something to take my mind off the real world. Something I haven't done in a while.

After checking the time, I grab my yoga mat from the closet in my office and make a run for it, determined to get to the studio for the next class in seventeen minutes.

It's been months since I took time out of my day to practice yoga. Hell, it's been months since I took time out of my day for anything. I deserve the break, and yoga always helps get me out of my head. It's one of the only things that ever works to help me escape. That and the beach.

With yoga, I can lose my mind to the moment. If they tell me I'm in a forest, I'm there. Poolside, I've got my sun hat on, ready to go.

It's always helped me to completely unwind, and I don't do it enough.

If I'm out for drinks with friends, I'm undoubtedly thinking of work. Watching a movie, thinking of work. Having sex, you bet your ass I'm thinking of work. Not that I've had sex in a while. Hell, I can't remember the last time I orgasmed without my own fingers doing the work.

The point is, work takes priority, and even when I'm not there, it's never far from my mind.

But yoga. That's always been my thing.

I wonder if sex after a yoga session would—

The elevator doors open in the underground parking lot and I move to rush out, jumping when Sal appears in front of me. "Jesus." My hand flies to my chest.

"Are you okay?" He grabs my elbow to steady me, and I laugh at the concern in his expression.

"I'm fine. I was just trying to sneak away, and I clearly got caught."

"You're sneaking away?" His eyes drop to the mat in my hand and he grins knowingly. "Ah. You're off for a moment of Zen."

"I am. It's needed."

"Understandable. It's been a busy week. I won't hold you up."

"Thank you."

He holds the doors open and gestures for me to walk through, waiting until I've reached my car before letting the doors close, waving as they shut.

I smile as I get in, laughing over his constant need to make sure everyone's safe, and it's not until I'm halfway to the yoga studio that I realize I haven't thought about my stresses once.

Maybe just the idea of yoga does the trick. Either way, I'm feeling better already.

Chapter Two

SALVATORE

The room buzzes as the morning rush moves around me. The rich smell of coffee tickles my nose, and I fight the urge to have another cup. I've already had three and it's only nine a.m. If I have another one before I get to the office, I'll be bouncing off the walls.

My eyes flit between the news on my phone and the entrance to the restaurant as I wait for my daughter, Paige, and the moment I see her, I smile.

Like always, I stand as she approaches, waiting until she sits down opposite me—her face in her phone until the very last second. "Sorry, it's been a morning. How are you?"

She grins softly, but her weary expression has my chest tightening. "Everything okay? How's Isaac?"

Her grin lifts into a sassy smile, and I preemptively roll my eyes.

Am I obsessed with my grandchild? Yes. I can't help it. He's a perfect little human who came into my life when I was least expecting it, and now, I wish I could spend every day getting to know him properly. Paige and Isaac's dad, Easton, got together when Isaac was three, and at the time, he only had Easton's mom when it came to grandparents. Now he's got me, and I'm making sure I uphold my grandfather duties to the nth degree.

"Isaac is good," Paige reassures me. "I promise."

"Good to hear. What about you?" I stare at her pointedly and she laughs.

"I come in second now?"

"Yep. I'm not going to lie. Sorry, Kid." I hold back a smile for as long as possible, but when Paige jokingly pouts, I chuckle. She feels the same. As soon as Isaac bounced into her life, he was her number one priority. Even Easton knows he's second in her eyes, and he's more than happy with that.

"You know, I think you're number one in his eyes too," Paige interrupts my thoughts. "You and Rochelle." *Easton's mom*. "Equal firsts."

"That's because we spoil him. What Isaac wants, Isaac gets."

Paige glares and another laugh rumbles out of me. "Within reason, obviously." For her sake not his.

"Obviously." Paige shakes her head.

If it was up to me, I'd give him the world. I was always controlled with Paige and her brother, Marc. I wanted them to learn the importance of hard work despite the fact that they were born with silver spoons in their mouths. Who am I kidding; their spoons were 24 karat gold with diamond-encrusted handles. They had it all.

But they had to give back too. And while Paige is much better at it, I'm still pleased to say that both of them have grown into generous and kind adults. Though Marc has some questionable personality traits. Namely his inability to take anything seriously and his constant need to be liked by all. In Marc's case, there's such a thing as *too* generous. Otherwise known as being irresponsible with money.

"Anyway, back to my number two."

"If I'm number two, does that make Marc number three?"

"On a good day, yes."

"And on a bad day?"

"Your mother rises above him."

Paige covers her mouth before she laughs out loud. Her mother and I talk often, despite divorcing over ten years ago due to my inability to put my family above my work.

I'm the first to admit it took me far too long to see the problem, and by the time I did, I'd lost them all. Paige wouldn't speak to me, and Marc only called when he needed something. I was what you'd call a poor excuse of a father.

Luckily, I've been given a second chance with Paige, and I'm working on things with Marc.

I'd deluded myself into believing I was giving them everything. I made sure they never went without and protected them with all that I had. Only I failed to give them my time or attention. These days, I'd like to think that I'm better, but I still have my moments.

"You know I'm going to tell Marc you said that."

"He knows. He never calls me anymore. Apparently, your mom is giving him extra attention now that you're living here permanently. I've been forgotten." I pout. Paige knows I'm joking. At least about playing favorites. I *wish* I was joking about the fact that Marc never calls. Or answers my calls or texts.

"I'm sorry, Dad." Paige's light expression morphs into one of concern, and I wave her off.

"Don't be. He'll come back when he wants something." I wink, hoping to lighten the mood. I was supposed to be finding out the cause of *her* stressful morning, not talking about me. "Enough about your brother. You were going to tell me what's going on with you."

"I was?"

"You were. Please."

"Okay. But you're not allowed to help. This is something I have to figure out for myself."

My lips thin in contemplation and Paige notices, raising an eyebrow until I agree. "Fine. But you know I hate when you ask me to stay out of it."

"I do." She grins not so innocently. "And if you must know, Easton wants me to consider publicly showing my art."

"That's great—" My eyes light up until Paige shakes her head with a frown. "That's great...coffee over there. Have you tried it?"

Her eyes roll toward the ceiling at my attempt to change my response, before she sighs. "I know he means well. But it's a big deal, Dad. One I'm not sure I'm ready for."

"What about..." I trail off when she tilts her head, her eyes pleading with me *not* to get involved. And God, it's a struggle. "What about you have some breakfast while we're here?" I once again change the topic, blowing out a breath when Paige smiles in thanks.

"Maybe I will. If you're paying."

"Deal."

"Thanks, Dad."

"Anytime. You know that, Kid."

She nods, her appreciative smile confirming that she's aware I'm not talking about breakfast. I'd do anything for her, if only she'd let me.

My afternoon is significantly less chaotic than the coffee shop was, and I'm grateful for the peace. Yet, it's now eight p.m. and I'm still in my office. Just like every other night.

You'd think I was avoiding my apartment. In fact, I'm pretty sure that's an exact argument I had with my ex over and over. "Are you spending all your time in the office because you don't want to be here? You don't want to spend time with me and the kids. Is that it?"

It wasn't.

I always made Camilla out to be the bad guy, making her feel like she was the one causing issues in our relationship. That it was *her* fault. All because I refused to accept responsibility. To accept the truth. The truth being that I'm a workaholic. And I mean that in the sense of being addicted to working. If I miss a day for whatever reason, I get anxious. It's a huge problem that I didn't see until it was too late.

But I'm working on it. At least, I'm trying.

Leaning back in my chair, I cross my ankles beside my desk, angling my body so I can stare out the window. Through the darkness, I can just make out the lightning bolt logo on the field, and a small smile tugs at my lips. I own this fucking team. I own the San Francisco Storm.

I made my ten-year-old self's dream come true, and I'm goddamn proud of that.

Sure, I've aged dramatically since deciding I could do this *and* keep my business running in New York. I've also never felt younger.

Or happier.

I've got Paige back in my life, my beautiful grandson, and—

A loud clang breaks into my thoughts and I pause, listening out for a follow-up noise.

When it happens again, I'm out of my chair so fast, I cover the distance to my door in record time, throwing it open as my muscles tense.

"What's— Keeley? Are you okay?" She startles at the sound of my voice, spinning to face me, her perfectly manicured eyebrows arched in annoyance.

"I'm fine. Or at least, I'd be fine if this stupid door didn't jam all the time." She blows out a breath, and I watch her glossed lips until she sucks them into her mouth.

"Do you need help?" My gaze shifts back to her eyes.

"No. I've got it." She pushes the door open and flattens her palm against the frame, yanking the door so hard that the lock clicks into place. "Finally. See?"

She turns to face me again, a satisfied light brightening her eyes, and I couldn't stop my smile if I tried.

"I never doubted you for a second." I raise my hands in innocence, and her gentle laughter fills the air, filling me with warmth like it always does.

Keeley's another big contributor to my happiness. She's been a godsend since we met on my first day, and I don't know what I'd do without her. I'm praying I never have to find out.

What started as a bubbly social media liaison willing to help out the new man on campus has led to a friendship unlike any I've had before. If I go a day without seeing her, it's been a bad one. She's the first I call when I need to talk something out and the only person I trust to give me an honest answer—my opinionated daughter aside.

Keeley's my rock, and I'll forever be grateful for that first day she hid in my office.

"Why are you here so late on a Tuesday? I thought you went home," I ask, taking a step closer.

"I did. I took a couple of hours off this morning to take Mom to an appointment. I *was* going to let myself have the time off without making it up, since I've well and truly earned it. But when I was sitting around at home, doomscrolling and being hit with far too many reels on anti-aging products, I decided to come back, needing to catch up on a few things I missed ahead of the sponsorship meeting tomorrow."

"You know you must have clicked on something about anti-aging for them to start showing you reels."

"I do. And I did. I was curious about my skin-care routine. I've been noticing more fine lines lately and I wanted to get ahead of it." She frowns as she pats the skin beside her eyes.

"Never one to let anything catch you off guard, are you?" I bite back a smirk, and Keeley's infectious laughter returns, making the lines on her face more prominent on her high cheekbones, still looking as perfect as ever.

I can't imagine anyone suggesting Keeley needs anti-aging anything. Least of all me.

She tucks her deep red hair behind one ear as her laughter softens to a smile, the dip of her dimples drawing me in.

"You know me. I'm always one step in front of the ball. I even knew you'd be here." She points my way and I feign shock.

"Really? And yet, you jumped when I called out."

"Yeah, well I didn't expect you to throw open the door like that."

"I heard a crash; I was worried." I shrug like it's no big deal.

"So...you came running to save me?"

"I didn't know it was *you* specifically."

"Fair enough. Are you going to be here much longer?"

"Probably. You?"

"A couple of hours."

"My office or yours?"

"Always yours." Keeley's quick to respond, grabbing her bag from the floor. "I call dibs on the couch."

"As I've said many times before, you are missing out. My desk chair is like a cloud on your back."

"I know. And ergonomically tested." She bounces her eyebrows, and a chuckle bubbles out of me. I've clearly talked about this chair often.

"Get in my office. I'll grab us some snacks." I smirk as I walk past her and she waves, singing her thanks as she glides toward my door.

"Don't come back without chocolate," she calls out, and I wave over my head without turning around.

"I never do." *Does she think I don't know her by now?*

Chapter Three

KEELEY

I inhale deeply as I move through Sal's office, letting his spicy cologne relax me as I make myself comfortable. I swear I work better here than in my own office, as though his scent triggers my productive mind. It's probably why I end up here whenever I'm working late or when we're both here on a Storm day off. *Which is almost a weekly occurrence.*

"Are you in the mood for milk or dark chocolate?" Sal asks when he reappears in the doorway, his hands behind his back.

I smile up at him before lowering my gaze and tilting my head, attempting to see around him. "Are you trying to make the vending machine candy sound more decadent than it is?"

"Not at all." He chuckles lightly. "I came prepared. I had these in my car." He holds out two blocks of my favorite handmade chocolate, only available from a cute little store an hour away, and I gasp.

"You went to Hamilton's Chocolates? When?"

"I took Isaac last Tuesday. It's actually a coincidence that I brought it today."

"I bet he loved that."

"He did. He knew exactly what he wanted when we arrived. I'm going to go out on a limb and say his aunt has given him some before? He seems to follow in your footsteps when it comes to being a chocolate connoisseur."

"Someone had to introduce him to it. Don't worry, I made it clear it was a *sometimes* food, otherwise Easton's likely to ban me from seeing him again."

"I said the same. But I lied."

Sal fakes a wince and I laugh softly. "Me too. What's the point of having aunts and grandparents if they're not going to spoil you?"

"Exactly. So which one?"

"Dark, please. Like my heart."

"Keeley, your heart is so far from dark, it's practically sunshine."

"That's quite the poetic notion."

"I try."

Sal hands me the beautifully wrapped bar of dark chocolate and opens his bar as he walks over to his desk, swiveling his chair to face me. "What are you working on tonight?"

"I've got—" My loud ringtone blares from somewhere in my bag, and I groan as I search around for it, smiling when it's Reed.

"One of your players is calling me after hours." I fake a frown and Sal laughs.

"Reed, it's late. What did Luke do this time?" I smile at my own joke until silence ensues. "Reed?"

"Sorry. Hayley was showing me something on her phone. I don't mean to be calling so late." His flat tone sets off alarm bells ringing through my mind.

"Is everything okay?"

"No. I should have called you sooner, but I haven't exactly been thinking clearly. The Jacksonville police called me earlier today." He sucks in a breath and my own catches in my throat. "Landon passed away. This morning. Hayley and I have to report for more questioning."

"Jesus. Have you spoken to Zane?" At the mention of Zane, I catch Sal stiffen from the corner of my eye, before he gets up and moves closer.

"He won't answer his phone. Hayley and I have been calling since we found out and nothing, not even..." He trails off and my stomach sinks.

"Has anyone tried going to his apartment?"

Sal lightly grabs my arm, physically turning me to get my attention, his wide eyes making my heart ache.

Reed begins to speak at the same time Sal opens his mouth to question me, and I hold my hand up to stop him.

"I don't know where he lives, Keeley, and I doubt any of the others do."

"Shit. I can look it up. I might head there now."

"Thank you. Let me know if you have any luck."

"I will. Try not to stress. I'm sure he's just ignoring the world while he processes the news."

"I hope that's all it is. Talk soon."

"Bye, Reed."

I hang up and Sal's panicked voice rings through the air. "What happened?"

"Landon died."

"Fuuuck."

"I know. I promise I'll make a few calls regarding the team in the morning, but tonight—"

"The team will be fine," Sal cuts me off, waving away my concern. "Controversy's our thing. I'm worried about Zane. Sounds like he's MIA?"

"Yep. I'm going to see if he's home. We have his address on file."

"I'm coming with you." Sal doesn't wait for my response before rounding his desk and grabbing his keys. "We can—"

"I don't know if that's a good idea, Sal. He'll see it as an ambush if he's self-loathing."

"I'm *coming*. I'll stay in the car if you think that's best. I can't stand around and do nothing, Keels."

"Okay. I'll meet you downstairs in five."

"Thank you." He smiles in appreciation before a loud sigh escapes him, the sound full of anguish. And I feel it too. Zane's a confident man, and you wouldn't be off base in thinking nothing ever fazes him. But it's all an act. I've seen the cracks in his tough exterior, and I can't begin to imagine how he's feeling right now. Especially with everything the media has been throwing his way.

"We have to find him, Sal."

"We will."

Sal's gaze turns sympathetic, and he takes a step toward me, maybe to comfort me, I don't know. Either way, I wave him off, throwing my things into my bag. I don't need comfort. It's time to get moving. Zane needs his friends, whether he thinks he has them or not. "I'll see you in a few."

It's after midnight by the time Sal's driving me back to my car. Zane's entitled concierge wouldn't let me up to his apartment, and when she refused Sal too, I almost slid over the counter to attack her. *"We take our residents' privacy very seriously."*

I wanted to show her how serious this was, and I would have, if I wasn't almost certain Zane wasn't there.

I'd like to believe she would have been more accommodating if he was.

We pull up next to my dark gray Volkswagen, and Sal switches off the engine in his Aston Martin, turning to face me with a weary expression. After my almost catfight with *Kate,* we'd driven to a few places that Zane had once mentioned in passing, but had no luck finding him. I was ready to call the police when Reed texted to say Zane had messaged in their group chat, letting them know he was fine and that he'd miss practice tomorrow.

I'm sure he sent it assuming we'd give up our efforts trying to get in touch with him.

Too bad he's wrong.

It only worked to relieve the extreme tightness in my chest before I called him again, begging him to answer.

"He's okay, Keeley." Sal reaches over and grabs my hand, giving it a squeeze. "We'll keep calling him tomorrow until he picks up. We can't do anything more tonight."

"I know. I'm just—"

"Worried?"

"Extremely."

"Then, how can I help? What can we do?"

"You've already helped. Thank you for keeping me company tonight."

Sal smiles as he circles his thumb over the skin on my hand, and I return his smile while the warmth of his touch heats me from within.

"I'm here for you, Keeley. Whenever you need me."

"I know. And I appreciate it. I should try and get a few hours of good sleep before facing the media tomorrow. I'll see you bright and early."

"You sure will. Good night, Keeley."

"Night, Sal."

Neither of us moves for a beat until Sal clears his throat and removes his hand, his knuckles white when he curls his fingers around the steering wheel again.

Sal and I could talk for hours without stopping, our conversations always flowing and comfortable. Until it comes to these little moments. The blips in our otherwise professional relationship.

This isn't the first instance we've lost time due to lingering touches or staring into each other's eyes for longer than we should. And I know with absolute certainty that it won't be the last.

While it's not something either of us has ever acknowledged out loud, I've thought about it often. I've even concluded that it stems from my complete lack of a love life and the fact that Sal's an incredibly handsome man.

He'll be fifty-two this year, but other than the salt and pepper in his hair and laugh lines decorating his skin, you wouldn't know it.

I'd be lying if I didn't admit I've thought about what it would be like to take things further between us. It's impossible not to. You'd be hard-pressed to find a woman that isn't attracted to him or his charm.

Only, it's not meant to be. There's too much standing in the way, and I'd never let a quick, or not so quick fuck ruin the relationship we have. It means too much to me. *He* means too much to me. Things are perfect exactly as they are.

"Night," I repeat, reaching for the door handle until Sal stops me, his hand shooting out to curl around my arm.

"Wait."

I smile at his touch, and I don't have to ask to know what's coming. "You don't have to do this every time I get out of the car." I giggle, the tension in the air dissipating slightly.

"I know I don't have to. I *want* to. What am I if not a gentleman?" He smirks and my laughter grows.

"Fine. I'll wait."

"Thank you."

He jumps out and jogs around the car, standing behind the door as he opens it. There was a time when he used to offer me his hand too, until Paige convinced him he was taking his chivalry a little too far. He opens the door for her too. And his ex. And any other females he might have in his car. Although, most of the time he has a driver, so it's his driver's responsibility. Either way, it's sweet and I'm happy to indulge him.

"Now we can say good night." He nods in thanks. "I'm sorry I forgot myself for a moment."

"Look at you oozing old-school charm."

"Good night, Keeley."

"Night, boss." I wink and he shakes his head, waiting for me to get settled in my car before walking around to his driver's side door and climbing inside. He lifts a finger in a wave as I drive past, and I can't stop my eyes from drifting to the rearview mirror.

Sal is like no man I have ever met. And it's not only the fact that he's almost twenty years older than most of the guys I know... He's real. Honest. And way more decent than he gives himself credit for. He's convinced himself that he no longer deserves love after fucking it up the first time, and he won't be told otherwise. I've tried. I doubt he even allows himself many of life's little pleasures anymore. It's all work and no play when it comes to Salvatore D'Angelo. The only people that ever get his time outside of the workplace are Paige and Isaac.

Although, for all I know, he could be in a casual relationship that he's keeping on the down-low. It's not like the topic of his love life comes up regularly. After our initial discussion where he proclaimed to forever be a bachelor, we haven't spoken about it. Things may have changed since then. Though I doubt it. I'm a workaholic and whenever I'm here, so is Sal. If he did have a woman in his life, I can't imagine she'd be too happy about their situation.

My phone chimes with a text as I'm pulling up to my building, and when I stop, I glance down to see a message from Hayley.

"Shit." Here I am thinking about Sal's goddamn love life when we have far more important things to worry about.

Zane's missing. Sure, he claims he's okay, but I have no doubt he's hurting. First thing tomorrow I plan to track him down. Whether he wants to be found or not.

Chapter Four

SALVATORE

My leg bounces as I pretend to be listening to Hayley and Reed's discussion about the unseasonal weather. They're trying to distract themselves, and if it was another time, I might partake in the conversation. Right now, though, I couldn't give a fuck how much rain they've forecast for the next few days. All I can think about is getting this plane off the ground. And fast.

Where is she?

Keeley was supposed to be here fifteen minutes ago and she's late.

"I'm here." Her voice filters in from outside, the metal staircase clanging from her heels as she makes her way up. She appears in the doorway, the glow of the tarmac lights giving her a halo, and I struggle to hide a relieved sigh as some of the tension leaves me. "Sorry I'm late. Let's get this plane moving."

There are plenty of seats for her to take yet she beelines straight for me, sitting down in the empty chair beside me.

"I was trying to reach a media contact of mine, wanting to get ahead of it in case the news breaks. I actually arrived on time. I've been pacing the hangar, waiting for her to call me back."

"Do they know about Landon, or Zane's arrest?"

"Not yet." She offers me a soft smile, the edge of it only lifting for a brief moment.

After our panic yesterday, Hayley contacted Blair, Zane's girlfriend, and discovered that Zane was not only out of the state—back in his hometown—but that he'd been arrested for issues unrelated to Landon.

Without hesitation, I chartered a flight so we could be there for him, and now, we're finally on our way.

"I guess that's a shred of good news." I sink back into my seat.

"It is. I just wish we had more. He needs a win."

"I know." *God, I hope he gets one.*

The flight takes longer than expected due to the bad weather Hayley and Reed were discussing, and by the time we touch down on the runway, it's the middle of the night.

We're all silent on the way to the hotel, robotically going through the motions up until we walk through the glass doors into the foyer, and Reed curses out loud. A very un-Reed-like outburst. "How the fuck are we staying in a five-star hotel when Zane's spending the night in a cell?" He throws his head back and sighs.

"Would you rather I booked a shithole?" I snap, hitting him with a little outburst of my own, and Hayley snorts out a laugh from beside me. "Would that make you feel better? We're here to help him, Reed. We're doing what we can."

"We should be doing *more*."

"Like what?" Hayley cuts in before I can ask the same question. Because if Reed has any ideas of what else we can do, I'm all ears.

Reed sighs again, pulling Hayley into his arms. "I don't know. I feel kind of helpless."

"Right now, he needs friends in his corner." Keeley steps forward and squeezes Reed's arm. "Us showing up for him is more than he's had in a long time. Get some sleep. There's nothing more we can do tonight."

She walks toward the front desk and we all follow, checking in before agreeing to meet back downstairs early tomorrow morning.

We say our good nights, and as Hayley, Reed, and Keeley step off the elevator toward their rooms on the floor below mine, an anxious energy surrounds me.

I'm slow to walk to my room, but after dropping my bag, I'm back out the door in less than a minute, too keyed up to sleep. I've just sat down in the lobby bar when, as if on the same wavelength, Keeley walks out of the elevator, her weary eyes instantly meeting mine.

"I knew you'd be here." She smiles brightly as she approaches, sitting down in the chair opposite me.

"Likewise." I hand her the drinks menu and wave to get the server's attention. "We didn't really get to talk on the flight. I wanted to check how you were doing."

"I'm good," she lies unconvincingly. "I've got a few more calls to make in the morning but otherwise—"

"I don't mean workwise. I mean *you*, personally. How are *you* doing?"

"Oh? I'm fine with a capital F."

"Fine?"

"Good." She rolls her eyes. "I'm more worried about Zane than myself. As should you be."

"Believe it or not, I can care about more than one person at a time." I wink, keeping things light for both our sakes.

"You're just an all-around good guy, aren't you?"

"Always. So… are you going to continue to lie to me?" I pointedly raise an eyebrow before continuing on. "Or…"

"Okay. Jesus. I'm tired, stressed, and going crazy because I feel like I'm missing something, or that I'm going to say or do something to fuck this all up for him."

"Like what?"

"I don't even know." She throws her hands in the air, and I reach forward to grab them, giving her fingers a squeeze.

"He's going to be okay," I say as the server walks over. "One way or another, I'm going to make sure of that."

We order our drinks, me a whiskey and Keeley a red wine, and sit in silence until the server walks away.

When he's gone, Keeley stares at me for a beat before raising her brow just like I did. "You're going to make sure? Like you did for Paige?"

"What did I do for Paige?" My shoulder lifts in an innocent shrug, and Keeley's beautiful laughter echoes through the quiet bar. Her way of calling my bullshit.

When Paige was blackmailed by her ex-boyfriend's family last year, I may have gone to great lengths to protect her. Not even Keeley knows the full story of my confrontation with the Mikklesons. Let's just say, I would have done almost anything to ensure her safety.

I will always protect my family, and while Paige is my flesh and blood, my team—the *players*—are my extended family too. I'd never do anything that put Paige or Isaac at risk, but I'd do pretty much anything else. Especially for Zane. I don't know what it is about him. I got the sense early on that he didn't have anyone in his corner. He's been through so much, he deserves a break.

"I'll do whatever I have to do, Keels."

"He's lucky to have you."

"And you. He needs all of us tomorrow."

Our drinks arrive and we change the topic as we drink, talking about Isaac to keep our minds off the following day.

Keeley yawns after taking her last sip of wine and my chest tightens. "You should get some sleep."

She laughs, rolling her eyes. "What's that saying? You can't take the dad out of the man."

"I don't think that's a saying at all. If you're trying to say that I care too much or that I'm overprotective, guilty as charged."

Keeley's strawberry-colored lips curl into a soft smile, and it draws my gaze, my heart pounding as her tongue swipes out to lick the gloss. "You're a good man, Sal. I'll see you in the morning."

She stands, the movement pulling my attention as I stand with her. "You will."

I walk her to the elevator and wait while it arrives, holding the door open until Keeley's inside.

"Good night, Keeley."

"Night, Sal."

Just like she instinctively knew I'd be down here, she also seems to know I'm not ready to go back up. Not yet. I couldn't sleep if you hit me over the head with a brick. I may have argued that there's nothing we can do, but it doesn't mean I'm a hundred percent convinced. There has to be something. I just have to figure out what it is.

I'm exhausted after my sleepless night—my whirring mind keeping me awake—and when I meet the others at the restaurant for breakfast, their weary faces suggest we're all in the same boat.

"I'm guessing you all got about as much sleep as I did?"

Reed scoffs as though my question is absurd. "If you mean none, then yes."

Silence falls as the server takes our order, and as we're waiting for our food, we keep the conversation on football rather than the reason we're here. It's not until we finish eating that Hayley addresses the elephant in the room, attempting to perk us up.

"By the end of today, Zane's going to be free, we're going to be able to put this behind us, and give him shit for stealing so much attention. He'll love it."

"Hayley's right, mostly." I smile. "Zane's going to be cleared. On both counts. We have to stay positive."

"For everyone's sake."

"Fuck, yes." Reed stands, nodding a few times. "Positivity is key. Let's do this."

Hayley smiles while Keeley nods in agreement, both of them jumping up, ready to go.

I pay the bill and follow behind them, ignoring my own positivity spiel, while my mind spirals, thinking about a plan B. If there's any way I can help Zane, I'm going to find it.

When we arrive at the address Blair gave us, we're guided through the diner to a private area off to the side, with windows facing the police station.

And my stomach sinks.

Zane's been there all night, and I'd put all my money on him spiraling more than I am, probably to the point of believing he deserves it.

Reed's the first to walk into the room to meet Blair, with me sliding through last, taking in the deafening silence following the creak in the door.

"Hi." Reed waves enthusiastically until he seemingly reads the room. "Sorry, that was a little too cheery for the situation."

Hayley snorts, and I lift my gaze in time to see a young woman step forward, grinning in response.

"We'll welcome any cheer we can get." An older woman joins her, lifting her hand in a wave. "I'm Florence; this is my husband, Tim." She gestures to a man beside her. "And I think you know Blair." Her attention shifts to the young woman, and Hayley bounces in anticipation.

"We do. At least Keeley and I do. Hi, Blair."

We introduce ourselves, and while Blair and Florence offer warm smiles, it's easy to see Tim's more unsettled, and if the protectiveness I'm feeling stems from being a dad, as Keeley seems to think, I'd bet I know how he feels.

"Thanks for coming." He steps forward, his eyes flashing to his family before he straightens his posture. "I'll let Blair and Florence fill you in on what we know. I have somewhere to be."

"Wait." Blair grabs her dad's hand, stopping him from leaving. "What's going on?"

"I think I know how I can help Zane," he tells her, barely loud enough for us to hear, and I stiffen, opening my mouth to speak until Blair voices my question.

"How?"

"I'll tell you everything when I get back." He squeezes her hand and takes another step toward the door. "Excuse me for rushing off."

I'm about to stop him when Reed gets there first, doing it for me. "I'm coming with you," he states matter-of-factly, his expression serious. "I'm here to help."

Like hell he is.

"Not a chance, Coombs." I move in front of him, my expression stern. "You're staying out of this. You're here for support and to provide your statement to the police on another matter. You're not getting involved."

"I'll be back soon," Tim says, trying to pass by, only I can't let him leave. Something in my gut is screaming at me to go with him.

Following Reed's lead, I step forward, tapping him on the shoulder before he's even managed a step.

"Can I help?" I ask, leaning back, my hands in my pockets as I stare him down, showing him I mean business.

Tim eyes me slowly, his gaze thoughtful, before he offers me a nod. "Come on. You can be my witness."

Witness? Jesus. What the fuck is he going to do? Whatever it may be, I nod and follow him out the door, only stopping when he pauses on the sidewalk.

"That's my car across the street," he tells me, pointing to a modest SUV before he takes off walking in that direction. "The passenger door is unlocked. I have to grab something from the trunk."

I nod, taking my time to walk around to my side, and I've just opened the door when my phone vibrates in my pocket. Without checking, I know that it's Keeley.

KEELEY: Do you know what you're doing?

I smile, imagining that the lack of knowledge is driving her crazy. She'll be hating that she has no idea where I'm going or what I'm going to do.

SALVATORE: I don't. But I'm quite capable of keeping myself out of trouble. You don't have to worry about me

KEELEY: I wasn't

SALVATORE: Sure, you weren't. 😉

I picture her standing tall and projecting her strength to the others around her, and my concern deepens. I'm sure she's putting on a front, always making sure she's helping others first.

She doesn't respond, and that's all the confirmation I need as I silently vow to make this all better.

Tim sighs as he gets in the car, running a hand down his face.

"What exactly are we doing?" I ask hesitantly, and he immediately perks up, turning my way with a grin.

"We're paying Zane's dad a little visit. Long story short, he goaded Zane into throwing the first punch yesterday, and he's been manipulating Blair for the past seven years."

"Jesus. I'm guessing you want to hurt him?" I wouldn't usually encourage violence, but I know without a doubt that if someone was hurting Paige, I'd stop at nothing to make them pay. I've been there. Only the issue was resolved before I had to take that particular path.

"I would love nothing more than to rearrange his cowardly face," Tim seethes. "But that's not my plan. I'm here so he can beat the shit out of me."

"Come again?"

"I need you as my witness. This time, I'm doing the goading, though I don't think it's going to take much effort on my part. One mention of Zane should do it."

"I can't believe any of this is happening. Have you seen him?"

"Only after the fight. None of us have seen him since the police took him away."

My heart pounds in my chest but I smile through it. "He's lucky to have you."

"And you, I hear. Blair tells me you arranged a private jet to be here today."

"I did. The commercial flights would have taken too long." I shrug softly, though he's not even looking my way. Still, he smiles.

"I've followed football my entire life. My dad played for South Carolina. I'm proud to say I know a lot about the sport in general. I can't think of another team owner that would go to bat for his players like this."

"I'm here because I'd made the assumption that Zane didn't have many people in his corner. I'm happy to discover I was wrong."

Tim points out Zane's parents' house when we pull up across the street, and within a few minutes, Zane's dad appears at the front door. Possibly on his way to Zane's hearing. Who knows.

"Wait here." Tim nods before jumping out of the driver's seat and jogging across the road. "Ron, I think it's time we had a word."

Ron's eyes widen, moving from Tim to his car and I duck, hoping he doesn't notice me. I wait a few seconds before taking a look, and when my eyes lock on Ron, I'm the one that's seething.

Tim was right. It's not going to take much to push his buttons. He's ready for a fight.

Chapter Five

KEELEY

The clock ticks ridiculously loud above my head, and it takes everything in my power not to rip it from the wall and throw it across the room.

Hayley suggested we write character statements for Zane while waiting for news, and while that was good in theory, it only worked to make me feel worse about the position he's in.

I thought I knew the gist of what was happening to Zane before I arrived, until Blair filled us in on more details after her dad left. And I still can't wrap my head around everything that's happened.

Zane's dad pushed him into a fight and then called the police to have him arrested. *His dad.* I can't even fathom what kind of a person, what kind of *parent*, could disown their child, then accuse him of trespassing when he came back.

That's shocking enough on its own, but to then start a fight and blame him for it? *What the actual fuck?* A wave of nausea hits me, thinking about all that Zane's endured.

It's just one thing after another. He's stuck in a cell alone just for visiting his childhood home, while we're here writing about how good of a guy he is.

Needing a moment to myself, I sneak out of the private dining room and through the halls of the diner, looking for somewhere to find some peace. The dining room was quiet, silent in fact, and yet it was so loud in my head, I was struggling to concentrate.

I'm not even sure who I'm most worried about at this point. Yes, Zane's in jail, awaiting a trial, but the determination set in both Sal's and Tim's features has me believing he's going to be okay. That they're going to find a way to ensure he's cleared.

My concern comes from wondering what the hell they're going to do to themselves in the process. Sal's a smart man, but I wouldn't put it past him to do something stupid, especially when it comes to protecting the people he cares about.

It's been over an hour since they left.

What the hell could they be doing?

Sal's a communicator, always, so his radio silence is *killing* me.

After taking a deep breath, I lean back against the brightly colored wall near the bathrooms at the back of the diner, and close my eyes.

The loud pop music works to block the chaos in my mind, and I'm surprised to say it relaxes me a little. But it's the vibration of my phone that really has me sighing with relief.

SAL: We're on our way back. I'll fill you in when I get there.

KEELEY: Thank God. The hearing is starting soon. Will you make it?

SAL: We're only five minutes away

KEELEY: Did it help?

SAL: I really fucking hope so.

I don't respond because I want to be back in the dining room when he gets there. Rushing this time, I walk through the doorway to the private area to find that Blair's a complete mess.

"He's going to miss the hearing, Mom." She tugs on the strands of her hair, pacing the floor.

"He's not," I cut in before her mom responds. "Sal's been texting me. They're on their way back."

"From where exactly?" Blair asks, her tone suspicious.

"He didn't say." And truth be known, I'm just as suspicious as she is. *What the hell did they do?*

Blair's previously panicked demeanor turns to frustration now that she knows they're on the way, but she aims her questions back at her mom, while the rest of us watch the exchange. Helpless. Waiting.

Barely a minute passes before the door finally opens and Sal and Tim step through.

A little of the tension leaves me when I see that Sal's okay, until Blair's mom gasps, and I turn to check what has her so frantic.

Sal may be fine, but Tim looks like he's been beaten with a metal rod, and it doesn't take much to guess who was on the other end of that beating. Zane's dad.

God. I hope this works.

I'm usually cool, calm, and collected in high-pressure situations, but here in the courtroom, I feel like a completely different person. I can't stop my leg from shaking, my heart is racing at a million miles per minute, and the pit in my stomach is so deep, it rivals the Grand Canyon.

Zane, on the other hand, is the picture of calm, relaxing back in his chair, his eyes on the door to the judge's chamber.

I doubt he's calm at all. He's just putting on a front, likely for Blair.

The judge walks into the room, and my body—that moments ago couldn't stop moving—stills, my racing heart frozen and my limbs paralyzed. This is it. This is the moment. There's nothing more anyone can do.

I listen to the judge's every word as he runs through the charges, my gaze darting between him and Zane, and it isn't until he's ready to announce the next steps that a shudder runs through me.

Sal's giant palm curls around my thigh, giving me a reassuring squeeze, and my entire body finds equilibrium. My pulse slows, and I feel like I can inhale deeply for the first time, a calming breath seeping back into my lungs.

I'm about to silently thank him when his hand disappears, and I glance up to find him focused on the judge, as though I imagined the entire thing.

After mentioning the new evidence he received that morning—which

I'm certain has to do with Sal and Tim—the judge shockingly dismisses the case, citing insufficient probable cause. *Just like that.*

The relief I feel is so overwhelming I struggle not to cry.

I am *not* a crier.

Zane's not out of the woods yet, but at least he's over the first hurdle, and I'm holding tight to hope that he'll be cleared of any fault in Landon's death too. There's no other acceptable outcome. He didn't do anything wrong. He saved Reed and Hayley.

We all exit the courtroom when Zane's dismissed, and while everyone's celebrating and hugging Zane, I sneak away, shifting into media-control mode.

I stalk the hall toward the front desk and pray they have somewhere I can work.

"Hi." The receptionist lifts her gaze as she places her book on the desk in front of her, offering me a tight-lipped grin. "How can I help?"

"I'm sorry to bother you. But I was wondering if you might have a room I can borrow for a few minutes. I have to make some time-sensitive calls."

"Does this have anything to do with the football star over there? My husband is a huge fan; I recognized him right away."

Jesus. Yep. That's *exactly* why I need to make these calls. I wouldn't be surprised if she's already messaged her husband to tell him Zane's here.

"It's not, sorry," I lie. "Do you have anything?"

"I think meeting room B is available."

"Great. Thank you. Where would I find that?"

She points me in the direction of a room with a weathered door that looks like it could pass as a janitor's closest, and when I walk in, I'm surprised to find it's bigger than I perceived.

I spend all of two seconds assessing my surroundings before sliding my phone from my pocket and making my first call, my fingers crossed for luck as the phone rings.

I'm on my fifth call by the time someone answers, and after finally getting through to three more contacts, I think it's safe to say no one's aware of Zane's arrest. At least, not yet.

Still, I keep going.

I've just hung up from another unanswered call, when a text comes through.

SAL: Where are you? Are you okay?

KEELEY: I'm fine. Just trying to get ahead of this news

SAL: What can I do to help?

KEELEY: Nothing. I've got this

SAL: You're my rock, Keels. Let me be yours.

My gaze lifts to my faint reflection in the window, and I physically deflate while my heart jolts in my chest.

It's moments like these that I struggle to remember he's my boss and almost twenty years my senior. *Why does he have to be so good to me all the time?* He doesn't even realize he's *my* rock too. He instantly calmed me today with one simple touch. The way my body reacts to him is unnerving.

For the past year, I've been pretending those moments don't mean anything, but now that my emotions are shot, it's a struggle to convince myself to maintain my practical approach when it comes to the two of us.

Am I physically attracted to Sal? Absolutely.

Am I emotionally attracted to Sal? Yes, in the sense that he calms me and being in his orbit makes me happy.

Do I have feelings for Sal? That I can't answer. Not now. But if asked, I'd say *no.*

I'm smart enough to realize *that* road is a complete dead end. But is that my response because I know that?

He's my boss first, though we're also friends, and right now, I'm confused if it's more than that. On both our parts. Either way, I'd never act on it.

SAL: Where are you, Keels? You're killing me here.

I inhale a deep breath, trying to shake off the image of Sal's demanding presence before rushing to find him.

I open the door and gasp, almost bumping into Zane in the doorway, and an embarrassed warmth coats my cheeks. "Zane? You nearly gave me a heart attack."

"Sorry." He cringes as I glance back over my shoulder, hastily closing the door, as if I left behind evidence of the inappropriate thoughts running through my mind. When I look back at him, Zane's pale face makes my chest tight. He's been through so much and— "I just wanted to say thanks," he rushes out, stilling me.

"Thanks? What for?"

He stares at me deadpan and I can't help but laugh. *He's thanking me?* "You're such an idiot, Zane. After all this time, you still don't get it. We *all* care. We're a family. And nothing you do is going to change that."

"I bet—"

"*Nothing*," I repeat sternly, my eyes locked on his, begging him to understand.

After a few beats, he nods. "Thank you. I promise, I'm starting to see it."

"Good. The next few weeks are going to be trying for you and the team, but we're going to get through it. Together. One day at a time. And by the end, everyone is going to love you. More than they already do. You know people crave a redemption story."

"Thanks, Keeley. If you ever need anything, I'd love to return the favor."

"Don't like being in debt, huh?"

"Definitely not."

I laugh lightly, but while I'm projecting happiness on the outside, the tightness inside my chest fails to dissipate.

We rejoin the others and say our goodbyes, while I remain a little on edge. I want to make this as painless as possible for him. But how?

I'm wound so tight on the flight home that when we land on the tarmac, Sal pulls me aside, his expression pained. "Let me help. Please. How many times have I called you into my office over the past year, needing you for one thing or another?"

"They've all been issues that were *my* problem too, Sal. My job. I was supposed to help you."

"And you don't think this is *my* problem as much as it is yours? A player on *my* team is being questioned over the death of another player, Keeley. *That's* my problem. More than anyone else's."

"You—"

"I'm helping. Do you want to go to the office or—"

"The office," I interrupt him, my feelings from earlier resurfacing at the thought of a more intimate setting. "I try not to work too much at home, if possible."

"Of course." Sal pauses as he visibly swallows, quickly replacing his unease with a smile. "We'll go to the office. It's time I took over some of your stress."

Like always, calm washes over me the second I sit down on Sal's couch, feeling the soft leather beneath my hands. This is familiar. Safe. Comforting.

In this room, I'm in control. The noise doesn't feel as chaotic when the deep mahogany scent of Sal's office permeates the air.

The view helps too. Football has my heart, so seeing the practice field while I work is like walking through a peaceful garden to me.

Everything about this space puts me at ease, including the man walking through the door.

Only try as I might to keep my thoughts at bay, the emotions from the day overwhelm me once more, and my stupid heart picks up speed.

This is going to be harder than I thought.

Chapter Six

SALVATORE

I smile at the sight of Keeley comfortable on my couch, her posture casual, her legs crossed at the ankles, a lightness to her expression.

Like she belongs there.

Maybe because she does.

I once told her this office was big enough for the two of us, and I meant it. I wouldn't hesitate to move her into my space. Any time. It would mean I wouldn't have to call her in here so often.

She adjusts her position as I join her inside, curling her feet up underneath herself, while I reveal the reason she arrived before I did. "I came prepared with more chocolate. Do you want some?"

"Always." She beams up at me, but her tired eyes give away the toll today has taken on her. On everyone. "I hate to ask..." She hesitates for a beat, her eyes flashing to the chocolate in my hand. "Should we order dinner first?"

"What?" I fake shock. "I've been told there's nothing wrong with chocolate for dinner." I wink. "But yes, we should order something more substantial. What do you feel like?" I stew over the question myself, knowing she's about to throw it back to me, like anyone I've ever asked that question to. We'll undoubtedly go through that "I don't mind" bullshit. It always—

"Pizza?"

"What?" My eyes bulge as I stare at her, stunned.

"Pizza. Is that a problem?"

"No. Not at all. Pizza is good." *Has anyone ever actually made a decision about dinner that quickly?*

"Good. You get it from Riccardo's, right?"

"Riccardo's? No. I haven't—"

"Oh my God." Her eyes flit shut and she moans in ecstasy, biting down on her bottom lip.

And for the first time in her presence, my cock twitches.

What the fuck is that about?

Keeley continues on, none the wiser, and I smile, hiding my panic when she opens her eyes. "You have to try their pizza," she gushes. "It's honestly the best around. You won't be able to beat it."

Her words pull me out of my thoughts and I almost laugh. *Is she seriously telling a New Yorker that San Francisco has the best pizza?*

I stare at her for a beat, a brow raised in challenge until she throws her head back with a laugh. "I'd go as far as to say it will rival your favorite in New York."

It's like she read my mind.

"We'll see."

Keeley's laughter subdues as she grabs her phone, bringing up the menu before passing it over so I can give her my order. When we're done, she runs through her concerns for Zane while we wait, her switch into work mode helping my little problem. Which I'm hoping remains just that—a little problem. The last thing we need is for it to become...*bigger*.

"I need a statement ready for when the news breaks," Keeley tells me. "While I'm usually a pro at statements, I don't know how to tackle this one. The world knows Landon attacked Reed and Hayley, and that Zane came to their defense. That's old news. They've moved on. However, when they find out Landon didn't survive, they'll circle like vultures, focusing on how Zane's act of protection resulted in his teammate dying, despite it being self-defense. They're going to be divided and they're going to be loud about it."

"You're right and because of that, this one needs to come from me. It *should* come from me. I know you're going to argue but I need to be the face of this. It's my job to protect my team."

"Some fans will hate you."

"Let them. I'm prepared to put in the work to rebuild their trust."

Keeley sighs, briefly massaging her temples, and I imagine myself taking over until she continues speaking. "I didn't agree to let you help so that you'd take it all on."

"I know." I nod, shaking off my thoughts.

"But you're going to do it anyway?" She glances up at me, her expression knowing.

"I am. You're not going to talk me out of it."

"Okay. Fine." She fakes a huff, but the hint of a smile gives away her appreciation.

"Thank you for not arguing. Let's get to it. How can we word it to protect Zane while also being mindful of the deceased?" I frown in thought and Keeley mimics my expression.

"That's the million-dollar question. But we've got this."

We're lost in a sea of ideas and notes when Keeley's phone rings, with security telling her our pizzas are here. I offer to go but she pushes me back into my seat and darts away, returning ten minutes later accompanied by the aroma of pizza and a concerned expression.

"What's wrong? Fuck. Has Landon's death been released?"

"No, I'd be far more worried if it had. This bag is way too heavy for what we ordered."

Amusement fills me at her trivial response and my interest piques. "Freebies? Great. Let's check it out."

"Freebies? Says the multibillionaire."

"I'm not a multibillionaire."

Keeley hits me with a glare that screams *bullshit*—she's good at those—and I chuckle under my breath.

"Fine. I *was* a multibillionaire. Until I decided to blow it all by buying a financially fucked football team." *Now I'm about half a million off.*

"So, you're broke?" She pulls that "bullshit" look again, and I shrug nonchalantly.

"I get by." My lips thin and it's Keeley's turn to laugh.

"Yeah, okay. How's that Armani suit?"

"It's Prada, and I bought it before I bought the team."

"God, you're full of it. Either way, let's find out what we've got."

Keeley opens the bag and her eyes widen before she stifles her amusement. "Shit. I forgot my next order was going to include a bottle of wine. Look how well they packaged it. It didn't move." She shows me the inside of the bag, and I have to admit, I'm impressed but confused.

"They sell wine? The images on the website suggested it was one of those hole-in-the-wall-type places."

"It is. And no, they don't sell wine. I've kind of become acquaintances with the owner's son, since I frequent there a lot. Along with about five other restaurants nearby because I never have time to cook. Anyway, we got to talking a few weeks ago and five minutes turned into an hour or more, and he bet me that I couldn't handle the spiciest pizza on their menu. Stupid bet really since he barely knows me. But it happened. Last week I tried the pizza and I won." Her beaming happiness returns, and this time it reaches her eyes, sparking a strange tightness in my chest. Is that happiness for him? Or because we've made a little headway on the statement and she's a little less stressed?

Ignoring my feelings, I meet her excitement. "Let me guess, it wasn't *that* spicy after all, and he just wanted to get you back there? He used it as an excuse to see you again." *What?* Jesus. Why do I sound jealous right now?

Thankfully Keeley laughs. "Actually, no. He was surprised when I ordered it and God, was it hot. I'm not going to lie. I thought I was going to pass out. I finished the two pieces I was required to eat for the bet, then faked a call so I could leave. I was so traumatized that I completely forgot about the wine." She picks up the wine and assesses the bottle. "It looks like a good one. It was worth the pain."

I don't know whether to laugh or stare at her in awe.

"Do you want some?" she continues on. "I don't have any glasses that are good enough for wine, but after the day we've had, I'm not sure I care."

At that I chuckle. "You worked hard for that bottle. You should save it for yourself. Or share it with the owner's son."

Keeley snorts before her face contorts. "God, talking about him brings back memories of the rest of that night and...wow, you do not need to hear about that. Moving on. I'll get the glasses." She shakes her head before handing me the bottle and pizza. "I'll be right back."

She walks away without waiting for a response, and I stare after her.

Was she going to tell me they ended up in bed together? Is that what she held back? I run a hand through my hair, my body tense and… Why the fuck do I care?

Keeley returns after a few minutes with a tall smoothie glass and a paper cup. “Sorry, the rest of the glasses were in the dishwasher and someone forgot to turn it on.”

“I actually have whiskey glasses in my cabinet over there,” I say with a smirk, pointing to said cabinet. “Would you rather use those?”

“Hell, yes. Why didn’t you lead with that?”

“I forgot until just now.” *You distracted me with your half-finished story.*

“Do you have whiskey too?”

“I do. Do you drink it?”

“Not usually. I was just curious. I’m filing that away for the things I know about Salvatore D’Angelo.”

“Wow, okay. Is the file big?”

“It’s growing.” She smiles to herself as she heads over to the cabinet, grabbing the whiskey glasses before pouring us both a glass of wine.

“To Zane being free of his heartache,” she says, raising her glass in the air.

“To Zane.” I clink my glass to hers and take a sip of the wine, scrunching my face when I taste it.

“What’s wrong?” Keeley laughs before she’s able to take a sip of her own. “Too posh to drink wine out of a whiskey glass? At least it wasn’t the paper cup.”

“Too posh?” I scoff. “I’ll have you know I can rough it like the best of them.”

“Best of who?”

“The people who rough it. I don’t know. Just taste the wine. You’ll see why I pulled a face.”

“Oh no.” Keeley gasps as her hand flies to her mouth, stifling a grin. “Is it bad?”

“Not bad exactly. But something’s not right.”

She takes a sip and her eyes immediately widen, her expression much like my own. “I think I’m too posh to drink wine out of a whiskey glass. You’re right. It’s nice but there’s definitely something going on.”

“It’s the glass, not poshness. It’s suppressing the qualities of the wine.

The shape doesn't allow for the wine to breathe properly, affecting the aroma, which in turn affects the taste."

Keeley stares at me blankly, then releases the most infectious but obnoxious laugh. "It's both."

"What do you mean?"

"It's the glass *and* your poshness. Do you hear yourself? The glass suppresses the aromas." She mocks my voice as she puts her glass down, and something propels me to grab her hand, pulling her into me as I press a finger to her lips.

"Wealthy, yes. Posh, no."

Keeley's breath hitches and it's only then that our close proximity registers in my mind. She peers up at me intently, her crystal-blue eyes boring into mine, forcing me to look away as my heart slams against my rib cage. My gaze drops to my finger on her mouth at the exact moment her lips part. Her chest lifts as she sucks in a shaky breath, and I'm powerless to resist her, as all rational thought exits my brain.

My pulse spikes as I lift my hands to her cheeks and stare into her eyes, the world around me fading to black. My muscles tense. My fingers itch to be curled into her hair. And an inner battle rages inside me with every instinct telling me to walk away.

Keeley doesn't break my stare, but her tongue swipes across her already glossed lips as she takes a step closer.

And I'm fucked.

I close what's left of the space between us, pausing with my lips a breath away from hers, my chest buzzing with nervous anticipation. Keeley's eyes grow round, and I'm unable to hold back anymore, pressing my lips to hers, taking her mouth in a possessive kiss.

She stills momentarily before melting into me, her lips parting to welcome my tongue. Déjà vu hits me and the idea that we've done this before catches me off guard, sparking a jolt in my chest.

A soft mewl escapes her and my attention shifts, a groan trapping in the back of my throat, as I crowd into her, lifting her chin to deepen the kiss.

Our tongues dance until Keeley clutches at my shirt and pulls back breathlessly, her tender doe-eyed expression reaching inside me.

She shakes her head in shock, and the movement snaps me out of the moment, even before she tries to speak.

"I—"

My eyes stretch wide and I release her, my sudden retreat halting her words.

"Fuck, Keeley." I run a hand down my face, my voice raspy as I struggle to process what happened.

What the hell was I thinking?

"We shouldn't have done that?" Keeley asks when I don't elaborate, preempting my words as she stands tall.

I shake my head, finally meeting her gaze. "No, we shouldn't have."

"That's a shame because it didn't feel wrong." Her voice lacks warmth and emotion, and I can't decide if that's because she's reverting back to professional mode, or protecting her feelings from what she thinks is a rejection. Or both.

I'm about to apologize when her lips curl into a smile. "You're one hell of a kisser, D'Angelo."

I'm still reeling, but the smallest of smirks tugs at the edge of my lips. "Have I ever told you that I admire your lack of filter? You always convey whatever's on your mind."

"Not always."

"No?"

"I wanted you to kiss me just now, and yet, I stayed quiet and waited for you to make a move."

"I know. I didn't need words. You let me know by other means."

"Wow." A laugh bursts out of her but she doesn't shy away. "Good to know you can read me, Sal. Not many can."

I smile before my shoulders drop and I force myself to look away.

"The funny thing is, I can read you too," she says, drawing my attention. "You can save the explanation. I get it."

"Do you?" I move to be closer to her again before thinking better of it and subtly rocking back. "I'm terrified, Keeley." I run a hand through my hair, gripping the back of my neck. "I don't think I could have survived the last year without your support. I'm—"

"That's not going to change." She cuts me off, grabbing my hand to still me. "It was a kiss, Sal. A kiss in the moment during an emotional time. Nothing to worry about."

Something about her casual tone has me curling my fingers through hers, my hold forceful as I pull her back into me when she tries to walk away. "Just a kiss?"

"Yes." Her voice comes out breathy. "Just a kiss."

"So you don't think it'll affect us working together?" My heart races as I wait for her response, and when she smiles reassuringly, a little of my panic subsides.

"It won't. I promise. But I agree we shouldn't do it again."

CHAPTER SEVEN

KEELEY

"So you don't think it'll affect us working together?" Sal asks, stepping forward, his intense gaze boring into mine.

"It won't. I promise. But I agree we shouldn't do it again."

"After tonight."

"After—" Sal sinks his hands back into my hair, rendering me speechless as he lifts my face to his, his dark eyes holding me hostage, a question in his gaze. He wants this, me, but he's not going to do anything until I tell him I'm with him.

"After tonight," I agree and he sighs before his mouth descends on mine, sealing our lips in another intoxicating kiss.

His hand lowers to cup my cheek, and a groan escapes from the back of his throat, the sound sending a shiver down my spine.

Somewhere in the back of my mind, I know this is wrong, but when he walks me backward and lifts me to perch on the edge of his desk, I'm too far gone to care.

"Take me," I whisper against his mouth, before leaning back onto my elbows. Our eyes meet and the look of desire and lust staring back at me sends a gush of wetness between my thighs.

"As you wish." Sal drops to his knees and opens my legs, staring between them as—

...

My alarm blares and I jolt awake with a gasp. *Goddammit.* Was I about to have a sex dream? About Sal?

I pause for a second, trying to recall the dream, and when it hits me, I burst out laughing. Stupid alarm. I could have used a happy ending. It's been too long.

We may have agreed not to kiss again, but no one said anything about using each other to get ourselves off. Even if it's only in a dream.

Although, I have no doubt that Sal's far too much of a gentleman for that.

His loss. Not mine.

Switching off my alarm, I close my eyes and try to find my way back to my fantasy until the real world hits me.

Goddammit. I have responsibilities that affect others, and those are far more important than any fantasy dream I was trying to continue.

My toes curl as I stretch my body, listening for the satisfying crack of my back as I twist, and by the time I'm out of bed, my dream is nothing but a distant memory.

Probably for the best.

After prepping my morning smoothie, I lean on the edge of a stool in my kitchen and scroll through my emails, holding my breath for what I know is coming.

And just as expected, it's there.

Subject: I'm sorry. The news has gone wide.

Fuck.

At least Zane had a day to himself before the chaos began.

I read through a few emails, gathering as much information as I can before texting Zane. Not only has Landon's death been announced, the media also know about his arrest, meaning every dirty detail is about to come out.

KEELEY: Landon's death has hit the news and someone leaked that you were in lockup yesterday. We've got this. I'm not worried and neither should you be. But we're going to need to talk

My message turns to *read* but Zane doesn't respond, and if I'm being honest, I didn't expect him to. At least not right away. He needs time to process it all. The last few days have been hell for him.

He deserved more than twenty-four hours of respite.

After inhaling a calming breath to center myself, I throw on my workout gear and secure my earbuds to walk while I call my contacts—killing two birds with one stone—advising everyone that Salvatore D'Angelo will be making a statement later today.

It's just past nine when I make it to the office, having already put in a couple of hours of work. I'm ready to take on the rest of the day, but as I turn the corner, Sal spots me and my heart jolts. *Please don't be weird, please don't be weird.* I couldn't handle it if last night changed things between us. He pauses briefly, until I smile and his eyes soften with relief as he beelines toward me, ignoring his assistant when she calls out.

"How's your morning been? My phone's been blowing up since seven."

"And I've been blowing up other people's phones since around the same time. Are you sure you want to make the statement?" I finished writing it last night when I got home. After our brainstorming session, it didn't take long.

Sal straightens, his confident stance giving me his answer before he voices it. "Send it through, and I'll be ready whenever you need me."

"Eleven?"

"Sounds good."

I turn to walk past him but his arm shoots out, wrapping around my waist before he quickly lets go. "About last—"

"There's nothing to talk about. We're good."

"You don't even know what I was going to say."

"I don't?"

"Nope. I was going to ask about the pizza. I couldn't stop thinking about it. I'm pretty sure it featured in my dream."

"The pizza?"

"Yeah, the pizza."

My dream from last night comes back to mind and I laugh softly. "Me too. Told you it was amazing."

"It sure is...was." He shakes his head with a chuckle. "Anyway, where was it from again?"

"Riccardo's."

"Thanks. That's all I needed. Now I better go and rehearse my speech."

"No one will fault you for reading from a script."

"I know. But..."—he pauses, his smile fading—"I want to get this right. I want it to sound genuine because I genuinely care."

"You're a good man, Sal."

"Not all the time." He squeezes my arm and walks back toward his office, stopping by his assistant's desk before heading inside. My brows furrow as I watch him, but when Wes calls my name, I snap out of it, instantly reverting back to business mode.

Though I can't help wondering, was he really talking about the pizza? *Because I know I wasn't.*

The media crowds our practice field, and when I note the disgust on some of their faces, I'm relieved that Zane stayed away. And that Blair's with him.

Sal stands to deliver his statement, and before he even says a word, Jeff from *Sports Unfiltered* bellows out from the crowd, "Have you dropped Zane from the roster? With this being a family team, I'd say it goes against your belief system to have a murderer in your lineup."

I cringe as my stomach sinks, my fists clenching at my sides as I struggle to hold back from ripping into him.

"Thank you for the valid question," Sal says calmly, his stance confident, his gaze directed Jeff's way. "Though if you'd waited a few minutes like everyone else, you wouldn't have wasted your breath voicing it."

I stifle my amusement while others around me aren't so polite. "In other words, keep your mouth shut until question time," one of the reporters from *News Break International* calls out, and I have to stop myself from yelling *hear, hear.*

Chatter begins throughout the crowd until Sal waves his hand and clears his throat, the simple actions bringing everyone to silence.

"Thank you all for coming on short notice. As you will have heard by now, one of our rookie players, Landon McKenna, passed away a few days ago. His family asked that the news be kept quiet until they could arrange a private burial for him, but that didn't go to plan as they had hoped. No matter the circumstances surrounding his death, we are all saddened by the news, and have sent our condolences and support to his family during this terrible time.

"But while a young life was lost, there are others who are suffering because of an incident that never should have happened in the first place. Zane Fitzpatrick being one of them, along with Reed Coombs and his partner, Hayley."

Sal pauses, subtly swallowing back his emotions, and while I know he's nervous, because he told me as much, you wouldn't know it by looking at him. His voice is even, his stance remains tall, and his composure is solid. He's a man of great integrity and right now, it's pouring out of him through his words.

"As Jeff so kindly pointed out, the Storm franchise is a family-oriented team, and Zane is and always will be one of our family members. We ask that you don't throw stones until the police have finalized their investigation. For now, Zane has not been charged with anything surrounding Landon's death, and it's likely to stay that way."

Murmurs begin but Sal's quick to shut them down. "I will not hear any ill will toward either Zane or Landon now or in the future. If you have a genuine question, I'm here to provide answers to the best of my ability, but I will not tolerate false accusations or negativity. I can't stop you from publishing your gossip, but I refuse to be a part of it. Now, I have five minutes before we have to clear the stadium for our closed practice today."

A sea of hands shoot up and I search the faces, pointing to one of my college buddies who I pray does me a solid.

"Mr. D'Angelo, how is Zane's mental health in all this?"

I breathe a sigh of relief, making a note to thank him later. These are the types of questions I wanted, but I don't expect it to be all that smooth sailing when their articles go live later today.

After Zane is officially cleared, as he should have been from the start, I spend the next week fielding question after question about his life—past, present, and future—while doing my best to keep the impact on his mental health as minimal as possible. Which is not easy.

I know it'll pass. The news is fresh in everyone's minds, and despite proving his innocence, there are still some assholes out there that need someone to blame. Supporters that want answers, believing they've somehow been wronged or lied to.

The San Francisco Storm is once again in the heat of controversy, but this time, the entire team is rallying for their teammate, refusing to let anything bring them down.

I head home early after a particularly stressful day drowning in emails—trying hard not to pull out my hair after another Storm fan decided to spread some bullshit about Zane's past.

My phone buzzes multiple times when I walk through my door, and I welcome the fact that it's likely to be the group chat, needing the distraction.

HAYLEY: So… I've just realized that the guys' group chat is like a beacon for love

PAIGE: A what, now?

My thoughts exactly.

HAYLEY: A beacon for love. A matchmaking service. Whatever you want to call it. Think about it. First it was Luke's support group and he found love with Amelia. Then it was Easton's turn. Then Reed. You see where I'm going with this…

I snort out a laugh until I give it some thought. She's not wrong. What I wouldn't give to be there when Easton learns that little tidbit. He's going to shut that chat down so fast the guys won't know what hit them.

AMELIA: Does that mean it's over? I think it's only Dylan and Thomas left on the group chat and they're both married

HAYLEY: They added Zane, so they can add someone else

AMELIA: Who?

HAYLEY: Reed and I have someone in mind

PAIGE: Shit. Hayls, what are you doing? Easton just showed me the guys' chat

HAYLEY: What? It's a great idea

PAIGE: I'm not so sure she's going to agree

She? *Fuck*. I don't like the sound of that. As the only single one in our friendship group, it doesn't take a genius to know who "*she*" is.

KEELEY: Dare I ask?

HAYLEY: It's you

Of course it is.

PAIGE: They've decided to call the group chat Keeley's support group even though you're not on the chat. Apparently, it's your time. Easton's not happy

I'll bet. Neither am I.

PAIGE: I think it's kind of cute

KEELEY: It's not cute or necessary

HAYLEY: Wait. Reed said Zane's defending you. What does he know that we don't?

What in the world? I groan comically as I fall back onto my bed. My guess is that he's defending me because he still feels indebted to me.

KEELEY: He knows nothing because there is nothing to know

I'm being honest, at least about Zane knowing anything, but something tells me they're not going to believe me.

HAYLEY: I love you, but I don't believe you

And there it is. Right on cue. Gotta love them.

Channeling my grumpy younger brother, I remove myself from the group chat, laughing as I do. Because this is all harmless. I hope.

KEELEY LEFT THE GROUP

I don't need help with my love life. Nor do I want it. But I guess, what does it matter if they name their little chat after me? It's not going to work. I don't have time for love in my life, and I give it a few weeks before they figure that out and get bored.

PAIGE ADDED KEELEY TO THE GROUP

PAIGE: I'm sorry, Keels. It's official. They've changed the group name. Easton's just as pissed as you are

KEELEY: I'm not pissed. But it's pointless. Although, since my life's goal is to irritate my brother, maybe it won't be so bad

HAYLEY: That's the spirit. The love of your life is out there waiting and this is going to attract him

An image of Sal comes to mind and I laugh even harder. Nope. We are not going there again, even if he did light me up inside from only a kiss.

A kiss... I have an idea.

KEELEY: I don't know about love, but I'll take a hookup. If the group chat can work on that, I'd greatly appreciate it

Might as well put their meddling to good use. Can't have them wasting their so-called power.

PAIGE: Thank you for making my night hell, Keeley. Easton just read that text

KEELEY: Whoops

Sorry, not sorry. This is going to be fun.

Chapter Eight

SALVATORE

The second my office door closes, the smile drops from my face and I sink back against the wall, closing my eyes.

Another day, another goddamn press conference. Only this one wasn't like the others.

One second I'm defending Zane's honor, despite believing everyone had finally moved on, and the next my integrity's in question. All because some dickhead decided to look into my past, mentioning my once fractured relationship with Paige, accusing me of focusing more on the players on my team and my job over my own family.

And the worst part is he wasn't fucking wrong. Back then at least. Now it's different.

I know my faults; I own them. A comment like that wouldn't normally get me enraged like it did, except that he also asked about the impending court case for the Mikklesons—Paige's ex-boyfriend's dad and uncle. A case I might have to testify in. A case *she* might have to testify in. And it completely rattled me.

When Paige first moved to San Francisco, she was being blackmailed by her ex's family, the Mikklesons. All because she'd overheard her ex-boyfriend's mom and aunt talking about some of his dad and uncle's illegal dealings within their company. Since our relationship was still a little fractured at the time, she didn't tell me what was going on. Instead, she decided to hire my private investigator, Austin, to dig around for proof that she could take to the police.

Being the strong, sometimes stubborn woman that she is, it wasn't until she was worried about her mom that she finally confided in me. As it turned out, Camilla had been sleeping with Gabriel Mikkleson, Paige's ex-boyfriend's dad.

The last thing Paige needs is to be thrown into the spotlight again when she's finally managed to find herself a semi-private life. As private as one can get in a high-profile relationship. These days, she controls the narrative, and I want to keep it that way.

What the hell is wrong with people?

How can they care so little about another person's feelings?

My cell rings at the same time my assistant buzzes my desktop phone, and I snap out of my mood. I've got shit to do and no time to wallow.

I answer my cell as I stride toward my computer, messaging Tabitha to ask her what she needs before spending the next hour putting out fires.

Client conflicts at D'Angelo Construction—the business I'm still meant to be running in New York.

Salary cap budget restraints.

Sponsors questioning whether or not they want to continue to support the team.

My ex-wife panicking over our son's recent headline.

I've just hung up with my fourth call in the last twenty minutes when someone knocks on the door, and I silently groan, banging my head onto my desk. "I'm not here," I call out, assuming it's Tabitha again.

"For me, you are. I'm coming in." My head snaps up at Keeley's voice and my mood lifts.

"What makes you think you're so special?" I ask as I get up from my desk and walk toward the door, instantly regretting my words since I've yet to figure out if we can joke anymore.

"We both know the answer to that." Keeley winks and I relax. "Now move out of the way; I need to sit down." She ducks under my arm, and her wildflower perfume assaults my nose, the familiar scent working like a drug, warming me as I breathe her in.

"That was awful this morning, but you handled it well. How are you feeling?" She launches straight into work talk as she sits down on my couch, and though it shouldn't, it catches me off guard.

I close my office door and hover near the entry, hesitating as far away as possible.

We haven't been alone in my office since I kissed her weeks ago, and for some reason, I assumed this moment would play out differently.

Our working relationship may have returned to normal, but this office will never be the same. "I'm fine," I recover, lying. "As you said, I handled it, and we can move on."

"Can we?"

"Yes."

"Sal, I was calling your name from the moment you walked away and you didn't hear me. The only reason I didn't barge in here sooner was because Wes needed me."

"Come on." I finally leave my position near the door, walking behind my desk. "That didn't happen." It's not possible. Keeley only has to whisper and I pay attention.

"You're allowed to admit when something affects you."

"I'm fine," I growl, standing taller as though that will prove my point. "Zane's the one you should be worried about. They ripped him to shreds back there."

"No, they didn't. They *tried*. You protected him."

Of course I did. Apparently being cleared of any wrongdoing in Landon's death means *nothing* to the media, along with some of our less forgiving fans. Zane's been forced to relive every dark moment of his past over and over since the case was ruled an accident, and I have to give him credit—he's handling it better than I would.

Although, for all I know, he's slamming the door when he gets home, wanting to bang his head against the wall like I am.

I'm thankful he has our team to support him. And, as Keeley's gaze softens, as though privy to my inner musings, I'm grateful I have her.

If anyone truly believes that women are the lesser sex, they are sorely mistaken. The women in my life are among the strongest people I know. Men, including me, would be lost without them.

"I did what anyone would have done in my situation." I shrug and Keeley scoffs incredulously.

"Sal, they brought up Paige and Camilla."

"They did," I say calmly, thinking back to the moment they mentioned my ex-wife. "I handled it. Now it's time to move on."

"You can hide your feelings from the world as much as you want. You can't hide them from me."

"I'm fine. Was it shitty to have my faults thrown in my face? Yes. Of course it was. Doesn't mean I have to dwell on it after."

"If that's what you want, I'll drop it. After one last point."

I glance her way, my lips curling into a small smile.

"You wouldn't be you if you didn't always have more to say."

"Exactly. And you better damn well listen."

"I always do."

"Good." She stands up, walking toward my desk, and I subtly step back. "You are not the man they described back there. That's the Sal from five years ago. Don't let those fuckers get to you."

"It was probably closer to three years if we're being honest, but who's counting?"

I wink and Keeley's lips press together in a frown, but she lets me off the hook, dropping the issue as promised, both of us falling back into a comfortable existence, and an ease takes over me.

I've always been able to go it alone, to get things done, to do what I had to do without getting others involved. And I liked it that way. Until I didn't. Now, I have to admit, it's nice having a teammate.

It's nice getting to share the load.

Zane's a formidable force over the next couple of months, and while football is a team sport, he's a big contributor to our success in the lead-up to the playoffs. I'd go so far as to say he channeled his rage into the game, and it shows. With the media furor surrounding Landon's death finally dying down—now that they have other topics to focus on—we're all working hard to put that chapter behind us.

If only I could put all the Storm chaos behind me. Instead, I have new problems to tackle almost every day, each accompanied by a giant billboard that says, "you can't avoid this anymore" and a flashing red danger sign.

I used to think Paige would be the death of me. Now I'm not so sure. The Storm franchise is working its way up to that top spot.

As though my thoughts conjured her, Paige calls as I'm hanging up with the Storm chief financial officer, and I smile as I answer. "Hey, Kid. How's your day?"

"Busy as always with an almost five-year-old. How are you?"

"Busy as always surrounded by five-year-olds."

"Oh, dear. Who was it this time?"

"It doesn't matter. I'd much rather talk about the *almost* five-year-old that can actually do things that are asked of him."

"There's a bit of a difference between brushing your teeth and running a billion-dollar empire."

"Hey, I'm the one running those empires. Their jobs are to control their fucking departments. Oh, ship, you don't have me on speaker, do you?"

"Nope, I learned my lesson the hard way. Let's just say that Isaac doesn't say 'ship' when something goes wrong."

"Ah, fudge. I'm sorry."

"No need to be. It wasn't you. It was Mom."

"Oh, good."

"Good?"

"Yep. I want to be the favorite grandparent on your side."

"I'm happy to hear that because Isaac asked if you could come over for dinner tonight. He said something about a secret club?" Her voice is hesitant, and I laugh out loud for the first time in what feels like weeks.

"I don't know what you're talking about. There's no club."

"What did he say?" Isaac's sweet little voice filters in from the background, and my heart fills with so much love.

"He said there's no club," Paige tells him, and I bite back a smile.

"Good. Is he coming over?"

"I sure am. Give me an hour."

"He's coming."

"Yay." Isaac's cheers work to chip away at the wall I'd erected to get through this week, and I make a mental note to thank him for it.

"I'll see you soon."

"Thanks, Dad. Maybe you can stay after he's gone to sleep? We can chat about your work?"

"We'll see. Love you."

"Love you too."

After hanging up with Paige, I have another three calls that threaten to bring down my mood, but it doesn't work. I'm off to see my little man, and nothing is going to affect me.

Since Paige and Easton gave me a key, I announce myself on my arrival then listen out for Isaac's footsteps as he runs toward me.

"Poppy!" He skids to a stop, with his socks gliding along the floor, and when he reaches me, I swoop him up into my arms.

"Careful, old man, you wouldn't want to break something." Paige appears at the end of the hall, welcoming me with her sassy grin.

"Who are you calling old? I still hit the gym five times a week. I can keep up with the best of them."

"What gym are you using? Because you don't use the one here."

"He uses the one at the stadium." Easton appears behind her, his expression stoic as he leans against the wall. "I can vouch for him. I've witnessed it with my own eyes," he says matter-of-factly and Paige snorts.

"Suck-up," she jokes, making me chuckle.

"Why would he need to suck up? It can't be because of you. You never listen to my opinion."

"You're right. I was referring to you being his boss."

I internally cringe, shifting in place as I smile through it. Another reminder of why I should *never* have kissed his sister.

"Easton has nothing to worry about," I tell Paige, pulling myself from my thoughts. "I don't make player cuts."

Isaac's eyes bounce between us all until he grabs my face and draws my attention his way, seemingly over the ridiculous adult conversation. "It's time for the club," he whispers loudly, his eyes flashing back to his parents. "They still don't know."

That may be true for now, but they'll know by the end of the night, because from the look on Paige's face, she is not letting me leave until I've explained myself.

I shrug at Paige, feigning ignorance before turning back to Isaac. "Let's go to our base. They won't hear us in there."

Isaac and I play secret spies in our secret club until we're called for dinner, and as soon as we're finished, we continue our game until it's Isaac's bedtime. The game's not overly innovative or complicated—all we do is make up our own little spy adventures—but it's ours, and I missed out on games like this with my own kids. Something I'll regret for the rest of my life.

I don't check my phone until I'm back in my apartment—only ever completely switching off like that when I'm with Isaac—and I find a message from Keeley.

KEELEY: I came by to ask about the budget meeting just now and to my utter surprise… you weren't there. On a school night 😉

I smile to myself as I respond before setting up my laptop for a night of work.

SALVATORE: Shocking, I know. I was with Isaac. Just got home.

KEELEY: Did you play secret club?

What?

SALVATORE: YOU KNOW ABOUT THE CLUB?!

I chuckle to myself, picturing Paige's face when she finds out Keeley's involved too. I snuck out before she could ask about it tonight, mostly because I could tell that she and Easton were both tired, so I'm waiting for her to call me.

KEELEY: I do. Isaac accidentally mentioned it when I was there yesterday. He panicked at first because he said it was supposed to be something between the two of you

Oh, shit. Poor Isaac.

SALVATORE: ...

KEELEY: Don't worry though. I put his mind at ease. I told him you and I play secret club too

I choke on thin air, coughing as I reread the message. *What the fuck, Keels?*

SALVATORE: Thanks.

I think?

What do I even say to that? And why has my mind gone somewhere it absolutely shouldn't? She's clearly joking, and yet, now I have our kiss back in the front of my mind. Not that it ever really left.

Keeley sends me back a laughing emoji, and since I have no clue what the hell she means by it, instead of replying, I distract myself with work.

Maybe it's not Paige or the Storm drama that's going to kill me. Maybe it's Keeley.

Chapter Nine

KEELEY

TWO MONTHS LATER

My heels clack against the polished concrete floors as I rush through the halls, needing a moment to myself after the day I've had. Tension coils in my shoulders, but when I'm close to Sal's office, I lift to my toes, softening the sound of my heels to sneak past unnoticed.

It's not that I don't want to see him, because that's usually the highlight of my day, but he's had a lot going on, and if he sees me right now, knowing I just finished a meeting with our sponsors for the season ahead, he's going to want to talk about it.

He might be a boss when it comes to his delegation skills, but he still loves to take on more than is necessary. And right now, he has bigger issues to work through. Namely the budget. It hasn't looked good since our previous owner fucked us out of the television series deal.

I've just made it around the corner when Luke calls my name from where he's standing in Sal's doorway.

Dammit. I tried.

"What can I do for you, Luke?"

As Luke moves toward me, Sal pops his head out of his office and raises an eyebrow, his way of questioning how I'm doing. I smile back as his phone rings, and he waves apologetically before walking inside, closing the door behind him.

Saved by the call.

At least until Luke smirks. "I'm not going to like this, am I?" I walk toward my office and Luke follows after me, leaning his shoulder against the doorjamb while I put my notebook and laptop on my desk.

"You're going to love it," he tells me. "I found you another man."

Ugh. I audibly groan, but cough to hide it. "Thank you, Luke. I appreciate all that you do, but as I've said for the past few months, I don't need your help."

"Sorry, Keels. You know I can't stop. It's all part of your support group."

"I don't—" I cut myself off, curling my lips into a grin. "I know you want to help. But no offense, the last three were..." I trail off, unsure how to describe Luke's epic failures.

I never had any intention of actually going along with the "Keeley needs a man" bullshit until I heard about the misery it was causing Easton every time Luke mentioned setting me up. After that, I couldn't help but play along. Easton's my brother; I live to make him miserable.

Only it came back to bite me on the ass. Because where the hell did he find the guys he set me up with?

Guy number one wanted to know which of the players I'd "hooked up with."

Guy number two couldn't understand why I worked for a football team and asked if I was going to quit when I had kids.

And guy number three tried to kiss me before we'd even sat down for dinner.

If I didn't know Easton better, I'd wonder if it was him getting me back. Except that's not something he'd ever bother doing.

"I know." Luke cringes, pushing off the wall to walk closer. "They were duds. In my defense, most of my friends are either taken or football players and you won't date either."

"I won't date guys that are taken?" I question, my brows raised.

"That came out wrong."

"It did. But I promise. I'm happy. If and when I want a man, I'll find one."

"What about Coach or someone else on the staff?"

"You want me to date Pierce?" My eyes bulge though it's not Pierce that popped into my head.

"God, no. I'm just trying to get a gauge on other people I know. Are coaches and staff off-limits? What about agents?"

I stiffen but Luke's lost in thought, most likely trying to come up with more ideas, so he thankfully doesn't notice.

"I think you're going about this all wrong." I try another tack, and Luke's forehead creases as he glances back at me.

"How so?"

"Well, when the rest of you found love, you found it on our own. The group chat worked its magic without your help."

Luke's confusion deepens, and I internally curse myself until his eyes light up.

"You're right." He clicks his fingers and I breathe a sigh of relief. I should have mentioned that months ago. "But..." Luke's voice cuts into my internal celebration and I pause. *Damn buts*. He always has them. "That will only work if you promise to get out more. You're never going to meet someone if all you do is work. It's the offseason, Keeley. You should be on vacation or joining a group of like-minded individuals to go... shit, I don't know. Do you have any hobbies?"

"How do you know I'm not going on a vacation?"

"Amelia."

Dammit.

"Well, rest assured, I'll be spending plenty of time with 'like-minded individuals.' I don't plan on spending all of my time here."

"It's seven p.m." He points toward my window, and I turn to see it's dark outside. Which is nothing new.

"So?"

"It's the offseason," he reminds me again, staring at me pointedly and... *Jesus*. When he says it like that, it sounds bad. I had no idea of the time. That meeting must have gone a lot longer than I thought. Time flies when you're having fun.

"Okay." Point made but what do I... Hang on... "You're here." I raise an eyebrow and he laughs.

"I am. Only I'm here because the big boss called me in to talk about the fundraiser I'm hosting with the D'Angelo Foundation, and no one says no to D'Angelo."

Dammit again.

"Fine. I'll try harder to meet someone. In fact, I'll message Paige now and see if she wants to go out next weekend."

"Great idea." Satisfaction beams across his face, and my eyelids briefly drop.

"You're like an annoying brother. You know that, right? More annoying than my *actual* brother."

"I'm giving you the full-sibling service since Easton's so grumpy all the time. This is how it's supposed to be."

"Oh, so you set Lainey and Thomas up, did you? That was sweet."

"Fuck, no. They kept that shit quiet."

"I wonder why."

"Maybe a brother is the wrong word. Think of me as a concerned friend."

"How about an overbearing coworker?"

Luke laughs, not at all perturbed by my put-down. He thrives on banter like this. "That works," he says, proving my point. "Get out more and I wouldn't have to stick my nose into your business."

"Why do you care?"

"Why do I care?" He scoffs as though I've offended him, and a little part of me feels bad until the hint of a smirk shines through. "I love messing with you, Keeley. You know I think highly of someone when I annoy the hell out of them. It's my thing. Just ask Amelia. And Lainey. And Hayley. And—"

"Thanks, Luke." I smile genuinely, my chest warming. Because deep down I know what he's trying to say. He cares. That's Luke. He's like an annoying brother, sure, but he genuinely cares. And since I would go to bat for any of these guys and their partners, like they're my own family, I get it. "You're a good guy. Despite what everyone says."

"What? Who's saying something?"

I bite my tongue until his face drops and I burst out laughing. "I can tease with the best of them."

"Okay. Okay. I get it. You can do it on your own."

"I can. And I will. When I'm ready."

"Okay, Keeley. Have a good night."

"You too."

He backs out into the hallway, laughing before he walks away, and I

follow to close my office door behind him, my eyes flashing to Sal's office before I do. It's seven p.m. on a Friday night during the offseason. Maybe we both need a life.

I'm not sure why, but Luke's words are still running through my mind when I arrive at the salon the next morning, and I hate to admit, he got to me.

"You're never going to meet someone if all you do is work."

He's right. Only there's no part of me that wants to change. I love my job. It stimulates and challenges me on a daily basis. And I love the Storm football team. I love keeping busy. It's my thing. I'd be lost without it. But... at some point I am going to be ready to settle down, and if I have no life outside of work, that's going to make finding someone difficult.

A future-Keeley problem.

Matt, my hairstylist, settles behind me, pulling me from my thoughts as he plays with my hair. "How's my favorite boss of the babes?" He smiles, grabbing his cart before sitting on the stool beside me.

"I'm good, thanks." I return his smile.

"And..."

"The 'babes' are good too."

"I miss them. Why aren't any of them in the news right now?"

"It's the offseason." I shrug as though that's an answer.

"So? Shouldn't that mean more time to get into trouble?"

"Definitely." *Let's hope that doesn't happen.* "Though it seems like the hockey men are stealing the focus."

"They sure are. Did you hear about the drama with the San Francisco Power?"

"I did, and I'm almost tempted to call their media team to find out what the fuck they are doing over there. He's a rookie. He shouldn't..." I trail off when Matt's eyes widen like he's about to get some insider information. And that right there is why the media are having a field day with that story. "Moving on. What are we doing with my hair?"

Matt huffs dramatically as though I've ruined his fun before recovering with a beaming grin. "I've got an idea for something different."

"Different?" I've kept my auburn hair the same length since college. I was joking when I asked what we were doing. I like consistency in my life, and my hair is something I can control. "I don't know about—"

"Hang on. I want to show you a photo."

He walks away without letting me argue, and I playfully roll my eyes as my phone buzzes with a text in the girls' group chat. He can show me what he wants, but it doesn't mean I'm going to like it.

AMELIA: Oh. My. God. I am so sorry, Keeley. Luke just told me about your conversation last night

I stifle a laugh, shaking my head as my hair concerns drift away.

KEELEY: He means well

It's annoying as fuck, but he means well. At least that's what I keep telling myself. Hopefully he backs off after our chat last night. Actually, I'm hoping they all back off.

HAYLEY: What did I miss?

AMELIA: Luke asked Keeley if she'd consider dating Coach Pierce

PAIGE: WHAT?!

HAYLEY: Oh Luke

I glance toward the back room to see Matt flicking through a magazine, giving me time to respond.

KEELEY: Technically he was trying to find out whether or not I'd be open to dating a coach. Or staff. Since I've blacklisted athletes

HAYLEY: That makes sense

KEELEY: Except that I don't need to be set up

I feel like a broken record saying that over and over. It's been months since they started the "Keeley support group" and while yes, I agreed to three dates during that time, I never once wavered from my "I can do this myself" approach.

HAYLEY: Is there something you're not telling us? I still remember what Zane said when all of this started

I start typing to defend Zane but Blair beats me to it.

BLAIR: Zane doesn't like being indebted to anyone. That was his way of saying he wants no part of this

KEELEY: And he's kept up his end of the deal. Even when Jenna tried to set me up with Blair's brother

I love Blair's bestie, Jenna, but what a disaster that was. Blair's brother is a good guy, However, he's not my type. I need someone a little more serious. Not to mention someone that's *not* four years younger than me.

BLAIR: Zane may love Cade again now, but he's got your back, Keeley

KEELEY: Tell him his debt is paid. (Laughing emoji) and tell the rest of the guys that I'm good. I've got this on my own

PAIGE: Easton will be happy about that. He cringes every time your name is mentioned. Although he did speak up when Jenna suggested Cade. I don't think he liked the idea of you moving away, since Cade doesn't live here

KEELEY: Aww he does love me

PAIGE: You know it

"Who's got you smiling like that?" Matt asks when he returns, hiding something behind his back.

"Paige."

"Oh, I love that girl."

"You and me both." I'll always be relieved that Easton found himself an amazing woman. His track record wasn't great.

"I'm seeing her this week to talk wedding styles," Matt tells me, and excitement wells in my chest.

"No way." I spin to face him. She's been keeping quiet about the wedding.

"Way." He covers his mouth as though he's said too much and I laugh. Matt's been Paige's hairstylist since she moved to San Francisco, and she introduced me after we became close.

"I can't tell you any more about Paige due to client/stylist confidentiality." I snort but he waves me off. That's definitely not a thing. "So...let's get down to business. What do you think about this?"

I reluctantly shift my gaze, armed with excuses as to why I need to keep my hair exactly how it's always been, but when I see the image, I'm intrigued.

Maybe if I change this part of my life, it will be easier to consider changing other areas. If anything, it's worth a shot.

Chapter Ten

SALVATORE

I dodge a few kids running around the lobby as I step out of the elevator, the sound of their laughter reminding me of Isaac, and a smile lights up my face. In the past I would have scowled at their parents, silently telling them to control their children, but now, you could say Isaac's softened me. A little. And I don't completely hate it.

It wasn't that I didn't like kids. Because I always have. In small doses. It's the chaos that I find difficult to handle. The unpredictability.

All things I've been working on since moving to San Francisco and reconnecting with Paige.

Speaking of my darling daughter… For the first time in as long as I can remember, she's waiting for me in the restaurant at our building, faking annoyance as I walk through the door a minute later than planned.

"What time do you call this?" She taps the simple gold Rolex I bought her for her birthday, and I chuckle under my breath.

"I'm terribly sorry, Paige. I know how much you love punctuality."

"I'll forgive you this time. Don't let it happen again."

"Noted. Why are *you* early?"

"Because I thought we were meeting at nine." She shrugs and I wince.

"Shit. You've been waiting for thirty minutes?"

"No. I just sat down."

"Of course you did." Another chuckle rumbles out of me, this one a little louder than before and Paige shrugs again. I can always count on Paige for consistency. Her lateness never fails.

"The usual?" I ask, scanning the room for a server.

"Yep. You know me."

Since the restaurant's busier than usual, I jump up to order our breakfast at the bar, hoping to bypass some of the patrons waiting for servers to arrive. When I sit back down, Paige is laughing at her phone.

"Sorry." She briefly glances up as I place a glass of water in front of her. "I promise you'll have my full attention in a second."

"What's so funny?" I take a sip of my water as I sit, enjoying the lightness to her expression.

"Apparently Luke wanted to set Keeley up with Coach Pierce."

"What?" I cough, choking on my drink, inhaling the liquid instead of swallowing it down. "Pierce?" I rasp.

"Yep."

A weight presses down on me at her nonchalant response but I ignore it.

"Well, there you go." I laugh softly, trying to cover my shock, and it hurts as though the water burned the back of my throat. "Interesting pairing. Is she going out with him?"

I cough again. *Why the fuck would I ask that?* Since when do I gossip with my daughter?

Paige laughs out loud, waving me off. "Of course not. He's like twenty years older than she is."

"Of course." I fight to stop the frown I feel forming because it has no business in this conversation. Paige is *not* wrong.

I force a smile and Paige eyes me curiously before her lips curl into a grin. "She's humored Luke a few times, going out with the guys he set her up with, but it was a hard no for Pierce."

"Right. I never pictured Luke as a matchmaker."

"Oh, you have no idea. It's become like a sport to him."

"With all his friends?"

"Nope. Just Keeley."

"I bet she *loves* that." The words are out of my mouth before I can process it, and Paige doesn't bother hiding her intrigue.

"Your sarcasm is spot on. She hates it. I think it's because she's hiding something. You two don't talk about that stuff?"

"What? No. We talk about work."

"All the time?"

"Yes."

"But you're friends, right?" She raises a brow and I nod in confirmation.

"We are." After everything happened with Zane, it was harder to hide the close friendship Keeley and I had, since Hayley and Reed had seen it firsthand. Only our friendship isn't exactly traditional in the way Paige is thinking.

"So...it can't all be about work." Her brows knit together, and I know it stems from her concern for my lack of a social life. I'm surprised she hasn't asked Luke to try and set me up.

"Do you think we sit around painting each other's toenails while talking about our love lives?" I smirk and Paige shakes her head, her concern instantly gone, exactly as planned.

"I would pay to see that. I'm not sure if I've said it before, but I'm glad you have each other. You both work too hard. I feel better knowing you're not alone."

You and me both, Kid. "It's nice knowing someone else is in the building at all hours. Only, I'm an old man; I don't have anything else going on. Keeley should go out more. Maybe you can help with that."

"Maybe I can." Paige nods with a smile, and while I'm the one that suggested it, a pit forms in my stomach. A selfish pit. Because I like having her around. "Maybe we need to take a different approach when it comes to her love life. Thanks, Dad."

"Happy to help."

What the fuck did I just do?

With the draft approaching, the topic of Thomas's replacement surfaces again now that it's apparent our second QB isn't going to be fit enough to play. And it's safe to say, it's elicited an acceptable level of panic. We won the Super Bowl last season, and to be without a star quarterback now is less than ideal.

I'm the first to arrive for our Monday morning meeting, and as the room fills, I scan my notes, glancing up every time the door opens.

With a minute to spare before we begin, Keeley walks in looking like the epitome of a fucking bombshell with a new, wavy shoulder-length bob, and my eyes bulge before I quickly recover. Not before opening my big mouth.

"You cut your hair," I rush out the second she sits down, silencing everyone at the table.

"I did. Thank you for noticing." She rakes her fingers through the strands, her expression confident, despite the fact that it's probably not something I should have mentioned.

I almost tell her it's hard *not* to notice, but I manage to hold back the remark, turning my attention to our general manager, Wes. "And you got glasses?" I smile, my tone lifting, thankful that he too walked in with a new look.

"I did. For reading. Thanks for noticing." He chuckles to himself as I tap my papers on the table.

"What can I say? I'm an observant fucker when I want to be."

"It's appreciated," Wes jokes before launching into the reason we're all here—our lack of a quarterback—and my chest tightens. "As I'm sure you've heard, Lawrence injured himself again playing a friendly game of football with his family last week, *after* he was cleared to play by the team trainers and the third-party doctors who assured us he was fit. It's no one's fault; it was a freak injury, but it now leaves us down two quarterbacks for next season." Wes is so calm you'd think he was discussing dropping his sandwich at lunchtime, and it settles my mind. If he's not worried, I shouldn't be either. "We already planned to secure one in the draft, but we need star power and we don't have the picks to secure that," he continues, stating the obvious. "The team and I have a suggestion."

"One suggestion?" *Dammit.* I force a smile while my stomach knots again. I trust Wes. I'm sure he knows what he's doing.

"It's a good one," he confirms, putting me at ease. Wes is a straight shooter. It didn't take long for me to learn there's no smoke and mirrors when it comes to him. He says what he thinks and he always does what's best.

"Let's hear it."

"Beckett Myers." He pauses, letting the name sink in, and I'm pleasantly surprised. "Current quarterback for the Colorado Cougars, known for his precision and record-breaking strike rate. He never misses his mark. It's usually his teammates that fuck it up for him."

Wes isn't wrong. Myers is a great player. One of the best. He's a solid choice. The only problem being that, despite his teammates letting him down, he's been with the same team since he was drafted, and there has to be a reason for that. Loyalty, maybe?

"What makes you think he's interested in a move?"

"His agent."

A laugh escapes me and it's echoed around the room, drawing my gaze back to Keeley. She brushes a loose strand of her hair behind her ear, and I picture my fingers entwined in the waves, tugging her head back as I… *Jesus.*

"That's a good place to start," I rush out when the laughter dies down. "I'm guessing he's a free agent?"

"He is. We've been told he wants to retire in a few years but that he's hungry for a Super Bowl win. Desperate for it, in fact. And while we can't guarantee that for him, our odds are higher than most. I've also heard through the grapevine that he's not happy. Hunter, his agent, didn't say that when we spoke, maybe to protect his reputation if he ends up staying with the Cougars. But a reliable source mentioned that he's one person in the spotlight and another person entirely when he's around his teammates in private. They're not the bonded team they claim to be."

"Okay. What does he want?"

"A three-year contract, and a guarantee that the team is out to win. Even if they don't."

"I meant money."

"As crazy as it sounds, his agent alluded to the fact that money didn't matter as much as his other requests."

"Seems too good to be true."

"Well…" Wes trails off, removing his glasses before eyeing me apologetically. "Our reputation isn't exactly glowing right now, and Beckett, understandably, has reservations. He's concerned about what he'd be walking into."

Fuck. I love this team, but most of my time is spent cleaning up messes, with a majority of them caused by outside forces or staff from the past, Landon's death aside. "Let me talk to him. Can you send me his agent's details? Maybe give him a heads-up that I'll be in touch?"

"I sure can."

"And if that fails... Are you telling me we don't have a backup other than our current backup who isn't ready to be a starter and our draft pick?"

Wes falls awkwardly silent and I have my answer. *We'd have to secure two quarterbacks in the draft.*

Keeley smiles from across the table, and I raise a brow in question, my eyes betraying me as they drop to her lips. "What Wes's silence is saying is... don't fail and all will be fine."

A laugh bursts out of me as I shake my head. "Thanks, Keeley. I'll do my best."

"You've got this. And if not, I know a wide receiver who I could bully into giving it a go. And you know Easton. He'd love it."

She's joking, of course, but I appreciate the humor. We have to stay positive. Beckett's our man. And we're going to secure him.

After another fifty minutes of the team running through realistic ideas in case my talk with Beckett doesn't go well, we end the meeting no better off than we started. When it comes down to it, Myers is the best fit, and until we know for sure what he's thinking, we're stuck in limbo.

Keeley's caught in another conversation when we leave, so I wait for her in the hallway closer to her office, reading through the millions of emails I've received in the hour I've been away from my phone. Or, at least, trying to read them.

I'm distracted.

Despite managing to hold very official discussions, I haven't been able to stop thinking about Keeley's goddamn hair since she walked into the conference room. And I can't for the life of me figure out why. It's a haircut. It's not a big deal.

She turns the corner, and the second she smiles I'm taken back to our kiss. It's been months, and yet I'm always taken back to that goddamn kiss, which is really fucking inconvenient.

"Are you waiting for me?" she asks when she spots me, tucking her new hair behind her ears, drawing my attention to it.

"Why the change?" I blurt, launching right into it, making her laugh.

"Are you saying you don't like it?"

"Did I say that?"

"No." She sucks her lips into her mouth, biting back a grin. "It was hard to miss the shock."

"I thought I hid it well."

"From others, maybe, but I saw it. When the attention shifted to Wes and your eyes flashed to mine."

"I wasn't expecting it. You never mentioned you were getting it cut."

"I didn't, and—"

"Why would you?" My shoulders drop as I chuckle lightly. Like I told Paige, work has always been Keeley's and my main topic of conversation, although before our kiss, we were definitely moving toward more personal topics. Now, we're back to strictly work talk. Our conversations may have changed, but the support and comfort she gives me have never wavered. And I like to think that's remained something she values from me too.

"Exactly." Keeley confirms my thoughts. "We're colleagues. Actually, we're not colleagues. You're the boss and my brother's future father-in-law."

Complicated as fuck is what I am.

Tension knots my neck while Keeley laughs as though she's read my mind and finds it utterly ridiculous, except that's the exact reason I never brought up the kiss again after it happened. Should we have had another conversation about it? *Probably.* But we're both adults, and at the time we decided it was a one-off lapse of judgment during an emotionally charged moment, nothing more. So that's how I'm treating it.

And she's dating now anyway.

Keeley nods a few times before gesturing toward her office. "I've got some work to do. Did you need me? Other than to ask about my hair?"

"You never actually answered me."

"Someone said I needed a change. Something new in my life. This is that, I guess." She laughs to herself.

"Good. I like that. And I like the haircut. It suits you."

She shakes her head as though I'm just trying to be nice, but she's wrong. She's more beautiful now than she was before and I didn't think that was possible. She's... Keeley. That's who she is. *Motherfucker.*

"Thanks, Sal. I like it too. *And* Wes's glasses." She stares at me pointedly and I can't stop the belly laugh that rumbles out of me.

"Yes, definitely. They were very striking. Me and my attention to detail." Code for… I fucked up again and almost admitted that I care for Keeley on a deeper level than that of a colleague.

I may not care about what anyone thinks of me, but I wouldn't want her to suffer because I couldn't keep my mouth shut. Thank God for new glasses.

"Have a nice afternoon, Keeley."

"Thanks, Sal. You too." She hits me with a sassy grin as she walks into her office, and it stays in my mind long after she's gone. My head is a messed-up place to be right now.

What the fuck is wrong with me?

Chapter Eleven

KEELEY

It's late, so the stadium's quiet as I spin around in my chair, putting my feet up on the edge of my desk. "Are you sure you don't have another angle?" I ask Liz from *Sports Unfiltered*. "The team's been through a lot. I'm not presenting this to Mr. D'Angelo unless I have your word."

"Trust me. He *is* the angle. That man is fine with a capital F. Not to mention rich and powerful. People are intrigued."

They want to do a puff piece on Sal, and I'm not sure he's going to go for it.

"Okay." I huff under my breath, imagining the look on Sal's face when I fill him in. "I'll try and catch him tonight. If not, I'll put in the request tomorrow."

"Thank you, Keeley. This will be a big win for me."

"Don't thank me yet. He hasn't said yes."

"I know. The thanks is for asking."

I hang up the phone and laugh to myself. Fine with a capital F? She's not wrong. But really? Does she think it's going to work if I pitch it to him that way?

Checking the time, I slip into my heels, a smile locked in place, ready to find Sal. I only make it around my desk when my phone rings again, my smile widening when I see the name on the screen.

"Callum? It can't be."

"Yeah, yeah. It's me. Don't get used to it."

My best friend never calls me. I call him regularly and he's happy to chat. Well, as happy as a strong, silent type having to listen to his bestie get everything off her chest can be. But he never calls.

I laugh to myself until reality sinks in. *He called me.* "What's wrong?" I try to keep my voice even, but fail to hide the hint of panic in my tone.

"Nothing's wrong, Keeley. Do you think I'd call you if it was?"

"Yes. Why wouldn't you?"

"Because you're on the other side of the world. How are you going to help if I jammed my finger in the door or cut my foot open?"

"For a serious guy, you're a real comedian. And an idiot. There are these things called emotions and feelings. You can have issues that are not physical."

"Right. Nah, I'm good."

"But you're calling me?"

"I am. Mum was asking about you and filling me in on your mum, so I called." I can picture him shrugging, and it almost makes me laugh.

"How is Bonnie? Is she there?"

"She's good. She was over last night."

"Last night? Oh, I forgot it's early in the morning in Scotland. Are you on your way to work?"

"The gym then work. So, what's new with you?"

"You're asking questions now? Who are you and what have you done with my best friend? Wait. I think I've figured you out. Your mom asked about me and you didn't have answers, did you?"

"Not a single one."

"What did she ask?"

"How you're coping with your mum's illness. Whether or not you're getting enough sleep or time to yourself. If you're *dating*."

"No wonder you couldn't answer. I usually only talk about work."

"I know that. But as your friend, I should be asking about the rest. Apparently. So..."

"So...what?" I tease, trying not to laugh as I pretend to be confused, making him work for it.

"You know what I'm asking."

"I really don't."

"Dammit, Keeley. How are you coping with your mum's illness? Are you getting enough sleep and time to yourself? Are you dating?"

"That wasn't so hard, was it?" I bite back another laugh, and he groans.

"Just answer the questions."

"God, you and Easton are so alike, it kills me. Although, maybe that's why we're so close. I'm used to it. In answer to your questions... I'm okay. I'm trying to be there for Mom as much as I can be, while also making sure she doesn't feel like I'm suffocating her. You know Mom; she likes her independence. Which I'm sure you understand with your Grandad. Am I getting enough sleep or time to myself? No. But I'm okay with that. I love my job. And as for my dating life. There's no one."

"Not even the boss you can't seem to stop talking about?"

"What?"

"You heard me." He delivers his response with no humor and I shake my head. What a way to get back at me for teasing him.

"You're so funny. I'm *not* dating."

"But if you were?"

"I'm not."

"Okay, well, thanks. I have my answers. Next time Mum's over I won't look like such an asshole."

"I don't think anything's going to change that. She knows you're an ass."

"Now who's being funny?"

"Always me. And I have more to say."

"Is it about work?"

"Of course."

"Then it can wait."

"See... asshole."

"I just pulled up at the gym and I need to be quick so I can get to the job site before my crew."

"You mean, your castle?"

"It's not *my* castle. But yes."

I picture one of the many castles from Disney movies and my chest warms. Callum's job fascinates me, and I'll never tire of hearing about it. There aren't many openings for castle restorations here in the USA, but in Scotland, he's never short on work.

"Have you ever wondered what it would be like to live in one of the castles you restore?"

"I do live there in the winter. I can get more work done that way. They're nothing special."

"Nothing special." My jaw drops. I will never understand my friend. "One day I'm coming to visit."

"Come during demolition time. Ask Easton—it's much more fun." His dry delivery has me snorting.

"The excitement in your tone tells me all I need to know. I'm in."

"Bye, Keeley."

"Love you, Cal."

Callum hangs up before I've finished speaking and I laugh out loud, almost missing the soft knock on my door.

"Coming."

I open up to find Sal leaning against the wall, his arms folded across his chest, his lips pulled into the smallest of smirks. Looking at him standing there has me thinking things I should not be thinking. Namely how I'd like to see that smirk from between my legs.

I may not be dating, but God, I'm in need of a good dicking. Sal is not the man for that, I know, but he's the only man I ever spend time with, so my imagination runs wild.

"What can I do for you, Sal?" I ask before remembering I was about to go and find him myself.

"I don't know. I was answering emails, trying to get ahead before a meeting for D'Angelo Construction tomorrow, and I had this urge to get out of my office."

"And you ended up here?"

"I did. I saw the light under your door."

"I'm here. As always." A slight twinge nags at my stomach and I internally wince. Luke's right. I really do spend all my time at work. It's nine p.m. Why am I here?

And Callum asked if I was dating. Yeah, right.

"I was actually about to come and look for you."

"Oh, yeah?" His face lights up and I smile because of it, knowing I can always count on Sal to make me feel wanted.

"Yes. I just got off the phone with *Sports Unfiltered*. They want to do a puff piece on you. What should I say?"

Sal's face contorts into an expression I haven't seen before, and I'm thoroughly amused. "What the hell is a puff piece?"

"Come on." I bite back a grin. "I thought you were smart. I'll give you an example. Storm owner Salvatore D'Angelo is not only one of the youngest owners in the league today but also the most hands-on. He's the first in the office and the last to leave, and always willing to get his hands dirty. While facing rumors and criticism head-on, he's transformed the team into the family-oriented franchise you see today. Etcetera. Etcetera."

"Please go on. You forgot to mention my power and charm."

I did. But the magazine certainly won't. "Do you want to do it or not?" I press my lips together and Sal chuckles, pushing off the wall to make his way inside my office, sitting back on the edge of my desk.

"Honestly? It sounds like hell. Are you asking me to do it or recommending I do it?"

I raise my hands in the air. "Neither. I'm just presenting the question." I close my door and take a few steps closer.

"That's a strange reaction." Sal frowns when I reach him. "Do you know the journalist?"

"I do."

"And..."

"And, what?"

"What aren't you telling me?"

"Nothing." *Why am I acting so weird?* Why do I care if he does it or not? I should be thinking about what's best for the team. "I owe her a favor which is why I'm bringing this to you. It's up to you to decide whether or not you want to do it."

"Is she honest?"

"Yes." Sometimes *too* honest.

"So this isn't something else disguised as a puff piece?"

"No. I asked the same question. She said their readers are interested in you and how this all came to be."

"To ask why I decided to neglect my business in New York City to play around in San Francisco?"

"What? I don't think anyone's thinking that. Are you?"

"Sometimes." Sal releases a sigh, and I walk closer, pushing him over so I can sit beside him.

"I thought your business was thriving?"

"It is. But it's doing it without me. Growing on its own. Like another child that blossomed without needing my influence."

"Is this really about your business?"

"Of course it is."

"Hmmm. I'm not a psychiatrist, but I can imagine they'd have a field day with that one."

Sal chuckles before running a hand down his face and standing up. "You're right. Paige said she has daddy issues, but fuck, I think I have kid issues. I had grand plans to be better and here I am, married to my work. Again."

"Sal, I don't—"

"I'm flying to Colorado on Monday to meet with Beckett." Sal changes the subject, grabbing his phone to presumably check his calendar. "I could probably find the time to answer some questions on the flight, if she wants to send them through."

"I think she wants to do a face-to-face interview." In fact, I know she does. Though emailed questions sound a lot more appealing.

"Face-to-face?" Sal frowns, tapping a finger on his leg. "Then, no. I don't have time for that. I don't have time for anything." He mumbles the last part under his breath, and a sarcastic laugh escapes me. Even though it's not at all funny. He's clearly worried about something, more than he's letting on.

"You sound like me," I confess, hoping to lighten the mood. "I had Luke telling me I need to get out more."

"Luke?"

"Yep. A few of the guys have taken an interest in my personal life."

"I may have heard that from Paige. I'm glad they're looking out for you."

Paige too? God, I'm fucked. "You're right. It's sooo sweet." My voice drips with sarcasm and Sal smirks, his delicious lips quirking just enough to reach his eyes.

"You sound thrilled. They mean well."

"How would you feel if..." I trail off, an idea coming to mind. "You work just as much as I do."

"Gee. Thanks, Keels. Isn't that what I was just saying?"

"Sorry, I wasn't finished. You need a better work/life balance. And we're like-minded individuals."

"Oh-kay. I'm not sure I like where this is going, but please continue."

"We're going out."

Sal's brows raise almost comically. "What?"

"This weekend we're doing something together." Sal opens his mouth to speak, undoubtedly ready to remind me that we often spend weekends together, but I'm about to shut him right up. "Something that *isn't* work."

"Didn't I just say that I don't have time for anything?"

"Yes, but you're going to find time for this."

"Right. What did you have in mind?"

"Absolutely nothing at the moment. I will come up with an idea. I've got a few days."

"You do that. And I'll see if I can squeeze it in depending on—"

"*You're coming*. Block out Friday night. It's the offseason. We deserve a break."

I stare his way, unyielding, and he eyes me curiously, his brow furrowed as though he's questioning his life choices, and it further cements my idea. We both need this. It'll be good for us.

I just have to think of something we'd both enjoy.

I smile widely, bringing out Sal's frown, and I snort at his concern.

"Don't look so worried." I squeeze his arm, excitement coursing through me. "It's going to be fun."

I hope. For his sake and mine.

Chapter Twelve

SALVATORE

Keeley marches into my office Friday morning with a notebook in her hand and a Cheshire-cat grin lighting up her features.

Meaning… I'm totally fucked.

She hasn't mentioned our little outing all week, most likely because I spent the last two days in New York, and I thought—*hoped*—she'd forgotten.

Wishful thinking.

It's not that I don't agree with her. How can I not, when everyone else is telling me the same thing? Paige. Easton's mom, Rochelle. Even Camilla said it again jokingly. Making light of the breakdown in our marriage.

I should have a better work/life balance. The problem is I don't even have time to think at the moment, let alone have fun.

Though when Keeley bounces her eyebrows, excitement reflected in her eyes, it's impossible to deny her.

"This isn't work-related, is it?"

"Nope." Her smile widens, as if that's possible.

"Okay, what are we doing?"

"I know I said to keep tonight clear. But what about tomorrow? I was thinking we could learn to surf. Unless you already know how. I just assumed you didn't."

"You assumed?" *Should I be offended?*

"Something about you screams 'I can't surf.'"

"Wow. You're right. But I'm not sure how I feel about it. What is it about me?"

"Does it matter? Are you in?"

"You know I'm fifty-two, right?"

"What? Since when? I could have sworn you were only fifty-one."

"Ha. Ha. That was my way of saying, I'm not surfing." Face-planting in the waves and getting sand in places that should never see sand is not my idea of fun.

"Lucky for you, I have back-up ideas."

"Of course you do." I bite back a smile, but a little of my amusement sneaks through. "I'll bet you added our little outing to your to-do list and blocked time for it."

"I did. It was color coded *purple* for '*fun.*'" She uses quote fingers for "fun" and I chuckle.

"How often do you use that color?"

"Every day. Work is..." She trails off when I cock an eyebrow, her lips thinning as she suppresses a laugh. "Fine. Never. It's new. But I plan on using it a lot more in the near future."

"Good for you. What other ideas do you have to torture me with?"

"Bowling."

My face contorts without my consent and I find myself apologizing. "Sorry, bowling is—"

"Not it. Moving on. What about live music?"

My brows lift as the idea of that sparks excitement in my chest. "Live music. I'm listening."

"Oh, yay. We're getting somewhere. Amelia, Luke's wife, is working with Poetic Nightmares on their new album. She's creating music videos for their first two releases. She mentioned they're performing their last album in its entirety this weekend and she can get us tickets."

I stare at her, racking my brain to see if I've ever come across the name Poetic Nightmares, but I've got nothing. I love music. Only now that we can stream everything, I tend to listen to music I know I'll like—bands or singers I'm familiar with.

I'm lost in thought when Keeley throws her head back and laughs out loud. "You've never heard of them, have you?"

"Nope. I couldn't name a single song."

"Okay. Poetic Nightmares is out, but music is in. Progress."

"I didn't say that. I said I haven't heard of them before. That doesn't mean I won't like their music."

"Do you like rock?"

"I do."

"With an emotional twist."

"Isn't all music emotional?" I frown, confused.

"I wouldn't say that. Surely, you've heard the very famous song 'Who Let The Dogs Out'?" Keeley bounces her eyebrows and I stifle a laugh.

"I'd say that's highly emotional to someone who lost their dog because someone else left the gate open."

Keeley snorts before covering her face in her hands. "How about I try a different approach? What music do you like? Actually, don't answer that. Let me guess." She stares at me intently, her eyes wide as she twists her lips, drawing my attention to her mouth. I watch her as she thinks, her bright red lipstick bringing back memories that I should not be conjuring.

"Elvis?" she asks, pulling me out of my head.

"*Elvis*?" I balk. "I have nothing against Elvis or his music, but he's not exactly my jam."

"Your jam?"

"Yep. Try again."

She giggles softly before staring at me some more, this time with her pointer finger trapped between her teeth. If I didn't know better, I'd swear she was doing it on purpose.

"I bet you love "Summer of '69" by Bryan Adams."

Dammit. She got me there. "What's not to love? It's a good song."

"I knew it. Is that your era? Do you like the older stuff?"

"I may be old, Keeley." *A lot older than you*. "But I'll have you know I listen to a lot of different eras. Only I'm not familiar with anything that was released after streaming began."

"Why is that?"

"Because I use music to lift my mood, and it's easier to choose something I know I'll like, rather than try to find a diamond in all that new *music* they're producing daily."

"You're right. You're old. That's such an old man thing to say. You're practically saying 'in my day.'"

"Guilty." I roll my eyes and Keeley once again hits me with her infectious laughter. "Music was just better back in my day. In fact, I bet I can play five songs from the different eras I enjoy, and you'll not only know them, but love them. Maybe even get a little emotional."

Keeley raises a single manicured eyebrow, her lips quirking in intrigue. "I'm up for that. Where's your phone?"

"Uh-uh. You said we had to have an outing, right? Let's make this an outing."

"Oh-kay."

"I'll meet you downstairs by my car at eight p.m. tomorrow. Assuming you're going to be here."

"I'm always here. But tomorrow?" It's her turn to frown, only hers is in confusion.

"Yep. It's my turn to do some planning." I have to find a decent cover band, and I have to find it fast.

My driver, Jeffrey, stops in front of an old dingy-looking bar, and Keeley's eyes dart to mine, her gaze puzzled as I help her out of the back seat.

"This is *not* where I pictured you taking me tonight." As she stands, her eyes rake over my body and she huffs out a laugh. "Although, I should have guessed considering your casual attire. I don't think I've ever seen you in anything other than a suit."

"Where did you think we were going? The ballroom at the Ritz?"

"Something like that." She smiles as she shrugs and I can't help but chuckle.

"Oh, Keeley. You are about to get schooled on music."

"Schooled? Really?"

"Yep."

"Bring it on."

With my palm resting against the base of her spine, I guide her past the entry and the line of people hovering outside, leading her to a weathered metal door at the side of the building. Keeley gasps quietly, her eyes once again flashing to mine. "Who are you?"

"I'm the same man you knew earlier today."

"Just more fun."

"The fuck? I'm fun."

"Yeah, okay, Mr. Workaholic."

"It takes one to know one, *Ms*. Workaholic." *Jesus*. What is with me? If Paige heard me talking like that, I'm pretty sure she'd disown me again.

Keeley laughs so hard you'd honestly think we were drunk, but I'd say it's more likely that we both need to get out more. Maybe then, we'd be acting normal right now. Whatever normal is.

"So, Mister? *Sir*." She stares at me pointedly when she says "sir" and I bite back a growl. She knows how much I hate that.

"Yes? *Miss*. Ma'am." I raise a brow in triumph and Keeley rolls her eyes.

"How do we get into this fine establishment?" She gestures to the door and I bounce my eyebrows.

"Allow me." I step around her and knock on the door, waiting patiently for the band manager to open up. The band I found was incredibly agreeable to my plans. Turns out, they're San Francisco born and raised and huge fans of The Storm. All it took was the promise of six tickets to the season opener, field level, and I had them eating out of my hands.

"Sal, my man." Nick, the band's manager, holds his fist out for me to bump it, and I don't need to look at Keeley to know her eyes are alight with amusement.

"Nick. Thanks for hooking us up tonight. We're looking forward to it."

"Anytime, man. Come on in."

I turn to Keeley, gesturing for her to walk in first, and find her biting back a grin. "Hooking us up?" she mouths, unable to suppress the sparkle in her eyes.

"Shh." I hold a finger to her lips before grabbing her hand and leading her inside, ignoring the warmth of her palm in mine while we follow Nick as he guides us to the main bar, seating us at a table near the side of the stage.

After a self-introduction to Keeley, one that's a little flirtier than I would like, Nick disappears backstage and Keeley turns my way.

"We couldn't line up like everyone else?"

"No."

"Why? Because this saved us, what? Five minutes."

"Nope." I chuckle. "Turn around; I think you misjudged the line."

Keeley turns and her eyes bulge as she bursts out laughing, grabbing my hand in the process. "Who are we seeing? I thought it was a little cover band. How did I not notice how big this place was?"

I stare down at our connection before following her gaze to where hundreds of people are filing in. My eyes drift back to Keeley's awed expression as she watches the huge warehouse quickly fill up.

From the outside, this place looks tiny, but looks can be deceiving. And this "little cover band" is about to tour with one of the biggest names in the country. They're performing tonight as a thank you to the fans that were there at the beginning of their careers. Before they wrote their own music. Music that, like Poetic Nightmares, I had never heard before this morning.

"This is Time Persuasion. You may have—"

"Bullshit. I thought you liked older music?"

"I do. Tonight, they're doing a covers set with a few of their own songs thrown in. I heard two of them today. They're not bad considering their generation." I wink and Keeley laughs even harder, affirming my decision to set this all up. She needed a break from our all-consuming world, and if I can give her even a night to unwind, I'll be happy.

"I have to admit, I'm surprised by all of this. By *you*."

"I had a life once. I wasn't always Mr. Workaholic. I just had to remember how that life works."

"You did good. Did you have help?"

"Of course I did. Tabitha held all my calls and canceled my meetings, while I ran around like I was in my twenties again, trying to find the perfect gig."

"And you struck gold. I can't believe we're here. I love Time Persuasion." Her eyes sparkle again, brighter this time, and I can't remember ever seeing her so *giddy*. If that's the right word. It's beautiful to witness.

"Good to know I've still got it. I used to be the man with all the plans in college. The guy my friends turned to for a guaranteed good night out."

A server appears with two drinks that we didn't order, and I glance toward the bar, finding Nick talking to a much younger bartender, shamelessly flirting without a care in the world. He looks over and waves in acknowledgment as I offer my thanks.

Keeley picks up her glass of red wine, taking a sip before smiling in appreciation. "This is my favorite. How—" She cuts herself off and laughs. "You think of everything, don't you?"

"Didn't you hear me the other day? I'm an observant fucker when I want to be."

"So it seems. Thank you."

"You're welcome."

"To like-minded individuals." Keeley raises her glass to cheers and I follow suit.

"To like-minded individuals and old man's music that you're going to love."

Chapter Thirteen

KEELEY

A stranger pulls me up to dance, and Sal laughs as I'm dragged into the mass of bodies pressed up against the stage, swaying their hips to the beat. I've been up and down all night, between dancing and sitting with Sal, all while he watches me, amused by my antics.

Time Persuasion starts playing one of their most famous songs, and I want to squeal when Sal starts to mouth along, having mentioned that he listened to a few of their hits during his "research" today.

I'd ask him to dance if he hadn't hit me with a firm "no" the first time I broached the subject, citing that he was too old for mosh pits, once again highlighting our difference in age. Not that this is anything close to a mosh pit.

The song ends, and I sashay my sweaty ass back to my seat, collapsing in a heap beside him.

Sal hands me another drink, this time a fruity cocktail, and I thank him with a grin.

I can't remember the last time I had this much fun on a date. And it's not even a date. We're four songs into Sal's "challenge" and he was right. Not only have I known *all* of the songs he asked Time Persuasion to play, but they're amazing recreations of the original versions. All with their own emotive qualities, each one making me feel something new.

Time Persuasion have been incredible. They've been mixing Sal's song choices in with their own, and I have loved every second of our night.

"What's the name of the last song?" I ask over the music, fanning my face with my hand.

"You'll have to wait and see." Sal raises an eyebrow, and that, paired with his relaxed demeanor, makes him at least twenty percent sexier. And he was pretty damn sexy to begin with. Especially tonight. While he's still wearing a dress shirt—I doubt he owns anything else—he's paired it with jeans and sneakers, and even left the top buttons of the shirt undone. Very un-Sal like. I love it. "The next one was a last-minute change in the roster," he continues, oblivious to my inner thoughts. "I noticed the singer had another talent."

My eyes flash to the band, but I didn't have to see it to guess. "Saxophone?" I ask. "Ralph's got a gift. He also produces a lot of their music."

"Ralph? You know these guys by name?"

"I do."

Sal stiffens slightly and if that's jealousy, I want more of it. It's been a long time since someone was jealous over me.

"I've been a fan for a while. They're still indie, but I have a feeling that's about to change after their tour."

"I can see that. They're a talented group. And credit to *Ralph* since he plays my favorite instrument." The way he says "Ralph" has me biting back a smile as a giddiness runs through me. He's totally jealous. He may be "too old" for me, but that doesn't mean he's a man without needs.

"What you're saying is that you saved the best for last?" I ask, keeping the conversation flowing while I swoon, my body swaying to the music, or perhaps because of the alcohol coursing through me.

"If you want a song that makes you *feel*, throw in a sax. This song is no exception. It's not necessarily the lyrics that evoke emotion—although, they always get me thinking about my life—it's the saxophone riff. The power of the notes. You're going to love it."

The way Sal speaks about music evokes a feeling of its own. His passion is infectious. If I wasn't already always drawn into every word he says, I'd be listening intently now.

He speaks about music like it's color. Or something tangible that you could reach out and grasp. When he tells you music is for the soul, in that deep raspy voice of his, he makes you want to sing to the heavens. And I mean that *exactly* as it came out, dirty connotation and all.

"I can't wait," I say excitedly, and while I'm referring to the song, a little part of me pictures something else too.

"Any guesses?" Sal asks, his mind still on our seemingly innocent conversation.

"Not yet. But the suspense is killing me." *That and the tension.*

God, I've had too much to drink.

Sal nods before his gaze flits back to the band, and there's something almost childlike in his expression. This is the Sal no one gets to see. The man I'll bet his ex-wife first fell in love with. If only she could see him now.

My stomach twists at the thought of his ex. My best friend's mom. Until I realize what's happening and cut those thoughts off faster than they came. I'm just as jealous as he is. Over nothing.

God, this is messed up.

I focus on the music for the next fifteen or so minutes, and when a certain seventies song comes on, I know instantly that this is for Sal.

I glance his way as I smile, and when the saxophone comes in, I melt into my chair.

Once again, he's right. I love this song.

"Oh, 'Baker Street,'" I announce proudly over the instrumental opening, drawing Sal's attention, watching his mouth as his lips curl.

"That's right. Do you know who originally sang it?"

"Definitely not."

Sal laughs before confirming it's Gerry Rafferty, his smile telling me this song is a favorite of his.

"Fine, you win. For now."

"For now?" He shakes his head.

"I was thinking that maybe next time I can find the band, and challenge *you* with some songs." Sal's brows furrow and I laugh out loud. "Trust me. You'll know them all and you might even love them." I paraphrase his words to me, and his chuckle morphs into a full-on laugh.

"Maybe." He bites his lip as he winks, and fuck me, that just about does me in.

"In all seriousness," I rush out, attempting to stop my thoughts from running rampant. "Thanks for finding this place. And for setting it all up. I've had fun."

"Me too, Keels. I think we nailed this whole 'getting a life' business."

"Absolutely." I laugh again, squeezing his hand just as Ralph sings the opening line.

I t's late by the time we leave the bar, and I'm thankful for Sal's driver when he pulls up in front of the exit, saving me from having to walk when I'm feeling a little lightheaded.

Who am I kidding? I'm drunk. And if I'm not mistaken, Sal's a little tipsy himself. Which I didn't think was possible. He seems like a seasoned drinker. A man that knows his limits and never dares to cross them.

After "Baker Street," I stayed off the dance floor, spending the rest of the night discussing music with Sal, getting to know him outside of work. And just when I thought he couldn't be any more decent of a human, I was wrong.

Not only does that man have the D'Angelo Foundation that he set up with Paige, and his business in New York, but it turns out, he's been quietly donating millions to various charities around the country, some that include funding instruments for disadvantaged children who want to learn, and another more recent charity to support grassroots football teams.

This man follows his passions.

And it kind of makes me want to be something he's passionate about.

As always, Sal opens my door and waits for me to slide in before walking around to the other side, waving off his driver when he gets out to help.

"We're dropping off Keeley first, Jeffrey," he tells his driver, gripping the back of the front passenger seat as he leans forward, offering me a healthy dose of forearm porn now that he's rolled up his sleeves. "She'll give you the address," he adds, turning to me when I'm not ready, catching me staring.

Whoops.

I smile, unaffected, and after relaying my address, I lie back against the headrest, closing my eyes.

My mind swirls with images of the night, and it feels like barely a minute has passed when Sal's palm curls around my thigh, the tip of his pinky brushing my skin where my dress has risen.

"We're here," he whispers, his gravelly voice sending a shiver right through me, ending between my legs.

"You shouldn't be allowed to whisper, Sal," I whisper right back. "It's confusing."

I open my eyes to find Sal's puzzled expression, and I giggle uncontrollably. "Oh, Sal. For a wise old man, you can be incredibly clueless at times."

The car comes to a stop, and Sal's quick to jump out, walking around the back to open my door. "I'll walk you up," he says loudly, as though trying not to whisper.

"Thank you."

I link my arm through his as we walk up the steps to the front of the building, and when we reach the entry, I let go, spinning to face him. "Thank you again. This was fun. How long do you think we can hold off before we have to do it again? You know, to ensure we keep that balance everyone speaks of."

Sal chuckles when I frown. "A good month. Maybe two."

"Oh, perfect. That works for me."

I rustle around for my key in my bag and open the front door, holding it ajar as I say goodbye. "Have a good night, Sal. I—"

"I'm walking you up."

"What?"

"To your apartment."

"I can find the way. I'm not that drunk."

"I never said you were. Indulge an old man, would you?"

My jaw shifts as I gesture for him to walk through. "Age is simply a number, Sal. You know that, right?"

"Just walk." His stern tone has me almost skipping ahead, and when we reach the elevator, I link my arm through his once more.

"Are you leaving me here, or escorting me to my door?"

"Your door."

"How very kind of you, Sir." Sal grumbles at my use of "sir" and I can't help but laugh. "I don't know why you're so opposed to it, Sir. It suits you."

"It suits me?"

"It does. You're very *Sir* like." For some reason I put on a very deep voice when I say that and Sal snorts.

"You know, some people may not like your 'say what you think' nature, but I quite enjoy it." Sal's eyes sparkle and I fake a frown.

"I can't tell if that's a compliment or—"

"Always a compliment, Keels. I can't imagine ever saying a bad thing about you."

"Another compliment. Thank you."

When we reach my door, I pull Sal into me, wrapping my arms around his neck, giving him a squeeze. Trying to be funny, I press a kiss to his cheek, only when I pull back, the energy shifts between us. "I really did have fun tonight," I whisper, my arms still locked around him, jolting when his palms settle on my waist. "Thank you."

"You're welcome. It's been a while since I let myself relax and switch off."

"Well, we have to change that." I blink slowly as I stare up at him, and I may be imagining it, but I swear Sal's palms clench around me ever so slightly. My fingers dance across the skin at the back of his neck as my heart beats frantically in my chest.

Why? I have no freaking idea, but I think I want him to come in.

Sal's eyes darken, and this time, I'm certain his palms tense.

"Sal?" I question, with no clue what I'm asking him.

His eyes drop to my mouth, and it's only when he sighs that I realize I have my lip trapped between my teeth. I release a breath, and a pained expression crosses his face before he lets go of me, his body unmoving.

"I should go." His words come out raspy, and it takes me a second to respond.

"Okay," I whisper, disappointment filling me, but he's still not backing away.

"Do you—" One of our phones emits a loud beep as a text comes through, cutting me off while simultaneously breaking Sal's trance.

"Fuck, sorry. I'm going." He steps back this time, forcing me to release my hold. "Thank you for tonight. I'm in the office all day tomorrow, but I've arranged for Jeffrey to take you back to your car. Just let me know what time works."

"You don't have to do that."

"I know. But it's done. If you don't text me, I'll have him wait for you out front, and he won't be impressed about that." He raises an eyebrow and I smile at the demand, glancing away to hide it.

"Okay, I will."

"Good night, Keeley."

"Good night."

Sal waits until I'm inside before he walks away, and I hold my breath, listening for the distinct ding of the elevator, only moving when I hear it.

I have no idea what the hell that was, but as much as it pains me, I want more.

Chapter Fourteen

SALVATORE

I almost fucking kissed her. Again. *What the hell is wrong with me?* She's twenty years younger than I am. She's not even ready to settle down yet, while I'm thinking about retirement. Okay, I'm not actually thinking about retirement, but some people my age definitely are.

Regardless, we are at completely different stages in our lives. So why the fuck did I let myself go there for a second time?

Once was bad enough. We moved on from that. We found balance again.

If I—

"Knock knock." Wes's voice sifts through my slightly ajar door as he raps his knuckles against the wood. *I'm late.* I pride myself on never being late. I'm busier than I've been in my entire life, I'm delegating more than I ever have, I'm dropping balls left, right and center, but I am never late.

"Come in. Sorry. I was just finishing up a call."

"You're fine. It's been a day for me too. I would have left you alone, if this wasn't important."

Dammit. I was worried about that when he set up the meeting last minute. "Take a seat." I gesture to the couch, internally cringing when Wes stays standing.

"Myers turned us down."

"He turned us down?" *Fuck.* That explains why he canceled our meeting today. "His agent said he wasn't feeling well and needed a recovery day. They rescheduled our meet and greet for Wednesday. What's going on?"

"Your predecessor."

"My what?"

"Storm's previous owner is releasing a book."

"And..."

"A passage from the book is being shared on social media. He mentioned the team's abysmal culture. He said he left because the staff and players were 'not the type of people he wanted his family associating with.'"

"He said that? Abysmal. Are you fucking kidding me?" My body tenses as my blood boils. "That fucker almost drove this team into the ground financially. He cheated Storm out of millions of dollars from that damn TV show. He stole—" I stop speaking, having already said too much.

When I bought the team two years ago, I made a promise that I'd never burden anyone else with the issues I walked into. That man was a crook. There's no other way to describe him. But instead of rotting in prison, he's living the high life as a wannabe film producer, and *apparently* selling his soul for a bestsellers list. Once again dragging us into the spotlight.

Wes stares at me as I calm myself down and offer him a smile. "You didn't hear any of that. The team is fine."

"Are we?" he asks, concern marring his features.

"Yes," I reply, hopefully putting him at ease, and I can honestly say that at this moment in time, it's the truth. "Other than our reputation being put through the wringer again."

"So...I don't need to start looking for another job?"

"What?" My eyes grow wide until Wes laughs.

"Sorry, I couldn't help myself. As I said, it's been a day."

"All good. You have nothing to worry about. I've been working behind the scenes to get the team out of debt, and I'm happy to report we are almost in the clear. Almost. But there's only so much I can do to tackle the hurdles we keep facing when it comes to our reputation."

"I've never been one to chase trouble," Wes begins and I turn to face him, giving him my full attention. "I apologize if I'm out of line here, but could we fight fire with fire? Discredit him a little."

"Wow." I raise an eyebrow with intrigue. "I never thought something like that would come out of your mouth."

"Me either." He laughs incredulously.

I haven't known Wes for long, but I quickly discovered he was a man of integrity. He plays by the rules. He's honest. He's also loyal, though, so I imagine this stems from his loyalty to the team.

"The thing is, I value right and wrong, and from what you accidentally shared, that man is in the wrong."

"You're right. You are. But we can't leak anything related to him without bringing more negative attention to the team, and we need to keep things positive. Having said that, when we've secured our quarterback and the media speculation has died down, I might 'accidentally' say something I shouldn't."

Wes smiles. "Sounds like a plan. In the meantime, how do we secure our quarterback?"

"Do we have any other options?"

"We do, but we haven't looked into them enough, because at a glance, they didn't look like a good fit."

"We may need to change shape."

"I agree. Let me talk to a few contacts I know. I'll see what I can find out."

"Thanks, Wes. I'll do the same, while also tackling our little image problem. That book couldn't have come at a worse time. Myers is all about upholding his good reputation. I can understand his hesitancy to leave one negative team for another."

"I hate to say it, but you're right. When I heard the news, I couldn't fault him for it."

"That's why we have to fix it. And fast."

I pat Wes on the shoulder as he leaves, releasing a long, drawn-out breath before Tabitha announces herself. "Sorry to interrupt, sir. If you don't need anything, I have that dinner..." She trails off, cringing when my eyes meet hers.

It takes me a second to process her words before I rush to apologize. "Sorry. Of course. You were supposed to leave thirty minutes ago."

"Wes looked anxious when he walked past, so I wanted to wait in case you needed me."

I smile in thanks. We've come a long way, Tabitha and I. At first, I didn't think it was going to work out between us, but other than her annoying habit of calling me "sir," she's been a godsend. "I appreciate you waiting, but you can go. I know tonight is important to you." And while I'm certain I need help, it's not Tabitha I want.

"Thank you, sir. Would you like me to come in early tomorrow?"

"That's not necessary. Enjoy your anniversary." In the almost two years we've worked together, Tabitha has only ever requested this night off. Both years. For her anniversary. And while I'd never expect her to work the long hours that I do, she never asks to go home. She always waits until I dismiss her, and sometimes, I forget. No matter how many times I tell her she should just leave when it hits seven, she never does, unless I say goodbye.

I once found her out here at nine p.m. and immediately gave her a raise.

Sometimes I wonder if I need an assistant to manage my assistant. Or...I could work on leaving the office earlier myself. I could embrace the whole work/life balance bullshit and take my work home instead.

Though, I'm not sure that's what the term means.

Tabitha pulls my door closed behind her as she leaves, and the second I hear the soft click, I'm retrieving my phone and messaging Keeley. Did I promise myself I'd try to rely on her less after our moment on Saturday night? Yes. Am I failing on day two? Also yes.

This is an emergency. And if anyone can calm me during a crisis, it's her.

SALVATORE: Any chance you want to help an old man out?

I cringe as I press send, but it's too late to take it back.

KEELEY: Stop trying to remind me of your age, Sal. Just tell me where you want me

Just tell me where you want me.

Where I want her?

Fuck. I *want* her in my bed, on her back with her legs spread. I *need* her in my office to sort out this shit storm of events and...*Jesus Christ.*

SALVATORE: My office in an hour. I'll buy dinner. It might be a long night

A long, purely platonic, disaster aversion, work colleague, business only night. Nothing else.

KEELEY: I'll be there

Keeley arrives fifty-five minutes later, and a loud sigh escapes me, releasing the tension I'd been holding since Wes walked out of my office.

It's crisis after fucking crisis here at the Storm headquarters, and I don't know what I'd do without Keeley by my side.

She glides in without so much as a knock and makes herself comfortable on my couch, talking about one of the coaches interrupting her on her way in. "Why is he even here? It's almost eight."

She glances up at me for the first time since she walked through the door, and all I do is smile as relief fills me. She's here.

She's always here when I need her. And I have no idea what the fuck I'd do if she wasn't.

I inhale slowly, letting my shoulders drop.

"Are you okay?" Keeley waves to get my attention. "You're scaring me a little."

Huh? My eyes focus, alerting me to the fact that I'd been staring at her while I contemplated the idea of her one day being gone. "Sorry. I was lost in my head. Thank you for coming. What were you saying?"

"It doesn't matter." Her lips lift into the most glorious smile, and I force myself to keep my eyes on hers instead of her mouth. "Anyway, I'm starving. There was a promise of dinner?" She changes the subject, rubbing her stomach for visual effect.

"Yes, there was. I'll order now. Riccardo's?"

Keeley raises an eyebrow, her expression stoic until I laugh. "What can I say? I'm kind of obsessed."

"Are you ready to admit it's better than any pizza you've had in New York?"

"Never."

"Then I'm ordering. I have a feeling I can change your mind." She bites her lip with a smirk, and my fucking cock twitches. Until I remember the mention of the owner's son the last time she ordered.

"I'll order. Just tell me what I need to get. It's my turn."

"What if my order comes with another free bottle of wine?"

That's exactly why I'm ordering. "I've got wine here if we need it."

"You do?" Keeley's eyes widen before her gaze darts to the cabinet in the corner of my room. "Since when?"

Since I realized you like a glass or two to wind down. "Someone gave me a few bottles for Christmas. And lucky for you, it's your favorite."

"That's convenient." She grins, her gaze once again darting to my makeshift bar. The bar I stocked with her drink of choice. Just in case she needed it.

"It is," I lie. "Anyway, what am I ordering?"

I order the gourmet special that Keeley insisted I try and my usual, just in case, then it's down to business.

"What can I do for you?" Keeley asks, kicking her shoes off before crossing her legs and leaning back into the cushions. My mind conjures far too many inappropriate responses before settling on the correct answer. "As you're probably aware, Gregory Winston is releasing a book. Turns out, he wasn't a fan of the Storm culture. Claims the players and staff were 'not people he wanted his family associated with.'"

Keeley cringes. "I saw it. His views are all over social media. Or should I say his lies? I was here while he was here. There was nothing wrong with our culture. And if there was, it came from him and his sidekick, Tray."

She tenses when she mentions Tray, the team's general manager when I first took over, and my mind drifts back to when I sought her advice over whether or not I should let him go. I always sensed there was something she wasn't telling me, and her reaction just now hasn't changed my mind. "It's like one thing after another," she continues, mindlessly running her fingers through the strands of her hair. "We've barely come up for air after the Zane 'scandal' and now..." She trails off when her eyes meet mine, wincing before she laughs. "That's not helpful. You know what we're facing. You don't need a recap."

"I don't, but it's nice to have my anger reflected back at me. It makes my reaction feel justified."

"You have every right to be pissed after everything you did for this team to protect them from the chaos he left behind." Her cheeks flush from her anger on my behalf, making my chest knot. She only knows half of it. I wanted to protect her too.

"There's more," I tell her with a wince of my own. "Beckett's seen the posts or somehow been told about the book, because he's declined our offer."

"*God-fucking-dammit!*"

"My thoughts exactly." I huff out a laugh.

"Sorry, once again that wasn't helpful."

"On the contrary...your little outburst lifted my mood."

"Good. Have you spoken to Wes?"

"He's the one who told me. He's looking for options while I figure out what to do about the book's claims."

"What are you thinking?"

"I'm not. That's why you're here. I need your help to get ahead of the fire."

Keeley nods a few times before her lips lift into a knowing smile.

"You were already doing that, weren't you?" I ask, realizing I'm an idiot. Of course she'd be on top of this.

"That's what I do best. And it's been all over socials all day."

"All day?"

"Yep. It was impossible to miss. I'm surprised you only just found out."

"I don't do socials, Keeley."

"You don't? We should fix that. It'll help your image."

"According to your writer friend, I don't need help with that. Power and charm, remember?" I wink and Keeley bursts out laughing.

"How could I forget?"

She smirks back at me, and instantly, it's clear our almost kiss is forgotten, just like our actual kiss was.

And it needs to stay that way. No more kisses or almost kisses. I'm not sure our relationship would survive another one.

"Back to the task at hand. What are *you* thinking?"

"That we leak something proving he's not the guy he says he is." She smiles innocently and it's my turn to laugh. "I know you've got more on him than you've told me. You're hiding something."

"What? I wouldn't dare. Though it's funny you say that. Wes suggested the same."

"Wes? Really? I never pictured him as the type to go for petty revenge."

"Did you picture me as that type?"

"Definitely. So let's get planning."

Ignoring the urge I have to ask why she thinks I'd go for something petty, I nod and move around to my desk, bringing my computer to life. "Yes. The sooner we figure this out, the better."

"Thank you. I've got a nanna night to get home to."

"Your nanna's still alive?"

"No." Keeley giggles softly, her expression playful. "Monday nights are my nanna nights because I can start later on Tuesdays. I get into my pajamas the instant I get home, then I curl up on the couch with a blanket, a book or movie, and a mug of tea or glass of wine. And that's where I stay until I fall asleep, or I force myself to go to bed at some ungodly hour of the morning."

"That actually sounds appealing. Perfect even. I'd much rather be having a grandpa night than tackling this issue. In fact, I wish most of my nights were like that."

"I bet you do." She beams brightly and my jaw drops.

"What does that mean?"

"It's fitting because you're an old man and a literal grandfather."

"Now who's bringing age into our conversation? I thought age was merely a number?" I tease despite telling myself I wouldn't mention the other night.

Keeley's about to respond when my phone rings, and I jump at the welcome interruption. "Sorry, I better take this."

I grab my phone and check the screen, my gaze locked on Keeley as she scrolls through her own, the smallest of smiles pulling at her lips.

And fuck. I really need to keep our conversation more professional. Less flirting, more work.

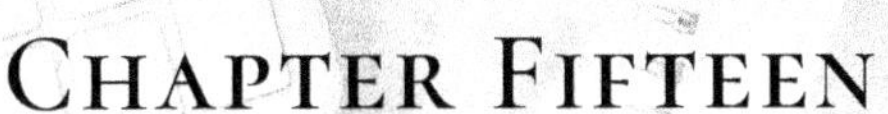

CHAPTER FIFTEEN

KEELEY

Sal hangs up from his call and paces the floor in front of his wall of windows, his usually perfect hair messed up from how often he's been running his hand through it.

Before I left to collect our dinner from downstairs, he was laughing, and now, he looks like someone killed his cat.

"Fuck, it just gets better and better, doesn't it?" He spins to face me, his expression pleading for me to make it all work out. And I'm trying.

"What happened?"

"Apparently Gregory didn't just mention our poor culture. He was specific in what he said."

"What?" I grab my phone, searching through my alerts, but nothing comes up other than the information I already knew. "I don't have anything here."

"The book hasn't been released yet. This is coming from a friend of mine that got early access. She's a sports critic."

"She?" *Jesus*, what does that matter? "I mean, who?"

"Bronte Welles. Do you know her?"

"I don't, but I know who she is. Was that her? What did she say?"

"She was giving me a heads-up. Gregory mentions substance abuse and bullying. He said he only agreed to the TV show if they promised to keep that information out of the narrative. He claims he wanted to get ahead of the issue and promote the team in a positive light before someone found out. Apparently, he was *helping*."

I stare at Sal, my eyes wide as his words sink in. Then I laugh so hard that I snort.

"Please tell me you don't believe that garbage? While I'm certain no team is untouched by substance abuse—even us—our starters, the guys on the roster? Hell, no. Some would say they need a little corruption in their lives. Except maybe Zane."

Sal frowns, and the little crease between his brows is so prominent that I want to rub it away. "Of course I don't believe it. The problem is...I don't think I'm the one he's trying to convince."

He drops his head into his hands and I regret laughing. It's so hard to picture these guys as the team he's portraying them to be. The closest they've ever come to bullying is Easton and the guys hating on Zane for sleeping with Easton's girlfriend at the time. And that was warranted in my opinion. At least it was until I got to know Zane. Turns out, he was misunderstood.

"I didn't mean—"

"No, you're right. I should be laughing about how preposterous this all is. But instead, I want to rip that fucker to shreds."

His eyes blaze with a fierce protectiveness, and my heart jolts. Ignoring it, I cross my arms over my chest, as though that'll help calm my reaction. I *cannot* allow myself to process this new side of Sal because I like it a little too much.

Sal shakes his head as his entire body stiffens.

"Your shoulders are tensing again," I muse, smiling in sympathy.

He drops them and stands tall, towering over me without my heels on. "We have to get ahead of this."

"We will. I promise. You need to relax."

"Relax?" His eyes bulge as though I've offended him, and I almost tell him to suck it up until he smiles, his fingers massaging his neck.

My hands itch to touch him, to relieve some of his tension, and before I can run through all the reasons why I shouldn't, I'm moving toward him, acting without processing the consequence.

"Let me." I remove his hands, replacing them with mine, immediately brushing my thumbs against his neck.

"You don't have to do that." Sal tries to step out of my grasp, but I move with him.

"Give me five minutes and we'll get back to it. I can't let you stand there in pain."

"I'm fine."

I dig my thumbs into a knot where his neck meets his shoulder, and he jolts forward, cursing under his breath. "You were saying?"

"Okay. You win. Do what you will."

"Thank you." Though it's best I don't take that literally because the things I want to do...

Last month—hell, even last week—I'd moved on from our kiss and placed Sal firmly in the friend zone.

That was until he looked at me like he wanted to worship the ground I walk on while getting me off. It's been so long since I've had sex that my brain can't stop replaying that image.

I cherish our relationship. Other than Callum, Sal's the closest man in the world to me. But...I can't stop thinking about what it would be like to kiss him again. And more. He's a friend that I want to sleep with. The two ideas aren't mutually exclusive. I can want to have my cake and eat it too. Right?

Either way, this moment isn't helping.

Lifting to my toes, I tilt Sal's head to the side and work the tight muscle at the base of his skull. He subtly groans, clearing his throat to cover it. "You're a woman of many talents," he rasps, his voice barely above a whisper.

"I am." A giggle escapes me. "Some you haven't even discovered yet."

My head falls back as I laugh to myself, further cementing my need to get laid. Maybe if I do, I might have the chance of forgetting about this. *Might*. Maybe. Probably not.

Sal doesn't respond to what I said. Instead, he sucks in a breath before falling silent.

With each passing moment, the tension builds, engulfing me like a warm hug, tightening my chest as a spark runs through me.

I close my eyes, letting the rest of my senses take over—the smell of his rich cologne, a blend of rum and leather, the feel of his warm skin beneath my fingers, the sound of his breaths picking up speed.

My mouth waters, desperate to get in on the action, and I bite down on my lip, terrified that if I don't, I'll whimper.

This isn't just a friendly neck massage anymore, and while I could be the only one that feels it, Sal's soft sigh suggests that I'm not.

I pause when I'm done, my fingers still lightly pressed against his skin. "Is that better?" I lean in as I whisper, careful not to ruin Sal's rare moment of peace. He doesn't get to stop very often. In fact, I'm not even sure he slows down. He deserves a break. He deserves this moment. "I'll give you a—"

Sal spins to face me, his dark, dazzling eyes bouncing between mine, his expression pained.

And I panic. "Shit. Did I make it worse?"

I've barely gotten the words out when he grabs my face in his hands, his thumb brushing my lip before he leans in and replaces it with his mouth, kissing me with a force I'm not prepared for.

I gasp at the welcome attack and reach out, curling my fingers around his tie, pulling him closer as I meet his fervor.

We stumble back toward the wall, and I brace for impact until Sal releases one of his hands and slows us down, his palm hitting the drywall before we do.

When we're still, Sal glides his hand down my back, his touch burning a path through the silk of my shirt. He pauses at the waistband of my pants, as though the little bunching of material is a warning sign, and I make a mental note to start wearing more dresses, imagining what could have happened if he didn't have that barrier.

My legs clench, and the smallest of moans escapes my lips, giving Sal access to swipe his tongue through my mouth and... *Oh. My. God.* A fire runs through me, arousal pooling at my center. My fingers clench against the soft material of his shirt as I lift to my toes, deepening the kiss, needing more but also unable to remember a time I ever felt this satisfied from a kiss alone.

You'd think I'd never been kissed before with the way my body responds to everything he does.

Sal groans as our tongues clash, and my heart skips, expecting him to pull away.

Only he doesn't.

We kiss for God knows how long until we're both breathless, gasping for air as we simultaneously split apart.

Neither of us speaks for a few seconds, our eyes locked, lips raw from practically mauling each other, and I almost laugh.

Almost. Instead, I smile, the first of us to break the trance. "I'm ready for more."

"For what?"

I raise an eyebrow, and he curses under his breath before huffing out an incredulous chuckle. "Fuck, Keeley. What are you doing to me?"

"Do you regret it?"

"No." He glances away, his pained expression returning. "How the fuck could I regret that? You're beautiful and... It doesn't matter."

"Doesn't matter?"

"*No*, because we shouldn't have done it. *I* shouldn't have done it. I was caught up in the moment and I'm sorry."

"Why?"

"My reasons haven't changed." He shakes as though the idea of that kills him, and I decide to push the issue.

"I get it. Believe me. I do. But you want it. You want me. And I want you too. We're adults. It's not like you're proposing marriage. You don't need permission to fuck me."

"Keeley." His pained expression intensifies, and I snap out of whatever messed-up spell I was under. "I hate to keep bringing this up, but I'm fifty-two. And your brother's future father-in-law. The dad of one of your best friends. Say for argument's sake that I threw you onto the couch and fucked you, as you say—" He winces at his choice of words, and I almost smile at how decent he is. "What happens after that? Do we go back to this? Can we still face each other at work? At family functions? You're not wrong. I want you. But one of us has to be practical here."

His words burn despite the fact that he's right. Still, I open my mouth to argue.

"I think we're beyond—"

Sal's phone rings and while he ignores it, I can't help glancing at the screen. It's late. After nine. The only late calls I get are important. So are his.

"It's Wes."

"Shit." Sal blows out a breath, running a hand down his face. "I better..."

"Yep."

He picks up his phone, turning away as he answers. "Wes, tell me you have news."

I can't hear Wes's half of the conversation, but Sal visibly relaxes the longer he listens.

"That's perfect. You think he'll say yes?"

Sal's eyes meet mine, and the relief in his expression elicits my own. They've found a solution. One problem solved. One to go.

When Sal hangs up, his smile warms my chest, and the "us" conversation drifts from my mind. "He found someone?"

"He did. Another free agent player that wants to leave his current team. He found out through an ex-teammate, meaning it's not common knowledge, but he seems to think we have a shot at securing him."

"That's amazing. Am I allowed to know who?"

"Vance McMillan." His smile widens like the cat that got the cream, while my stomach sinks and memories of the past flood my mind.

He's a vile, pathetic excuse of a man, and he's not right for this team. Especially considering the accusations Gregory is about to put out into the world.

The knot in my stomach turns to nausea, but I smile as Sal tells me how perfect Vance is. And he's not wrong. He's a great player, who, for the most part, has avoided controversy. *In the public forum.* The rumor mill, however, is rife with talk of his inappropriate behavior, only it's just that—talk. Because no one will speak out. Including me.

So, how do I tell Sal he needs to forget about Vance as an option without admitting what happened between us?

The one thing I keep close to my chest.

It's hard enough being a female in a male-dominated world, but if I were to publicly accuse a football player of assault, I'd never work again. Even Sal would have trouble keeping me on the team. The board would vote against him. It would be my college experience repeating itself again.

Controversy with players needs to be handled delicately. We need to be seen as supporting our men. When it comes to staff behind the scenes, particularly women, it's easier to cut ties and move on.

I learned that lesson the hard way. During my junior year at college, I interned with our college athletics department, working across a few different sports, including football. Vance was a senior and the star quarterback for the team. I didn't have to meet him to know who he was. Everyone knew him.

From his freshman year, he was praised for his talent, touted by everyone like he was going to singlehandedly secure our D1 college the championship each year.

And he did. Once.

I couldn't imagine the kind of pressure that comes with that tag, and I admired him for how well he held himself considering all that attention.

It didn't take long after I started with the football team to befriend a few of the players, and through them, I officially met Vance. He was so focused on football that I was intrigued by him, and when he asked me out, I didn't hesitate to say yes.

Our date was fine but we didn't click. It was apparent early on that we didn't have much in common. I thought it was obvious we'd part ways as friends.

Vance didn't feel the same.

He got angry and stormed off, calling me all the names under the sun before coming back and apologizing, insisting on driving me home.

I thought that was it. Names I could handle. And he apologized.

But I was wrong.

I reported Vance to my boss a few days after he assaulted me, needing some time to process what had happened, and within a few hours, I was being politely asked to leave.

It's likely I only have a job now because they promised to give me a glowing reference if I let them deal with the fallout privately. Being a naïve twenty-year-old, I signed my rights away. But never again. That moment changed something in me. And I don't plan on ever becoming that version of myself again.

"That's great, Sal." I widen my smile, praying my words sound sincere. It is great that they've found a solution to a problem we did not need right now, but not great that it's Vance.

Sal nods a few times, running a hand through his hair, further messing it up. "Thank God, right?"

"Thank God." I force another grin, nodding a few times in return before grabbing my phone and bag. "I'm going to head home. I'll work on Gregory and his bullshit tonight. If I come up with anything, I'll let you know. And if you come up with any brilliant ideas, feel free to send them my way.

I turn to leave but Sal rushes forward, grabbing my wrist. "Keeley, wait. We haven't even eaten. About what happened... I'm—"

"Don't apologize, Sal. You're entitled to feel how you want to feel. I promise to keep things purely professional from now on. The pizza's all yours. The special tastes just as good reheated for breakfast." I wink but it lacks the spark it usually has.

"Keels?" He pleads for me to say more, misconstruing my mood as something to do with us. But it's not.

I wish it was that.

"I'm okay. We're okay. I promise. Good night."

Relief hits me when he lets me walk away, but it's short-lived and I almost crumble on the way to my car. I'm going to have to find some way to tell him or Wes. Either way, I have to face it all again.

Chapter Sixteen

SALVATORE

I'm not sure how long I stared at the door after Keeley metaphorically slammed it in my face, but it must have been a while, because by the time I broke myself out of my trance, she was long gone and the pizza was cold.

When I finally peered out my door, her office was locked up, and the lights in the hallway were off.

It was as though she'd never even been there.

A little part of me wishes that were true because *what the fuck am I doing?* And why am I constantly asking myself that very question when it comes to Keeley?

It's been years since I let a woman take over my thoughts—not since Camilla, and look how well that turned out.

Yes, I have two amazing children, and an incredible grandchild because of that marriage, but while I don't regret it, I'm the first to admit I am not cut out for relationships.

Life with Camilla was great in the early days, but when my business took off, that part of my world consumed me, and there was no *work/life balance* where I was concerned. It was as though life was in color, but I could only see black and white.

I was a shitty husband, father, friend, son. I hadn't spoken to my mother for a month when she was rushed to the hospital after suffering a heart attack. And despite praying that she would survive it and give us more time, when she did, I barely changed.

It took years for me to wake the fuck up, and when I finally did, it took another few years before anyone would accept me back in their lives.

I'm only just managing to juggle family time with Paige and Isaac. There's no way I could consider throwing someone else into the mix. Especially not Keeley. She deserves better than that. Not that she wants a relationship, but still. I can't commit to anything, even a one-night stand.

I'm on edge when I arrive in the office the next morning—nervous to see Keeley—and I hate that I'm relieved to hear she's working from home. Until it hits me that I'm likely the reason why.

Wes arrives just before lunch and gives me a full rundown on what he knows about Vance McMillan, and a spark of hope ignites in my chest, though it's not without a dark shadow hovering above it.

I want Beckett Myers.

On paper, McMillan ticks all the boxes, but it's what I can't find that has me concerned.

Wanting to distract myself last night, I did a little digging, and the results raised more questions than anything else. There are no skeletons in his closet, no reports of playboy ways, or any of that "I'm a football star, I do as I please" gossip. He's squeaky clean and I don't like it.

Even Beckett, who *is* squeaky clean, has a past.

It took me all of five minutes to find gossip from his college days, talking about an incident with a reporter in front of his childhood home. While never charged, it's said that Beckett punched the guy in the face when he questioned Beckett's mom about her personal life.

A nonissue in my mind. He was protecting her, further convincing me that he'd fit in well with this team. We protect our family. I may have been absent from my loved ones, but if they ever needed me, I was there.

When it comes to Vance...there's nothing. And that worries me because I know how easy it is to keep things quiet. I'm guilty of using my influence and money to do it myself.

Vance is from a wealthy family. Is he doing the same?

No matter what, I'm not prepared to give up on Myers. Not yet. And I have an idea to win him over. Turns out the book excerpt leak yesterday may not have been the bad thing we thought it was. It gives me a chance to lay it all on the line. To talk to Beckett knowing the controversy coming our way.

You could say, it's going to put me ahead of the game.

If my plan works.

The airport is as chaotic as my head when I arrive in Colorado Springs ahead of my meeting with Beckett.

My phone rings as I'm exiting the arrivals lounge, and I stiffen until I see that it's Camilla. Better her than Beckett's agent or Wes. Ever since Beckett agreed to keep our meeting, after I all but offered my first-born child—sorry, Paige—I've been waiting for him to cancel.

I send Camilla to voicemail and shoot off an apology text. She couldn't possibly be more disappointed in me than she was when she ended our marriage, so I've stopped worrying about what she thinks of me now. I actually think it's improved our relationship. I don't feel guilty all the time, and she doesn't resent me since she knows what to expect.

Doesn't stop her from messaging me back, despite me letting her know I'd call her when I was free.

CAMILLA: Heads up… Marc got himself in a little bit of trouble again. Nothing illegal. But I know your name's in the media again so wanted to let you know.

I was wrong. Hearing from Camilla was *not* in fact better than hearing from Wes.

SALVATORE: Is it public yet?

CAMILLA: Not yet. But there's only so much I can have swept under the rug. It's your turn now.

SALVATORE: I'm not sweeping anything away. He can face the consequences of his actions.

CAMILLA: Even if it tarnishes the D'Angelo name?

SALVATORE: Even then.

I love that kid, but he needs to learn to avoid trouble rather than driving head-on into it. We've been bailing him out for far too long.

CAMILLA: I'll let him know.

Of course she will. Better to let me be the bad guy.

I pocket my phone as my driver comes into view, his professionally printed sign standing out in a sea of handwritten posters.

"Mr. D'Angelo?" he asks as I approach.

"That's me. Nice to meet you."

"Nice to meet you too. I'm Tony. This way please."

The icy morning air hits me as we walk away from the building, no longer in the safety of the wind barrier. It's cold as fuck compared to San Francisco, and I'm only now remembering I didn't bring a coat. I didn't bring anything other than my laptop, notebook, and phone. The plan is to fly in, get this deal done, and fly out.

Yes, we have Vance as a potential waiting in the wings, but I want Beckett. I was set on securing him for the team, and no asshole ex-owner is going to stand in my way.

"Still heading to the Broadmoor Hotel?"

"Yes, please."

"With the morning rush, it's likely to take us thirty minutes. Would you like a coffee for the drive?"

God, yes. "That would be great. Thank you."

"Not a problem. I know a place five minutes down the road."

I nod as Tony opens the back door of his blacked-out Audi. "I have a special in-car desk if you need it."

"Wow. Yes, thank you."

Tony walks around to the trunk and returns with a desk that fits perfectly in my lap while not actually resting on my legs.

I'm admiring the structure as Tony sits down in the driver's seat. "Did you make this?"

"My son did."

"I need one of these for home. Does he sell them?"

"No, sir. It's a one-off. He's a man of many talents."

"I'll say. Please pass on my thanks."

Tony nods before focusing his attention on his job, while my mind flashes back to Keeley's comment from the other night. When I told *her* she was a woman of many talents.

I think that's the line that shifted the energy in the room, and it's my fault.

When it comes to Keeley, I thought I'd drawn a deep line in the sand, placing her on the side marked "friend." The problem is, I can't stop fucking thinking about her as more than that, not lately anyway. All she has to do is touch me these days and I'm picturing myself throwing her over my shoulder and taking her to bed.

I'd love to say it's because we spend so much time together and there isn't anyone else. Maybe I just need a good fuck? Maybe I need to relieve some tension the way only having sex can.

But...to do that, I'd need to entertain the idea of being with someone else, and at the moment, I can't.

I may be a workaholic, but I pass by beautiful women every day —in my building, when I'm out for a run, on the goddamn magazine stand while I line up to pay for my groceries. Without sounding too cocky, I could use my wealth to seduce almost anyone I wanted. Almost. But while I *can* do that, I never would. The thought alone makes me uncomfortable. And not all of those feelings stem from my moral high ground. It's also the fact that I don't *want* anyone else.

Only I don't want Keeley either. I mean I do...but I don't.

And that's a fucked-up predicament to be in.

After a quick stop for coffee, we pull up in front of the Broadmoor Hotel, and I glance down at my laptop, the screen still black. I was raving about the fancy car desk, and yet, I was so far inside my head that I didn't even use it.

Fucking Keeley.

I'd love to be annoyed, but of course, I can't be. Nothing she does annoys me. And that's part of the reason I don't want to mess with what we have, with her age and brother coming in a close second.

Tony opens my door as I pack up my unused laptop, and when I step out, I find a concierge waiting for me.

"Mr. D'Angelo?"

"Yes?" I say curiously, now wondering if I'm recognizable, or if I have my name written somewhere on my clothes.

"Mr. Myers is waiting for you in our private dining room. He asked me to escort you when you arrived."

"Thank you. Lead the way."

"I'll wait for you in the parking lot, sir," Tony confirms and I smile in thanks before I leave.

We pass a tank of a man in a tight black tee and sleeve tattoos as we enter the dining room, and my brow furrows as my eyes lock on Beckett sitting alone at a table by the bar. Did he bring security?

Is this his way of saying he doesn't trust me or my team?

Beckett glances up as I approach, and a warm smile tugs at his lips as he stands. "Mr. D'Angelo, it's good to meet you, sir."

"Please, call me Sal. It's great to meet you too, Beckett. I've got to be honest; I was worried you'd cancel again."

"Sorry about that, sir. I mean, Sal. If *I'm* being honest, the latest reports about the team freaked me out a little. I've been with Colorado since I was drafted. I'm ready for a change, but it has to be a change for the better."

"I completely understand, which is why I wanted to meet with you in person. I want to lay it all out. Tell you what's going on with the team. The truth about management and the players behind closed doors. Some of what I'm going to tell you isn't even known by them. But I'm here to gain your trust and to show you that we are not the team we're portrayed to be."

"I'm listening."

"Thank you. I'll start by saying that the reports about our culture are utter bullshit. At the heart of it, we're a family-oriented team. We have each other's backs and protect our own. I'm not going to sit here and pretend the controversies we've faced lately haven't been warranted. I have no intention of lying to you. But I will say that what you read on Monday was so far from the truth that it's defamatory.

"Our previous owner—and this is the part no one else knows—drove the franchise into the ground, putting us in a hell of a lot of debt to launch his production company. And from what I've found out since hearing about the upcoming book, it's not doing so well. My guess is that he's written this book as a way to draw attention to his new venture as a producer, and we've been caught in the crossfire because controversy sells.

Especially after our Super Bowl win last year. We're working on getting the Storm name cleared again. But while I can't guarantee you won't face questions if you choose to sign with us, I can promise you that after spending five minutes with the team, you'll be convinced you made the right choice."

"How can you possibly know that?"

"Because I know my players. I know my staff. And we are not who they say we are."

"Okay."

"There's also a good chance we'll make the Super Bowl again—we've won two in the last three years—and I happen to know that's something you're striving for. Can any other teams offer you that?"

"With all due respect, you can't really offer that either. But I agree, the odds are higher."

Beckett's serious expression has me pausing for a beat until he finally smiles, making me relax.

"Do you have any questions for me? I'm here to provide all the answers. I'm an open book. We want you on the team. So hit me with your concerns."

Beckett's quiet for a beat before he leans back in his chair, visibly relaxing. "I've got some questions. But I promise not to take up too much of your time."

Chapter Seventeen

KEELEY

My eyes crack open as the sun shines through the gap in my curtains, and I groan out loud. Another sleepless night, another morning beginning with a headache.

For the first time in years, I worked from home for the full day yesterday, and if I didn't know Sal was away on business today—according to his calendar—I would have done it again.

I can't face him. Not because of what happened between us. That is what it is and something to worry about after this little breakdown.

For now, my concern is Vance fucking McMillan and how I'm going to get through this unscathed.

After dragging my ass up out of bed and getting in a quick run at my building's gym, I head into the office, faking a confidence that I'm currently lacking.

My morning is thankfully uneventful, giving me time to think about what the hell I'm going to do.

I have to tell someone. Apart from the fact that I don't want to work with the creep, I'm not the only woman who works here. We have female athletic trainers and physicians. Not to mention our social media manager is a young girl only a year out of college. I can't knowingly put any of them through what I went through.

Everyone here is like my family. Vance doesn't belong here.

I'm at the point of seriously considering putting names in a hat to decide who to talk to when someone knocks on my office door. My heart jolts until Paige calls out.

"It's me."

My shoulders drop as I relax, jumping up to let her in.

"Hey stranger. How are you?" I pull her into a warm hug before dragging her inside. I could use a friend right now, even if that friend is the daughter of the man I'm stressing over.

"I'm good. I stopped by to talk to Dad about the wedding but he's not here. I'm guessing he's in New York?"

"I actually have no idea. All I know is that he's away on business."

"Ooh, why so secretive?" She laughs and I laugh along with her, but it's obviously lacking.

"So...the wedding?" I smile giddily, changing the subject so we don't have to talk about her dad, and she waves me off.

"You know we're only doing this for Isaac," she says as she walks farther into the room, glancing out the window.

"I know. That's not going to stop me from getting excited and treating you to the full bridesmaid service. I'm still a bridesmaid, right?"

Paige and Easton have been engaged for close to a year, despite the fact that neither one of them wanted to get married. Especially Paige. She did, however, want to adopt Isaac, and they concluded that getting married would make that process significantly easier. She asked me to be a bridesmaid months ago, but other than searching for a dress, which I only learned about from our hair stylist, I haven't heard a thing since.

"Of course you're still a bridesmaid." She turns my way, smiling without her eyes, and I wait for the *but*. "But...you may not want to be one when I tell you something."

"Please tell me it's hideous dresses. I can get behind that." It's highly unlikely since Paige used to be a fashion model. Still, the idea of that amuses me.

"It's not hideous dresses."

"Okay."

"The wedding is in August."

My eyes widen for the second time during this conversation. "August? During the preseason?" Easton had told me he didn't think they'd have it until after the season, next year. A year from now.

"Just after," Paige confirms and I bite back my shock. "We've decided to have it in between preseason and the first game. Easton doesn't want to make a big deal out of it. He thought if we had it during the offseason, it would become bigger than it needs to be. And I tend to agree."

"You're not wrong. It also gets Easton out of planning because he'll be too busy."

"Actually, he wants to be involved in the planning. He just doesn't want the guys to plan an epic Vegas-style bachelor party."

I imagine Luke running wild with ideas and I nod with a laugh. "August is sounding like a great idea. I'm excited. Let me know if I can do anything." My giddiness returns as I mentally start planning.

"That's why I'm here. I'd love your help."

"Of course. Anything you need."

"Thank you. I know we've got a lot to do between now and then, but I'm ready to throw myself into it all. Now...spit it out."

"What?"

"What's going on with you? You're enthusiastic, sure, but there's something off about you. Your smiles aren't reaching your eyes like they usually do."

I blow out a breath and prepare to tell Paige about the past. Even before she and Easton started dating, I had a good feeling about her, and we became close. Since then, we've become more like sisters.

And I kissed her father the other night.

Not weird at all.

All hail my sarcasm.

Paige is one of the few people who know the reasons behind my reluctance to date athletes, and since she's always been honest with me, I know I can trust her.

"Wes and your dad are looking at a QB from my past." I sit down on the edge of my desk, my legs suddenly shaky.

"To replace Thomas?"

"Yep." I clench my jaw as I think about it.

"By the look on your face, I'm guessing you didn't have a good past?"

"He's the guy that got me fired, the guy that forced himself on me, and..." I trail off because she doesn't need to hear the details to know what I'm implying.

"Oh, fuck, Keeley. You never told me that he made it to the pros."

"I try not to talk about him at all." Or think about him for that matter, when he's not a hot topic.

"Understandably. So…what did they say?"

"Who?"

"My dad and Wes."

"Oh." I cringe and Paige sighs in understanding, her expression sympathetic.

"You haven't told them?"

"Not yet."

"You should at least tell my dad. He's not going to want to sign him if he knows what he's like."

"I know. But that was years ago. What if he's changed? What if he's a genuinely good guy, just like his reputation suggests?" *What if they choose him over me?*

"What if he's not?" Her words hang in the air and my chest tightens at the thought.

"This could open a whole can of worms and ruin his career." *Or mine.*

"Is that really what you're worried about?"

"Yes." My voice lifts, giving away my lie.

"What's going on?" Paige reaches forward and grabs my hand, giving me a squeeze.

"You know that your dad and I are close, right?"

"I *do*." She speaks slowly, and it would make me laugh if Sal and I hadn't had a moment the other night. That's not what I'm referring to here.

"I'm worried he'll go into protection mode," I lie again, though now that I think about it, that's another possibility.

"Oooh." Paige's mouth forms an O before she visibly cringes. "He's definitely going to do that. I don't think it's avoidable."

"So what do I do?"

"You tell him anyway. It's better he knows now than when you start acting uncomfortable around his QB and he demands to know why."

"You're right. Thanks."

"Any time. Good luck."

"Ha. Thanks for that too."

"I'm not going to lie; I don't envy you in the slightest, but I'm here if you need me." Paige squeezes my hand again and I smile. This talk may not have solved any of my problems, but at least I know what I have to do.

My heart jolts as I think about Sal's reaction, and I'm not sure if it's because I'm worried about what he'll do or excited by the idea of his protectiveness. Either way, I'm going to find out.

"Sal, I have Keeley here to see you." Tabitha smiles my way as she speaks, both of us pretending it hasn't been years since I asked her to announce me to Sal.

Sal's silent for a beat, but I swear I can hear the faintest of sighs. "Thank you, Tabitha. Please send her in."

I smile at Tabitha, hoping to convey the depth of my thanks without words, and walk across the hall to open Sal's door.

"Hey, sorry to bother you—"

"That's not possible, Keeley, and you know it." He gestures for me to come in, and I let out a soft laugh. Since when have I cared about that? I usually confirm he's alone and then barge right in. I've interrupted calls, his lunch, and hell, I once walked in on him changing his shirt. That one was my favorite.

Now, I'm hesitant and it's not for the reason he thinks.

"I was actually going to come and find you," he tells me, brushing past me to close the door. "Take a seat. I have news."

News? Dammit. He's about to tell me they signed Vance. I know it. Despite the awkwardness between us, there is a lightness to him, a relaxed energy that only comes with knowing a few of your problems have been solved.

"Before you tell me, I need to talk to you about something."

Sal freezes, his eyes wide before his head drops back. "I'm sorry. I promise I haven't been avoiding you. You were out of the office and then I was away on business. Which is what I was coming to talk to you about."

"That's not—"

"Is there any way we can go back to the way things were? I can't lose you. And more than that... I don't want to."

My stomach knots and I feel bad for letting him believe I walked away the other night because of our kiss.

"We're good, I promise."

"Are you sure?" His expression is so hopeful that my chest aches.

"I'm sure." *Please don't hate me when I finally tell you why I held back.*

"Thanks, Keeley." Sal's relieved sigh makes me smile until he shifts the conversation back to what he had to say. "Ready for the exciting news?"

"No."

"We signed Mye— No?" Sal frowns, pausing when he notes my response. His eyes rake over me, concern etched into his features. He studies me for a second before cursing out loud, perhaps registering my panic, though there's no need. Was he going to say Myers?

"I'm an idiot. I—"

"I'm fine. No, I'm good. Did you say Myers?"

"I did, but that's not important right now."

"What?" I jump to my feet, my own lightness now matching Sal's. "How can you say that? Securing Beckett is incredible news."

"It is." He speaks slowly, watching me curiously. "What's wrong?"

"Nothing."

"Nothing?"

"No, I'm good. And relieved. How did you do it?"

"Keeley—"

"Is that where you were yesterday? Did you fly to Colorado? What's he like? Is it all official or just a verbal deal at this point?" I know it's wrong to slam him with questions, and from the look on his face, he can see right through my attempt to distract him. Yet, when I stop talking and offer him a genuine smile, he relaxes.

"It's official. His agent called about an hour ago confirming the news, and to reiterate the deal, Beckett called himself. I only just hung up with him when Tabitha buzzed me to tell me you were here." Sal frowns when he says that out loud, his brows pulling into a furrow. "Why was that?"

"Why was what?"

"Since when do you have Tabitha announce you?"

Since I was awkward about the information I no longer have to tell you. "I have no idea what happened there. I've been so busy, I don't know whether I'm coming or going."

"Are you sure?"

"Yes, like I said before, you and I are good."

"Okay. Good. Great. Want a drink to celebrate Beckett?"

"A drink? At eleven a.m.?"

"Yes. I'm in desperate need of a coffee. "

"Oh, right, yes. I just have to grab my purse from my office."

Sal stares at me pointedly, his face pinched as though I offended him. "You don't need your purse. I've got it. I need to get out of here. It's been a long, stressful morning."

"Okay." I laugh. "Let's go."

Sal's palm hovers near my lower back as we exit the office, and I swear I can feel an electric current between us. None the wiser, he waves to Tabitha as he walks past. "Coffee, Tabitha?"

"No, thank you."

"Are you sure?"

"Yes, sir."

Sal nods as we continue on our way and for the first time, I don't comment or laugh when Tabitha says "sir," signifying a shift in our relationship. One that neither of us acknowledges.

And a weight settles in my chest. Only...

Maybe it's for the best.

I have to be a professional. Both of our lives will be so much easier if we can go back to the way things were. And I, for one, am going to try.

Chapter Eighteen

KEELEY

FOUR MONTHS LATER

It's so dark in my room when my alarm goes off that I picture the birds telling me to shut the fuck up and go back to bed, making me smile as I open my eyes.

Four a.m.

It's like the first day of school. Or in my case...preseason training camp is raring to begin.

I'm a night owl, always have been, so my early-morning workouts during the season are a killer.

When it's the offseason, I walk on my lunch break, or head home early to exercise at night. That's not possible when my workload ramps up. It's the workaholic in me. But since I also value my fitness, my alarm is waking me before the sun.

I sleepily rub my eyes as I make my way to the bathroom, anticipating the warmth of my massage shower as I start to strip down. I don't usually shower before a workout, however since I'm completely changing my routine, I'm allowing myself this little comfort before putting my body through hell.

With a yawn, I turn on the tap, holding my hand out to check the temperature, rolling my shoulders as I wait.

And nothing happens. At all. No warmth, no cold, no goddamn water.

Today of all days.

Turning the tap off, I stalk through the house and grab my phone, ignoring the time as I call our building manager, putting it on speaker so I can flick through my emails to make sure I haven't missed a message about the outage.

I haven't.

There's nothing.

My call redirects to the after-hours line, and as the hold music plays, I run through what I'm going to say, getting more frustrated every time I hear the "your call is important to us" bullshit.

It's eleven minutes before a husky voice comes on the line, and the second she speaks, I know I'm not the first person to call. Her own frustrations are dripping from her tone and all she said was hello. I wonder who else in my building is waking up at four a.m. Maybe we can work out together.

"Are you calling about the lack of hot water?"

"No, actually. I'm calling about the lack of water *in general*."

There's silence on the end of the line, though I swear I hear the faintest "fuck" coming from under her breath.

"Thank you for reporting it," she says, her now robotic voice telling me she's said that very line many times already. "We have someone looking into the issue. We will let you know when it's resolved."

"Thank you. May I suggest you email everyone in the building to let them know it's out?"

"No one checks emails at four in the morning."

"I did. It would have saved you this call."

"Noted."

"Thank you. Have a nice day."

She scoffs as I hang up, and I run a hand down my face while I groan. I probably wouldn't be having a good day in her shoes either. Though I bet she has water at her home, so I can't give her too much sympathy.

Instead of heading to the gym in my building, I change plans, getting dressed and packing my outfit for the day before driving to work, mentally preparing myself to use the facilities there. Something I have never done. I'd much prefer to uphold the illusion that I naturally look perfect every day. No one needs to see me as the frazzled mess I become at the end of a workout, especially my mostly male work colleagues.

Let's hope I'm the only one up this early. Otherwise they're in for a treat.

After an uneventful and private workout, I managed to cool down and make myself presentable before anyone else had graced the office with their presence, and I'm grateful for that.

It's nice to keep the mystery alive.

My morning is spent fielding calls from contacts of mine, trying to get the inside scoop on what I can tell them about our roster for the season ahead, and just like I do every other year, I give them the same response.

"It's too soon to know. We'll announce it to the world when we're ready."

They're like broken records. Still, I admire them for trying.

I manage to catch the end of the first drills session, before Pierce calls time and I smile when I see my friends back in the action. I've seen a few of the guys during the offseason, and while they've been here for organized team activities, namely Reed, Luke, and Zane—and Easton, obviously—this is different.

They are on and ready for the season ahead.

When we get back to the locker room, someone finger whistles to hush the room, and I naturally look around for Thomas. That was his thing. Not the whistle specifically, but I could always rely on him if I needed to get the guys' attention. I miss him. It's not going to be the same now that he's retired.

My eyes lock on Luke's, and his knowing smile has me stifling a laugh. He misses him too. They may be brothers-in-law and still see each other regularly, but I'll bet it's not the same. Other than a few years when Thomas played for Seattle, they've been teammates their whole lives. I'm surprised that Luke's playing for another season. I always thought they'd retire at the same time.

The room finally falls quiet and I tap my clipboard, running down the list of names I need to see after they shower. "I need Rivers, Coombs, Jeffries, and Wilder in my—"

"You mean your brother?" one of the rookies calls out and I roll my eyes. It's day one of training camp, and we've already identified the new comedian.

Guess what, James? I, too, can be funny.

"I have a brother?" I fake a gasp and all but Easton and James laugh. "Yes, Easton is my brother. For those of you that find it so fascinating, let me tell you something that will blow your minds... We share a mother and a father too."

Luke mimes his head exploding before shooting me a wink, and I shake my head. That's exactly how he reacted when he first found out I was related to East, but that's mainly because he considered us friends and thought that he knew me.

He was half right. We *were* friends. We *are*. I didn't tell him because Easton asked me to keep our connection quiet when I landed the job not too long after he was recruited. He didn't want anyone to think he'd helped me get the role. I may complain about him often—especially since he never told me that was his reasoning until last year—but he's a good guy at heart.

Doesn't mean I'm going to stop driving him crazy.

"And before you ask," I continue, smiling when I note the beginning of Easton's scowl, "he is grumpy all the time. It's no different around his family."

Easton flips me off, and I take that as my cue to get the room back in order. If I don't, he's likely to cut me off, and I'd miss my nephew far too much for that.

"Anyway, back to my list. If I named you, I need you in my office after you've showered. Thank you."

I jump down from the bench seat and stumble over an abandoned cleat, falling into strong arms.

"Are you okay, ma'am?" Beckett's gaze softens in concern and I smile in response.

"I'm good, thank you, Beckett. We haven't really had the chance to talk yet. How are you settling in?"

Beckett packed up his life in Colorado and moved here a couple of months ago so he could train with the team. When I saw him coming out of Sal's office on his first day, I almost hugged him for how grateful I was to have him here. If he hadn't taken a chance on us, I would have had to come clean about Vance, and I'm ninety percent sure my life would be completely different right now.

I'm not sure how it would look, but it wouldn't be the same.

Beckett offers me a whisper of a smile, and I see the moment he switches over to professional mode, as though I'm interviewing him during the post-win celebrations. "I'm good. Great even. Thanks for asking."

"And everyone's treating you well?"

"Of course."

"No issues?"

"None."

He's a man of few words, but I don't think he's lying. The team respects the hell out of him as a player, and it only took a day for him to prove himself as a good leader during some of the team workouts. Even if he mostly keeps to himself.

"I'll leave you to it then. Thank you for saving me."

"Any time, ma'am."

Ma'am. If I was really a ma'am, I don't think Sal would have an issue with the two of us sleeping together. But since I'm very much not a ma'am, I'm destined to continue on the path of self-love.

Yes, I'm still obsessing over this months later. *What the hell is wrong with me?*

I glance up in time to catch Sal across the room, the hint of a scowl marring his features as he watches Beckett walk away from me.

And that's why I'm still obsessed. Talk about mixed fucking signals.

The sad part is that I can't hate him for it because he means well. He's trying to do right by me. Or, at least, trying to do what he *thinks* is right for me. He's almost twenty years older than I am. He has a daughter close to my age. A daughter who happens to be my future sister-in-law. It's a mess of epic proportions. But I don't want to marry the guy. I just want him to service my needs.

I'm the girl that goes after what I want because I've learned that life can fuck you over when you least expect it. There's no time like the present. And right now, Mr. Salvatore D'Angelo is the only man on my mind. It's been that way for a *long* time.

And I've done nothing to try and change that.

My phone chimes with a text and when I read Hayley's group chat message, I laugh. It's as if she read my mind.

HAYLEY: I haven't discussed this with Paige yet —don't hate me—but I'm thinking it's time for that girls' night we keep talking about. We can celebrate her last few weeks of freedom. What do you say, Paige? Saturday night?

Paige refused a bachelorette party, but she mentioned at the time that she'd love to go out with her close friends, and Hayley's finally taking action. I could use a night out.

PAIGE: Just the girls?

HAYLEY: Of course. Only those of us on this group chat

PAIGE: That sounds perfect. Let's do it!

AMELIA: I'm in

BLAIR: Me too. Where are you thinking, Hayley?

HAYLEY: Nowhere yet. I'm open to ideas

HAYLEY: Keeley, what about you? You deserve some fun

AMELIA: Agreed

PAIGE: I second that

AMELIA: If you can

I smile at the support of my friends, support for both Paige and me. They know work usually takes precedence over fun. And they'd never push me. But it's nice to know they haven't ruled me out completely. Because in this instance, I want to go. Hayley's right; I deserve some fun—a night out —and more than that, I want one.

Another message comes through as I'm lost in my head, this one outside of the group chat.

PAIGE: Everything okay? How was day one?

I'm confused as to what warranted her message until I realize I never responded to the group chat.

KEELEY: I'm good. Today was good. I'm coming out with you all. I've just been busy. I'll let the girls know

KEELEY: But if you don't want this, I'm happy to try and shut it down

PAIGE: No way! You know I love spending time with you all. As long as it's nothing like a bachelorette party, I'm ready to go

KEELEY: Great, I can't wait

PAIGE: Love you

KEELEY: Love you too

Though I know her response is genuine, a twinge of guilt settles in my stomach. I'm usually the first person to talk about my problems. Only... how do I talk honestly to Paige when the problem is my infatuation with her dad?

Even more of a reason to move on.

KEELEY: I'm there!

I text the group chat.

KEELEY: And I know a place we can try

Chapter Nineteen

KEELEY

As though stepping into a time warp, we push through the deep-red velvet curtain into another world, and my jaw drops.

I found a quirky bar online that moonlights as a burlesque club during the summer months, and when I sent it to the girls, it was a resounding yes for our night out. Since I hadn't actually been here before, the images online could have very well been too good to be true, but I'm happy to say, on first impression alone, I don't think that's the case.

A circular stage sits prominently in the center of the room, adorned with the same velvet curtains and gold trim. Dancers line the stage with opulent corseted costumes embellished with sequins and lace. In front of the stage is a wooden dance floor, while the rest of the dark room houses three deep mahogany bars, cabaret seating, and burgundy leather sofas.

I'd go as far as to say the picture online did not do it justice.

"Welcome to The Satin Rose. Do you have a reservation?"

The girls all look my way, and I laugh at the concern in their expressions. "I sure do. It's under Keeley Reynolds. I reserved a booth."

"Ooh, a booth." Hayley whistles under her breath. "I love this place."

The host directs us to our table and lights a dusty-pink candle before handing each of us a menu. "You'll find all our cocktails here, but if you don't see a favorite, rest assured, our bar staff are just as talented as our dancers. Have a lovely evening."

She wanders away and all eyes are on me. "This place is incredible, Keels."

"Right? I can't believe we haven't been here before. Have you been here?" Paige asks, her eyes wide as though I have a secret she doesn't know about. And I suppose I do. It's just not this.

"When do I ever go out?"

"You went out a few months back. With my dad."

"What?" Hayley chokes on thin air, her eyes sparkling with gossipy joy while I stiffen beside her. "You had a date with Daddy D'Angelo? Sorry, Paige."

"Ugh," Paige groans. "I really wish you wouldn't call him that." She tries to pout but her smile shines through, and I squeeze my leg under the table.

"Why? He's your dad and he's a D'Angelo. Daddy D'Angelo. Right, Keeley?" She elbows me in the side but I raise my hands.

"No. Please leave me out of this."

"Because you're dating him?"

"No! Jesus. We're friends who went to a concert together. That's all. And it was *months* ago. Despite it being the offseason, I've spent all my time between work and home."

I didn't know Paige knew about it. Sal and I haven't spoken about it since. And we definitely haven't planned round two.

My eyes flash to hers and she smirks back at me. "I should probably let you know that Dad tells me everything."

My heart seizes for the briefest of seconds, but I hide it behind my smile, ensuring it never once wavers. "I love that. I'm glad the two of you have that relationship now."

Paige releases a soft laugh, and I'm not sure if it's because she sees through my attempt to remain calm or she's about to agree with me. And it's the longest three seconds of my life before she does.

"I love it too, but he's also still my dad. I don't need to know *everything*. And you definitely need to go out more. I didn't realize it had been that long since the two of you went out."

Relief fills me when she smiles, and it doesn't appear to have an underlying connotation. "You're probably right; either way I haven't been here. I'm excited for the night."

"Should we order a cocktail?" Blair asks, having been quiet since we walked in.

"Hell, yes!" Hayley's quick to respond. "My girl needs alcohol. Her brother's staying with her and Zane."

"The two of them are driving me crazy." Blair frowns. "It was better when they'd stopped being friends. It's like revisiting my youth."

"I can't even imagine. There's no way I'd let my brother stay with me." I shiver and Paige not so subtly raises an eyebrow. "No offense, Paige. But come on, even you can admit he's hard to live with."

"Actually, I can't. I don't have a bad thing to say about him."

"He's brainwashed her. We have to help her before she ties herself to that ogre forever."

"If Amelia can put up with Luke, I think Paige can handle Easton," Hayley adds before shuffling closer to me, out of Amelia's reach.

"You're not wrong." Amelia shrugs and we all burst out laughing before waving to a roaming server and starting our night with his favorite cocktail recommendation.

"To Paige and her future husband." I raise a glass, winking her way as she smiles.

"To Paige and Easton."

"To me."

"Okay, girls. Let's knock this back quickly." Hayley takes a gulp of her *Wandering Eye* cocktail, her gaze shifting to the dance floor. "It's time to dance before the next show begins."

My thigh-length silk dress clings to my body after I've spent the last hour dancing with Hayley, and I need to sit down.

We're on hour three, and while I'm somehow still standing, Paige, Amelia, and Blair snuck back to the table a while ago.

"I need water. So much water."

"I need thongs," Hayley calls out louder than necessary, her face pulled into a pout while I laugh at the confused stares she's getting around us. "I've spent the past two months wearing runners and my feet have grown accustomed to not being tortured." She rubs the top of her foot while I laugh harder.

"She means flip-flops and sneakers," I fill the strangers in, and Hayley waves me off as we walk back to our table. It's become a running joke of ours for one of us to translate for her every time she uses Australian terms.

"I just can't get on board with flip-flops," she says as she drops into her seat. "They'll forever be thongs to me. Either way, they're much more comfortable than heels on a dance floor."

"I beg to differ. You won't see me in anything lower than three inches unless I'm at the gym. I think I have Barbie feet. They're naturally inclined to accommodate my heel."

"And that's why you're the boss." Hayley gives me finger guns, and I throw my head back with a laugh.

"Far from it, Hayls, but thanks."

"In the team's eyes you are," Amelia adds, drawing my attention. "Just ask Luke. He once said he wouldn't be surprised if you take D'Angelo's gig one day."

"Ha. Could you imagine?" I roll my eyes until all of my friends freakishly yell yes at the same time before their laughter surrounds us.

"I think you four spend *way* too much time together."

"And we wouldn't have it any other way."

The clock strikes midnight, and as though they're all Cinderella, Amelia, Paige, and Blair call an end to the night, with Hayley giving me another hour, despite having to get up at five.

"Are you sure you're happy to stay?" I ask her before the others disappear out of sight. Now that I'm out, I'm not ready to leave, but I'd never force someone to stay just to keep me company.

"Definitely." Hayley laughs as though my question is absurd, and pulls me toward the bar, offering our table to a woman celebrating her thirtieth birthday. "My scene tomorrow is a morning-after scene. Consider this method acting. I'm getting in the mood."

She finishes her drink and lowers it to the bar, bouncing her eyebrows as she does, and I can't help but laugh along with her. This is not usually my scene, but God, am I having fun.

"To late nights and early mornings without regret," I say, lifting my glass to my lips and finishing it off, feeling the burn as the fruity concoction glides down my throat.

"I'll have another, please..." I trail off, looking for a name tag on the man behind the bar.

"Nico," he confirms, instantly registering what I'm doing.

"Thank you, Nico. I'll have another."

Nico's deep-brown eyes crinkle with his smile, and when he winks, a spark ignites inside me. "You weren't here before. Right? Did you just start?" The girls and I were alternating between ordering from the bar and our table, and I don't remember seeing him. He definitely has a face to remember.

"I asked my friend to swap," he tells me. "I've been serving over there." He points to the smaller bar across the room and my gaze follows, finding the server we've had for most of the night.

"Why'd you swap?"

"You."

"Me?" My eyes go wide while the little spark morphs into more of a fire. "Are you sure you don't mean the beautiful Hayley Jackman?" I point to Hayley as she watches the dancers, oblivious to our conversation.

"She's beautiful, sure. But I prefer redheads."

"Okay."

Nico moves away to make my drink and I watch him as he goes, comparing him to a man that could very well be his father—in age and in looks. I'm clearly attracted to a strong jawline, a light dusting of stubble to run my hand over, and piercing dark eyes, because they're a match where those features are concerned.

I'm completely lost in my ogling until Hayley jabs me under the ribs, and I jolt with a squeal. "*Hayls*!"

"Oops." She smiles innocently while I shake my head with a laugh.

Nico returns with my drink, complete with a little umbrella in the top, and our hands brush as he passes it over. I smile flirtatiously, wishing for that fire to move between my legs, but it doesn't happen.

This guy is gorgeous. He's about six feet—which is shorter than Sal but taller than me and that's what counts—he's got tattoos covering his muscular biceps, the ends of which disappear beneath the sleeves of his tee, and his eyes... My God, they could melt panties.

Just not mine.

Dammit.

"He's cute, Keels." Hayley winks, glancing his way. "Do you want me to disappear?"

"No, thank you. I don't need your matchmaking services right now."

"Matchmaking? God, no. He's not the guy you take home to meet the parents. He's the guy you fuck in a bathroom and never think twice about."

I suck my lips into my mouth, biting back the thought.

"Just look at him. He knows what he's doing with that smirk. And I have no doubt he's done it many times before."

"I don't disagree. Only I thought you'd all decided it was my turn to find a man."

"Oh, we have. But this guy is not him."

"Any ideas who is? I have pretty high standards."

"As you should. You need someone who matches your boss-babe energy and respects the hell out of you for it. An equal. I've been thinking about it a lot." The smallest of smiles tugs at her lips before she hides it away.

"Okay. Let me know when you find him."

"I will. Just to be clear, you're definitely a no to athletes?"

"A hard no. Always."

"Shame. Beckett is one fine-looking man."

"You noticed that too?" I question and she nods as she bounces her eyebrows.

"How could I not?"

"He's gorgeous, but even if he wasn't a football player, he's too quiet for me."

"You're right. I'm sure I'll come up with someone else. In fact, I'll bet there's someone right under our noses, if only we could find him."

"If only." *Dammit.* What is she alluding to?

"Anyway, that's for another time. For now, ask Mr. Smoldering Eyes what time he gets off work. You know, so he can get you off."

Hayley's eyes sparkle as she laughs at her own joke, and I can't stop the snort that flies out of me. "I'll think about it."

I've just got to stop thinking about someone else.

Chapter Twenty

SALVATORE

"Thanks, Bronte. I appreciate you keeping me up to date." Thank God for friends in high places. If it weren't for Bronte and her publishing contacts, I'd be completely out of the loop on Gregory's damn book. I should also be thankful that she's still friendly with me since she was Camilla's friend first.

"Anytime, Sal. I'll be in San Francisco next month; we should meet for a drink. It could be a good time to talk about your own memoir."

"Mine?" I chuckle under my breath. "No one wants to read that story. I'm boring as hell."

"A billionaire workaholic who ran his marriage into the ground before moving halfway across the country to buy a football franchise, while continuing to run his business? Not to mention your adventures assisting in the arrest of two crooked businessmen, saving your daughter from public humiliation."

"Wow. Something tells me you've thought about this. Also...you know way too much about me."

"You know Camilla and I will always be close."

"I do. I just didn't realize she was still talking about me."

"I love her, but she'll talk about anyone for attention."

Anyone? My hackles rise and a tightness works its way into my chest. "Even the kids?"

"No," Bronte's quick to reassure me. "I promise. She doesn't talk about the kids. Not in a gossipy way."

"Good."

"Anyway, moving on. I have contacts. I could find you a ghostwriter."

I chuckle again, my brows furrowing. "Thank you. If I ever decide to go down that path, I'll keep you in mind."

"Please do."

"Talk soon."

"Definitely."

I hang up and immediately pour myself a whiskey, the idea of sharing my life with the world eliciting a dull pang in my stomach. Gregory's tell-all is sharing enough; I don't need any more out there, even if he doesn't mention my name. He's attacking my team and that's like a personal attack on me.

Thank God for the delay in the release. It turns out, the Storm football team wasn't the only team he mentioned in his book, and he's currently being sued for defamation over one statement he made about another franchise's general manager stealing money from his players to support his luxurious life. Of course, his claims come with no reasonable proof.

What the hell kind of publishing company lets shit like that through?

I probably owe them a drink, because without that, we'd be thrust back into the spotlight again at the start of a new season. Here's hoping the case goes to trial and takes years to be resolved, and maybe they'll scrap the book altogether.

After sitting down at the desk in my home office, I roll the bottom edge of my glass on the dark wood grain finish, staring at the liquid as it swishes close to the edge.

I needed this news, and while it could still go either way, it feels like a temporary victory. Meaning, it's back to normal programming for me. And that means budgets.

I've been spending more time in this office over the past few months, working on D'Angelo Construction during the Storm's offseason. But that's all about to change now that we're back in the swing of things.

It felt wrong to work full days in the Storm office when I wasn't doing anything for the team, so it made sense to move my work here. It had nothing to do with avoiding the temptation of a beautiful redhead. Nothing at all.

Time passes slowly as I stare at the numbers in front of me, unable to process a single thing as that beautiful redhead haunts my mind. I'm so out of it that when my phone vibrates across the desk, I jolt, my heart racing as though I've been caught with my mind wandering where it shouldn't.

Which is exactly what was happening.

Instead of thinking about the task at hand, I've been thinking about Keeley. Replaying her moment with Beckett in the locker room.

It wasn't even a fucking moment and yet... *What the fuck am I doing?*

It's been months since we kissed, and I still can't stop thinking about the softness of her lips and the light whimper that escaped her.

I can't have her. Plain and simple.

We work together, she's my daughter's closest friend, her goddamn sister-in-law, and more than that, she's twenty years younger than I am. We've been over this.

So why can't I accept that truth? She has. She seems to have moved on easily. Business as usual.

My phone vibrates again, reminding me I missed a text, and I absentmindedly pick it up, unlocking the screen without looking at the sender.

KEELEY: Hi

Keeley? *Hi?* My eyes bulge over a two-letter fucking word, and I stare at it for a beat before deciding how to answer. If I was to scroll back through our message chain, I'm certain I'd discover that the last time either one of us texted about something that wasn't work-related was right around the time that we kissed. Although, since she only said hi, I'm making the assumption that it's not about work.

SALVATORE: Hi back.

KEELEY: Why is it awkward between us now?

SALVATORE: I didn't think it was.

KEELEY: You know it is

I laugh at her response though it's not exactly true. When we're at work, it's like nothing has changed. Only we no longer have after-hours working dinner dates, long chats in my office, and we don't talk about anything personal. She could have a fiancé and I'd have no idea.

Okay, that's not entirely true because Paige would have mentioned that, most likely in the sense that Easton was grumpy about it. The point is that I don't really know what's going on in her life. Like what she's doing at—I check the time and groan—*one thirty in the morning*. What the fuck?

SALVATORE: It's not awkward, though I did think you'd given up on me. As a friend.

There's so much more I want to say right now, but it's none of my business.

KEELEY: I haven't given up on you. As a friend

SALVATORE: Okay. This is work-related then?

KEELEY: Definitely not. I don't talk about work when I'm drinking

Fuck. I reread her previous text and laugh at myself. She hasn't given up on me *as a friend*, just as someone to give her more than that.

SALVATORE: Where are you?

KEELEY: Wouldn't you like to know?

Yes. Dammit.

SALVATORE: That's why I asked, Keeley.

KEELEY: I'm out. With friends

KEELEY: Actually, I WAS out with friends, but they left

SALVATORE: Where are you?

I have to stop myself from calling her or overpunctuating the text to show my frustration. She's in her thirties and not my responsibility. I need to calm the fuck down.

KEELEY: I'm out

Goddammit, Keeley. I clench my fist and tap it against my lips, taking a deep breath through my nose. *I don't have to worry. I don't have to worry.*

SALVATORE: Are you having a good night?

My fingers stab the letters a lot harder than necessary while I say the words out loud, my teeth clenched.

KEELEY: I am, thank you

SALVATORE: Good. Who were you out with? Anyone I know?

Please tell me it was Paige. She mentioned something about wanting to sleep in tomorrow so that could be why.

KEELEY: Hayley, Amelia, Blair, and Paige. But they went home to their men

KEELEY: The guys on your team. Your players

KEELEY: I'm happy to report there are no players here tonight. Well, no SPORTS players. Wait, I guess the guys could be athletes, though I don't recognize any. Maybe they're rookies

Christ, she's not just drinking, she's drunk. And she's texting me.

SALVATORE: ...

KEELEY: Are you sure you want me to be single? There are a lot of fine-looking men here

Fuck. I have no right to want her to be any way—single or otherwise—but I don't like where this is going.

SALVATORE: Don't do something you regret in the name of pissing me off.

KEELEY: Believe it or not, I only do things for myself

I believe it. Still...pissing me off would bring her a lot of joy right now. I blow out a breath and stand, pacing the floor of my office, abandoning the glass of whiskey I never actually got to sip. *What the fuck do I do here?*

I pass my desk, and a photo of Paige comes into view.

Paige.

SALVATORE: Hey kiddo. Were you at the Westerly tonight? A friend thought he saw a photographer following you around. I wanted to check in.

PAIGE: It's 1:30, Dad. You worry too much. But thank you. I wasn't there. I was at The Satin Rose

She was where? I've never heard of that place. Even so... Thank you, Paige.

SALVATORE: Good. But I'll always worry. That's not going to stop anytime soon.

With a sigh, I sit back down and grab my glass of whiskey, a little of the tension leaving my body as I finally take a sip.

PAIGE: You need a girlfriend

I choke on the liquid, coughing a few times as I rub my chest.

I don't need a girlfriend. Worrying about Paige is a full-time job, and now look at me worrying about Keeley.

I'm too old for this shit.

Speaking of Keeley, what the hell am I going to do?

SALVATORE: Can you please look after yourself, Keels?

KEELEY: Always. Someone's got to do it. Have a good night, Sal

SALVATORE: You too.

I lean back in my chair, crossing my ankle over my knee as I swirl my glass. It's one thirty a.m. I should be going to bed. And I will. I'm going to finish this drink and go to bed. It's the smart thing to do.

I'm a goddamn billionaire running a construction company while being a hands-on owner of a football team. I'm a smart man.

I'm going to bed.

Chapter Twenty-One

KEELEY

Nico announces last call at the bar, and I pout as if my expression will elicit a change of the rules. "You don't have to leave." He laughs softly. "We just can't serve alcohol anymore. We officially close in thirty minutes, if you want to wait."

"What would I be waiting for?"

"Me."

Of course. I bite back a smile, but before I can respond, he gets called away, and my mind once again drifts to Sal.

I wonder what he'd think about my innocent flirting. I'm not actually going to sleep with Nico, and I'm ninety percent sure he knows that. Though I will admit I'm enjoying the attention from someone who's not afraid to give it to me.

Unlike the man in my mind.

As Nico chats with a gorgeous blonde at the other end of the bar, I study his features, trying hard to picture him in my bed, between my legs. I imagine his palms wrapped around my thighs as he spreads me, the veins in his forearms bulging below his rolled-up business shirt sleeve, his dark eyes boring into mine as his deep voice penetrates my thoughts.

"I've wanted to do this for so long, Keels. I hope you're ready for me." His head lowers to the apex of my thighs, and I moan as I grab his salt and pepper hair, his— *God-fucking-dammit.*

I shake myself out of my head and Nico smiles, catching me looking in his direction. God, how long was I staring his way in a daze?

It's another couple of minutes before he appears in front of me, and when he does, I have my apology ready to go. As much as I'd love him to fuck the idea of Sal right out of my mind, I'm not sure that's possible. Especially in my slightly inebriated state. My mind is too messed up to think clearly. On a normal day, I'm smart enough not to insert Sal into my fantasies. It does no one any favors.

"Your place or mine?" Nico asks and I laugh.

"I'm going back to mine. Actually, I'm going back to a hotel because a water pipe burst somewhere in my apartment building days ago and we still have no water. It's really... not the point. I'm going alone."

"You sure?" Nico doesn't bother hiding his disappointment, and I feel bad about my constant flirting. If he knew my mind was elsewhere, though, I doubt he'd argue.

I don't apologize because I have nothing to be sorry about, and instead pay my tab, giving him a decent-sized tip. More than I'd usually give.

After one last smile, I grab my phone and contemplate how to get home. I should Uber, but I once made a promise to my mom that I wouldn't Uber alone if I'd been drinking, and I kind of want to keep my word.

Pulling up my contacts, my finger hesitates over Easton's number, my nose crinkled uncomfortably. He's going to kill me. But once he hears my reasoning, he'll reluctantly agree that calling him was the right thing to do.

Doesn't make it any easier.

I should have gone home with the girls.

My phone rings in my hand as I'm staring at it, and Sal's name flashes across the screen. *What in the world?*

Glancing up as I answer, I frown as my eyes find a man with a lot of Sal's distinct features looking back at me from across the room. *God, I'm drunk.* Maybe I should have picked *that* guy to go home with, then it wouldn't have been such a stretch.

The man matches my frown as I watch him, his frame getting bigger as he stalks toward me.

"Come on, we're leaving," he snaps when he reaches me, grabbing my hand to pull me up from my comfortable stool.

"What?" I shake my head, confused until his voice registers in my mind.

"We're leaving."

"Sal?"

He pauses, his eyes wide and he stares at me, confused. "Who the fuck did you think I was?"

"Why are you acting like Easton?"

"Easton? Trust me, you don't want to be making that comparison right now."

"Why not?"

"Because I want to throw you over my lap and spank you. What did you think was going to happen when you messaged me drunk and alone at a bar in the middle of the night?"

I don't even remember doing that, but since he's here. "Take me home, Sal."

"Fuck, Keeley." Sal covers his pained expression with his huge palm, and I study the veins bulging on his skin. "That's why I'm here."

"Good." My eyes lift to his and I smile. "I'm ready. I have been for a while now." I frown at my own words, not even sure if I mean that to say I've been ready to go home, or ready to go home *with Sal.* Both are true.

And from Sal's quiet groan, that I'm sure he thinks I can't hear over the music, I'd say he thinks the latter, and he's not at all happy about it.

My mind spins as I stare out the window of Sal's sports car, the passing lights making me drowsy as I close my eyes to block out the brightness.

"Thank you for coming," I say softly, fighting a yawn. "It would have sucked to have no way home on top of everything else."

"Everything else? What's everything else?" Sal tries to keep his tone even, but the slight uplift at the end makes me laugh as I glance his way, catching his frown before he schools it.

"Despite pissing me off, you're a good man. But you don't have to worry about me. I can handle staying in a luxury hotel for a few more nights. It's not like it's a hardship."

I yawn and turn back to the window, resting my head against the glass.

"What do you mean by hotel?"

"I'm staying in a hotel." Another yawn escapes me as my eyes drift shut. "My bed is like a pillow." I picture the cloudy goodness and imagine myself snuggling against the mountain of pillows right now. I sigh as my body sinks into the softness, my throbbing feet finally getting to rest.

Bright lights assault my eyes, and I scrunch my face before rubbing them and slowly opening them just a touch. Through the slit in my eyelids, I can see we've stopped moving.

"Where are we?"

"My apartment building."

"What?" I straighten in my seat, getting caught by the seat belt. "I thought you said you never take anyone to your apartment."

"I know what I said, Keeley. This is different. You passed out after mumbling something about staying in a hotel, and I couldn't wake you."

"Wow, I must have been out of it. I'm not usually a deep sleeper."

"No, I mean, I didn't try. To wake you."

My chest tightens as I stare up at him, seeing through the man I have no reason to be pissed off at. My Sal. My gentleman.

"Thank you. We can go to my hotel. It's—"

"We're here now."

"At your apartment building."

"Yes."

I raise a brow pointedly because he's clearly not seeing the issue here. "The building your daughter also lives in?"

"She knows we're friends, Keeley." Sal all but rolls his eyes, and I almost groan until I remember what Paige said earlier tonight. She knows *everything*.

"So I heard."

"What does that mean?"

"She said you tell her everything. She knew about the concert we went to. What else—"

"I know what you're asking, and no, I haven't told her that I kissed you."

"Twice."

"Twice."

"And you don't think she'll question me spending the night in your apartment?"

Sal shakes his head. "I'm not worried, if you're not."

"Of course you're not worried. I have no doubt your gentlemanly mind isn't thinking what I'm thinking. But Paige might."

"Christ, Keeley. Nothing is going to happen. I won't have to lie to her so I don't see the issue."

"Perfect." I smile when I really want to curse the heavens. *Why the hell didn't I go home with Nico?* Now I have to spend the night in Sal's apartment, *not* getting lucky.

Sal smiles back at me, oblivious to my sarcasm. "Can you walk or..." His gaze darts to the window behind me, and I almost turn to check what he's looking at.

"I can walk." I definitely don't need him helping me inside. Or touching me in general.

"Okay. Wait there." He gets out of the car and I do as he asks, waiting for him to open my door.

Sal holds his hand out for me to take, and I let him help me out, not entirely convinced I can do this part on my own. Walking is fine. Our eyes lock when I'm standing, and the intensity of his gaze penetrates my chest, making my pulse spike. I bite my lip, and his eyes briefly drop to my mouth before he glances away, clearing his throat.

With a quiet huff, I pull away from his grasp, taking a step toward the glass door, only to pause as realization hits me.

"Easton lives here."

Sal scoffs and it sounds suspiciously like a chuckle, drawing a scowl his way. "He lives with Paige, Keeley. Why is that only just sinking in?"

"Because I don't tend to think about my brother when talking about my sex life."

Sal visibly swallows, and I almost return his half-scoff, half-laughing reaction. "We weren't talking about your sex life."

"Weren't we?" I raise an eyebrow, and he stares at me stunned until his gaze hardens and he shakes his head.

"Come on. It's time to go inside." He holds his arm out, gesturing toward the doors, and when I walk ahead, he once again ushers me forward protectively, only this time his hand hovers much farther away. As though that makes all the difference.

And maybe it would, if I couldn't feel the electricity hovering between us. He doesn't have to touch me to pass on his warmth.

"What are we doing when we get to your apartment?" I ask, as the doors open.

"Going to bed."

"Exactly. I told you we were talking about—"

"*Keeley,*" Sal grates, his teeth clenched in frustration, and I swear he follows it with *"I'm trying here,"* but he's mumbling under his breath so I can't be too sure.

Either way, a smile tugs at my lips as we walk.

Sal came to my rescue. He found out I was drinking, alone, and he hunted me down. Sure, he's protective. It's in his nature. It would be easy to believe that's the reason we're here.

If he hadn't looked at me like my face haunts his dreams.

I'm also ninety-nine percent sure there was mention of a spanking.

He wants me. There's no doubt about it. Only he won't touch me now that there's alcohol coursing through my veins.

When I'm sober, however, that's a different story. I have a feeling he's not going to be able to deny me again.

And I want to find out.

Chapter Twenty-Two

KEELEY

My head's throbbing the next morning as I sneak out of Sal's apartment, an image of his locked jaw and tense gaze playing on my mind. I still plan on calling him out on his attraction to me, but doing it wearing last night's dress and morning-after smudged makeup is not the way to go, even if I did attempt to wash it off.

I type a text to Sal as I ride the elevator, though I'm almost certain he wasn't there. It was too quiet when I woke up at nine a.m., and Sal is both a night owl and morning person. He's like a robot; he doesn't need sleep to survive.

After hitting send, I lean my head back against the mirrored wall and close my eyes until the elevator stops, jolting me to open them again. I glance over at the door, my eyes drifting past the floor level on the screen, and my stomach drops. I'm on Easton's level. Of course I'm on Easton's goddamn level.

I hold my breath, my eyes wide as the door opens, and fuck... One internal groan later, I'm smiling by the time Easton glances up from his phone.

"Hi."

"Keeley?" He frowns, his eyes bouncing around the small space as though he's going to find something to clue him in on this strange occurrence. "What are you doing here?"

Good question. "I came to visit."

"I'm on my way to the stadium."

"I know. But I..." *I what*? What am I doing here?

Easton folds his arms over his chest, waiting for me to continue until his eyes bulge. He scowls as his gaze moves from my face down to my disheveled dress, and a grumble flows out of him.

"Are you doing the walk of shame? Fuck, Keeley. Did you sleep with someone in my building?"

"No. Jesus. Of course not."

"The elevator was coming down. You were coming from a higher level."

"I was. But only because I forgot to push the button for your floor."

Easton leans back against the wall, his blue eyes clouded with suspicion. He doesn't even speak and I fold, another lie spilling out of me.

"Fine. If you must know, I drank myself into an emotional state and needed my mom. I slept in the spare room. I've been feeling—"

"Nope." He holds up a hand to stop me. "I don't need the details. I believe you."

"Are you sure? We could go out for breakfast and I could fill you in on everything going on in my life."

"Where are you going? If not my floor?"

"Back to Mom's. I forgot something."

"Fine." Easton pushes the button for Mom's level and the underground parking lot, then turns back my way. "Are you okay?" he asks after a beat, the hint of concern marring his features.

My lips curl into a smile as a warmth flows through me. Try as he might to keep up the grumpy-asshole persona, it's been fading since Isaac was born, and even more so now that he has Paige. Some days you wouldn't even know he was grumpy at all.

"I'm good, I promise."

"Okay. Good."

"Thanks, Easton."

He nods as the doors open to Mom's floor, and I squeeze his arm as I walk past, grinning until the doors shut behind me.

"Goddammit," I mumble under my breath. Me and my stupid lies. Now I have to convince Mom and Phil to pretend I slept here last night. In case Easton decides to get nosey.

Inhaling on a groan, I knock on the door and listen as movement sounds on the other side. I force a smile preemptively, just as my mom's boyfriend, Phil, opens up. "Hi, Sweetheart. How are you?"

His eyes briefly flit to my dress, and his brows furrow to hint his concern, but unlike Easton, he doesn't voice it, putting on a smile of his own as he waits for me to respond.

"I'm good, thanks, Phil. Is Mom around?"

"She is. Come in. She's having a shower but shouldn't be too long. Anything I can help with?"

"Actually, yes." Phil gestures for me to walk through to the kitchen, and I nod before following behind him, filling him in on my predicament. "I need you to tell Easton I spent the night here if it comes up. No questions asked. *Please.*"

He stops abruptly and I almost bump into him. "Wow. Oh-kay. Yep. Sure. No questions asked." He nods to himself, and the smallest laugh escapes me. I'll forever be grateful that my mom found him later in life.

"Thank you, Phil." I can always rely on him to help me out—that or he's terrified of me because he doesn't have any daughters himself.

"I'm asking questions." Mom joins us in the kitchen, her eyes beaming with intrigue, and I curse under my breath. "Why are you asking Phil to lie to my darling son? I'd never—"

"Oh, stop. You lie to him all the time. 'Of course I didn't let Isaac watch TV before bed.'" I put on my best Mom voice and Phil laughs.

"Okay. You're right. I still want answers."

"Of course you do. I drank a little too much last night, and one of my friends let me crash at his place. Easton saw me leaving just now."

"*His* place?"

"Yes."

"A friend?"

"Yes, Mom. Jeez."

"Do you work with this '*friend*'?"

"What? No. He's not an athlete."

"I never said he was." Her eyes sparkle with mischievous wonder, and I have to fight myself not to groan. *Does everyone secretly think Sal and I are something more than we are?*

"So...we're *not* covering you for a one-night stand?"

"No. I can promise you, there was no inappropriate behavior." I hold my gaze steady and Mom nods. While I often like to pretend otherwise, Mom always knew my tells. It was impossible to lie to her. Easton, on the other hand...

"I believe you. Only...sex isn't inappropriate. Who taught you that garbage?"

Goddammit. Now I know how Easton felt when I let it slip that Paige had been staying over at his place when they first got together. I laughed at Mom's teasing.

Oh, how the tables have turned.

I glance at Phil, hoping he'll save me, but he simply shrugs, his eyes full of their own humor.

"I didn't mean it like that, Mom. I just meant that my sleepover was purely platonic."

As much as I wish that wasn't the case.

"Okay. He's a good guy, that one."

"What? Who?" My stomach sinks and I frown to keep the fear out of my eyes.

"The man who took care of you. Most guys these days would try and take advantage."

"Not this one." He's a true gentleman. Not that I say that aloud. The less I say on the topic the better. "So, now you know the why? Can you please lie for me?"

"Of course. A little white lie never hurt anyone, and you know I'd do anything for you. All you have to do is ask." She smiles sweetly and I groan.

"*Mom.*"

"What?" She raises her hands in innocence and I roll my eyes, my gaze once again drifting to Phil for assistance. But he's no use. He's too busy staring at Mom like she hung the moon.

"Okay. Well, thanks. I'm going to go."

"Have a nice day, sweetie."

"You too."

I spin on my toe and stalk toward the door, desperate to get home. But Mom has to have the last words.

"Oh, and Keeley?" she calls out as my hands wrap around the door handle, my eyes closing in resignation. This is not going to be good. "Say hi to Sal for me. We haven't seen him for a couple of weeks."

I wince internally, but on the outside I'm the picture of calm. "Will do. Bye." I wave, refusing to look back, because while that could have been an innocent request, I'm not so sure it was. Especially after her questions about my "friend." Mom's always been observant. But I can't for the life of me think of anything Sal and I have done to arouse suspicion. And yet Hayley hinted at the same.

Not that *anyone* has anything to be suspicious about. There's nothing going on between us. At least there's not *now*.

With my phone pressed to my ear, I absentmindedly stare out my window as I return Callum's call, brushing my fingers through my freshly washed hair.

"You're alive," he answers slowly, his usually gruff voice holding no hint of concern until he adds, "Are you okay?"

"Yes, why wouldn't I be?"

"You called me three times."

"What? When?"

"Your middle of the night."

"Oh. Sorry about that. I was pretty drunk. I don't remember calling you. Why didn't you answer?"

"Because I was working. Different time zones, remember? I called when I got back to my car. Why didn't you answer *my* calls?"

"I was sleeping. In another man's bed."

"Uh-huh."

"And yes, it's the man you're thinking it is."

"I wasn't thinking of anyone, but now I know who. A part of me wants to say I told you so, but if he took advantage while you were drunk, I—"

"He refused to sleep with me. At all. He wouldn't even sleep *next* to me. Despite me asking him to." I hate that I can remember that. There may have even been begging.

A strange noise comes through the line and I roll my eyes.

"Did you just snort?"

"No."

"It sounded suspiciously like you tried to suppress a laugh and snorted. But the Callum I know doesn't snort. Or laugh for that matter."

"Exactly. So it can't be that."

"You like him, don't you?"

"I haven't met him so I can't say for sure."

"*But...*"

"But I think he's good for you. And if he wasn't Easton's future father-in-law, I think Easton would agree with my assessment."

"Of course I'd be attracted to the one man that Easton would care about me dating. Other than Sal, he couldn't care less about my love life."

"Have you told him?"

"God, no. I'm not stupid. There's nothing to tell."

"That's true."

That's true. Callum's delivery is so dry that you'd think he was teasing me about that notion, but he's just stating a fact. A fact I want to change. And I will. Soon.

"Anyway, are you coming over for Easton and Paige's wedding?" I change the subject, needing to move on from last night. "I know last time we spoke you were looking into it. Easton would love it if you could. As would I. But I know you're busy."

"Actually, the timing worked out. I've been contracted for another castle construction that's starting early in the new year, so I've hired a few extra people to make sure this one's done before winter."

"So many castles, so little time."

"You're hilarious."

"I am, aren't I. I can't wait to see you. It's been too long."

"You could visit."

"I know. One day I might."

We chat for another few minutes, and I almost don't want to hang up knowing I'm going to have to face my day. It's been a long time since I was last drunk. So long that I'd forgotten how awful the morning after is.

I think I'll be working from home today.

Chapter Twenty-Three

SALVATORE

With my arms folded over my chest, I watch the team training camp from the comfort of my office, and I'm proud to say they look strong.

What I'm not proud to say is the fact that I'm currently hiding in my office.

Keeley wasn't in yesterday. I had a feeling she'd be MIA before I even looked for her car. It was the sneaking out of my apartment that clued me in.

I'd lain awake all night after getting her settled, not moving from the spare bedroom in case I woke her, my mind swirling with questions for the morning. *Should I make her breakfast? Do I need to research a hangover cure? Or leave a towel and some clothes in the en suite so she can freshen up before leaving my room?*

My room. That's another thought that kept me awake. Keeley slept in my bed. And she looked damn good in it too with one hand tucked under her cheek while the other lay flat on my side, exactly where my chest would usually be.

God, it was hard to look away. Until I remembered it was highly inappropriate to be staring at someone while they slept. Especially when I'd already rejected that someone four times within the past year.

Keeley had every right to wake up and punch me. Or worse, cut me from her life.

Instead, I wasted all of my worrying because she snuck out as soon as she woke up. At least, she tried to sneak out. I'm guessing she didn't think I was home considering how loud she shut the front door.

Now I'm here, trying to prepare myself for every possible reaction when I see her again.

Is she going to be embarrassed? She shouldn't be. She didn't do anything to be embarrassed about.

Is she going to be mad? I wouldn't blame her if she was. Hence, the reason I was planning breakfast.

Those two options were fairly easy to prepare for. It's indifference I'm most worried about.

Is she going to walk in here like nothing happened, leaving us to continue on with this weird relationship we have? With both of us pretending there isn't a strange energy floating between us.

Sure, that sounds easier than having to talk it out. But we're adults. It's about time we grew the fuck up and got it all off our chests.

Someone knocks on my door and I freeze, wondering if I'm going to have to face that conversation right now, until Paige pokes her head in.

"Hey, Dad. Have you got a minute?"

"Of course. Come in. What's up?"

"I wanted to drop this off." She closes the door and hands me a drawing from Isaac, warming my heart.

"He made this for me?"

"He sure did."

"I love it. I'm going to put it up somewhere in the office. Thanks, Paige."

"You're welcome." She smiles cheerily and I can sense more.

"You know I always love seeing you, but when do you ever visit just to drop off some of Isaac's artwork? Is there something else?"

"Yeah, so... question. Are you aware that you're famous?"

"What? No, I'm not." I shake off her crazy idea. Paige can have her fame and I'm proud of everything she's done, but I'm more than happy to stay out of the headlines, unless it's in relation to my business or the Storm...and it's positive.

Paige bites back a smile and I frown. "You're not?"

"No. What is this about?"

She pulls her phone from her bag and I panic. The book? God, don't tell me more came out from that fucking book. I almost wish there had been something in there about me personally so I could sue his ass too. It's much easier to sue as an individually named person than as a team, when he was smart enough not to get too specific. It's just enough to bring us back into the negative spotlight but not enough to get him in trouble. If only he'd thought about that when mentioning the other team.

Paige spins her phone to face me, and I hold my breath, ready to unleash my rage. Until I see the image.

Fuuuck. Who the hell cares about photos of me?

"Okay." I play it straight, pretending I'm not fazed that she's holding an image of me outside The Satin Rose, after she told me she was there Saturday night. "That doesn't really make me famous."

"It means you're sellable."

"Yay for me."

Paige laughs before her smile turns mischievous. "I didn't know you'd been to The Satin Rose."

"I haven't. You can see my car in the image. I'd just parked there."

"Oh, okay. Either way, I thought you should know that people are interested in your life."

"What people?"

"I don't know. Storm fans. Women who find workaholics attractive."

"Very funny. Thank you for the heads-up. Is that all you came for?"

"No, actually. I also came to talk to Keeley. Did you know she spent the night in our building on Saturday?"

"What?" I choke on nothing, and Paige laughs so loudly that I double-check she closed my office door.

"Okay. Fine. I was worried about her because she messaged me drunk. She passed out in my car without telling me where she was staying, so I let her stay at my place. I slept in the spare room. That's all it was."

"What?" Paige's jaw drops, but she fails to hide the sparkle in her eyes. "Easton told me she'd stayed at her mom's."

"Stop lying. You didn't believe that."

"You're right." She smiles. "I didn't. But I do believe *your* story. Such a gentleman."

I'm really fucking not. Just because I didn't touch her, doesn't mean I wasn't thinking about it.

"Thanks, Kiddo. Can you do me a favor?"

"What's that?"

"Maybe don't bring it up to Keels?"

"I wasn't going to."

I huff out a laugh, but I should have guessed. She just wanted me to spill the details. Fucking gossip magazines.

A thought hits me and I panic. "Were the photos just me?"

"Yep. The photographer must have left by the time you came back out with Keeley."

"Oh, good."

Paige's previously happy expression morphs as she eyes me curiously, her lips parted as she furrows her brow. "Is there more to this friendship? More to you and Keeley?"

"No. I care about her a lot. But we're just friends."

Paige nods, and while I'm not technically lying at this point in time, the words taste bitter in my mouth, as though I've never been so dishonest in my life.

My stomach swirls with discomfort.

I'm not sure how long that line will remain true, and I'm terrified of what that will change.

After continuing to hide out for most of the day, apart from my two meetings, I pour myself a glass of whiskey the second the clock ticks over to five, and give myself a pep talk.

The longer we leave this, the harder it will be. It's just a talk.

I've had much tougher conversations in the past. I can do this.

Sort of.

Because I'm a chickenshit, I buzz Tabitha and ask her to arrange a meeting with Keeley for seven p.m., knowing she'll still be here, then dismiss Tabitha for the night.

When seven hits, Keeley waltzes through my door, her lips curled into a radiant grin, and my shoulders fall in relief.

"You came."

"You asked. You're the boss; what was I supposed to do?"

"Tell me to fuck off," I say seriously. I deserve it.

Keeley beams in amusement, and while I smile back at her, her reaction concerns me a little. This is what I was worried about—the calm.

She should be pissed off at me. I once again hit her with all the mixed messages. I rushed to her side to pick her up, embracing her in the process, then refused to sleep next to her when she asked.

Having her in my space confirmed something I've been fighting for a while.

I want her.

More than I want anything else in my life right now. And it sucks doing the right fucking thing. Turning her down Saturday night was one of the hardest, and easiest, things I've ever had to do. Hard because she was staring up at me with her dazzling blue eyes boring into mine, her vulnerabilities on full display as she begged me to stay. *Easy* because I would never take advantage of someone not of sound mind, and Keeley was more intoxicated than she was letting on.

If she'd been sober, she never would have asked me to stay like it was killing her if I didn't. She would have sassed me. Told me the ball was in my court. Flirted.

And I have no doubt I would have given in.

If she hadn't been drunk, I'm not sure I could have walked away.

But she was.

"Why would I tell you to fuck off?" She walks over to my couch and sits down like she always does, and my eyes follow her as I respond.

"For the other night."

"For taking care of me?"

"No, you should be thanking me for that. Why didn't you go home with the girls and—" *Fuck*. I sound like her father. "Ignore that. You're old enough to make your own decisions."

"You never got to do this with Paige, did you? Never picked her up drunk from a party?"

"Can you please not compare our situation with my situation with Paige?"

"Why not?"

"Because she's my daughter, Keeley, and you're..." I trail off because I'm not sure where I was going with that.

"I'm what?" She bounces her eyebrows and I huff out a laugh.

"A brat. That's what you are." Keeley snorts before standing again and walking closer to my desk, making me take a few steps back, moving under the guise that I need another drink.

"I've been called worse things." She shrugs and my chest tightens.

"From whom? What?"

"It doesn't matter. Why am I here?"

"Keels?"

"Come on. I have places to be."

"Right. Okay." The tightness in my chest morphs into a burn, and I ignore the fact that it could be considered jealousy.

"I thought we should talk."

"Talk?"

"Yes. About the other night."

"What do we need to talk about? I got drunk at a burlesque club, and my friend took me home to sleep it off."

"How much do you remember?"

"Most of it."

"Okay, well, I'm sorry."

"For what?"

"For letting you believe it was leading somewhere it wasn't."

"What?" Keeley laughs through her response. "I never once believed that. I know you, Sal. And I know the kind of man you are. I never for a second thought you'd take me home and have your way with me. I merely hoped for it." She grins and I bite back a groan. She's not going to make this easy.

"Do you remember us dancing?"

Keeley frowns, her face contorting before she laughs. "We didn't dance."

"We did. We were on our way out when they announced the last song from the burlesque dancers. It was slow and..." *Really fucking sultry.* Not that I need to paint that picture for her. "You asked me to dance. Actually, no. You didn't ask. You told me we were dancing and dragged me to the edge of the dance floor. You wrapped my arms around your waist and settled yours on my shoulders, leaving a space between us until I pulled you close."

The more I say, the more I relive the moment, the fire it ignited when I touched her skin where her dress dipped low at the back.

We danced for the entire song, never once breaking our stare while my heart slammed in my chest. Just like it's doing now.

"You smelled delicious," Keeley whispers, and my eyes widen as she glances away, lost in thought.

"You remember that?"

"Yes. Flashes of it are coming back."

"There's not much more to say. When the song ended, everyone cheered and you told me you were ready to go. For real this time."

"And the next thing I remember, I was waking up in front of the valet of your building."

"That's right."

"And you wouldn't sleep next to me."

My shoulders drop. Of course she'd remember that part. "I thought, given the circumstances, it was best if we stayed in separate rooms."

"And now?"

"Now?"

"Yes. What's best now?" Her ocean eyes bore into mine as she stands confidently, forcing me to admit what I'd do if the circumstances were different. Only I don't want to answer.

Because I have no fucking idea where it will lead.

Chapter Twenty-Four

KEELEY

If Sal's trying to hide his guilt and regret, he's doing a shitty job of it. While part of my memory is sketchy—like the fact that we freaking danced—I can remember everything that happened after we got to the apartment. *Unfortunately*.

I should be embarrassed, and for a moment the morning after, I was. I shamelessly begged him to sleep next to me and he rejected me—again—opting to sleep in the spare room. Which in hindsight is probably just as comfortable as his master suite, which begs the question. Why didn't I sleep in the spare room?

That's where *I* send my guests whenever I have someone staying over. To the spare room.

It's strange that he offered me his bed, and yet, I like it. There's something a little possessive about it.

At least, there would be if it was anyone other than Sal. Knowing him, he was doing it out of some gentleman's code—*the lady shall hath the best bed*.

I almost laugh at my own thoughts, picturing him standing at the end of the bed with those words running through his mind, until a memory hits me.

My hand lifts to my head absentmindedly and I cover it up, tucking my hair behind my ear.

Did Sal kiss me?

When he thought I was asleep?

Seconds before I drifted off, I have this faint recollection of him coming back into his bedroom, straightening the comforter that I'd already managed to twist, and pressing a kiss to my forehead.

It's possible I dreamt it, but when my gaze lifts to his, and his penetrating eyes stare back at me, I don't think I did. I think it was *real*.

You do want me, don't you, Sal?

I was right. And the fact that we danced only makes it more obvious.

He refused point-blank to dance with me at the concert months ago, yet he danced with me at the club. God, I wish I could remember more. I'd love to relive it. To have it in my memory bank to replay over and over. To remember the emotion of the moment. More than anything else, I want to *feel* it.

Was the energy electric?

Was my heart beating out of my chest?

Was his?

Could he feel the spark that always hovers between us? Sometimes out of reach, sometimes stronger than the pull of gravity.

I have no doubt in my mind anymore...

He wants me.

He just *doesn't want* to *want* me. And he prides himself on his morals. On doing the right thing.

Taking the first step is going to kill him.

Only we can't deny it anymore.

At least, I can't.

I'm done.

"You don't have to answer that." I let him off the hook from having to tell me what he wants. For the time being anyway.

Sal huffs out a laugh, breaking our stare before pouring me a glass of wine. I wait quietly as he brings it over, and after taking it from his hand, I walk to his side of the desk and sit down, crossing my legs as I lean back in his chair, my skirt bunching around the slit. "How is it possible that we have the same chair and yet yours feels so much more comfortable than mine?" I change the subject, needing him to relax a little more before I propose we take things further.

Sal pauses for a second before catching up, a light chuckle escaping him. His eyes drop to the chair until he seemingly realizes that means he's looking at my legs, and he's quick to lift his gaze. "My ass groove?" he asks, softly clearing his throat.

"Very funny."

"Jokes aside. You look good sitting there, Keels. Maybe you should take over after I've retired." He chuckles again, taking a step closer, as though finally loosening up.

"That's not how your job works, Mr. D'Angelo. I'd have to buy in, and I will never have that kind of money."

"What if I gave it to you?"

"The money?"

"The team. Paige doesn't want it, and there's no way in hell I'm giving it to Marc."

"Why not?"

"The maturity factor for one."

"Okay. Even so, you are not giving me a whole-ass football team. Why would you?"

"I have my reasons." He walks around to my side of the desk and sits on the edge, folding his arms over his chest.

"I'm listening."

"Reason number one." He gestures to me, waving his hand from my face to my heels. "You look comfortable. Like you belong here."

"That's not a reason to hand over a billion-dollar franchise."

"Why not?"

Leaning forward, I peel off my heels and lift my feet up onto the desk, relaxing farther into the chair. Sal's eyes flash to my legs and his throat bobs, his lips parting briefly before he controls his reaction.

"The job is yours. Look at you making yourself at home. You definitely look more comfortable than I do."

Sal may be talking about comfort, but he's wound so tight I'm itching to work out his kinks again. Not that he'd let that happen. Not after where it led last time.

Which is a real shame.

I smile at my inner monologue and he smiles back at me, confusing my expression, because while I am definitely more comfortable than he is, this position isn't as relaxing as I thought it would be. His desk must be higher than mine.

I subtly wriggle, stretching my toes when my calf cramps and Sal notices immediately.

"Are you okay?"

"Of course."

"My desk is too high, isn't it?"

"Jesus. It's like you read my mind." I giggle to myself or rather *at* myself and begin to move until Sal lowers himself to his knees and grabs one of my legs, his eyes on the floor as he massages my muscles. *Returning the favor.* I stare at his hands, watching as his fingers expertly rub my calf, working the tension until it eases.

It's so good that I can't control the moan that escapes me.

"You don't have to do that," I whisper on a sigh, my voice holding a plea that he never stops.

Sal chuckles, most likely because he said the same to me last time and I didn't listen. So why should he do the same?

"You're always taking care of others. Including me. Let me take care of you."

"Okay, but once you start something you have to finish it."

"*Keeley*," he warns, making me smile.

"It's only fair."

"I'm happy to help. With the massage. If that's what you're asking."

"It's a start."

Sal coughs without looking up at me, and I bite back a grin.

"You know I have men lining up for me. I could name three right now that would drop to their knees and crawl to me if I asked." I'm exaggerating, a little. If I was into football players, I'm sure I could win over a few rookies. Hell, I know at least one of them would drop to his knees if any woman showed him her bra. But that woman isn't me.

If I'm showing anyone my bra, it's not going to be a boy with no experience. It's going to be a man who knows his way around a pussy, and I have a feeling that man is Sal.

"I don't doubt it, Keels." Sal looks up at me, his smile locked in place while his strained voice gives him away. "Have you ever asked?" His voice lifts at the end and I almost laugh. Is he jealous?

"Maybe." I shrug noncommittally, and Sal releases a raspy sound from the back of his throat, somewhere between a laugh and a grunt.

"Good." He recovers, releasing my leg to grab the other, and a beat passes between us. "You deserve to be worshipped." His eyes rake over me, traveling from my feet to my eyes, and my heart picks up speed. God, I want him to touch me. I want his palms to follow the path his eyes just took, gliding along my skin, his thumbs slipping between my legs as he brushes past.

My legs clench just thinking about it, and Sal curses under his breath.

"What are you doing, Keels?"

"Enjoying my massage. What are *you* doing?"

"Enjoying your massage."

"What?"

"*Jesus.* I meant, giving you a massage."

"Sure you did." I raise an eyebrow, and Sal huffs before increasing the pressure on my calf, digging his thumb in deeper until I moan again, laying my head back and closing my eyes.

"God, this feels good."

"Maybe you should spend less time in these heels?"

I should what? My eyes fly open as I lift my head, scowling at him in offense. "Hell, no. My heels are part of my personality. The only time you'll see me without them is when I'm working out, taking a quick five-minute break, or—"

"Here?"

Oh, Sal, you walked right into that one. "Having sex."

"Goddammit. I'm not fucking you on my desk, Keels."

Sal lets go of my leg, and it naturally falls with my legs spread slightly. I'd normally be quick to be a lady, but when his gaze lowers to my center, I hold back.

"What am I doing?" Sal grates, his expression frantic.

"I don't know."

"Then what are you doing?" Sal stands, taking a few steps back as he throws the question my way, and I answer honestly.

"I'm wishing we were back in your apartment."

"Fuuuck." He runs a hand through his hair as he turns away, flustered. "Why?"

"Because you didn't say you wouldn't fuck me just now. You said you wouldn't fuck me *on your desk*. You're being a gentleman."

Sal spins back around, his expression pained, a wildfire in his eyes. I open my mouth to apologize until he stalks closer, flattening his palms against the desk as he leans over me. "Is that what you want?"

"Yes."

He grabs my thigh with his free hand, lifting it to wrap around him. "And this?"

"God, yes."

He smirks momentarily as though happy he's affecting me, and I smile back at him until my breath picks up speed and my pulse spikes at having him so close, his eyes so intense. I'm usually the confident one in a relationship, but right now, he has me at his mercy. If he told me to beg, I'd be dropping to my knees to plead so fast he'd get whiplash.

"Christ, Keeley. We can't."

He doesn't pull away. On the contrary, his palm squeezes my thigh, and it sets off a chain reaction, ending with a throbbing between my legs.

"Why?" I whimper, no longer able to hide the desperation in my tone.

Sal curses again, and I know I've pushed him too far, too soon. But instead of stepping back like I expect him to do, he closes the space between us, his body crowding me in.

"If you don't want this," he growls, his deep voice vibrating through me, "I suggest you tell me now."

Unable to speak, I zip my lips, and Sal laughs incredulously. "I need words, Keeley."

"I want this." I look him in the eyes, my stare unwavering as I lift my other leg, wrapping that around him too, the motion putting my white lace panties on full display.

"Fuck, Keeley." He stares down at the undoubtedly wet material, the fire in his eyes burning out of control. "I want to rip these hot-as-fuck panties from your body. But once I do, there's no going back for me. At least not tonight."

"Good. I want you to destroy me, Sal. I want it all. *At least for tonight.*"

Sal's gaze lifts to mine, and a moment passes between us, both of us knowing this is going to change everything, yet unable to stop it.

"We should probably set some ground rules," Sal rasps, his eyes meeting mine as he slowly runs his palms along my thighs, exactly as I pictured it.

"We can talk about that later," I rush out, my chest heaving as I wriggle in anticipation.

"As you wish." I barely have time to process his words before he has his hands on my hips, lifting me to sit on his desk the second I wrap my legs around his waist.

I let out a gasp, and he slides me farther back, spreading my legs before he lowers himself to his chair, dragging it closer so his eyes line up with my pussy.

I hold my breath, watching with rapt attention as he lifts my panties away from my skin, ripping the silk with his fingers while leaving the rest intact, turning them into a crotchless pair.

And my body convulses in need. "Oh. My. God."

"Rule number one," Sal grates, the tip of his thumb gliding toward my clit. "And this may be my main rule... I want to hear you moan *my* name, not God's, when I'm making you scream. I've spent far too long thinking about how delicious it would sound. I'm not giving someone else the credit."

Holy shit. My breath hitches as I nod, until Sal raises a brow, once again expecting an answer, with words. "Yes, Sir. *Sal.* I can do that."

Chapter Twenty-Five

SALVATORE

Sir. *Fucking sir.* I hate that term, and yet, when it's whispered from Keeley's perfectly glossed lips as her pleading gaze begs for more, my fucking cock hardens.

All this woman has to do is look at me with a fire in her eyes and my body reacts.

That doesn't mean that it's right. I still don't know what the hell I'm doing. But I can't stop.

Not anymore.

Deep down I knew if I ever allowed myself to do more than just kiss her, I'd never go back. And this right here is exhibit A.

"Please," Keeley whimpers again, and I sit back to look her in the eyes.

"Tell me what you want?" I ask, needing to please her now that I have her begging.

"Anything. Just touch me."

Christ. I close my eyes and do as she asked, spreading her legs and gliding my thumb through her slick heat. I bite back a groan, my mouth watering at the thought of running my tongue through her arousal. Only I can't. Not yet.

I'm not ready for that.

I haven't really thought past ripping her panties.

I've gone fucking mad.

Too bad I want this just as much as she does.

Keeley mewls softly as I begin—my fingers exploring as I stare at her glistening core. Her breathing picks up, and she lies back, angling her hips to give me better access and a better view.

As I gently roll her clit, I bite my lip to restrain myself just as Keeley hisses under her breath, her own lips trapped between her teeth when I glance up at her.

"This is so good, Sal. Fuck. Just like that."

With a nod, I circle her bud one more time before spreading her bare lips and rolling my chair closer, suppressing a groan as my cock aches.

Keeley sits up so fast that I chuckle. "Oh, God. I mean, oh, Sal, are you going to—" She leans forward, grabbing my shoulders, and I shake my head.

"Lie back, Keeley. I can't do anything with this angle."

She glances down at my fingers almost squashed into the desk and laughs. "As you were."

After lying back again, she brings her knees up to her chest and *holy fucking shit*, I've never really thought about a pussy being beautiful before, but fuck, is she beautiful.

She writhes on the desk as I stare at her, her hips subtly rolling as though she's fucking the air.

And I want to shower her with compliments, tell her I want to spend every day worshipping her goddess-like body, only I shouldn't. Not yet. Neither of us is ready for that. I shouldn't even be thinking about it.

"Please touch me," she pleads impatiently, bringing me back to the moment.

"I am." I tap my thumbs down where I'm spreading her, and I don't have to look to know she's rolling her eyes.

"Sal."

"Okay. I'll stop making this about me and focus on you." A breath rushes from her mouth, and I smile as I lean forward, blowing on her clit, my fingers gliding through her heat.

"Like this?"

"Yes, oh, yes."

"And this?" I rub her clit, playing with the bud, and her body jolts.

"Yes. Yes."

I tease her for a moment, moving slowly toward her entrance, only pausing to glance up at her. And when our eyes lock, her wanton expression completely does me in.

"Fuck, Keels. You look perfect right now."

She's so wet that I slide a finger easily inside her, an unrestrained groan flying out of me when she cries out my name. "*Sal.*"

With my teeth clenched, I watch as her pussy sucks me in, coating my finger in her arousal.

Holding my breath, I pump my finger a couple of times before adding a second and scissoring them inside her, my gaze never once moving from between her legs.

She bucks her hips, rolling her pussy against my hand until I press my thumb against her clit, grinding it a few times with increased pressure.

"Yes. Fuck. Oh G... Sal."

"Good girl."

"Jesus. This is. Ah. Don't stop."

I continue with my ministrations until I can't wait any longer, my need to taste her taking over my mind.

And that's not something I've ever needed before.

Keeley groans when I release my fingers, and I chuckle as I lean in, only stopping to spread her lips again, immediately running my tongue through her heat.

And *fuuck.*

"Oh, God. Sorry. Sal. I can't."

Her flustered state pulls a smile from within me as I lick a path toward her clit, circling the bud before making my way back down, repeating that movement a few times as I add my fingers again.

Keeley wriggles as I penetrate her, my fingers working her pussy while I suck her clit, her sounds alone making it almost impossible to resist freeing my cock so I can get some relief.

She moans, mewls, squeals, and huffs, all while I quicken my movements, feeling her walls tighten as she glides closer to the edge.

I twist my hand, curling my fingers against her wall as I bite down on her clit.

Keeley arches off the desk as her lips part, and the most glorious moan escapes her. "I'm close. So close."

"I know." I glance up at her from between her legs, my face still close enough for my breath to warm her. "I've got you."

She cries out as I lick her again, giving her what she needs, alternating between nibbles and sucks as my fingers work her into a frenzy.

Her ragged breaths stop, and she falls silent as her head flies back and her body bucks into me.

Two more pumps, and she covers her mouth, screaming my name into her hand, her body shaking as her orgasm hits.

I don't stop until she cries out again, the shaking more of a thrashing now as she grabs my hair, lifting my head to look at her.

She shoots me a glare, and I smirk back at her, my cock twitching as she takes control. I love that she's comfortable showing me what she needs.

"Fuck, Sal." She huffs between breaths, shaking her head with a laugh. "That was exactly what I wanted."

I snort out a laugh of my own because me too, Keeley, me too.

With a sigh, she lies back and closes her eyes, lowering her legs to wrap around me when I stand. And I feel the bead of pre cum soaking my briefs.

As if aware of my inner thoughts, Keeley smiles with her eyes still closed, her lashes fluttering against her flushed cheeks, and I continue to watch her as she comes back down to earth, her breaths slowing to a more even pace.

"You're really not going to fuck me, are you?" She opens her eyes, pulling her lips into her mouth to smother her teasing grin.

"I'm really not. I'm a man of my word."

"What if I want it?"

"It doesn't matter. I'm willing to admit you have a lot of control over me, Keels. But that's one argument you won't win. *If* we ever get to that stage, I'm going to take my time."

"That's not an issue. We can go slowly here. There's no one around."

As if her words were the switch for our practice field, the lights come to life behind us, bathing us in brightness. "Fuck," I growl loudly, lifting her back in my arms, and spin around, lowering her to my chair, so her back is to the windows. "Fuck, fuck, fuck." The fucking windows. How the hell did I forget that?

"Not that I don't love you moving me around like that. But...what's the matter?" She giggles behind her hand, sitting up to look over her shoulder.

"I'm not an exhibitionist, Keels."

"This is actually better for us."

"What do you mean?"

"Have you ever looked at your office from the field?"

"Yes. No. Maybe. I don't know. I'm a busy man."

Keeley giggles again, and it's easy to see she's making fun of me. But I don't mind.

"It's mirrored during the day." She shrugs and my eyes flash to the windows.

"Well, fuck me." We just gave a show to anyone out there.

"I'm trying."

"Jesus. You really love driving me wild."

"I live for it."

"As I said, not tonight. We should go."

"You actually said 'if' that ever happens. I like 'not tonight' a whole lot more."

I glance away, laughing through my frustration. She's making it really hard not to bend her over my desk right now. "You're killing me here."

"Fine. I'll stop. I promise." My chair creaks as she stands up, and within seconds, I feel her beside me, the energy sizzling between us. My muscles tense as I turn to face her, expecting to find her grinning from ear to ear.

She's not. Instead, she's staring at me like I'm food, and that's goddamn worse.

"How about I return the favor?"

Fuuck. "Not tonight."

"Not tonight for that either? I think we're going to be busy this week."

"Keels."

"I know." She raises her hands in surrender, and I'm sucked into her playful side, loving how easy this is between us. For now. What happens when she wakes up tomorrow? After the moment has passed.

"Come on, let's go before you burst a blood vessel."

She straightens her dress, and all I can think about is the hole in her panties and her arousal leaking through, making my cock throb. I'm so fucking hard I might have to fuck my hand in the stadium showers. I'm not sure I'll make it home otherwise.

I just fingered my closest friend, massaged her walls while licking her pussy until she was screaming my name.

Keeley. A woman almost *twenty years* younger than me.

And I'm desperate to do it again.

Chapter Twenty-Six

SALVATORE

I arrive with the sun the next morning, in desperate need of a workout before my early meeting on New York time, and the second my desk comes into view, I falter. Scenes from last night roll through my mind, and I internally groan. How the hell am I expected to concentrate today with thoughts of Keeley covering her mouth as she screamed my name? Or mental images of her knees pressed into her chest and her pussy weeping for me?

How will I ever look at this office the same?

I won't. That's the simple answer.

Camilla and I were together for *years*, and I never once fooled around with her in my office. Not for lack of her trying.

My office is my space. The only place I have all to myself.

And yet, I want Keeley here. I've wanted her here since the moment we first met.

Now she's forever ingrained, because I am never going to lose the memory of last night.

After working out my frustrations, pushing myself to my limits at the staff gym, I barely make it to the New York call with my sanity intact. And by the time I get to my first meeting in person, I'm a mess.

She's taken over my mind, she's all I can think about, and I have never been consumed like this before.

As the room fills, I'm agonizing over what comes next between us, when Keeley waltzes in as though nothing has changed. Her bright smile flits my way, and she winks when nobody's watching.

She's completely unaffected. And I almost ask what's wrong.

I'm *not* as okay as she looks. So...is her appearance a front?

"Morning, everyone." Her smile widens as she sits down at the other end of the table, taking the head position opposite me, as though she's my queen. "Wes asked me to join you for five minutes to field any questions you might have regarding scheduled interviews during our training camp and preseason practices. We've already had reporters stalking the players to ask for exclusives with particular interest in discussing Beckett Myers, and I wouldn't put it past them to move on to you next. He's a hot commodity, and people are understandably interested in his story, with the big question being how we secured him over everyone else.

"Let it be known that like last year, we have restricted media interviews during the first two weeks of training camp. And while you may be approached, I ask that you check with me before agreeing to any press. Questions?"

A couple of people ask for advice, but I couldn't tell you what advice they're seeking because I'm too busy watching Keeley, in awe, loving the way she holds the room.

I wasn't joking when I said she could take over my job, not because she's the most qualified, but because of the way she commands attention. In a man's world, she confidently demands respect, and fuck, it's glorious to watch.

It's hard to picture that there was ever a time when she was vulnerable and raw, and yet, something tells me she's been there. She has to have been. We all have. There's always a story to tell, and I want to know hers. I want to know everything there is to know about her.

Sure, we talk, but I have this urge to discover all her deepest, darkest secrets. The skeletons in her closet.

Day-to-day she's an open book, but what's she hiding beneath that strength?

Keeley finishes up with her questions and waves as she exits, drawing my attention until she's out of my line of sight, never once looking back.

And while I called this meeting, I suddenly wish we were done.

It's another slow seventy-five minutes before I get back to my desk, and I've barely sat down when there's a knock at my door.

"It's me," Keeley calls out, and my shoulders drop as I stand up again, just as she announces, "I'm coming in."

Happiness radiates from within her as she glides inside and closes the door, her stride confident and familiar. After a quick glance around the room, she flattens her knee-length skirt and lowers to the couch, crossing her ankles while raising a brow my way.

"You wanted to see me?"

"I did?" I sit down slowly, my eyes flashing to my blacked-out computer as though I'm going to find a meeting reminder in the middle of the screen. I quickly bring the damn thing to life as I frown. I don't remember anything.

My calendar pops up first, and my confusion deepens. "This says that I'm currently free." I quickly glance her way. "I can't see anything for—" I cut myself off when she laughs.

"You're messing with me?"

"Am I? Or have you been thinking about me *all* morning and wishing I was here?"

Jesus Christ. Maybe she can read my thoughts. "I don't know what you're talking about."

"That's a shame." She fakes a pout. "I always thought we were on the same wavelength."

"Why are you here, Keeley?" I lightly scold her—despite knowing exactly what she's alluding to—and her eyes flare with a fire I saw for the first time last night.

"My answer to that comes in two parts. I'm not sure you're ready for the second."

Goddammit. The way my dick begs to be called into play, I'm certain he is. If that's what she's referring to. She's right about me, though; I'm not ready. "What's the first thing?"

"I wanted to check in. To see how you were doing after breaking your strict moral code."

I should be offended by her low-level teasing, but instead, I laugh out loud, this entire situation taking me so far away from my comfort zone, I can barely see it anymore.

"How are *you*?" I counter. "Does anything between us bother you at all?"

"It would be a lot easier if you weren't my brother's future father-in-law, my boss, and my best friend's dad, but does it bother me that you are?

No. It's not like we're getting married and I'm becoming..." Keeley trails off before her eyes widen and she laughs hysterically, her whole body shaking as she covers her face with her hands. "Oh, this is good."

"What did I miss?"

She straightens up, her eyes wild with excitement. "I want you to visualize it so you'll find it as funny as I did."

"Oh-kay."

"Picture Easton's face as he hears the news that his annoying older sister is now also his mother-in-law."

I freeze at her words. While I can definitely see the humor in what she's saying, I'm ninety percent sure all the blood just drained from my face, because I feel lightheaded.

When she puts it that way, it sounds so much worse than it is. "There are off-limits relationships, and then there's us." I shake my head, turning away. There are so many things wrong with that image.

"What? You don't find it funny? Did you picture it?"

"I'm not marrying you to get back at your brother."

Keeley snorts, and I have to admit her amusement is a little infectious, eliciting a smile without my consent.

"Ha. I told you."

"I'm not smiling over Easton's pain."

"Then what are you smiling about?"

"You. Your happiness. Your joy."

"Oh." The amusement drops from her face, and I almost apologize for whatever I said wrong, until her lips pull into the most delicately tight-lipped smile. "Thank you," she whispers. "That's actually really sweet."

It takes me a moment to respond, caught in the softness of her voice, and I clear my throat, chuckling softly. "Yeah, well. You constantly remind me I'm a gentleman."

"This is different though. So...thanks."

Her admission has my heart pounding and a million questions running through my mind, all of them left unsaid. Instead, I circle back to her earlier comment.

"I'm almost afraid to ask. What's number two?" Since we've established that the inappropriateness of us being together doesn't bother her, I'm guessing not much is off-limits in her mind.

"Are you sure you want to know?"

No. "Yes. Hit me with it."

Keeley gets up and walks over to my desk, the sound of her heels clacking on the floor like a warning, each step increasing the pace of my pulse. When she's standing opposite me, she flattens her palms on my mahogany desktop, exactly where I had her last night, and leans forward, her loose white shirt billowing to reveal a hint of her lace bra.

I subtly swallow a lump in my throat, worried that if I don't, I won't be able to respond when she finally speaks.

I'm a powerful man. People of all stature bow down to please me. Yet all it takes is one fierce little redhead, staring me in the eyes, and I'm the one ready to fall to my knees.

"I want another night, Salvatore," Keeley begins, and I hold my stare, watching her lips as she speaks, waiting for her to finish before I react. "I want...more licking, more fingers, more..." She trails off as her eyes drop to my crotch, and I thank the universe that I'm wearing black and she can't see the bulge forming.

Because fuck... I want that too.

"Most of all." She scrunches her nose in sympathy as though this next one is going to be the hardest to take, and I clench my fist under the desk. "I want to suck you dry."

God-fucking-dammit. I have a meeting in thirty minutes, and I'm a few choice words away from coming in my pants.

Lifting my fist to my mouth, I close my eyes and groan, ignoring Keeley's light giggles in front of me.

"I thought you were ready?"

"And I hoped you'd keep it PG in the middle of the day."

"I could have dropped to my knees and pulled down your pants."

Fuuuck. "You're right," I choke out. "This is better."

"Good. So what do you say?" She smiles sweetly and I choke again, this time on a laugh.

"I have no fucking idea."

"Let me help you out. The answer is yes. I'm not asking you to name a time or a place. I just want to know that if the opportunity arises, I can take it." She stands tall, resting a hand on her waist as she pops a hip.

"Another night?"

"Or day, I'm not picky."

"Like now?" My gaze flashes to the door, and for some messed-up reason, I seriously consider it.

"God, no. I have a meeting soon and so do you. I don't want to rush it."

"Okay."

"Okay?" She laughs incredulously. "I wasn't expecting that."

Neither was I. I lean back, trying to appear more composed than I am. "What were you expecting?"

"I'm not sure exactly." She furrows her brows.

"Then why did you ask?"

"Hope?"

"Thank you for always telling it like it is, Keels. I never have to guess when it comes to you." She laughs, but there's an edge to it that wasn't there before, and it brings me back to the last time that happened. The day I told her that we'd signed Beckett. Not that now is a good time to bring that up.

Tabitha buzzes my desk phone, and we both startle, as though released from a trance.

My eyes flash to my watch, and I curse under my breath. "Shit. I have to go."

"Told you."

"You did. So, ah..." I awkwardly scratch the back of my neck. "How does this work?" *What the fuck?* How does this work? I'm a grown man; I know how it works.

Keeley raises a brow and I roll my eyes. "We just see what happens."

"I can do that." *I think. Maybe.*

"Good. I'll leave you to it."

"Thanks. Hope you have a nice afternoon."

"You too."

Unlikely, since I'll now be thinking about whatever the fuck I just agreed to, and not much else.

Why can't I think clearly when it comes to Ms. Reynolds?

Although the bigger question should be... If I *could* think clearly, what would I want?

I'm almost afraid to answer that.

Chapter Twenty-Seven

KEELEY

The candle flickers beside my bath and I sink down beneath the water, moaning internally, the magnesium salts working their magic.

Thank God for the little joys in life. Like water. In my own damn apartment.

It may have only taken a few days to fix the "little" water issue in my building, but for the last four days, we've been advised to keep our usage to a minimum until they can be sure it's not going to happen again.

And rule number one was no baths.

I'm a rule follower by nature so…easy. Right?

Wrong.

I've never been a regular bath girl, but it turns out, if you make something off-limits, I'm like a dog with a bone—obsessed. It's been on my mind twenty-four seven.

Not only did I call my building manager on a daily basis for an update, I also walked past my bathroom longingly and contemplated breaking the rules, just once, or filling it halfway. Sometimes, I closed the door, hoping for an out of sight, out of mind scenario, or told myself that I didn't need it, trying to remember that I don't even like baths that much.

Nothing worked.

I've been unhinged, dreaming about this moment. Right up until fifteen minutes ago when I received the email informing me we were all clear. A giddiness ran through me, and I beelined for the bathroom so fast I almost slipped in the hallway.

Then it hit me.

As I turned on the tap, waiting for the relief... it wasn't the bath I was desperate for.

It was something else even more off-limits.

Sal.

I hadn't planned on putting myself out there and telling him I wanted more when I walked into his office the morning after he blew my mind. I *had* planned on keeping my cool, and only checking in.

Until I saw him and that wasn't an option anymore.

I never expected him to agree.

I assumed my request would fluster him a little, and that he'd give me that stern "Salvatore D'Angelo" look that says, "I'm a billionaire; I don't have time for your silly little games," or at least a "*Keel-ley.*"

What I wasn't expecting was for him to be agreeable, to ask questions, and go along with my idea to just "see what happens."

And now I'm the one that's a mess.

It's been four days with zero opportunities to see what happens, and I'm so worked up from constantly thinking about it, that I almost gave in and created one.

If I just *happened* to need him late one night, and we *happened* to be the only people still in the office...like last time. Or if my car broke down and no one else was available to help me.

Maybe we— God, I'm going crazy. I don't *need* Sal. I have my toys and my hand. What I need is to chill the fuck out. Since when did my next orgasm become something I obsessed over, or even thought about for that matter?

I've endured a lot to get to where I am today. I can get through this.

If it happens, it happens.

If not, business as usual. Literally.

My mind whirs as I run my loofah over my arm, up and down, lathering my skin from my shoulder to my fingers.

What am I even thinking by proposing anything to Sal? He's my *boss*. I wasn't lying when I said that him being Easton's father-in-law didn't bother me, but being my boss should.

Easton and I kept our sibling relationship a secret for years with him worried people would assume I got the job because of him. What would they think if they caught me with Sal? I'd never be able to progress within the Storm franchise without people questioning my true worth.

Hell, I'd probably never be able to progress within any football franchise without someone mentioning our relationship and using it against me.

Our relationship? God, I'm making this out to be so much more than it is.

Focus, Keeley.

You are a strong independent woman. Men do not make you go crazy and overthink things that aren't even a possibility yet.

I laugh out loud, almost snorting at how ridiculous I'm being. I don't need a man for anything. I never have. It's time to remember that.

After taking a deep breath, I bring my mind back to the task at hand, and it's only when I realize I've been washing the same arm for the past few minutes that I remember why I don't take baths that often—too much time to think.

And nobody needs that.

For the next week, it does in fact revert back to business as usual between Sal and me with work being the only thing we discuss. If and when I see him. If I was a dreamer, it would have been easy to believe I imagined our moment. Only I'm not a dreamer; I just got what I asked for. For life to return to normal.

Since we're in the thick of training camp, I expect to see Sal out and about, watching practice or catching up with the management team. I don't. He's MIA, and while I'm generally not a needy person, it makes me wonder if he's away because of me.

And we can't have that.

KEELEY: You better be in New York or I'm going to get a complex over you avoiding me

I laugh at my own joke. If he is avoiding me, that's more on him than it is me.

I put my phone away, assuming that if he is in New York, he'll be busy. Only it's less than a minute later that he responds.

SAL: I wouldn't dream of doing that. I'm on my flight home. D'Angelo Construction needed me.

KEELEY: You're a busy man, Mr. D'Angelo

SAL: What can I say? I get shit done. Shit that my team can't seem to manage without me.

KEELEY: You are the boss

SAL: Don't you forget it.

I smile before pocketing my phone again and watching the end of training, a smile on my face as Easton and Zane chat comfortably on the other side of the field. I'm just about to head to my office when someone loosely covers my eyes from behind.

"Guess who?"

Thomas's voice is like a song in my ears, and I jump before spinning around to face him. "You're here!"

"I'm here. Wes called me to come in and meet with him. He wants to talk to me about something. Any idea what?"

I zip my lips because it should come from Wes, but they're restructuring the coaching staff and there's an opening for a new quarterback coach. Obviously, Thomas would be perfect for it.

"I know nothing," I lie, while a giddiness runs through me. "You'll have to wait and see."

"Mmm. Okay."

"Thomas, my man," Luke calls out the second the whistle blows for the end of the session, jogging over. "Did you forget you retired last season?"

"How could I when you continue to remind me?"

"That's because you shouldn't have retired. When are you going to admit that you're bored?"

"I'm not bored. I'm here to catch up with Wes." Thomas subtly winces as he speaks, and I can't stop my smile. He dropped himself right into what's coming.

"What for? What's going on? Why didn't you tell me?"

"I think you're needed on the field, Luke." I try to help but it's no use. Luke is not going to give up on this.

"I don't know anything. I—"

"Thomas, you made it." Wes joins us, patting Thomas on the back as he moves past. His gaze shifts to Luke and he frowns. "Shouldn't you be on the field?"

I snort out a laugh as Thomas chuckles beside me. "I'm on it. But I'm going to find out what's going on here." Luke's brows furrow as his gaze moves between Wes and Thomas. Then with a laugh, he's gone.

"What was that about?" Wes asks, looking back over his shoulder to see Luke watching them.

"That was Luke being Luke."

"Okay, then. Are you ready, Thomas?"

"For what exactly?" Thomas raises an eyebrow, and I have to bite my tongue so I don't blurt it out.

"Come on, let's go to my office. If I don't see you before, Keeley, I'll see you at five."

"See you, Wes. Have fun, Thomas." Thomas rolls his eyes and I laugh as they walk away. I couldn't think of anyone better to join our team. After all, Thomas is still part of the family, and he knows our plays inside and out.

Fingers crossed he agrees.

After catching up with Coach Pierce, the reason I was watching practice, I power walk back to my office in time to take a media call and then I have a moment to breathe. A rare two hours, in fact. Enough time to sneak in a yoga session...if I rush.

I'm always freaking rushing. One day, I'd like to have a slow day, maybe a walk in the morning, outside in the sunshine, followed by a relaxing breakfast and a yoga session before I start work. One day I'd like to... Ah, who am I kidding? That sounds like hell. I love the hustle and grind. It's who I am. And if I go now, I might actually make it.

"Take a deep breath in. And out. And when you're ready, open your eyes and slowly sit up."

My eyes are open before she's finished speaking, and I'm sitting up ahead of anyone else. My instructor, Adhira, smiles, no longer perturbed by my tendencies to move quickly.

During the session, I'm always in the zone. The second we're done, however, my mind is back in the office and it's go time again.

"Thanks for another great session," I whisper as I stand, rolling up my mat.

Adhira joins her hands at the center of her heart and bows her head slightly as she whispers, "Namaste," and I tuck my mat under my arm to do the same. "Namaste."

"See you in a few weeks?" she jokingly questions me.

"I'm hoping to make it back sooner, but you know me."

"Anything is better than nothing."

"Exactly."

I wave goodbye as I walk out into the foyer, heading to the showers, a smile on my face until I'm met with an obnoxious *out of order* sign.

"You've got to be kidding me," I grumble under my breath, turning to face the receptionist.

What is it with me and showers lately? Talk about bad luck.

"Do you have other showers?" I ask as politely as I can.

She smiles sympathetically and I wish I hadn't asked.

I stare her way as she explains what happened, even though I tuned out the second she said no, drifting into planning mode. I could go home and shower, except that it would be at least a fifty-minute turnaround without including the shower, and I have my meeting with Wes in just under forty minutes. I could skip the shower—I've never been a huge sweater during yoga anyway—but I'm a creature of process and my day won't be the same if I don't.

An image of the staff changing room flits to mind, and I internally groan.

Beggars can't be choosers. It's that or nothing, and I've already established I can't do nothing.

"That must be so annoying," I interrupt the receptionist as she continues her rant. "I hope they get it fixed soon so you don't have to keep explaining yourself."

She laughs, and I use that as my chance to say goodbye.

I'm blessed by the traffic gods on my way to the stadium, giving me plenty of time to shower and get ready before I meet Wes.

When I get to the changing room, I'm grateful to be alone until I reach the cubicle and a throat clears behind me.

"Keeley," Sal's deep voice floats through the air, drawing my gaze to find him dripping with sweat, his towel draped over his shoulders, his chest bare. And my entire body tingles.

I clench my fist, biting back a moan.

How the hell have I never seen his body before?

Taking a step forward like a moth to a flame, I stare in awe as a bead of sweat rolls across his taut skin, dripping between the crevices of his abs, the lucky droplet making it all the way to the waistband of his shorts.

I swallow a lump in my throat as a strangled groan breaks my trance.

"Fuck, Keeley," Sal growls and I snap out of my ogling.

"Sorry." I choke on the word, coughing before trying again. "Sorry. You're back?"

"I am." His nostrils flare as his gaze drops to my stomach, visible below my sports bra, before darting to my face again, his expression pained. I have no doubt he's cursing himself for not resisting the urge to look.

"Did you have a good flight?" I ask, pulling him from his head. "I snuck off to yoga while the boss was away. Just going to shower and I'll be back at it."

I bounce on my toes and Sal seemingly relaxes.

"Thanks for letting me know." His lips thin into a suppressed smile and I laugh. "Enjoy."

"I will. You too."

You too? The thought of Sal showering beside me has me clenching my legs, and I internally groan for allowing that idea to play out in my head.

With a smile, I shake off my thoughts and step inside, closing the door behind me before I laugh into my hand.

Fuck. That can't be real. He can't be real. It's a figment of my imagination. It has to be. Because the alternative is that Salvatore D'Angelo is ripped like a god.

Closing my eyes, I lift my sports bra over my head, and another image of Sal's chiseled abs floods my vision. My mouth waters, and I bite my lip as my phone buzzes, snapping me out of my lust-filled daze.

WES: I need an extra thirty mins. I hope that's okay.

KEELEY: Works for me

I'm going to need that long just to cool the fuck down, and it has nothing to do with my hour-long yoga session and everything to do with the man getting naked in the cubicle beside me.

Basically, I'm fucked.

Chapter Twenty-Eight

SALVATORE

The treadmill clicks over to five miles, and I gradually slow the machine, my surroundings seeping back into view. I don't usually disappear into my head like I did just now, but when life is a fucking shit show, it's kind of hard not to.

After a five-minute cooldown, I grab my towel and wipe the sweat from my face, staring at myself in the mirrored wall as my breathing calms.

It doesn't last long as a vision of my charcoal-stained lot comes into view.

Of all the fucking things.

Arson.

I've owned my own business for over twenty years and never experienced a personal attack on one of my buildings.

And make no mistake, it had to be personal. A message.

Someone set fire to D'Angelo Construction's on-site office at one of our build sites, *and* the gardens surrounding it. They didn't touch the multibillion-dollar building itself. *Thank fuck.* And emergency services were there to help before anyone from my team had called them.

Before any of them had even found out.

My guess... the same person who lit the fire called 911.

I pissed someone off. Me, or Daniel, who's been running the company while I've been in San Francisco. And neither of us knows who.

Like I said, it's a fucking shit show.

I should have stayed in New York.

I *would* have stayed in New York if it wasn't for Daniel practically kicking me out of the state. *"There's nothing you can do here. I'll call you if we hear anything else."*

So, I made my statement, which gave the police fuck all since I had no idea who I could have possibly annoyed, then I was on my way.

Back here to hopefully get through the week without something else going wrong.

With one last look at my weary expression, I drag my T-shirt off over my head and wrap the towel around my neck, making my way to the changing room, checking the time to ensure I'm not running behind for my meeting with the board.

I'm not.

It's unusually quiet for the middle of the afternoon, but if I stop and listen, I can hear the occasional whistles coming from outside. My team is back in action—the rookies giving it their all to prove themselves during training camp, the seasoned pros showing them how it's done.

I have to admit, it's calming. The chaos of a football team *is* calming.

Who knew this place would be what I needed in my life to find zen?

I'm smiling to myself as I open the door to the changing room, until a vision of red appears ahead of me, and I catch myself before I groan.

Keeley's unintentionally teasing me in a tight little sports bra and yoga pants so perfectly sculpted to her body that you'd think they were painted on. She's facing away from me, and try as I might not to let my gaze drop to the curve of her ass, I can't stop it.

I'm a red-blooded man like the rest of them, and this woman is my weakness.

And it's not just her body that reels me in. It's the way she makes me feel.

My pounding heart beats in my ears as I stare at her.

I'm drawn to everything about her. Her happiness, her strength, her passion, and the way she controls a room full of men who think they're God's gift to women. She's incredible. And right now, she's making it hard to walk away.

My sports briefs tighten as the blood rushes to my cock, and I catch myself before I'm hard, adjusting myself as I clear my throat.

"Keeley." Her name escapes me without permission, and I internally wince. It would have been so much easier to let her walk inside, none the wiser of my presence.

She turns and without a word, she steps forward, her lip trapped between her teeth as she unabashedly ogles my body.

There are words exchanged, but I couldn't tell you what the fuck I said with my energy focused on getting into the shower before her eyes drop to my shorts to find my cock standing at attention for her.

We talked about opportunities presenting themselves, but as much as I'd love to taste her again, the staff changing room—where anyone can walk in at any moment—is not the place.

Keeley smiles before disappearing in the last cubicle, and instead of choosing the one I'm currently standing next to, the one farthest away, something pulls me forward, and the next thing I know, I'm under the water in the shower next to her, picturing her gloriously naked body as she lathers herself in soap. Slowly. Purposely. And...

Motherfucking fuck fuck.

I imagine her brushing her loofah gently over her skin, circling her breasts, one at a time, the bubbles coating her pebbled nipples. She steps farther under the shower, the water soaking her body as she lowers her hand, moving toward her glistening pussy.

Pre cum pools at my tip, and I fight not to wrap my hand around my cock for relief.

Needing a distraction, I squirt soap into my palm and massage it into my shoulders and chest while my mind drifts without my consent.

A soft mewl permeates my thoughts and I freeze, the hot water pelting against my back as I close my eyes, waiting to hear it again.

Nothing happens for the longest beat, and I almost laugh at my delusional messed-up mind until it happens again. Keeley's beautiful whimper sends a spark straight to my cock, and I'm done fighting it anymore. The way I see it, I have two options. I can stay here and fuck my hand while picturing Keeley fucking her own in the stall next to me, or I can—

Fuck this.

Without allowing myself time to back out, I turn off the water and quickly wrap a towel around my waist before opening the door and checking to make sure we're alone.

A nervous buzz runs through me, mixing with the adrenaline already coursing through my veins. I square my shoulders and knock on her door, listening for her reaction. And it doesn't disappoint. Her breath hitches a second before something falls to the floor and silence ensues. I give her a moment of grace before I knock again, this time a little more forceful. I've made up my mind, and I'm not walking away until I've watched her come apart from my touch.

"Open the door, please." My voice strains and I don't bother hiding it. If she feels even half of what I'm feeling, she'll understand the urgency of the situation.

She's quiet again, and I'm contemplating ways I can get in when she opens the door, her eyes shining with desire, her face flushed as the steam swirls behind her, her body—like mine—wrapped in a towel.

"About freaking time." She curls her fingers through my towel and drags me inside, reaching around to lock the door behind me. She's confident and full of sass now, but I have a feeling she needed a few seconds to work up to it. As did I. Because as soon as we're alone, she sucks in a shaky breath.

And I get it.

This is insane. I'm acting crazy. And yet I can't stop.

We're both still for a beat as an electric energy fills the space around us, crowding us in like a blanket of warmth. Keeley's lips part as her chest rises, and her beauty in the chaotic moment floors me.

I need to touch her.

After dropping my towel, I curl my fingers around the edge of Keeley's and lift my gaze to get her reaction. She nods, and I undo the knot above her breast, sliding the towel from around her, dropping it to the bench and grabbing her waist. I walk her backward, only stopping when she hits the wall, the water falling over us both.

Our eyes lock as I lower one of my hands, running my palm over her pussy.

Her head falls back as she quietly gasps, and I'm drawn to her neck, leaning forward to suck the delicate skin below her ear, my fingers exploring her heat.

She spreads her legs, opening up for me, and I groan, sinking a finger inside her, quickly following it with a second. She's so wet that my thumb easily slides over her clit, making her jolt in my arms, her whimper telling me it has nothing to do with the water.

I kiss a path across her shoulder, squeezing her waist as I groan against her skin, my fingers scissoring inside her warm pussy. Her walls constrict as she cries out, burying her face in the crook of my neck.

My cock twitches dangerously close to her body, and I stand tall, covering her mouth with my free hand as she bucks against my fingers.

"Cry out into my hand," I whisper, curling my fingers as her breath quickens. "I want to feel the vibration of your lips as I'm making you come."

She moans against my palm and grabs my shoulder for support, rolling her hips as her entire body trembles.

"I'm close."

I lean into her, the edge of my body pressed to hers as I stifle her whimpers, my fingers pumping into her while my thumb rubs her clit, picking up speed in time with her breathing.

She bucks and mewls, writhing against me, her pussy squeezing my fingers as she flies over the edge. She bites down against my palm, her screams silenced as they vibrate through my skin.

I bury my face in her neck, quashing my own groans as her orgasm takes over her.

She coats my fingers with her arousal, and it's only then I remember I wanted to taste her again, wanted to feel those juices coating my tongue.

I continue my ministrations, slowing my movements until her breathing returns to normal, then instead of washing my hand under the water, I bring it to my mouth, licking my fingers as she watches me through hooded eyes.

"Oh, God," she whispers almost breathlessly, and I can't stop the small smile that pulls at my lips.

"God had nothing to do with that."

Keeley rolls her eyes before her lips pull into a smirk, and she spins me around against the side wall, lowering to her knees. I'm ashamed to say the image of her sucking my cock delays my reaction, and she's almost to the floor when I grip under her arms.

"Not a chance." I pull her to standing, my cock pulsing as if to ask me what the fuck I think I'm doing. And I have to wonder the same. Only...

"We're not doing that today. Not here. Not now." I have to hold strong to that.

Keeley raises a single brow as she sucks her lips into her mouth, biting back a grin. "You may be the boss out there." She points toward the door before settling her finger at the tip of her mouth, her smile seductive. "In here, we're equals, and if I want to drop to my knees, I'll drop to my goddamn knees. Got it?" Her voice holds no room for negotiation, and my cock fucking knows it. The greedy asshole thickens to uncomfortable levels, my tip brushing against Keeley's stomach. "Good." She smiles, taking my erection as the response she needs to try again.

This time as she drops to her knees, I throw my towel on the floor, softening her fall, and her gaze snaps to mine, smiling in thanks.

I open my mouth to speak, until she silences me, wrapping her glistening lips around my tip, sucking me into the back of her throat. "Jesus Christ."

My hand shoots out to flatten against the wall behind her and I hunch over, my muscles contracting as her mouth works me into a frenzy.

She smooths her tongue against the base of my length, curling it and gliding a path back to the tip, the sensation making my pulse spike.

After wrapping her fingers around my shaft, she pumps me a few times before sucking me in rhythm, her movements picking up speed until I have to bite my arm to stop myself from cursing.

It's been years since I allowed anyone to get this close, and it fucking shows. It's only been a few minutes, and my balls are so tight I'm going to explode any second. "You need to stop," I grate, the words leaving my mouth with a breath.

Keeley shakes her head, pulling a groan from the back of my throat.

"You need to stop, *now*," I demand, trying to move back, only stopping when I hit the wall behind me, giving Keeley the chance to tighten her grip on my thighs.

My body shudders as Keeley drags me back into her, taking me so deeply that my tip hits the back of her throat.

"Oh, fuck." My cock jerks as my head drops back. I clench my teeth, trying to last longer until Keeley moans around me, the vibrations sending me over the edge. I jolt forward, unable to stop my cum from filling her mouth, apologizing as she glances up at me, swallowing with a smile.

She doesn't release me until I beg her to stop, and even then, she sucks one last time before pulling off with a pop.

"God, that was satisfying," she moans and I choke on a laugh.

"For you?"

"Yep. Hopefully it was good for you too."

She stands and steps back under the water, drawing my eyes to the way her wet hair clings to her face and to the water cascading down her naked body. A body I could stare at all fucking day.

"Looks like I'm going for the wet look today."

"What?" My gaze drops to her pussy before flashing to her eyes to find her biting back a laugh.

"I meant my hair." She turns the tap off and squeezes the water from the strands, her confidence back in place. "Sorry, did you need the shower?"

I snap out of my messed-up trance to match her conviction. I'm a powerful man, for fuck's sake.

Keeley leans past me, bending down to grab her towel, and her breasts brush against my cock, making me hard again. I turn in the hope that she doesn't notice, but no such luck.

"I can go again, if you want." She dusts her tongue across my tip, and I grunt as I step back, shaking my head, moving out of her reach this time.

I could go again too. Only we shouldn't be here. We both have work to do.

And on top of that, if I stay, this woman is going to be the death of me. I need to maintain some level of control.

Chapter Twenty-Nine

KEELEY

I wipe my mouth as I stand, while running the tip of my finger across his length, admiring his grooming. It's so Sal. Of course he couldn't be neatly groomed everywhere but his cock. He has to have it all. Even if nobody sees it.

Unless they do?

With a smile, I glance up to find Sal watching me, his gaze falling to my lips before his head drops backward on a sigh. "Fuck. It's been a long time since…" He trails off, laughing under his breath, answering my unspoken question. "What are you doing to me? We're in a goddamn changing room. At work."

"I'd love to say I'm sorry, but I'm not. Plus, you came to me."

His chuckles get louder before a groan rumbles from the back of his throat. "Fuck, I know. I have no words."

"How about you say thank you then leave me alone. I have to finish my shower and get to a meeting with Wes."

"Jesus. Are you late?"

"Not yet." I raise a brow, and he shakes his head, my strong powerful man now a flustered mess. And God, it's hot.

"Okay. Alright. I'm going." He turns toward the door before pausing suddenly and glancing over his shoulder, stopping me from sneaking a look at his ass. "Thank you." He winks back at me and I internally swoon.

"You're welcome." I bounce my fingers in a wave, and Sal chuckles again, wrapping the wet towel around his waist before disappearing out the door.

I listen until he's settled back into the stall next to me, laughing when I hear his soft growl.

That man is the whole package rolled into one, and he doesn't even know it. He's hot, powerful, kind, generous, swoony, a freaking god at getting me off... and the crazy part is that he thinks I'm the one in control.

I'm not. I may be able to push his buttons to get what I want, but if he were to tell me to do anything, in that deep commanding voice of his, I'd be putty in his hands.

I'm secretly hoping that scene plays out soon.

When we're not strapped for time.

With only fifteen minutes to spare, I rinse off and get dressed in record time. At least I thought it was a record time until I open the door to discover I'm alone. Sal not only finished before me, but he snuck out so quietly I didn't even notice.

I quickly reapply my makeup, focusing mainly on the lip area—hoping to hide the fact that my lips look a little more swollen than they did when I walked in here—and I've just made it back to my office when Wes arrives.

He knocks softly, and I'm pleased to say I am cool, calm, and collected, despite Sal giving me an incredible orgasm barely thirty minutes ago.

What an end to my workout session.

"Wes, come in." I motion for him to sit down at the round table in my room and grab my laptop on the way to join him.

"First things first. Was Thomas excited?"

Wes slumps in the chair, shaking his head ever so slightly. "He said no."

"What do you mean, he said no?" I stare at Wes bewildered, my eyes wide as I let his words sink in. Not once did I consider that an option. Thomas loved it here, and I know he's not doing anything else yet.

"He didn't think it was fair for Beckett to be coached by the guy he replaced, when they only started a year apart in the pros. He says it's like a teacher trying to explain a task to someone they went to school with, after they both learned the exact same thing at the same time."

"That happens. My next-door neighbor tutored me in music, and we went to the same school. She was the year above me."

"Yes, but were you both professionals in your field?"

"God, no. I sucked and she went on to play in the Boston Symphony Orchestra, I think." I glance away, puzzled, and Wes chuckles sadly.

"Exactly."

"Dammit." My shoulders drop as I catch up, understanding Thomas's reasoning. It's unfortunate, but it makes sense. "Any other options?"

"I have a couple. And if they don't come to fruition, we'll put the word out publicly."

"Best of luck."

"Thank you." Wes huffs out a laugh. "I might need it. Now back to tomorrow's media session. What do you need and when?"

Wes and I run through the plan for tomorrow, and he grunts and groans at the exact moments I thought he would. We've had media here all week; that's nothing new. The difference is that until now, they've had limited access to the field, and no interviews have been approved. Wes wanted the team to have the chance to train together without the thought of media requirements in the back of their minds. And while I respect that, I can only hold them off for so long.

We have a new starting quarterback this year after winning the Super Bowl, and everyone wants to know how the players are feeling, especially Beckett. Most other franchises are already allowing team interviews. The San Francisco crew is getting restless.

"I really appreciate you accommodating this, Wes. I know we need to focus on the game."

"It's a necessary evil. One I will never get used to."

I laugh and Wes's eyes widen. "No offense."

"None taken. I'm not the media; I'm the go-between. A babysitter of sorts."

"That's the most accurate description I've heard. They certainly need someone taking care of them. Making sure they don't fuck up."

"Not that it works."

"No. I'm afraid nothing will. Anyway, I've got to run. I've got a call with another potential coach."

"Ooh, can I have any hints as to who? Do I know them?"

"You might. I'll let you know how it goes after speaking with him. Keep your fingers crossed."

I almost pout like I would with Sal but thankfully stop myself, making me wonder if I've ever been professional with that man.

We certainly weren't professional while naked in the changing rooms. God, I wish I was back there now instead of...

Fuck, Wes. "Yes. My fingers are crossed. I look forward to hearing from you."

"Thanks, Keeley. Talk soon."

I don't see Sal for the rest of the day, and that's probably for the best. If I had seen him, I'm not sure I could have stopped myself from asking him to meet me in the gym or his office. Anywhere for a replay of what happened earlier.

That man knows what he's doing and— Nope. I am not going to think about *how* he knows because that's a recipe for me to spiral. He's had more years of experience than I have, and that's all I need to know.

For the next few days, I throw myself into extra, unnecessary work to distract me from thinking about Sal. That is, until I remember I'm supposed to be dedicating time to my bridesmaid's duties—helping to plan a rehearsal dinner for the man-I'm-not-thinking-about's daughter. *Dammit.*

Since Paige refused a bachelorette party, she decided to make the rehearsal dinner a bigger deal, a week before her wedding, and I'm giving it my all. At least, I'm trying to.

I'd consider channeling my inner Paige, otherwise known as the queen of event organization, if I hadn't realized how wrong that sounds.

Everything makes me think about Sal and the complicated situation we've found ourselves in. Meanwhile, Sal seems completely unaffected. When I pass him in the halls, he smiles, just like he always did. When he needs me, or I him, he's there ready for anything, as though nothing has changed.

Except it has. For me.

If I thought I'd be able to get him out of my system after a couple of incredible, mind-blowing orgasms, I was dead wrong.

I want more.

All the time.

I can't stop thinking about him.

The following Friday, I'm deep in thought, pretending I'm busy on my laptop when I swear I hear my name. I glance up from where I'm hiding away in the corner of my local café to find Paige walking toward me.

"Keeley, hi."

"Hey, Paige. How are you?" I smile awkwardly, my mind spiraling with how bad of a friend I am, until I subtly pinch my leg, snapping myself out of it. We've spoken plenty since I all but fucked her dad, and it was fine. Having her standing in front of me now is a different story. A little part of me wants to blurt it all out and beg her to forgive me.

Lucky for me, that part of me doesn't get a say in the matter.

Paige lifts her lips in a soft, hesitant smile, and I almost panic as she sits down. Until she speaks. "I'm good. If you don't count the fact that my mom and my brother have decided they're flying in four days before the rehearsal dinner. I thought they'd fly in the day before and fly out right after the wedding."

I bite back a laugh, instantly relaxing as I pass her the menu. "I can't believe you're getting married in a few weeks. Where are they staying?"

"I'm not sure about Marc, but Mom's staying at our place." She cringes and I immediately feel her pain.

"Your apartment? God, I'm surprised Easton agreed to that. You need cake." I gesture toward the dessert list, and Paige laughs before it turns into a strangled groan.

"Easton didn't agree. Mom invited herself and made it impossible for him to say no. You know, since she thinks we have a perfectly good spare bedroom. We don't. It's my art studio. But do you think that matters?"

I cringe on her behalf. "Shit."

"Yep. Dad offered for her to stay at his place, because he holds the empathy gene and could see we were both uncomfortable with it all, but she wasn't interested in that. Her exact words were, 'I want to be with my daughter before her wedding.'"

At the mention of Sal, a pang of guilt settles in my stomach, followed by the sting of jealousy. *He offered for his ex-wife to stay in his apartment?*

Was that before or after he was fingers deep in my pussy?

Said pussy throbs and I internally scold myself, crossing my legs to hide my pain, as Paige continues on. "Can I come and stay with you?" She holds her hands out as she jokingly begs, and I laugh as I take her hands, squeezing them in mine.

"You know you're always welcome. But she's your mom. She wants you there. And my guess is that Easton already has plans to move into my apartment with Isaac. If I know that brother of mine, you're on your own."

"Oh, I know. He asked your mom. You were his second choice. Followed by Reed. He's that desperate."

"Not desperate enough if he hasn't suggested Luke as an option."

"Not yet, but I'm ninety-nine percent sure he'd go there. He gets along fine with my mom, but since she's been in wedding mode, even I've found her insufferable. The only one she's not driving crazy yet is Dad. And that's because he's mostly stayed out of the planning."

Her easygoing smile drops, and I curse Sal under my breath. He's once again let work distract him, and I'm annoyed on Paige's behalf.

"Wait. No, I didn't mean it like that."

"Like what?"

"You look like you want to strangle my dad."

"Oh, shit. I do?"

"Yes." She laughs. "But the truth is, I haven't asked him to do anything. I didn't want to bother him with it. And now, I'm kind of regretting it. He'd be much easier to deal with than Mom."

Her hesitant smile returns, and my chest aches for Sal. He would have loved that.

"You should ask him. I'm sure there's some last-minute stuff to do. Double-checking the venue or taste testing the cake?"

"We've already..." She trails off when she catches my raised eyebrow and laughs out loud. "You're right. I should double-check both of those things. Thanks, Keeley."

"You're welcome. You know me. Always here to help you."

"*And* my dad. I'm a little jealous he gets to see you so much. I miss you."

"God, I'm sorry. I promise to be better."

"Don't be. You're fine. I'm just going a little crazy with the wedding coming up and the Mikklesons' trial not long after that."

"Shit. I heard about that."

"From Easton?"

"Ahh, yeah. Probably. Or maybe Mom." Definitely not your dad getting hounded about it in a press conference. "How are you feeling?"

"Nauseous. I'm going to be a witness during the trial."

"What?" My eyes grow wide as our server arrives. "She'll have the cake of the day, please. Actually, make that two." I order for myself and Paige before my focus is back on her.

"Does your dad know?"

Dammit. Why the hell would I ask that?

Paige shakes her head. "Not yet. But I promise to tell him soon." She stares at me pointedly, silently asking me to be her friend instead of her dad's, and I nod in return.

I'm not going to tell him. But it's going to break him when he finds out. He wants her as far away from that family as possible. They almost broke her once; he won't let them do it again.

I have a million questions, but I don't get to ask a single one before Paige moves the topic back to her mom, filling me in on the many over-the-top things she's done since finding out Paige was engaged. I laugh along with her, but the moment she's gone, my happiness fades.

What's going to happen when she finds out about me and her dad? Will I still be the friend she confides in?

You'd think all this talk of brothers and dads, ex-wives and family connections would have squashed any ideas I had for continuing to sneak around with Sal.

Yet, after spending the rest of my day racked with guilt, I'm right back where I started, wishing he was here to help me through it. A little part of me wonders if he's wishing he was here too. Or at least, hoping he's thinking about me. *Only* me. Not a past relationship that he never chose to leave.

I don't recognize the person I've become, but I can't stop myself from spiraling, and by the time I fall asleep, I'm struggling over what I'm going to do.

One thing is for sure though… I'm in this deeper than I thought.

Chapter Thirty

KEELEY

When the sun rises after my night of panic, I wake up feeling almost back to my normal self—the workaholic version of me. The girl who doesn't get caught up in her love life.

The person I became last week was someone reacting from a place of fantasy and delusion. The real me makes decisions based on practicality, and lusting after a man twenty-four seven is not that.

I'm not saying I won't end up locked in another shower with my lips wrapped around Sal's cock; I'm just saying I'm not going to let it affect me day-to-day. I need to look at it like a yoga session—something that gets me out of my head in the moment, and nothing more. Somedays I have time for a class, some days I don't. Hell, some *weeks* I don't and that's okay. Life goes on like always.

Preseason keeps me busy for the next two weeks, and before I know it, the rehearsal dinner has arrived.

I'll never claim to be an event planner—that job is way beyond my skill set—but when someone assigns me a task, I am all in, even if that task is something out of my comfort zone.

With an hour to go before the guests arrive, I'm buzzing around the hotel ballroom as though I'm high on sugar—straightening this, double-checking that. And by the time the guests start making their way inside, I'm a chaotic mess. But a mess who's dressed to perfection.

While Sal and I haven't found another moment alone since the shower, he did take the time to "casually" slip in the fact that he'd offered for Camilla to stay at his place. He worded it as though it would have been the biggest drag since he'd have to move into a hotel, easing my mind without me having to ask the question. If I didn't know Sal as well as I do, I may have wondered if Paige had noticed my reaction and told him to say something. But I'm confident in saying it wasn't her. That's Sal. It's like he knows what I'm thinking without me ever having to voice it.

As the guests file in, I'm tapped on the shoulder by the hotel manager, pulling me from my thoughts and back into organization mode, when I finally thought I was done.

How could anyone do this for a living? How could Paige put that much pressure on herself multiple times a year planning the fundraisers for the D'Angelo Foundation? I couldn't do it. I'm exhausted and the dinner hasn't started yet.

Paige, Easton, and Isaac arrive shortly after I've spoken with the catering manager about dessert, and when Paige walks under the floral archway and into the elegantly decorated ballroom, her glistening eyes make it all okay.

I did good.

Thank fuck.

At Paige's request, we don't have a seating plan, and since I'm still working until the very last second, I take the only empty seat available, which is thankfully next to my mom.

"Did you save this for me?" I ask, clutching her hand, giving it a squeeze.

"I want to say yes, because surely I'd get brownie points for that, but no. I hadn't even noticed you were still floating around."

"Gee, thanks, Mom. Aren't moms supposed to be moms until they die?"

She laughs out loud while my stomach sinks. I shouldn't be joking about that. Ever. And in her case, that reality is closer than I'd prefer to admit.

"I'm sorry, darling daughter. I should have been focused on you while attending the rehearsal dinner for my son's wedding." She raises an eyebrow and I finally smile.

"Thank you. I'm glad you've seen the error of your ways."

Mom laughs again before her eyes bounce around the room. "You did an amazing job, Keeley. And in case that brother of yours fails to say thank you, you should know he appreciates it. Just ask your sister. He actually said 'wow.'" She points to my sister, Addison, and I smile her way.

"That's huge. And thank you. You know I'd ensure nothing but the best for my baby bro. Though I still can't believe he's getting married."

"I can." She glances his way, her eyes welling with so much pride that emotion swells in my chest. "From the first moment I saw him look at Paige, I knew she was it. I'd never seen him look at anyone else that way."

Certainly not his ex. She was a piece of work. "He may drive me crazy, but God, I'm happy he found Paige."

"Honestly, I think she found him."

I follow Mom's line of sight to watch Paige and Easton smiling with Isaac, and my stupid eyes start to water.

"You're not getting emotional are you, little sister?" Addison calls out from across the table next to ours, drawing attention from a few people on our side of the room. She's not the type to leave anything alone. In fact, I have no doubt that if she lived here in San Francisco, she'd probably have sleuthed her way into outing me and Sal. She loves a good scoop.

"Never," I lie, poking my tongue out. "I got some mascara in my eye. Excuse me."

No one pays me any mind as I get up and sneak away, heading to the bathroom under the guise of a sore eye. In reality, I need a moment. Addie's right to be shocked by my emotions. And I normally wouldn't let them show except for the simple fact that my brother and best friend are getting married. Paige is going to be my sister, she's going to officially adopt Isaac, and they're going to have an amazing life together. They would've had a great life together whether they got married or not, but the adoption would have been more complicated, while next week's little ceremony ties it up in a nice little bow.

I take a deep breath as I stare in the mirror, smiling away my impending tears. If I'm a mess now, how the hell am I going to get through the wedding without fucking up my makeup? I'll be standing in front of the entire goddamn room.

And...dammit, Isaac's going to be a ring bearer.

Gently wiping under my eyes, I brush a stray strand of hair behind my ear where it belongs and straighten out my perfectly straight dress, laughing at myself. I'm Keeley fucking Reynolds. I don't get emotional at rehearsal dinners. I don't get emotional in general. I'm fine.

Satisfied with my little pep talk, I open the door to find Sal pacing in the hallway, his perfectly tailored suit molding to what I now know to be a ripped body. A body I've yet to get out of my mind.

He stops when he sees me, his shoulders relaxing as he releases a sigh.

"What has you so tense?" I ask, walking over to greet him.

Instead of telling me how he feels, he grabs my hand and drags me back in the direction of the bathrooms, pulling me inside the family restroom and locking the door behind him.

"*You*." He squeezes my hand. "I saw you upset and then you disappeared suddenly. Is everything okay?"

"God. Yes." I release a soft laugh. "It's stupid. I was getting emotional over Easton and Paige."

Sal's eyes widen before he chuckles. "You don't like showing any kind of vulnerability, do you?"

"Not unless I'm naked. With you. Then I don't mind it."

"*Keeley*."

"I know. Wrong place and definitely the wrong time."

"When have we ever been in the right place?"

"Very true." I jokingly grab the thin strap of my dress, and Sal rushes to stop me, his touch like fire when he brushes my hand away.

"I refuse to ruin this outfit. Have you seen yourself?" He spins me toward the mirror and settles behind me, trapping me with his arresting gaze.

I *have* looked at myself, obviously, and yet when his eyes lower to my dress, I follow, and it's like I'm seeing it for the first time. Through his eyes. My olive-green silk number clings tightly to my body with the V neckline dipping just below my breasts, the Hollywood tape working its magic to keep the material in place. The skirt falls below my knees, showing off my five-inch nude heels, the fit leaving no room for panty lines. Not that Sal would think about that.

"You're a vision, Keeley," he whispers, drawing my attention back to his eyes as I smile in thanks. "It's been a struggle not to stare at you since I arrived, and I'm afraid to say I'm failing."

"And now you're here."

"Now I'm here."

Sal slides one of the thin straps from my shoulder and gently kisses a path across my skin, his eyes closing as he lets out a strangled groan.

"Why is it impossible to stay away from you?" he whispers, the heat of his voice warming my skin while also making me shiver.

"God, if you find out, please let me know because I've been thinking the same thing all week."

I spin to face him, and we're so close our noses almost touch, and yet, Sal doesn't step back. He doesn't pull away like I expect him to.

I take in a shallow breath, and Sal's eyes drop to my mouth, his hooded gaze making me shudder.

"Sal?"

"We can't do anything tonight, Keeley."

"I know."

"But I can't walk away." His pained expression hits me in the chest, and I know how he feels.

"Me either."

We both fall silent as Sal gently cups my face in one hand, his other wrapping around me to settle on my back. "What are you doing to me?" He whispers the words as he leans in, gently pressing his lips to mine, his touch so soft, you'd think I wouldn't feel it. But I feel it *everywhere*.

My heart races as I slide my hands around his waist, under his jacket, pulling him closer.

He groans against my mouth, his lips caressing mine, his thumb curling under my chin to lift my face higher, deepening our connection.

The kiss is soft and purposeful, explorative and raw. And when it ends, it's over much sooner than I would have liked and yet it couldn't have been more perfect.

"Sorry, I..." Sal trails off as he steps back, running his hands through his hair. "Actually, I'm not sorry, only we probably shouldn't have done that at my daughter's rehearsal dinner." He cringes comically and I laugh.

"No, probably not. And now you've gone and messed up your hair." I walk forward and lift to my toes, tousling his locks until it's stylishly messy as opposed to the I-just-finished-kissing-my-daughter's-best-friend look he had going.

"Thanks, Keels. Your hair still looks perfect."

"I noticed you keeping your hands away from it. Always so thoughtful."

"I try." He shrugs and I laugh, straightening his jacket, as I smile up at him.

"Shall we get back to it?"

"Yes. We should."

"You go first and I'll slip through the kitchen. Our secret will be safe for another day." Sal nods, his eyes locked on mine as he brushes his thumb across my cheek.

"See you out there."

"You will."

He stares my way for another few beats before laughing to himself and heading for the door. "Oh, and Keeley. Why don't you get yourself a nice glass of wine, sneak out onto the balcony, and have a moment to yourself. You deserve it."

He doesn't wait for me to respond, opening the door, only pausing long enough to check that the coast is clear. And the déjà vu makes me smile.

When a few seconds have passed, I open the door to find Paige and Isaac heading my way, thankfully lost in conversation, not noticing I'm there. With my heart slamming in my chest, I sneak across to the kitchen, exiting into the opposite side of the ballroom in the hope that I don't draw attention.

Mom's eyes catch me across the room, and she raises an eyebrow in concern, until I give her a thumbs-up.

Though I have no idea why I'm saying I'm fine, as my pulse has never raced so quickly. If Paige had been walking that way one minute earlier, that could have ended in disaster.

I mingle as I calm down, keeping a straight face, and after the entrées are served, I confirm the officiant has arrived and that we'll be ready for the rehearsal once the main meals are done.

My shoulders ache, undoubtedly from the tension building, and Sal's words run through my mind.

"Why don't you get yourself a nice glass of wine, sneak out onto the balcony, and have a moment to yourself. You deserve it."

He's right. I do deserve it, only I feel bad for drinking on the job.

I subtly glance his way to find him already looking back at me, his expression pinched in concern. Most likely knowing I've had something on my mind all night. Sometimes he's too observant for my liking.

He raises his glass to his lips and bounces his eyebrows, reminding me to relax.

"Okay," I mouth back, rolling my eyes as I walk toward the bar.

"I'll have a glass of your house red, please," I ask the server as someone sits beside me, a man I don't recognize out of the corner of my eye.

Paige and Easton originally wanted a small wedding. Easton's exact words were "a handful of guests would be great," and he wasn't joking. The thing is, our family alone is more than a handful of guests, and they both have friends, and Easton's teammates on top of that.

I was right, of course. There are at least fifty people here, and while I'd still consider it to be small, to Easton, it's not.

The man beside me clears his throat, and I turn to find familiar eyes staring back at me, stifling a laugh when he smiles flirtatiously.

"I'm Marc," Sal's son greets me, holding his hand out for me to shake before leaning down and pressing his lips to my knuckles. It's safe to say he is not like Sal at all. Yes, Sal is old-school charm, like that gesture was. The difference is that Sal's charm comes without the corniness.

"If I'm not mistaken, you're one of Paige's beautiful bridesmaids. I saw you all taking a photo earlier but didn't catch your name."

"I'm Keeley." I stare at him pointedly and he smiles back at me.

"Keeley. Keeley."

He repeats my name as though he recognizes it from somewhere, and I huff out a laugh, waiting for him to catch up, but when he smiles again, it hits me. He's truly clueless. God, maybe the D'Angelos never talk about me. I guess that's possible.

"It's a beautiful name for a beautiful woman."

"Thank you." The server places my wine down in front of me and I spin on the stool, facing the crowd of people mingling in front of us. My gaze catches Sal's again, and he frowns as his eyes bounce to Marc beside me. I shrug as I stand. "I better get back to it. My poor brother looks confused over there."

"Your brother?" Marc glances over his shoulder, his eyes darting to where I'm pointing to Easton, and his jaw drops as he laughs out loud.

"That's why I recognize the name. We're practically family. Lucky I didn't hit on you."

"Lucky indeed."

"Although, technically we're *not* family, so..."

"I think you better look elsewhere." I take a sip of my wine and instantly feel better. Sal was right. I needed that.

"Mmm, I agree." Marc continues talking as I take another sip. "Easton's pretty huge. He'd probably attack me for just thinking about the things I could do with his sister."

I choke on the liquid traveling down my throat, coughing a few times with my hand in front of my mouth. "No doubt," I say with a croaky voice. "It's better if you don't test that theory."

"Noted. What about that Hollywood actress? Is she still dating that giant football player?"

"Very much so. You might want to find someone *after* the dinner. There are plenty of clubs around here."

"You're right. Good idea. Thanks, Keeley."

He smiles before jumping up and walking outside, the strange conversation pulling another laugh out of me as he disappears around the corner.

"I see you met Marc." Sal appears out of nowhere and I startle, almost spilling my wine. And yet, I'm not entirely surprised that he's here.

"I did. He's a *friendly* kid." I'm careful with my words and Sal groans.

"God, what did he say?"

"Nothing. We just spoke about whether or not it was appropriate to hook up with someone who's almost like family."

I smile while Sal chokes on nothing, a similar reaction to what I had. "Because of..." His eyes widen as he trails off, and I bark out a laugh.

"God, no. Not us. Me and him."

"You and... Did he hit on you?" Sal refuses to meet my eye, turning to face the rest of the room.

"Not exactly. Would it matter if he had?"

His head snaps to mine so fast, I startle again, until he shakes, glancing away. "No, it wouldn't."

"Okay. Good. I told him about a club he should go to later. I might meet him—"

"Do not finish that sentence, Keeley." Sal smiles as he seethes, and my heart races as a tingling sensation has me clenching my legs. I like seeing Sal jealous. A lot.

"So it does matter?" *Jesus.* So much for my panic over Paige almost catching us. It's like I'm addicted to him.

"We can't have this conversation here. But yes. I'll let you enjoy the rest of the night in peace; no more work talk. I promise."

Work talk?

I turn to find Luke and Amelia joining us at the bar, smiling when Amelia grabs my hand. "I need to borrow you for a minute," she says, her eyes full of apology. "If that's okay."

"Of course. I've got my drink. I'm good. See you both later." I wave to Luke and Sal, and follow Amelia over to the couches, sitting down on the armchair next to her. "Everything okay, Ames?"

"Everything's fine, but I noticed that other than scarfing down your meal, you've barely had a chance to sit, and I know you're not going to acknowledge that yourself. Take a second. Everything is running smoothly. We're all having a great time. You deserve a moment to enjoy it. I'll leave you be."

"Thank you, Amelia. You're right. But I don't want to be alone."

Because I've already taken a moment. I took a moment to shove my tongue down Sal's throat, and I should not have done that here.

I need to distract myself or I might try and do it again, and relaxing on the couch is not going to work.

"Tell me what's been going on in your life, Ames. How's Juliet?"

Amelia smiles, and I know I've bought myself at least thirty minutes talking about her daughter. Just in time for the rehearsal to begin.

Chapter Thirty-One

SALVATORE

Laughter rings out around me and I chuckle along, pretending to pay attention as Camilla regales a few of the guests with stories of Paige as a child. "And then she would…" Her voice fades into the background as I lose focus, once again drawn to Keeley, watching her as she floats around the room, shining like she always does.

My pulse races as I study her, smiling at the way her lips quirk when she's politely exiting a conversation, and the way she brushes her hair behind her ears, even when it's perfect. Maybe an unconscious habit from when her hair was long.

Keeley spins suddenly, knocking into Reed, and the two of them laugh out loud, with Keeley throwing her head back before jokingly burying her face in her hands.

She's beaming with happiness, and I want to be over there, soaking it all up, sharing in her joy.

"Do you remember that, Salvatore?"

"Of course. What?"

Camilla laughs, her eyes lifting toward where I was looking just as Isaac steps into my line of sight. Perfect timing, little man. Camilla's laughter softens and her lips curl into a knowing smile. "He's a pretty amazing kid, right?"

"He sure is. And you didn't think we'd have grandchildren."

"I didn't. But I'm very happy Paige found Isaac."

"He was definitely meant to be a part of this family. I mean, look at him in his cute little suit."

"Like grandfather, like grandson."

"Absolutely."

"There's a lot of love in the room," Easton's aunt adds, the warmth in her tone making me smile.

She's not wrong. Everyone I love is in this room right now.

I smile at Paige pulling Isaac onto her lap, her eyes bright as Keeley drops down onto the couch beside them. A spark of something new ignites in my chest and I quickly glance away, launching into a new conversation to distract me from whatever the fuck it is.

Now is not the time to process it.

The night ends much later than planned, and it's safe to say Keeley's not the only one that got emotional. My apparently cold heart melted at the sight of Paige walking toward Easton during the rehearsal, and I'm not ashamed to admit it had just as much to do with his reaction as it did hers. That man is completely smitten with my daughter, and I couldn't be happier for the two of them.

Yet, here I am, potentially fucking things up by messing around with his sister. With the way things are going, that secret is not going to be a secret for long. We're not being careful enough.

Keeley's still buzzing around as the guests depart, and when I offer to help, she waves me away, letting me know she'll see me tomorrow.

Her tired eyes make me anxious, and I almost demand that she lets me stay, until Rochelle catches up with me, linking her arm through mine to walk with me outside.

"Can you believe our kids are getting married?" She smiles warmly, her eyes locked on Easton and Paige. "You know I told Paige not to marry him?"

"You what?" My eyes bulge until I remember a conversation Paige and I once had, and it all comes back. "Are you referring to the day she had her epiphany? The day she decided she *wanted* to get married after being anti-marriage for so long?"

"That's the day. I'm glad she didn't listen to me. She's going to make the most beautiful bride and a wonderful daughter-in-law."

"She is. She's lucky to have you welcoming her into the family."

"Thank you. We all love her. I'm sorry about Easton."

"Easton?"

"Yeah, I'm not so sure he's going to make the best son-in-law, but he'll be a good husband, that much I know."

I chuckle when she winks, both of us turning to watch Easton grumble about something like he always does, while Paige's happiness never wavers. "They're a good match, that's for sure."

"They are. Two down. One to go." Rochelle nods toward Keeley, and I swallow a lump in my throat. "One day she'll put work aside and focus on her personal life. I hope."

"Want me to fire her?" I joke to hide the uncomfortable knot forming in my stomach, and Rochelle laughs out loud, drawing attention our way.

"Shhh. She'll kill you for even suggesting that. But even so, I'm going to say no. I've never seen her happier than she has been lately. And since she never leaves the office, that must be what's bringing her joy."

"Well, the guys are back. She's in her element." I pause as the words leave my mouth, shaking my head. "That came out wrong. I meant that we're all back in the swing of things and—"

"I knew what you meant." Rochelle smiles, a soft laugh bubbling out of her. "Keeley swore off athletes a long time ago. It's not the guys that are lighting her up. At least not in that way."

My brows furrow, but I hide it before Rochelle turns my way, my expression morphing away from confusion. Though my thoughts still linger. Keeley mentioned not being interested in dating the players on the team, but I always assumed it's because they work so closely. Is there more to it?

I walk Rochelle to her car and wait for Phil to arrive before saying goodbye, all while my eyes linger on the exit, waiting to see if Keeley comes out.

She hasn't surfaced by the time I make it to my car, and I'm about to go back inside when I notice Paige and Hayley waving goodbye to the guys before meeting Keeley in the doorway and heading inside together.

My driver, Jeffrey, jumps out when I walk toward the back of the car, but I wave him off, getting the door for myself. "Did you have a good night?" he asks when I'm settled inside, his eyes finding mine in the rearview mirror.

"I did, thank you. Everything was perfect."

"Good to hear."

My thoughts drift back to my moment with Keeley, and my lips tingle as a reminder of our kiss.

I hadn't planned to do anything tonight, but the spell she has me under is getting stronger by the day, and I'm not sure how much longer I can keep this up.

I'm not a casual relationship kind of guy. If I was, I would have been fucking around long before now. But with Keeley, I don't think it's casual at all. Which is a terrifying concept. There's so much at stake. And I don't know if I'm ready to take that step for either of our sakes.

If I got thirty minutes of sleep last night, I'd consider that a win. I can't remember the last time I tossed and turned so much, thoughts running on repeat through my mind, my anxious heart unable to slow down.

I'm up well before my alarm, and I've already worked out and showered before the sun's even risen to meet the clouds. I'm doing all that I can to keep myself busy, and still my mind won't stop whirring.

When it's finally a reasonable time to text Keeley, I ask her to meet me in my office and then pace in front of my windows. The practice field fills while I wait, a sea of turquoise and black painting the turf, as the players line up for practice.

My phone rings just as someone knocks on my door, and I check the screen to make sure it's not Keeley seconds before she pokes her head inside.

"You wanted to see me?"

"I did."

"What's up?" She wanders in and closes the door behind her, making her way over to the couch, smiling as she sits down. Her relaxed demeanor puts me at ease for what I imagine won't be an easy conversation. But I have to get it all off my chest.

"I wanted to talk," I blurt and Keeley nods, turning to give me her full attention. "About us." I clear my throat awkwardly, and Keeley's smile turns sympathetic. It's been decades since I've had to have "a talk" with anyone romantically. Camilla and I didn't even "talk" when we ended our marriage. There was yelling. Lots of yelling. But we managed to avoid the "let's sit down and talk about our future" conversation.

Keeley and I are past the point of avoidance. At least, I am. Now that it's keeping me up at night. And I'm praying we're on the same page.

"Why don't you come and sit down?" Keeley waves to the space beside her on the couch as my eyes drop to where I'd picked up my pacing again. I hadn't even noticed I was doing it.

"Sure. I can do that." I grin as I sit, angling my body to face her way, while still giving myself the option to avoid eye contact.

"What would you like to talk about? In terms of us," Keeley asks, her voice holding a warmth that instantly calms me.

"I guess I want to know what you're thinking. What you want." My voice comes out stilted compared to her smoothness, and I almost groan until she smiles reassuringly.

"I'm going to be completely transparent here." She twists to face me, sitting tall and confident, and I actually laugh.

"You mean you've been holding back up to now?" I stare at her deadpan until her eyes widen comically, and she laughs along with me.

"Fair point. I'm going to continue to be honest then. I want more of what we've been doing, Sal. I want us to have fun."

"Fun?"

"Yes. It's been a long time since I've been intimate with anyone other than you. The last time was before we met. I'm far too busy to date, apart from the few Luke set me up on, and they were never going to end in the bedroom. That man cannot matchmake to save himself. Anyway, I digress. I'm too busy to date. I tried *fucking* apps disguised as dating apps but even that was too much effort. I have a friend that works wonders, hitting the right spot every single time, but I need variety and there's only so much my hand can do."

My muscles tense as words escape me. There was a lot to process there, and I'm sure I should be responding about where this conversation is going. Only I'm stuck on her friend. Who the fuck is he? Or she. Didn't she just say she hadn't been intimate with anyone since we met? Is it not intimacy in her mind if it's a quick fuck? It sure as hell felt intimate to me when we were hiding out in the changing room.

"Are you okay?" I jolt at Keeley's soft touch, her words interrupting my thoughts as her hand curls around my wrist. "I know that was a lot, but I wanted to put everything on the table. So you knew exactly where my head was at."

What about where my head's at?

"I appreciate your honesty. Always. Only... I'm confused. What exactly does that mean?" It sounds a hell of a lot like a casual relationship which is what I was worried about.

"It means that I think we should help each other out. I'm busy; you're busy. We don't have time to get it elsewhere, so why not?"

Jesus Christ. Why does that sound worse than a casual relationship?

"If I'm helping you, are you prepared to lose the *friend*?"

"What?" She frowns, confused. "Why would..." She pauses, and a glint of humor sparkles in her eyes before she schools her features and straightens her posture. "I can't. Leo means too much to me."

Leo. Jesus. "I didn't need to know his—" Keeley's laughter cuts me off and my brows furrow. "What?"

"Have I told you I like seeing you jealous, Mr. D'Angelo? *Sir.*"

"*Keel—ley.*"

"Leo is my vibrator. You don't have to be jealous. We can share him."

Fuuck. I groan, dropping my face into my hands.

"I don't know if I'm cut out for this, Keels." She opens her mouth to speak, but I lift a hand to signal for her to wait. "Full transparency?" I ask, standing slowly, struggling to counter my erratic pulse.

"Please," Keeley whispers, the humor leaving her eyes.

"I don't want some kind of casual arrangement with fleeting preorganized encounters and strict boundaries. I don't want you to use me as a replacement for *Leo*, waltzing into my office so I can get you off." I pause as the thought of that pops into my head. "Okay, maybe I'm not opposed to that last one. But I want more. I can't do casual. Not with you. Only, I'm not sure I can do a relationship either. I'm at a loss here. There are far too many factors at play. I know I'm overcomplicating what I'm sure you thought would be relatively simple. I apologize for that. But this is bigger than us, Keels. As shitty as that is."

She's quiet when I'm done, and I have a feeling that's the first time I've ever made her speechless while she's been fully clothed. "Are you okay?"

"You want more?"

Fuck, yes. I think I want it all. "What I want doesn't matter. We have other people to think about." I blow out a breath as I glance away. I can't do casual because I'm already in too deep to pretend. And I can't ask for more, because I'm setting us both up for heartbreak when this undoubtedly ends in explosive fashion.

"If only our relatives weren't getting married, right?" Keeley whispers, pulling my gaze to find her suppressing a smile. "I'm kidding."

Her laughter brings me out of my heavy thoughts, and I smile back at her.

"You're kidding?"

"No, not really. It would make our situation a hell of a lot easier. I was kidding about bringing it up during a serious moment. I just wanted to cool the room a little."

"Thanks. Sorry. I really killed the joy of it all."

"No, you didn't. You were honest and real. Which is something I've always valued about you."

"Thanks, Keels. Why does this have to be so goddamn complicated?"

"It doesn't have to be. It is what we make it."

She locks me with her stunning gaze, trying to appear strong while a shaky breath gives her away, offering me a rare moment of vulnerability.

Something tells me it's too late for us both. We flew past casual in the private jet everyone seems to think I own.

And I don't think either of us know where to go from here.

Chapter Thirty-Two

KEELEY

Sal's gaze locks me in a choke hold, and I struggle to swallow the lump in my throat. He's right. About everything. He can always see through me.

I don't want a casual relationship any more than he does. The only reason I'm suggesting it is because it's less complicated that way. It's easier to ignore the various excuses screaming at us to walk away, trying to convince us that it's never going to work.

Because they're probably right.

"Maybe we should sleep on it? Who knows, one of us might come up with some brilliant idea for how this will work." I internally cringe at how ridiculous that sounds and smile to hide it.

"Sleep on it?" Sal lets out a soft chuckle. "I can do that."

"Good."

Good? What the hell am I doing? What the hell are *we* doing? We're both in denial. That's what. We're both deluding ourselves for one more day of hope before it all comes crumbling down. It was nice while it lasted.

"Was there anything else you wanted from me?" I ask, standing up, needing to get away before I start getting anxious. Something else Sal can always read through my actions.

His lip purse momentarily, and I busy myself straightening out my pants until he speaks. "No, that's it."

"Okay. Great. I have a meeting to get to. Talk soon."

"Always."

I smile as I'm leaving and then I'm all smiles for the rest of the day, putting on a front as I go about my business, until the second I'm home.

Earlier than usual. My front door barely has time to slam before I'm falling back on my couch, calling Callum on speaker as I cover my face in my hands.

"Keeley." Callum's voice croaks and he clears it as I say hi. "Do you have any idea what time it is over here?"

"Honestly, no. I don't even know what time it is here." Though it is still light out.

"Shit. What's wrong?"

"Nothing... Everything."

"That narrows it down."

"Shut up." His gruff voice makes me smile and I relax enough to uncover my face. "I'm obviously referring to my love life."

"*Obviously.*"

I laugh at the sarcasm in his tone and sit up, curling my legs up under myself. "I know none of this is going to interest you, but you're going to hear it anyway. And I'm not even sorry about it."

"Have at it then."

"I messed up, Cal. I thought it would be easy. I was wrong. It got complicated so fast, I never saw it coming. And I should have. I'm a well-educated woman. I can handle tough conversations with the most confident and self-absorbed men out there, *and* make them see my side of the argument. I can spot lies, read minds, argue like the best of them. Yet, I let my feelings creep up on me and then freaked the fuck out when they did."

I pause to give Callum a chance to speak, only he's dead quiet, making me wonder if he fell asleep, until he sighs. "You lost me. Actually, you never had me to begin with. Take a deep breath and explain it to me like I'm five and I don't speak your language."

"English?"

"Frantic woman."

"Oh, right. You need to learn that quickly if you want to get yourself a girl."

"When did I say I wanted a girl?"

"You didn't. However, you're not as young as you used to be. Midthirties are right around the corner and—"

"I thought we were talking about you?"

"We were."

"Then let's get back to it. If you want to talk about my love life, I'm going to need you to call back at a better time."

"When you're not so tired?"

"No, when I can't answer the phone."

I snort at his humor then stifle my laugh, knowing that's likely to prompt him to hang up on me, and I need to talk this out with someone that isn't related to the situation.

God, I wish that wasn't so literal.

"Back to me."

"Good. Now what are you talking about?"

"Sal."

"Your boss?" It takes a lot to make Callum smile, and I can tell by the rise in his tone that he's smiling right now. At me, not with me.

"Yes. My boss."

"What did you do?"

"We... ah... kind of hooked up a few times."

"Kind of?"

"Okay, no. We definitely hooked up. Twice. Once in his office and once in the staff changing rooms." I wince as his strangled laughter echoes through the phone. "Of course you'd laugh at this."

"I'm actually not laughing at what you did."

"Then what are you laughing at?"

"Like father, like daughter."

"What?"

"Didn't you tell me that Paige admitted to fucking someone in the bathroom of her building's gym, and you later found out it was Easton? Seems like the D'Angelos have a thing."

"What. Ew. Don't say that. They don't have a kink. An opportunity presented itself and we took it, that's all."

"Who the fuck mentioned kinks? And why are we talking about your sex life?"

"Because I can't talk to anyone else about this."

"You can talk to him."

"Who?'

"Your boss. It sounds like you're falling in love with him, and if that's true, you need to talk to him about it."

"Ugh. You're not supposed to offer me sound advice. You're supposed to tell me my situation sucks and that you'd hate to be in my shoes."

"Your situation sucks and I'd hate to be in your shoes."

"Thank you. It does suck. I appreciate the support." Callum groans at my craziness, and the fact that he's trying warms my heart. "What would you do?"

"If I'd fallen for my boss, who also happens to be my brother's father-in-law and my best friend's dad?"

"Yeah." My stomach knots at how bad that sounds, and I appreciate it when he doesn't laugh. But God, he's a good listener.

"I'd talk to him," Callum advises. "Or in my case *her*. I'd tell her how I felt and try to work through it together."

"He tried. And I brushed it all off."

"Why?"

"Because his concerns were valid, and I didn't have the answers he was seeking."

"It's not your responsibility to have the answers, Keeley. That's for the two of you to work out."

Ugh. I sigh, letting my head drop back to the couch. "You're right."

"I usually am."

"Since when?"

"Always. I just don't like talking in general."

"Isn't that the truth."

"Anything else before I go back to sleep? My alarm's going off soon."

I smile at my friend, my chest swelling with gratitude that I have someone I can talk to, even if it pains him to talk back. I miss him. "When are you flying in?"

"The day before the wedding. I can only stay two nights."

"Boo. You suck."

"Good night, Keeley."

"It's not my bedtime yet."

"I'm hanging up."

"Bye."

I smile as he ends the call, feeling a little lighter and a lot less confused.

As much as I hate to admit that Callum's right. He was telling me what I'd been telling myself since I walked out of Sal's office, only it doesn't change a thing. Telling Sal I feel the same won't take away the complications surrounding our situation; it will only add to it. And with Paige and Easton's wedding coming up, we should be focused on them, not us.

Picking up my phone, I bring up Sal's name and type out a text, pressing send before giving myself time to think it through.

KEELEY: I can't do casual either. Can we talk about it again when the wedding is over?

Or in other words, when the complication levels are at an all-time high?

SAL: I think that's a good idea. So… in case I don't get to say it on the day, you're breathtaking, Keeley. Never has there been a more beautiful bridesmaid.

Oh, Sal. My shoulders drop as my body relaxes and I laugh to myself, knowing Sal would have made a comment about me holding on to too much tension. Just like I do with him. I found an amazing guy. A decent human being who doesn't play games. Who wants me as much as I want him.

And he's completely off-limits.

KEELEY: You can't say that before you've seen me

I tease, needing to bring us back to the friends we once were.

SAL: I don't have to see you to know that's how I'll feel. You're always the most beautiful woman in the room and I wish I could say that to you more often.

My heart catches as my stomach swirls with regret. Why can't this be easy? Why does love have to be so goddamn hard?

Not love. Relationships. Why do relationships have to be so goddamn hard?

After shooting off a thank you message, I fall back onto my couch, doing a full three-sixty to where I was when I first got home. No better off than I was then.

I may have said we should talk after the wedding, but what is there to talk about? It's casual or nothing, and we've already established neither of us can do that.

Maybe the best idea is to try to move on. Or at the very least, pretend to try.

Because, what else could we possibly do?

Chapter Thirty-Three

SALVATORE

Preseason comes to an end with our last game this weekend, and I half expect more of Gregory's book of lies to be released. There's so much positive energy surrounding the team right now that I wouldn't put it past someone to try and bring us down.

Fortunately, I'm wrong, and as Paige's wedding approaches, it couldn't be more perfect.

Unless you count the cloud that's been hanging over my head since I told Keeley I couldn't do the casual thing anymore.

What a fucking idiot.

Who tells a stunning, intelligent, confident woman that they no longer want to have sex with them?

Hell, we didn't even have sex and I shut it all down.

All because I was catching feelings.

Me. The guy that puts work over everything else.

The guy that hasn't thought about a woman that way for too many years to count. And now that I have, she's all kinds of off-limits.

I'm sure a therapist could fill a notebook on that revelation alone.

I'm already awake when my alarm goes off on the morning of Paige's wedding, and I can't decide if it's because I'm excited or nervous.

On one hand, my daughter is getting married to a man that would give her the world if she asked for it. On the other hand, my daughter's getting married. Period. My baby. The girl who once asked me if it was still okay to hold my hand even with everyone calling her a big girl.

The woman I let down.

Fuck, I'm lucky I was even invited to the wedding. Had it been five years earlier, that may not have been the case.

I take my time getting ready, buttoning the crisp white shirt I bought specifically for the occasion, being careful when I take my custom suit out of the garment bag, gliding my fingers over the imported Italian fabric.

I'm about to put on my shoes when a knock at my door interrupts me, and I stand up, my brows furrowing.

"I'm coming."

No one can access my level unless they live in the building, and I know Paige stayed at the hotel last night after the game. Not that she'd be visiting her dad on the morning of her wedding.

After adjusting my tie, I open the door and come face-to-face with Camilla, her eyes wet with tears.

"She's getting married, Salvatore," she cries out as she lets herself inside, grabbing a photo off the table in my hallway. "I didn't think I'd get emotional like this, but now that it's here, it's sinking in. She's not coming home."

The first tear falls and I almost laugh. This has nothing to do with Paige getting married and everything to do with Camilla wanting Paige to live near her forever.

"She's been gone for years, Cami. You didn't actually think she was going to move back home, did you?"

"Yes! I thought she'd come to her senses and realize she was meant to grow old in New York. She's a socialite like me. It's where she belongs."

"Paige hasn't been a socialite for a while. I'm afraid that ship has sailed. And that's a good thing. She's found her place. The woman she was meant to be. She has Easton and Isaac. A career that she loves. A family of friends."

"We're her family, Sal."

"And she'll always have us."

"Easy for you to say when you live in the same state."

"Move here." I shrug, and the gasp I get in return is so loud, you'd think she was screaming.

"Move here? Leave New York?"

"It's not as hard as you think."

"Oh, really? Is that why you're still keeping one foot in the door? Still running your business as though you never left?"

"Daniel is running D'Angelo Construction. Not me."

"So you weren't there a couple of weeks back."

"There was a fire, Camilla. It's not like I flew home for the Monday morning catch-up meeting." *Although I do regularly call in for that.*

I expect Camilla to argue, but she shocks me when her face pales. "I didn't know there was a fire."

"I paid big bucks to keep it quiet, so I'm happy to hear it worked."

"Why?"

"Why what?"

"Why did you keep it quiet?"

"Because I didn't want it coming out that we had a disgruntled employee going around setting fire to our offices, wanting to send a message."

"A disgruntled employee. Is that what you think?"

"It's what I *know*."

"I think you're wrong."

"What? Why?" I frown until a thought comes to mind and I chuckle softly. "Camilla, this isn't something for you to get excited about, and it's not something for you to discuss at one of your gossip-fueled lunches. In fact, I'd prefer it if you didn't."

Camilla stares at me deadpan as she folds her arms over her chest. "That's not what this is."

"It's not?"

"No. Do I like gossip? Sure. I like it as much as the average person does." *I wouldn't exactly say that but I let it slide.* "This isn't gossip. I'm worried."

"Worried?"

"I increased my security the other week because I think I'm being followed." Her voice lowers while my heart jolts, and for the first time, I pause and give her my full attention, keeping an eye out for her usual tells. If this was one of her attention-seeking grabs, she would have told me about it the second she arrived in San Francisco. Or called me the moment she increased her detail. If she's only telling me now, it's not a game.

"What makes you think you're being followed?"

"I wish I could say it's just a feeling, but I've seen flashes of light, like someone is taking a photo as I'm leaving the building. I heard footsteps behind me and turned around to find no one was there. It's freaking me out. And it only started after I was officially called as a witness for the Mikkleson case."

"The Mikklesons. Fuck." Why didn't I put two and two together? Is it them trying to send me a message? Send my family a message.

I wouldn't put it past them considering what they did to Paige years ago, but I thought that part of our lives was over. I guess it's possible that now that the trial is approaching, they're back to their old tricks.

"You told Paige not to testify, right?" Camilla asks me, her expression neutral.

"I did. They've got plenty of evidence without her statement. After she agreed, I pushed it from my mind."

The second Paige told me about the Mikklesons blackmailing her after she moved to San Francisco, I took over the investigation with Austin, vowing to protect her. And with Camilla's help, thanks to her affair with Gabriel Mikkleson, we were able to secure the information we needed to bring them down.

Us. Not Paige. I want her as far away from this as possible.

"That's good for Paige, but I'm part of that evidence." Camilla sighs and my stomach knots with guilt. I somehow managed to avoid getting summoned.

"I know. Sorry. What can I do to help?"

"Nothing. I wouldn't have mentioned it if you hadn't mentioned the fire. I'm looking after myself."

"Are you sure?"

"Yes. I'm sure." Camilla huffs and I have to fight not to roll my eyes. "Believe it or not, I haven't needed you for over ten years, Sal. Even before we actually split up."

I wince at the personal attack but nod in agreement. I deserve that. Even if it's not entirely true.

"Anyway." Camilla smiles, her entire demeanor shifting back to her ever-confident self. "We don't have to concern ourselves with that now. We're all safe here in San Francisco." She says San Francisco like it pains her, and I huff out a laugh. "Let's talk about it *after* the wedding. Before I go home."

"Okay. After the wedding." I smile, while inside my stomach is churning. I have way too much to talk about after today. And none of it's going to be fun.

Let's hope today goes really slowly.

The morning flies by, and before I can blink, I'm being guided into Paige's hotel room, my eyes closed as Camilla tells me to get ready.

"Are people getting dressed in here? I can come back another time. I don't want to make anyone uncomfortable." Camilla laughs and I frown, hating the fact that at this present moment, she has more control over me than I'd like.

"Your eyes are closed as a surprise, Sal. You can open them now. No one is naked."

I never mentioned the word "naked" but of course now that it's out there, one bridesmaid comes to mind. At least until I blink my eyes open and find Paige standing in front of me, her back toward me as someone I don't know does something with her hair.

"Hi, Dad." She turns around, and my chest tightens as emotion wells in my throat.

"I… You… Paige." I laugh, shaking my head as though that'll rid me of the tears forming in the back of my eyes.

"Stop, Dad. You're going to make *me* cry."

"And you better not do that, Daddy D'Angelo, because her makeup is set." Hayley appears out of nowhere, squeezing my shoulder as she walks past. I laugh at her ridiculous name until I notice her long champagne-colored bridesmaid dress and falter. My mind conjures a picture of Keeley wearing the same dress, the long-split revealing her… *Jesus*. No.

"You look lovely, Hayley." I smile, bringing my mind back to the present while my eyes surreptitiously bounce around the room.

"Why, thank you, Mr. D'Angelo. Paige picked the perfect dresses for us all. Don't you think?"

"They're very nice indeed." I nod while my heart slams in my chest, knowing that if Hayley's here, Keeley's likely to be somewhere close by.

"I've been thinking..." Paige gets my attention, stopping me from spiraling. "Would you... Ah... Do you..." She trails off and my brows furrow.

"What's wrong?"

"Sorry, I'm fine. You don't have to look so worried."

"I can't help it. It's my job." I laugh and Paige smiles fondly back at me. "What have you been thinking?"

"I know I said I didn't want to make a big deal out of today. But, ahh... Would you be interested in walking me down the aisle?"

I'm still smiling from her calling me out, so when her question hits me, my heart jolts and I'm momentarily lost for words.

"You don't have to, of course. I was just—"

"I'd love to." I cut Paige off as she backtracks uncomfortably, my pulse jumping around like crazy. "It would be my absolute honor."

Paige's entire face lights up, and for the first time in far too long, I feel like I did something right. "Thank you, Paige."

"Don't thank me. It means just as much to me as it does you."

My emotions take over me again as more tears well in my eyes. "Dad. Stop."

"Sorry, I..." I choke on the words, before clearing my throat. "I just need a minute and I promise I'll be good."

"Thank you. Like Hayley said, I cannot mess up my makeup. There's not long to go."

"Five minutes, actually." I hear Keeley's velvety voice and I turn so fast, my neck twinges. Not that it bothers me. I'm distracted, once again rendered speechless, only this time by the incredible beauty standing in front of me. She's more breathtaking than I ever could have imagined, her eyes alight with infectious joy, her soft pink lips pulled into a radiant smile. I'm sure the champagne-colored dress clings to her beautifully and her hair is styled to perfection, but I'm too caught up in the captivating energy she just brought into the room and the warmth filling me.

"Don't look so shocked." Keeley laughs, flashing me a pointed grin as she seemingly covers for me, snapping me out of whatever the fuck that was.

"How can it only be five minutes?" I ask with fake wonder, spinning back to Paige when she laughs from behind me.

"You sound more nervous than I do."

"Not nervous." I shake my head. "I'm not ready to lose you just yet."

"What do they say? Don't look at it like losing a daughter; look at it like gaining a son."

Someone snorts to stifle a laugh, and I know without looking that it's Keeley, making me huff out a laugh of my own.

"Very true. Lucky me." Paige smiles knowingly, likely thinking I'm joking about Easton. And I am in a sense, just not the way she's thinking.

"It's time to line up." A woman with a headset waves to get our attention, and the room falls quiet until she's gone.

"I guess that's our cue. Are you ready, Kid?" I'm still not sure *I'm* ready, but I put on a front, ignoring my racing heart as Paige smiles back at me.

"Sure am, Daddio. Let's do this."

Let's do this. Here we go.

Chapter Thirty-Four

KEELEY

If I thought I'd expelled all my emotions during Paige and Easton's rehearsal dinner, I was sorely mistaken.

I've almost cried three freaking times today, and Paige hasn't even walked down the aisle.

First was when she glided out of the bedroom in her dress, looking like an ethereal being with the glow of the sun beaming through the window behind her. Next was when Isaac popped in to visit, and his eyes started to water as he told his "mom" she was beautiful.

Then my goddamn brother had to go and get emotional when he saw Isaac walking down the aisle with our mom, taking his role as the ring bearer very seriously.

Easton's like a brick wall when it comes to emotions, so it's impossible *not* to react when he does.

Now, I'm waiting in anticipation for Paige to walk in with Sal, his expression from earlier still fresh in my mind.

My body heats as I picture the longing in his eyes and the bob of his Adam's apple. He wasn't staring at me with attraction or lust. It was something else. Something I've never experienced before, and it felt bigger than it should be between us.

He's lucky I was the only one who could see his face. Hell, we were both lucky because we would have had a lot of explaining to do.

My stomach flutters just thinking about it, and I close my eyes to recover, taking a moment to compose myself. *I can do this.*

I can get through today without obsessing over a man. I *don't* obsess over men. It's not my thing.

The music changes and my breath hitches involuntarily. I shake off my reaction until Paige and Sal step into view, and my world stops as nausea consumes me.

I'm falling in love with my best friend's dad, and he's about to become family.

After making the mistake of glancing over at Easton again, at the exact moment a tear falls down his cheek, I lose it, choking back my own tears during the entire goddamn ceremony. Thankfully, I snuck my makeup bag into the bathroom near the reception so I can do a touch-up.

The ceremony runs for about thirty minutes, and when Easton and Paige kiss, I cheer them on while my heart cracks. There's no "working things out" when it comes to Sal and me. It's too messed up for that. We just witnessed our future become more complicated than one could ever imagine. The best we can be is friends.

The officiant presents Easton and Paige as husband and wife, and Easton scoops Isaac into his arms as they do the rounds, all of them beaming with happiness, my grumpy brother unable to wipe the smile off his face. I watch them with so much love swirling around my heart that my own troubles easily wash away.

They've been through so much and found their happy ending. That's all that matters today.

Before moving on to the reception, the photographer tries to get a few staged shots of Easton with his family and friends, but he refuses point-blank, giving her nothing until she's forced to walk away. He relaxes when she's gone, and I laugh when I catch her hiding behind a tree, snapping shot after shot of him candidly enjoying the moment.

I sneak away to get my first drink for the day—other than the small glass of champagne the girls and I had to toast Paige—and I've just taken my first sip when Sal's son, Marc, sidles up to me again, his smile tight as he unabashedly rakes his eyes all over my body.

"What's a girl like you doing alone at the bar?" He winks, his words slightly slurred before the night has even begun.

I raise an eyebrow, hiding my concern. For now. "A girl like me?"

"Yeah. You're fucking gorgeous and you know it. I can't believe I'm the only guy over here."

"I believe we've had this conversation already. I'm off-limits, remember?"

Marc frowns, his gaze dropping to my hands. "I don't see a ring. Are you a maneater or something?" He chuckles to himself and... What the hell? It's been less than a week. How is it possible he has no idea who I am?

"I'm something. And you seem to have forgotten what that something is. Rest assured, you won't have to wait lo—"

"Marc." Sal's deep voice cuts in from behind me and I smile. There's one of my protectors, right on cue. I knew it would be either him or Easton that came over as soon as they noticed us talking. "You better not be annoying Keeley."

"Keeley?" Marc's eyes widen before they crinkle as he smiles.

"That's me." I wave as I smile back at him, and Sal's gaze travels toward the sky.

"Jesus Christ. We spoke the other night. How the fuck did I forget that?"

"I'm wondering the same."

"Sorry." He cringes and leans in, whispering in my ear. "I was pretty fucking high if I'm being honest."

"Oh-kay." My eyes meet Sal's over Marc's head, and I can tell by his murderous expression that he heard what was said.

"Did I hit on you? I'm sure I would have, because, well, look at you."

"Thank you." *I think.* "You did. Hit on me. And—"

"Marc." Sal steps between us, subtly moving me backward.

"Shit. I almost forgot you were there, Dad. You're cramping my style."

"Believe it or not, I'm not here for you. I need Keeley for something."

"Do the off-limits rules not apply to you, old man?"

I suppress a snort as Sal's nostrils flare ever so slightly.

"We work together, Marc. Our situations are vastly different."

"Maybe so...but that doesn't mean everything's aboveboard." Marc raises an eyebrow while I quickly glance away, almost certain my amused reaction is going to give us away.

"Marc," Sal warns again.

"What?" Marc raises his hands in the air. "I'm kidding. Keeley knows I'm kidding. Don't you, Keeley?"

I turn to face him. "Of course." I smile softly. "Paige filled me in on your class-clown persona."

"That's me. Always the comedian." Marc's lips lift into a wide grin, but it holds a hint of something else, something darker, suggesting he doesn't love that little descriptor.

"Are you—"

"I guess I'll leave you to it. Enjoy your work talk." He walks away without waiting for a response, and when he's out of earshot, I turn to Sal, my chest tight with concern.

"I think you should go after him."

"What?"

"You're his dad, and something was clearly bothering him just now."

"I know my son, and trust me when I say he does not want me chasing after him."

"I just think—"

"I said he doesn't want me. But I noticed it too. I'll ask Camilla to go. They've always been closer than we have. If anyone's going to get him to talk, it's her."

"Thank you."

"Do you ever *not* worry?

"Do you?"

"Sometimes. But you don't even know Marc."

"He's your son and Paige's brother. He's hardly a stranger."

"You're right. He's family now." Sal forces a smile and I laugh out loud, drawing the attention of the guests close by.

"That didn't seem to bother him. Maybe we should take a page out of Marc's book."

"Mmm. Maybe."

Sal glances away a little distractedly, but when he looks back, he's the picture of calm once more. "I better get back to it."

"I thought you needed me."

"Oh, right. I just wanted to say you look stunning and that I hope you have a good night."

"Thank you." My pulse spikes as he flashes me a hint of the emotion he revealed earlier today. "You don't look too bad yourself."

"Thanks, Keels. I wish I could say more." He scratches the back of his neck, the emotion in his eyes morphing into regret. And he doesn't need to say anything else; I can read it on his face.

"I know. Me too."

I squeeze his arm and walk away in the opposite direction of Marc, glancing back over my shoulder before I catch up to the girls, finding Sal already looking away.

This isn't going to be easy, but it's the right thing to do.

Since we had a sit-down dinner for the rehearsal, Paige and Easton decided on a cocktail party for their reception, and when we're led into the ballroom, I finally spot Callum across the room.

"Why are you hiding away in the corner?" I ask as I reach him, giving him a tight hug which he doesn't reciprocate.

"I'm not hiding. I'm just easing into it. This is the most people I've seen in months. Maybe even years."

"Sounds like you need to get out more."

"Nope. I like my life exactly as it is. This is not my scene anymore."

"It would be if you hadn't been injured."

"Nah, even when I played football, I hated the crowds."

"You mean the fans?"

"Maybe." He shrugs, and I can't help the laugh that bursts out of me until his football career seeps back into my mind.

"Have you spoken to your dad?" Callum's dad is American and his mom is Scottish. They lived next door to us in North Carolina during our teenage years. Callum's between Easton and me in age, but they played football together when we were in high school, so they were much closer. Until Easton moved away for college and Callum and I stayed near home.

He injured himself before starting his second season in the pros, during an altercation with his dad, the same year his parents divorced. And when his mom moved back to Scotland to take care of *her* dad, he followed.

"No, but he tried reaching out. He heard about the wedding from your dad."

I cringe, my face scrunching in apology. Easton doesn't like me talking to Dad about his life. They don't speak. It's why his last name is Wilder and mine's Reynolds. He convinced Mom to change his name to her maiden name as soon as he was old enough to understand what sharing a last name means. My brother may not express emotion, but he feels it, and our parents' split hit him pretty hard.

I've always looked at it differently from him. I'm more pragmatic. They tried to make it work and it didn't. Was single parenting hard on Mom? Of course. But I imagine staying in a loveless relationship would have been a lot harder. And now she has Phil.

As if knowing I'm thinking about them, Mom and Phil wave through the window from where they're talking to my sister and her husband outside.

"I'm sorry about my dad. That's on me. I promise I never mentioned you. But I probably shouldn't have told him about Easton either. Although, I'm sure Mom or Addie would have said something too. Easton's the only one who cut him off."

"It's not your fault. And it's not hard to ignore him."

I almost laugh until Callum forces a smile, the edges failing to meet his eyes. Not that he ever usually smiles that wide.

"I think it's time we had a drink. What do you say?"

"Am I going to be attacked by your boyfriend?"

"Shut up. I don't have a boyfriend. And even if I did, I'm sure it would be clear that there are no sparks between us. At all. You're too much like my brother. So that would be wrong."

"But it's okay if it's your brother's father-in-law?" Callum raises an eyebrow, his melancholy gone, replaced with his dry humor. He didn't even smile as he delivered that blow.

"Stop. We're not talking about this today. It's Paige and Easton's day. I'm not ruining it by one of them overhearing that I have a thing for Paige's dad."

"It's a *thing* now."

"Callum," I warn and he raises his hands in the air.

"I'm stopping. But I'm not sure he's feeling the vibes you think you're putting out."

"What vibes? What do you mean?"

"I don't think he realizes you're repulsed by the very idea of hooking up with me. And I you. At least not from the glare he's shooting my way."

"First, repulsed sounds kind of mean, especially now that you're referring to me. And second, that's not helpful. I don't want to know that information. Okay?"

"Fine. He's not jealous. He's too busy flirting with a gorgeous mature woman who looks like she stepped straight out of a Hollywood movie."

"Dammit, Callum. That's his ex-wife." My chest burns as I fight the urge to look.

"*Damn.* I was only messing with you. Sorry 'bout that."

"No, you're not. Come on. You're buying me a drink."

"Aren't they free?"

"Yep. You still owe me."

Callum huffs out what could be interpreted as a laugh before he follows me toward the bar, and I make it all the way to the other side of the room before I glance back, my eyes locking with Sal's as he chats with Camilla.

It's Easton's wedding. It's Easton's wedding. It's Easton's wedding.

It's not appropriate to cause a scene.

No matter how much I want to.

Chapter Thirty-Five

KEELEY

After spending time catching up with Callum, I make my way around the room, mingling with family and laughing with friends. The more I distract myself—by actually enjoying the night like I normally would—the easier it is to push Sal from my mind.

At one point during the evening, Camilla taps her glass in an attempt to call for a speech, but Paige is quick to wave her off, reminding her that they want to keep things casual.

Around nine p.m., the lights soften in the grand room and the mood instantly changes. Guests relax, the vibe shifts from a wedding to a party, and the music changes to match.

Bodies drift toward the dance floor and the bar, while for the first time since leaving the ceremony, even Easton looks comfortable.

Hayley rushes over when the DJ plays a country song, and I preemptively laugh when Reed follows behind her.

"You have to see Reed boot scoot," she tells me.

"Boot scoot?" I mouth to Reed and he jokingly rolls his eyes.

"I already told Hayley, I'm happy to dance with her but I'm not *boot scooting*. That's something between her and me."

"Right." I raise my hands. "Best you keep that between the two of you. I think we should dance *without* any practiced moves."

"Ugh, fine," Hayley huffs, while her smile lights up her face. "Let's get this party started."

Paige, Amelia, and Blair join us on the dance floor, along with Luke and Zane. Zane reluctantly, but that man would do anything for Blair, even if that means shaking his ass while his friends give him shit.

For the next hour, I light up the dance floor, and while I can't see Sal—which is a good thing—I can feel his presence. The stronger it gets, the more I throw myself into the music, letting the beat consume me, taking me away from the situation I'm in.

I'm a hot mess when Paige beckons Easton over for what must be the tenth time tonight, and when he shakes his head again, I laugh loudly, taking over the fight.

"I have an idea," I tell Paige, before heading over to Mom and Isaac, calling in reinforcements.

"Isaac, sweetie. Do you think you could do me a favor?"

Isaac stares at me puzzled until my smile widens and I raise my eyebrows enthusiastically. Mom eyes me suspiciously and I have to say, her look is warranted.

"What do you say you help me get your dad on the dance floor? Your mom would love to dance with him."

Isaac's eyes light up at the mention of Paige and he nods, rushing off toward Easton.

"That's playing dirty, don't you think?" Mom purses her lips but she fails to hide the smile threatening to come through.

"It's his wedding day and he's refusing to dance with his wife."

"They danced."

"They swayed for about thirty seconds."

"It's not his thing."

"Come on, admit it. You were contemplating the same idea."

"Fine, I was. You beat me to it."

We both glance back toward the dance floor to find Easton walking toward Paige, holding Isaac in his arms, and I can't help the gloating grin that lights up my face.

"I know I give him a hard time, but that brother of mine is not so bad."

"Of course he's not. He's my son."

"You're so funny."

"I try." Mom shrugs and I wrap my arms around her, giving her a squeeze. "When do you think it'll be your turn to find a man?" she asks as she pulls back, her mischievous grin making me laugh.

"Not tonight, that's for sure. I'm going to dance some more; want to come?"

Mom glances over her shoulder toward Phil, and he waves from where he's talking to Addie's husband, his loving expression making my chest ache. *Do I want that?* God, I think I do. "I'm in," Mom says, grabbing my arm for support, pulling me out of my head. "I haven't embarrassed your brother nearly enough today."

My smile widens as we walk toward the dance floor, and it expands farther when I catch Easton's glare. I've signed myself up for some major payback, but I don't care. Seeing him dancing is worth it.

Mom sways to the beat, her feet unmoving while her beaming smile warms my heart. She can't move like she used to; she lacks the control over her body that she once had. But I know that being out here with the rest of us is important to her. If I have to hold her the entire time, I will.

Paige's mom joins us after a couple of songs, and I stupidly find myself looking for Sal. Wondering where he is. Who he's with.

My attention shifts for less than a minute and when I look back, my world spins on its axis, with everything moving in slow motion.

Mom's knees buckle as she falls toward the ground, knocking the side of her head on the steps leading to the bar.

My chest heaves as I rush forward, dropping to the ground beside her, seconds before Easton does the same. "Mom? Mom?"

I grab her hand as Easton lifts her slightly, cradling her head in his arms. "Mom, can you hear me?" Easton asks, his voice much less panicked than mine.

She doesn't answer, but squeezes my hand, pulling a relieved sigh from within me.

"She squeezed my hand," I rush out, my eyes still wide with panic as I search the room for Phil.

Easton's sigh matches my own, and he leans closer to whisper in her ear. "You're going to be okay, Mom. Just rest for now."

Phil and Addie push through the frantic bodies, joining us on the floor. And when it all gets too crowded, I stand and step back, my mind whirring with all the things that need to be done. "Can we get the music turned off and the lights brightened over the dance floor?" I call out, turning in circles as I bark instructions at anyone who will listen.

"We need to clear the area. Please." I turn to look for someone who might have a phone and find Blair holding up a cell, showing me that she's already calling 911. I mouth thank you and search for Paige next. "Paige?" I wave to get her attention, and she gives me the thumbs-up, letting me know she's listening. "I think you mentioned your uncle's a doctor?" Paige frowns momentarily before nodding and whispering to her mom, the two of them disappearing into the crowd, and it takes a second for me to realize her reaction may have been because it wasn't her that told me that fact. Only I can't think about that now.

After creating a circle of space around my family, I find a cushion from one of the lounges and hand it to Easton, moving on to calming Addie down. Easton and Phil take over caring for Mom, along with Paige's uncle, all of them assessing her condition while we wait for an ambulance to arrive.

I'm not sure how much time passes, and though it feels like a lifetime, it's probably no more than fifteen minutes later that Mom's being wheeled away toward the exit, with Phil holding her hand.

"I'll go with her to the hospital and call you as soon as I know anything," he tells us with a smile. "She's still squeezing my hand. She's going to be okay."

I stand, frozen, unable to look out the windows until the flashing lights disappear from my peripheral vision.

I have to stay strong. I have to. I've always been the strong one. I can't stop now. With a deep breath, I convince myself I'm okay. Only when I finally look up to find half the room staring back at me, my composure lasts all of thirty seconds before my entire body trembles from the shock.

My throat constricts, the air catching in my lungs, making it harder to breathe. I squeeze my eyes shut, trying to talk myself down. *I'm okay. I'm okay.*

"Keeley?" Luke's voice cuts into my thoughts, and I open my eyes to see Sal pushing through the crowd from outside, his determined gaze locked on mine. Luke must notice my attention being pulled away, because he turns and steps aside just as Sal reaches us.

"Fuck, Keels." Sal grips my shoulders, his fingers warming my skin as he stares into my eyes. Tears blur my vision, but I can see enough to catch Sal's anxious expression before he pulls me into him, wrapping me in his arms.

I bury my face in his shirt as my emotions overwhelm me, but it's not until Sal whispers in my ear that I completely fall apart.

"I'm here, Keeley. I'm here."

Every last ounce of strength leaves me as I pull back. "I asked her to dance, Sal. I should have been holding her."

"You didn't do this."

"I didn't help." My voice cracks as the first tears fall, and I curl into Sal once more, holding on to him like a lifeline as my head spins, thoughts of my mom plaguing my mind.

At some point, a warmth spreads through me from my head, as though Sal kissed my hair, but it's so fleeting, I have to wonder if I imagined it.

The lights dim as the soft tones of the music start up again and I reluctantly stand tall, smiling up at Sal. "Thank you," I whisper, the words catching in my throat.

"She's going to be okay. I saw her before the paramedics loaded her into the ambulance."

"You did?" I blink a few times, confused.

"I was outside when the ambulance arrived. I had no idea anything had happened until I saw her. Phil said she was telling him that everyone needs to stop being dramatic."

I snort out a laugh, wiping my eyes. "And here I am, more dramatic than anyone else. God, I don't know why I reacted like that."

"She's your mom. You don't have to be strong all the time."

"Yeah, I kind of do."

"Why?"

"Because when I let my emotions control the situation, I ruin really expensive, custom shirts." I gesture to the mascara stain on Sal's white silk shirt, and he huffs under his breath.

"I know what you're doing."

"What?"

"Deflecting. You're allowed to show your emotions."

"I'm fine."

"Really?" He waves a hand in front of his shirt, much like I did, and I let out something between a laugh and a cry. I'm about to apologize again when Sal's smile turns sympathetic, and another wave of emotion wells in my throat.

"Can I be real for a second?" I rasp, wiping at his shirt as if I can magically remove the black stains.

Sal grabs my chin, lifting my head to face him. "Of course."

My chest tightens at the concern reflected in his eyes, and the room around us fades away.

"I'm terrified, Sal. I don't want her to die."

Without saying a word, Sal drags me back into his hold, and I allow myself to collapse into him, feeling safe in his arms. Feeling supported. Loved.

And while I know I'll have to face reality again soon, for now, I'm exactly where I need to be. Consequences be damned.

Chapter Thirty-Six

SALVATORE

Keeley stays locked in my arms for another few minutes while I rub circles across her back, occasionally whispering words of comfort, ignoring the stares aimed our way.

The second I saw Rochelle, I knew I'd fucked up. I'd walked outside to hide away, acting the part of the coward I am.

I lost control of myself, working myself up as I watched Keeley having fun, hating the fact that it could never be me laughing by her side.

Because of that, I wasn't there when she needed me.

And now that I am, I'm not leaving until she tells me to go.

I'm not stupid; I know how this looks. I'm not a colleague looking out for my teammate, or even a friend offering support. Keeley has plenty of friends, all here tonight, and yet she chose me. She let me hold her. She broke down in *my* arms. And anyone that knows her knows that's a big deal.

The same goes for me.

My marriage ended because I couldn't see that my wife was hurting. Even when she was standing in front of me. With Keeley, I didn't have to see her at all. I *knew*. She consumed my every thought as I ran inside. I didn't have to be looking at her for her to be all that I saw.

And I'll be here for however long she needs me. No matter what happens because of that.

I'm not sure how long we're standing, frozen in time before the crowd disperses and the whispers calm down. Still, I hold Keeley until she pulls away again, her tear-soaked cheeks cracking my chest wide open.

"Sorry," she apologizes again and I scold her with a glare, making her laugh. "What? I am. I'll buy you a new shirt."

"I don't need a new shirt. I have plenty."

"But you had it made especially for today and—"

"Are you planning on wearing this beautiful dress again?" I stare at her pointedly, holding back from calling her out for deflecting again.

"No."

"Exactly."

"Point taken."

"Good."

Bright lights assault my eyes, and I blink a few times as Keeley moves away, putting distance between us as though we're no longer able to hide in the shadows. Not that either of us is mistaken enough to believe we were hiding.

I'd say the only people that won't be questioning our relationship are Rochelle and Phil, and that's because they were already gone.

It's safe to say the cat's out of the bag.

"I think the party's over." Keeley smiles softly before glancing over her shoulder toward the back room. "I'm going to grab my bag before everyone begins their goodbyes. I don't want to miss anyone."

"Take your time, Keeley. You see most of these people on a regular basis. They're not going to mind if they miss you."

She lifts her shoulders as she turns to leave, and I have no doubt she's going to ignore me. I'd laugh if Paige wasn't walking toward me, a hesitant smile gracing her lips.

"How are you doing, Kid?" I pull her into a hug, much like I did with Keeley, and she sniffles softly before stepping back.

"What a way to end the night." She huffs out a strained laugh while tears prick her eyes.

"She's going to be okay, Paige."

"For now. But it's not going to be that way forever. It's going to kill Easton and Isaac."

"Just them?"

"No." She shakes her head. "It's going to kill me too."

"I'll be here, Paige. Whenever you need me, I'll be here."

"Until *you* die."

"Whoa. Are you killing me off?"

"No, sorry. But for a girl that doesn't love facing deep emotions, it's been a full-on day."

She pouts and I bite back a smile. "It has. You got married. You're not my baby anymore."

"I haven't been your baby for a long time, Dad."

"No, but you've been a D'Angelo. Now you're a Wilder, and I have to rely on Marc to continue the family name."

A bout of real laughter escapes from Paige, and it eases my mind.

"Don't worry. He'll settle down. Mom said he was upset about that earlier. He hates that no one takes him seriously. Apparently, he wants what I have. And I've got to be honest, I feel bad that I've been neglecting him a little."

"You're not allowed to feel bad, Paige. Especially not today. Marc wouldn't let you in if you tried. Though, that does explain why he was high."

"He was high?"

"A little, yeah. At the rehearsal. And I'm the asshole that assumed he was rebelling again."

"*Jesus*. Does that mean he's spiraling?"

"I think so. Have you seen him? I better—"

"I think he left. And you're needed somewhere else anyway."

"Right, what did you want help with? What do we leave here and what needs to go home with you? I can fit some stuff in..." I trail off when Paige laughs before staring at me pointedly. "What?"

"I don't mean *me*." She points toward the back room as Keeley steps out, her bloodshot eyes visible from here. "How long have you loved her?"

"Huh." I choke, clearing my throat. "That's not... I don't... We—"

"Come on, Dad. You've been playing down your happiness for weeks now. At first, I couldn't figure out what it was until I noticed Keeley's happiness on the rise too. Then tonight... I hate to say it but everyone saw it tonight."

"Fuck."

"Yep."

"I don't even know what we are, and it's killing me, Paige." The words are out of my mouth before I've thought it through, and I instantly regret it. I should not be talking to my daughter about my love life with her best friend...and sister-in-law.

Jesus Christ, this is one fucked-up situation.

"Talk to her, Dad. You're a smart man. You know what you have to do."

"Thanks, Kiddo."

"Anytime." She shifts to walk away, but I stop her, my expression pinched uncomfortably.

"On a scale of one to ten, how pissed is Easton right now?"

"You sure you want to know?"

"Reluctantly, yep."

"About fifty."

"Great." I smile, my teeth bared as I grit them. *Way to ruin her day, Sal.*

"Don't worry." Paige squeezes my arm, her voice soft as she smiles sympathetically. "He'll come around. He has to. You know, since you came around to the idea of him."

For some reason that doesn't ease my mind, but when Keeley smiles, drawing my attention, I no longer care.

"Let me know if you need me for anything," I tell Paige. "Please."

"I will. But we're all good. For now, you need to look after your girl. We'll probably see you at the hospital."

"No, you won't." Keeley joins us, a hint of humor behind her tired eyes. "It's your wedding night. Mom will disown you both if you show up tonight. Addie and I will go. If Mom's not home tomorrow, you can visit then. But tonight is about you."

"What about Isaac? Your mom was going to look after him for the night, and—"

"I've got him," I cut in. "He's been asking for a sleepover at my place for a while."

"I thought you had some big meeting first thing in the morning?" Paige questions me and... *Fuck.*

"It doesn't matter. Being here is more important."

"Are you sure?"

"Yep." I smile while my chest tightens. If there was ever a time for me to push work aside, now is it. "Where is the little man?"

"He's asleep on the couch over there." She points to the lounge area near the glass doors leading to the gardens. "Mom's with him. He was already asleep when…" She trails off but she doesn't have to continue; we can fill in the blanks. And thank God he was sleeping. He didn't need to see that.

Paige hums, her expression wary as her eyes move between Isaac and me. "We should stay with him. Easton's not going to want to—"

"Mom's okay," Keeley cuts in. "I spoke to Phil a few minutes ago. I promise, she's okay. Easton knows that too."

Paige's eyes flash to something over my shoulder and I stiffen, her soft smile telling me Easton's about to join us. Though God knows what she's smiling about because I can't imagine this is going to be fun.

"Keels?" Easton squeezes her shoulder as he moves past, settling next to Paige, his eyes briefly flitting to mine. "Did you talk to Phil?" he asks, his voice flat, his expression neutral.

"I did," Keeley responds, seemingly unfazed. "He mentioned he'd already spoken to you."

"Yep. Mom said to say that if we don't have a proper wedding night, she's going to disown us."

Keeley snorts, while Paige laughs through a sniffle, and even I crack a smile.

"Told you," Keeley gloats to Paige.

"What do you want to do? Dad said he can look after Isaac." At that, Easton's forced to turn my way, and if looks could kill…

Easton gives off a murderous vibe on a good day, but now, I don't think I've ever seen anything like it. His nostrils flare as his wild eyes meet mine, and I stand tall, willing to take everything he wants to throw my way. He scoffs under his breath, and his expression changes, the anger replaced with hurt, and my stomach knots.

"Easton, I—"

"I want to stay home with Isaac." He turns back to Paige. "We can stay in a fancy hotel any night. Tonight, I want to be with my son."

"Easton…" Keeley tries to speak but he closes his eyes, his broken expression making her pause. "East?"

"You never stayed the night at Mom's, did you?"

He doesn't bother waiting for a response before stalking away, grabbing Paige's hand as he leaves. She glances over her shoulder, her gaze apologetic as she mouths something I don't understand.

"I hope so," Keeley says with a sigh, her expression defeated.

"What did Paige say?"

"He'll get over it."

"You don't believe her?"

"I do. I just don't think it's going to be anytime soon."

"Because it's me?"

"No, of course not," she lies, trying to smile through her pain. "He's pissed that I lied. Or that I held back the truth." She shrugs and... *It's definitely because of me.* And I have no fucking idea how to fix it. They need a book for shit like this. What to do if you find yourself falling for your son-in-law's sister.

If Gregory's pompous ass can release a book, why hasn't anyone written something like that? *Fuck*. They probably have.

"Tell me what to do, Keels, and I'll do it."

"You don't have to do anything."

"Keeley. This isn't all on you. It takes two to tango, remember?"

"God, you're old."

"Why? Young people use that phrase."

"Sure they do."

I fight not to smile but it shines through, and when Keeley hits me with a grin matching my own, I start to relax. "What about I ask Jeffrey to drive us to the hospital to visit your mom. I can come up or wait in the car—whatever's best for you."

Keeley's smile briefly falls before she widens it again, and I have my answer. "Thanks, but Mom doesn't want me visiting either, so I'm just going to help pack up here and head home."

"Do you need a ride?"

"No, that's okay. I didn't have much to drink and my last one was hours ago. You don't have to wait." She glances toward Easton and Paige, and my heart breaks for her. This was supposed to be a happy occasion. It wasn't supposed to end like this.

"I'll help you pack up. Just tell me what I need to do."

"You don't..." She begins to argue but trails off before I've even opened my mouth. "Thank you, that would be nice."

She directs me like we're strangers, and when everything is packed and we're ready to go, she gives me a brief hug goodbye before driving away.

Taking a part of me with her.

Chapter Thirty-Seven

KEELEY

After messaging Phil several times asking if he's sure Mom's okay, and him telling me she's good every single time, he finally sends me a video of her rolling her eyes with the accompanying text, "Do not come here. I'll see you when I get home."

Of course, I ignore her, and the second visiting hours begin, I'm hovering in her doorway. I need the distraction after lying awake all night thinking about Sal.

"Seriously?" Mom rolls her eyes when she sees me, mimicking her video from last night. "I thought you were a rule follower?" She raises her eyebrows, her face looking much gaunter than I remember it, her body looking frail as she lies in the hospital bed. Have I been missing the signs? Is she worse than I thought?

"Keeley?"

Shit. I smile to hide my spiraling thoughts. "Yes. I am a rule follower. That's why I waited until visiting hours."

"Yeah, well, I've barely woken up. So thank you."

"You're welcome." I smile, ignoring her sarcasm. "How are you feeling?"

"Like I stole the spotlight from my son."

"The perfect gift for him. Now you don't have to give him a present."

Mom stifles a laugh and I call her out on it. "You know I'm right. You have no reason to be embarrassed. We're all worried about you."

"Don't be. This is part of my life now. We have to get used to it."

"We don't—"

"Can we talk about you for a second?" she interrupts, changing the subject like always.

"What about me?" I let her off the hook. For now. We'll be revisiting this conversation later.

"It must have been hard seeing me fall like that. Did you have anyone to comfort you?"

I frown, puzzled, until the smallest of smiles tugs at her lips. "Dammit. Who told you?"

"Addie. You know she loves drama."

"We're friends and—"

"Uh-uh. Don't bullshit me. You've been more than friends for months, maybe longer."

"What? Where did you hear that garbage?"

"I didn't hear anything. I saw it. With my own eyes." She widens her eyes and waves a hand in front of her face, while I internally groan.

"When?"

"You've been happier lately. And so has Sal. But then there are moments when you're both grumpy. At the same time. I'll see Sal looking lost in the lobby one day and sure enough, that night when I call you, you're 'having a day.' Then suddenly, all is right in the world again. For both of you. Can't be a coincidence."

"Of course it's not a coincidence. It's work-related, Mom."

"I thought that at first. Until you showed up at my door early in the morning after spending the night at his place."

"That wasn't—" Mom's brows rise so fast that I stop speaking.

"You're really going to lie to me while I'm in the hospital?"

"Dammit."

Mom laughs out loud, prompting me to look back at the open door, thankful to find we're still alone. "Okay. I stayed at Sal's. We ran into each other when we were out, and I fell asleep in his car on the way home. It was the week I was staying in the hotel, so he didn't know where to take me."

"That was nice of him."

"It was."

"A friend would do that."

"Exactly." I smile, sitting down in the chair near Mom's head, relaxing a little.

"So...how do you explain the rehearsal dinner?"

Fuck. I stiffen as my heart stops momentarily before starting up again, galloping in my chest. "You were all smiles then," she continues, a soft grin on her lips. "Stealing glances. Moments alone."

"Again, that's—"

"Kissing?"

Goddammit. There is no way she knows about that. No one saw us. "How did you..." I trail off when Mom's eyes grow in surprise. She didn't know. She was bluffing and I walked right into it.

I sink my head into my hands and groan while Mom stays silent, letting me have my little freak-out moment. That kiss with Sal still plays on repeat in my mind. When we'd been fooling around in his office and in the staff changing rooms, it was easy to pretend we were scratching an itch.

After that kiss...well, that's another story. I understand why Sal gave me an all-or-nothing speech.

"We *were* more than friends for a little while there." I glance up at Mom, and all it takes is a second of her meeting my gaze before her face drops.

"Oh, Keeley. What happened? From the way Addie was talking, I thought you were together."

"I think I like him. No, I don't think that. I know it. Only it's so freaking messy. And on that note, how are you not judging me right now? He's your son's father-in-law. The two of you share a *grandchild*."

"Sounds like I don't have to. You're judging yourself enough for the both of us."

"What? That's not..." *Is that what I'm doing?*

"Isn't it?" Mom poses the same question, and I pause to think about it. People have been judging my life choices since I was a kid, and I never cared.

Are you really staying home to do homework instead of coming to the party?

You're so smart—you should be studying medicine, not PR and communications.

You're working for a football team? You?

I've been judged for every decision I have ever made. Why do I care now?

My family has never judged me. Not once. And their opinions are the only ones that matter.

"I'm self-sabotaging, aren't I?"

"I didn't say that." Mom shakes her head with a straight face until the edge of a smile gives her away.

"You were thinking it."

"I wish I wasn't. I've never had to worry about you. You've always made decisions based on what you want, not what anyone else tells you to do. And I truly admire that in you. But..." She trails off and I hold my breath, wanting someone to tell me what to do for the first time.

"But?"

"This is different. Love is a big deal. And—"

"I'm not in love."

"Stop. You know that's not what I'm saying."

Ugh, she's right. But the tightness in my chest tells me my heart wants out of this conversation.

"Love makes you vulnerable. Love puts your happiness in someone else's hands. Love can hurt. It can break even the strongest of souls. And you, my darling daughter, are one of the strongest people I know. You probably don't even realize you've had your walls up all this time. Telling yourself that you're too young, and that you'll focus on love when the timing is right. After you've got yourself a well-established career."

"What? No. That's not what I've been doing," I lie, badly. *That's exactly what I've been doing.* And Mom sees right through it. Like I knew she would.

"The thing about love is that you can't plan for it. It creeps up on you and bites you on the ass when you least expect it."

"Stupid Cupid." I pout, crossing my arms like a childish brat.

Mom laughs, but there's a sadness behind her eyes, and I know what's coming. "It's hard enough for most of us to let down our walls. But you, Keeley—you've had so many reasons to build yours out of steel. Don't let something as meaningless as age and labels stop you from finding that great love you truly deserve."

I choke back tears, biting my cheeks to stave them off, refusing to get emotional. I've been telling myself for years that I wouldn't let what happened to me shape my future. Turns out, I've been doing it without even realizing.

I suck in a breath as reality sinks in. Sal didn't change things between us by telling me he wanted more. *I* did by not telling him there and then that I wanted it all. He was baring his soul, admitting it was all-or-nothing, and I walked away.

An uncomfortable knot twists in my stomach, and I must physically react because Mom leans forward to grasp my hand.

"What's wrong?"

"I think I'm a lot more messed up than I thought I was." I throw my head back with a fake cry and mom laughs at my expense.

"Oh, Keeley. We all are. You're not special in that regard."

"Good. Any wise words for what I should do?"

"Are you actually going to listen?"

"Maybe. You seem to have your head on straight this time. You didn't make the best choice for your first partner, although I suppose you got three wonderful... one wonderful child out of it, and two that aren't so bad. This time around, you did good. Phil is a keeper."

"He is. But I'm afraid I can't take credit for that one. He did the chasing. You know me. I'd all but given up on love."

"Shut up. No, you hadn't. You were on that dating app for...more established people." I cringe and she laughs again.

"For old people, you mean?"

"Age is just a number, remember?"

"You're right. And I was on that app. But I wasn't looking for *love* if you know what I mean."

"God-fucking-dammit," Easton groans behind me and I spin around so fast, my neck hurts. As fun as it is to see him in pain, I did *not* want to run into him today. "Why? Why are you always talking about things a son should never have to hear?"

"I told you not to visit. Seems like I have two disobedient children."

"Three, actually." Addie walks through the door, and I internally groan. Yay for random family meetups.

"Hi, Addie." Mom waves while I blow out a breath.

"Hi, Mom." Addie darts around Easton and pushes past me to stand next to Mom's head, brushing Mom's hair off her face. "How are you feeling? Are the doctors looking after you? Where's Phil? I thought he was spending the night."

"I'm good. The doctors are great, and Phil wasn't needed here so I sent him home to check on the cat."

I snort at the same time Easton does. Mom doesn't have a cat. She's just trying to amuse herself during one of Addie's "mothering" moments.

"You have a cat? Since when?"

"That's not important. What's important is that I'm good. The doctors are sending me home this morning, so you all wasted your time."

"It's not wasted, Mom." Addie rubs her hand with a sympathetic smile. "We all want to be here."

"I don't," Easton announces, and Mom smiles appreciatively, always preferring honesty. "I hate hospitals and I kind of wish I'd called Phil before I came. Do you want a ride home? I'm heading to the stadium, so I'll be going right past our building."

"That would be great. Can you let Phil know he doesn't have to come in?"

Easton nods as he pulls his phone from his pocket, heading into the hallway. And I take that as my cue to leave.

"I'm going to go, Mom." I stand and squeeze Addie's arm before walking around to the other side of the bed. "I'll stop by later this afternoon. I've got some running around to do."

"Is that code for work or your boss?" Addie bites back a smile and I roll my eyes.

"It's code for running around."

"You owe me lunch. I need to know everything."

"I'll think about it."

"You better call me, bitch. I'm not leaving until we talk."

Dammit. "In that case, lunch today. Twelve o'clock at the Westerley."

"Sounds perfect."

When I turn to Mom, she's biting back a smile of her own, not at all taken aback by our sarcastic banter. "Love you, Mom. Thanks for the chat."

"Anytime. But I'm not the one you should be chatting with."

"I know."

"Good. Love you."

Addie waves exaggeratedly as I walk away, and I smile while screaming inside. I don't want to talk to Addie before talking to Sal, only I have to give her something. I just have to figure out what.

After waving back, I step into the hall and almost bump into Easton coming back inside.

"Sorry." I smile awkwardly while he grunts and moves out of my way, mumbling a sorry in return.

Silence falls between us, and it's so uncomfortable I have to fill it. "I'm heading home. Did you speak to Phil?"

"I did."

"Good. I'll see you later."

I force another smile, and once again, Easton doesn't return it. Not that he's a big smiler, but still… It's obvious from his folded arms and blank stare that he's not happy about being here with me. And I'm not in the headspace to buy into his mood.

I move to step around him until he holds a hand out to stop me.

"We need to talk about what happened." Easton's eyes flash to Mom's room, and I release a soft sigh. I'm sure he's right. But like Mom's constantly telling us, there's nothing we can do. Nothing any of us can do.

"There's not much to say. It's not going to change anything. Nothing either of us say is going to make a difference."

Addie calls out to Easton before he has the chance to respond, so I shrug and gesture for him to go inside, then walk away.

I'm happy Mom's okay. I just wish there was more we could do to stop this from happening again.

Should I have talked to Easton about it? Probably.

Can I handle dealing with him right now, knowing that he's only speaking to me because Mom's in the hospital? No.

I'll talk to him about it another day.

For now, I need to talk to Sal.

But first, I need to decide what the hell I'm going to say.

Chapter Thirty-Eight

SALVATORE

The boardroom boasts a similar view to my office, and I find myself staring out the window, lost in my head. The board members—the ones I rallied together after taking ownership of the team—are discussing the legal ramification of us suing the former owner over the release of his book. It's an important discussion that I should be paying attention to, and yet, I'm acting like a brat that inherited a business while knowing nothing about business in general, letting them handle the tough decisions.

"Does that sound like a good compromise, Sal?"

Fuck if I know. "As long as it keeps the team out of the spotlight, I'm happy."

Bryan, two-time Super Bowl champion for the Storm—who played when I was a kid—eyes me suspiciously. I recruited him for the board after hearing how much he's supported the team over the years. At first, I couldn't understand why he wasn't already on the board since he was a brilliant businessman in his own right before he retired. But after looking into the team's finances, I knew. Gregory didn't want brilliant businessmen or women on his board. He wanted yes people, or those that didn't look too closely at the bullshit he was pulling behind their backs.

"Sorry, Bryan. As you know, my daughter got married yesterday, and her husband's mother collapsed during the reception. I've been a little preoccupied, but I'm with you."

Megan, one of my board members from New York, gasps from the video screen, her hand flying to her face. "I'm so sorry, Sal. Is she okay?"

"She's in the hospital, but she's doing well." Guilt eats away at me. I'm worried about Rochelle; that's not a lie. Only, it's Keeley that has me distracted.

I messaged her last night to make sure she got home safe—despite the fact that I may have had Jeffrey follow her so I could see it for myself—and her reply was curt.

She'd texted, "I'm inside. Talk soon."

Talk soon? I didn't want to talk soon. I wanted to talk that second, to beg her to tell me where we go from here, because I'm at a loss.

Easton may be pissed, but Paige seems to be okay with us. And when is Easton not shitty about something? It's out there now, so I figure if I talk to him about it, man-to-man, I might be able to make him accept us.

But does Keeley want that?

I thought she did, until her complete one-eighty at the end of the night.

And I'm unraveling again. *God-fucking-dammit.*

"Can you please run through the plan again, Bryan? I'm all ears. Let's ensure that asshole gets all that he deserves."

We discuss attempting a cease and desist order, despite the fact that I don't think it will work considering he doesn't name anyone specifically, and by the time I get back to my office after two hours, I'm done.

I've just sat down when my phone rings, making me groan until I see that it's Paige.

"Paige. Hi," I rush out, answering as though I'm desperate to speak to her. Probably because I am. She may have been okay when I said goodbye last night, but that doesn't mean she's not pissed off with me now that she's had time to think about it all.

"Hi, Dad. How are you?"

"Better now. I've been wanting to call you all morning, only I wasn't sure it was a good idea."

"Easton's visiting Rochelle."

"How is she?"

"She's good. He just texted to say he's taking her home."

I sigh in relief, a little of the tension releasing from my shoulders. "That's good. How are you?"

"I'm good too. My feet are killing me from dancing, but I'm happy."

Happy is good.

"What a night. It didn't end the way any of us would have expected, but it was a beautiful wedding, Paige."

"It was beautiful, wasn't it? Though, I feel awful thinking about it. It was nice to have everyone together and enjoy themselves before..." She trails off and my heart breaks for her.

"You're allowed to be happy, Paige. You just got married. *Fuck*... my baby just got married." I groan jokingly and Paige laughs, as I hoped she would.

"That's right. It happened. Despite having such poor role models when it comes to relationships."

I relax at her teasing tone, hoping that means she still feels the same as she did last night.

"I'm happy you were able to see past our mistakes. I'm proud of you, Paige."

"For getting married?"

"No. For the incredible woman and mother you've become."

"Thanks, Dad. I'm not sure I would have chosen this path if I hadn't found Easton and Isaac, but I've never been happier."

And there's the perfect segue...

"Speaking of Easton... How is he?"

Paige laughs, and I shudder at the sound, anticipating what's coming. "Depends on what you're asking."

"You know what I'm asking."

"He's...processing. He knew the two of you were friends, but I guess he hadn't seen what the rest of us had."

The what? "What did you see?"

"The way you look at each other. I've been waiting for one of you to admit something was going on. I just didn't expect it to be so public."

"It's not like we kissed in the middle of the dance floor."

"Oh, I know." Her laughter softens, and I wish I was there to have this discussion in person. Until she adds, "It was way more intimate than that."

"Shit."

"Don't stress about it. Easton will come around."

"There's nothing to come around to." *Not yet.*

"Okay, Dad. Keep telling yourself that."

"Thanks, I will."

"God, you're hopeless. Talk to her."

"I've gotta go. I've got a call waiting."

"And you wonder how I knew you had feelings for Keeley. You're the worst liar."

"I don't know what you're talking about."

"Daaad."

"Okay. Okay. What can I do to help with Easton? Do you think I should talk to him?"

"Only if you have a death wish."

"Jesus." I mouth the word fuck and run a hand through my hair, blowing out a breath.

"I'm kidding. Talking to him is a good idea. Just give him a couple of days to cool off."

"A couple of days. Got it."

Paige giggles while I close my eyes. "Will you be home later today?" she asks, making me perk up.

"I will."

"Good. I can bring Isaac around if you like?"

"I'd love that. I'm heading home in the next hour."

"Good. I'll see you later on."

"Thanks, Paige."

"Love you, Dad."

"Love you too, Kid."

I hang up and blow out another breath before collapsing into my desk chair and staring at my computer screen for the next twenty minutes.

When it's apparent I'm not going to get anything done, I call Jeffrey to come and pick me up, deciding to call Keeley on the way.

After settling in the back seat, my finger hovers over her name, contemplating driving over there instead, when my phone starts ringing.

"Daniel, is everything okay?"

My chief operating officer sighs loudly, and I preemptively close my eyes, preparing for the bad news undoubtedly coming my way. "We're being shut down for unsafe practices on the Chamberland site. We have to stop work until the New York City Department of Buildings has conducted a full investigation."

"You've got to be fucking kidding me. In my twenty years of business, we have never even come close to a violation, let alone unsafe practices. Do you know who reported us? Have you spoken to Lyle?"

Lyle's our project manager on the Chamberland project and our most trustworthy employee. There is no way he'd let that happen.

"We don't know. But Lyle's taking the blame. He said he hired two new staff recently and caught them having secret talks on a few occasions, despite claiming they didn't know each other. The only reason he's not convinced it was them is because they turned up for work this morning."

Alarm bells ring in my mind, and I pray that I'm wrong. "When did he hire them?"

Daniel falls silent for a beat before cursing under his breath. "A few days before the fire at the Toddville site."

"Fuuck. Not that I ever questioned it, but this isn't Lyle's fault. It's mine. I'm on my way."

"You don't have to come here. I didn't call you for that."

"I know you didn't. I have to put a stop to this."

"How?"

"I'm not sure yet."

After ending the call, I stare out the window, trying to remain calm while inside I'm fuming. Unsafe work practices? Bull-fucking-shit. I hate to think it, but Camilla may have been right. We're being targeting by the fucking Mikklesons. It has to be.

The second Jeffrey pulls up to the curb by my building, I'm out of the car, waving him off when he steps out to open my door, beating him to it. "I'll be back in thirty minutes; can you please wait? I need to get to the airport fast."

"Of course. I'll be here."

I thank him as I run inside, and I've just made it to the lobby when Easton steps out of the elevator, his eyes wide when he spots me.

Just what I need.

I force a grin as he walks closer, silently cursing the world for putting him in my path.

"Easton." I nod when he reaches me, hoping he'll nod back and be on his way. We have to talk. I know that. This isn't the best way to begin our new life as official in-laws, but as Paige said, today is not the day. He's still processing, and I'm so worked up I'm likely to say something I regret, and that's not helpful for anyone.

"I didn't plan on running into you. But since you're here..." He trails off and I almost groan.

"We have to clear the air, I know. For Paige and Keeley's sake, but—"

"No buts," Easton cuts me off, and I pause momentarily before pleading my case.

"I'm not trying to get out of this, I just—"

"Have you thought about how a future with Keeley would look?" He talks over me again and I suck in a breath, remaining calm. A less patient man might have told him to stop being a dick. Not me though. Because I can't deny that he makes a valid point, and I appreciate the fact that he's looking after his sister.

"Yes, I've thought about it. A lot. The thing is...Keeley and I aren't officially together, Easton. We're—"

"So, you've spoken about kids and marriage?" This time when he interrupts me, I pause for an entirely different reason, feeling nauseous as he throws my biggest concern back in my face. "She's thirty-three. She has her whole fucking life ahead of her."

"Do you think I don't know that? Do you seriously think that I'd fuck around with your sister, my daughter's best friend, my colleague *without* thinking about the consequences?"

"She's not your colleague. You're her boss. How's that going to look? Half the football team was there last night."

"I was consoling a friend."

"Really? A friend?"

"Yes. That's exactly what I was doing."

"If that's true, then as her *friend*, I want you to pretend you just found out she was falling for a man twenty years older than her. What advice would you give?"

His words hit me like a blow to the stomach, and I physically wince.

"Paige seems to think you're in love with her," he continues, and this time it's more like a knife, the pang in my middle excruciating. "If that's true, then please, I beg you, think about her future and what she'd be giving up if things progressed between you."

He twists the knife, cutting me deeper, and it makes me want to vomit.

"You're a good brother, Easton." I smile through the pain. "I understand you're trying to protect Keeley, I do. I want to protect her too. But Keeley's a strong woman who has never let anyone make decisions for her. We have to trust that if she wants a relationship with anyone, she knows what she's doing."

I hope. Though I'm not entirely convinced.

Easton stares at me for a beat before nodding his head and walking toward the front door, denying me a response to my passionate plea. Does that nod mean he agrees, or that he's decided us talking is a lost cause? I stare after him, unable to move until my phone vibrates in my pocket, making me pause.

Fuuuck. I'm an asshole. I'm doing it again. Putting work over everything else.

At the worst possible time.

I shouldn't be leaving without talking to Keeley.

But if I don't go, how much further will the Mikklesons take this?

Chapter Thirty-Nine

KEELEY

I avoid all people for the rest of the morning, and when Addie calls to postpone our lunch—because Mom needs her—I sigh in relief. *And silently thank Mom for getting me out of it.* I have no doubt she lied to help me.

My mind whirs in the silence, so I get up and put on some music, smiling when "Baker Street" is one of the first songs to come on. I added it to my playlist after my night with Sal, and it's the perfect song for wallowing.

Though I shouldn't be wallowing at all. I promised myself I'd call Sal, and I've been putting it off. Despite the fact that he's called me twice.

The song changes, this time to Britney Spears's "Toxic" and I burst out laughing, picturing Sal's face if I told him this was one of the five songs I think *he'd* like.

My conversation with my mom comes back to mind, and a shiver runs through me. I was always the one telling Sal it wasn't a big deal—that our relationship and the age gap between us *wasn't* a big deal—and now I'm the one second-guessing everything.

Except my feelings. They haven't changed.

When he calls a third time, I take in a deep breath and sit down on the couch, curling my feet up underneath me.

"Hi," I answer softly, maybe a little more hesitantly than I normally would when it comes to Sal.

He sighs in relief, rushing out a "thank god," not bothering to hide how affected he is by me not answering his calls.

"I'm sorry. I—"

"You have nothing to be sorry about. How's your mom, now that she's home?"

"She's good. She wants everything to return to normal, and for us all to stop checking in on her."

"That sounds like Rochelle." There's a slight smile in his voice, but when he speaks again, it's gone.

"I have to go to New York. Only I don't want to go until I've seen you. Are you home?"

"You have to go to New York?"

"I do." My chest tightens until I realize that's probably a good idea. It will give us both a chance to think about how we want to move forward from here. I want Sal in my life, that much I know. It's the *how* that has my stomach in knots.

It's easy to tell myself I don't care what anyone thinks about me, or our relationship, but when those people are my friends, my colleagues, my *family*, it's harder to ignore.

"It's the worst fucking timing. There's an issue with one of my sites and I have to meet with lawyers and—"

"Lawyers? Is everything okay?"

"It will be. But we need to talk first. Can—"

"You should go. We can talk when you get back. Nothing is going to change between now and then. In fact, things may be better. They might have settled down a little."

"Keeley, I—"

"Please, Sal. D'Angelo Construction is important. How long will you be gone for? A week?"

"A couple of days, at most."

"There you go. You'll be back before anyone's even moved on from the gossip." I wince at the words coming out of my mouth, but it's the truth. We'll be a hot topic for a while; I have no doubt.

Sal's quiet for a beat until he clears his throat. "I'm coming over."

"What?"

"I'm coming over."

"Sal." I laugh. "You're being crazy. I'll be here when you get back. I promise. You have to go." I refuse to be a woman who holds back her man.

"I'm already pulling up out front. Let me up when they buzz you. Okay?"

I close my eyes while my heart beats frantically in my chest.

"Okay."

"Thank you."

I hang up to a slew of texts, one from Callum, checking in, and the rest from the girls in our group chat.

HAYLEY: Hi Keeley. Now that you've had a night of peace, I have to ask... Do you have something to tell us?

The girls all messaged last night asking about my mom, and I was surprised when none of them mentioned Sal. Now I understand.

AMELIA: Leave her alone. She'll tell us when she's ready

HAYLEY: Of course. Tell us when you're ready. As long as it's soon

BLAIR: Take your time, we're all here to talk if you need us

HAYLEY: The guys' chat is blowing up too. Blair's right. We're all here

HAYLEY SENT A PHOTO

KEELEY'S SUPPORT GROUP

LUKE: Did you know about that, Zane? Is that what you've been keeping quiet about?

ZANE: Hell no. I told you all. I knew nothing

DYLAN: I'm missing something

EASTON LEFT THE GROUP

LUKE: I'll add him back in soon. First, Keeley and D'Angelo are a thing

DYLAN: I don't really know him that well, but I can see it

REED: We should all be saying congratulations and leaving them alone

LUKE: Jesus, Reed. Chill. I'm only talking about it because of the group chat name. I'm happy for them

REED: Good

LUKE ADDED EASTON TO THE GROUP

I groan, burying my face into my hands. That was not the best way for everyone to find out about Sal and me. And I can't help but notice that Paige wasn't part of that group chat. She seemed okay last night. I have to wonder, is that still the case this morning? After she's had a chance to think it through or talk to Easton.

My intercom buzzes, and I stare at the machine on the wall before pressing the button to let Sal in, slowly walking toward the door. I hover in the entry, pacing anxiously, until he knocks.

With my hand curled around the handle, I take a deep breath before opening the door, and the second I see Sal, all of my pain, all of my insecurities, instantly melt away. He's like an off switch for my mind. When he's around, the noise disappears.

"Sal." His name leaves my mouth on a breath and I throw myself into his arms. He catches me easily, sighing into my hair.

"Thanks for letting me up."

With a rushed laugh, I step back and stare into his smiling eyes, shaking my head. "Did you think I wouldn't?"

"It crossed my mind. I wasn't sure where your head was at after yesterday."

"I'm not sure either. But I'm working on it." I gesture for Sal to come inside, and he grabs my hand as he walks past, shutting the door behind him.

"Talk to me, Keels. Let me help."

"Is that your way of saying that *your* head is all clear?"

"God, no." Sal comically winces and I huff out a soft laugh. "There's still so much we have to work through, so much to say. But when I saw you upset, none of that mattered. I wanted to be the guy you turned to. The guy to help you through it. Basically, there was no way in hell I was letting Luke pull you into his arms."

I snort, rolling my eyes. "He's married."

"Doesn't make a difference. At that moment, it had to be me."

"Good. Because you're the only one I needed. I'm not sure what I would have done if you hadn't come back inside."

Sal smiles before he gently cups my cheeks, angling my face toward him as he slowly glides his thumb over my cheek. "We made a mess of things, huh?"

"At least they all found out at once."

"Very true." He chuckles and the familiar sound warms me, while my chest fills with regret.

"I shouldn't have walked away last night," I admit, holding my breath as I wait for his response.

"And I shouldn't have let you leave. We're both idiots."

"What do we do from here?"

"First, I'm going to kiss that beautiful mouth of yours and then..."

"Then?"

"How about we agree to work through this mess together?"

"That's probably a good idea. We do work better as a team. First, back to the *kissing*."

Sal's lips curl into a delicious smirk seconds before his hands sink into my hair, and he leans down, pressing his lips to mine.

I melt at his touch, my lips parting on a sigh. A groan rumbles in the back of his throat and he increases the pressure, his mouth molding with mine, the feel of him all-consuming.

Sal does many things well, but his kisses are pure perfection. He kisses with passion, sending a spark of ecstasy through to my core, as he walks me back toward the wall.

My body hits the plaster and we both pause, breaths ragged as our gazes lock. "God, I wish I could take you to bed. But I don't have enough time to worship you like you deserve."

"I'm okay with a quickie."

"I'm not. Not for our first time. And definitely not before we've talked."

I smile before pulling him back into me, not at all surprised that we won't be taking things further tonight. That just adds to Sal's appeal.

Doesn't mean I'm ready to stop.

"I'll let you be a gentleman tonight, but you better kiss me like your life depends on it. Leave me desperate for more, counting down the seconds until you come home."

Sal's eyes widen, but I don't get the chance to ask why before his mouth descends again, his tongue tracing my lips as he seeks entry. Entry I easily grant him.

Our tongues swirl, and the feeling of warmth dances through my veins, lighting me up from my head to my toes, making them curl into the carpet.

Sal growls against me before his tongue disappears and he gently sucks my lip into his mouth, releasing me as I sigh.

He kisses the corner of my mouth, my cheek, my jaw, making his way down my neck with a fiery possession, burning a path across my skin.

I mewl as my breath quickens, tightening my hold on his shirt, pulling him closer until there's barely a space between us.

"I don't want to stop," I whisper as he nibbles on my shoulder, his hands curling into my hair.

"I'm not stopping," he rasps against my skin, the vibrations making me shiver while I laugh.

"You have to, remember?"

"No."

"Sal."

"No."

His phone vibrates once against me, and I jump at the feeling, my legs clenching as my body begs for more.

"You have to go."

"One more minute." He's barely finished speaking when his phone buzzes again, this time more incessant, a call rather than a text.

"Do you have a minute?" I ask with a giggle, and he pauses his kisses as he growls. He stands tall and checks his watch, cursing under his breath.

"Not really."

"Then go. It's only a few days, right? We can talk when you get back."

"Talk?" He raises an eyebrow knowing that's not what I meant.

"Among other things."

"Okay. I'm going. I—" He cuts himself off before pressing a chaste kiss to my lips. "Talk to you later?" He smiles, but there's an edge to it, a nervousness he doesn't need.

"Yes, please. Call me when you get there."

Something shifts in his eyes and I laugh. "Come on. You know I'm a mother type. I'm like this with all the guys." Sal's face drops for a split second before he forces a chuckle.

"Very true. I'll call you when I get there."

"In your private jet?"

"On the commercial flight Tabitha booked while I was on the way here."

"Boo. You're no fun."

"Do you want me to buy a jet, Keeley?"

"God, no. What a waste."

Sal chuckles again before pressing another kiss to my head, then my nose, and my mouth. "Bye, Keeley."

"Bye, Sal."

With another parting kiss, he leaves, and I couldn't wipe the smile off my face if I tried.

Maybe this is all going to work out okay.

My phone chimes from the kitchen, and I smile as I jog to check it, breathing a sigh of relief when I see that it's Paige.

PAIGE: Any chance you're free to meet for dinner tomorrow?

If that isn't code for "we need to talk" then I don't know what is.

KEELEY: Of course. Where were you thinking?

PAIGE: Second Chapter at seven?

KEELEY: I'll be there

PAIGE: Thanks Keeley. I appreciate it

She appreciates it? I'm the one that should be grateful. As if I was going to say no. It's time to tell her the truth. That I'm falling for her dad.

Chapter Forty

SALVATORE

My flight lands thirty minutes later than planned, so by the time I get to my apartment, it's a little after nine p.m. in San Francisco.

I'm about to pour myself a glass of whiskey, guilt swirling around me for canceling on Paige and Isaac, when I remember Keeley's request...and her subsequent reasoning. *"You know I'm a mother type."*

To think I basically told Easton to get fucked when he questioned me about my future with Keels, and he wasn't wrong to ask. She *is* a mother type. She cares for every one of those guys on the team, she looks after Isaac, and her eyes light up every time she sees him. I don't want more kids. I couldn't imagine chasing after a two-year-old in my fifties.

And on top of that, I can't have them. Camilla made me have a vasectomy the second we had Marc. It should be a no-brainer to stay away from Keeley.

I'm not even great with my grandkid. I was supposed to be home for Paige to bring Isaac around today but I failed her again. I'm not cut out for this.

The problem is that when I imagine my fifties, Keeley's there, by my side where she should be. *Fuck*. We should have talked about this before I left.

No, I *shouldn't have left.*

Since it's late, I text Keeley instead of calling, massaging my temples before pouring my drink.

SALVATORE: I'm here safe.

My phone lights up before I've had the chance to open the bottle of Macallan, and when I read Keeley's reply, I frown.

KEELEY: Where is 'here'?

SALVATORE: New York.

I swear I told her where I was going.

My phone rings, and my heart jolts at the sight of Keeley's name flashing back at me. I have so much to say, so many questions to ask, but I want to talk to her face-to-face.

If I wasn't certain she'd say no, I'd send Jeffrey to pick her up and arrange for her to fly here. In fact, if I was able to think straight around her these days, I would have brought her with me.

"Keeley," I answer, attempting to keep my tone light.

"You don't send check-in messages that often, do you?"

I pause before answering, trying to recall the last time I told anyone I'd arrived somewhere safely. And it hits me.

"Never."

"What do you mean, never?"

"I don't think I've ever sent one."

"Not even to Camilla?"

"Definitely not." She requested it. Often. My stomach knots as memories assault my mind. I was always too busy to remember, and in the end, she gave up asking.

"That explains it." Keeley cuts into my thoughts.

"Explains what?"

"Why you gave me such little information. It's quiet, so I'm assuming you're not on the tarmac or in the airport. Are you home?"

"Sorry, yes. I'm home. In my apartment. Safe and sound."

"Good. Thank you for letting me know."

"Have you been sitting up waiting?" My lips curl into a smirk as I picture her waiting by the phone until she scoffs.

"It's only nine p.m."

"True, but aren't you exhausted after last night? Since you missed your Nanna night for the wedding, I thought you might swap it to tonight."

Keeley laughs. "I should have. I can't believe you remembered that."

I remember everything when it comes to you.

"How could I forget? I've still got the visual you painted in my mind. An image of you curled up in an armchair, plaid pajamas on, a mug of hot tea in your hands, your legs covered by a hand-knitted blanket."

"Wow. Close. Only, it's summer, so I'm wearing silk pajamas and I have a glass of Merlot in my hand. No blanket. But while we're on the topic of a blanket, I don't own a hand-knitted one, and now I kind of want to."

"Do you know anyone that knits?"

"No, but I'm more than happy to buy one."

"Good idea. Are you reading or watching mindless TV?"

"I'll have you know I'm watching something incredibly intellectual."

"Oh, yeah?"

"Yes. It's a true crime documentary."

"You too? Camilla was hooked on those things, and what the fuck am I doing?"

I groan while Keeley bursts out laughing. "You're allowed to talk about her. I promise I'll only get a little bit jealous."

"You'll what?" My heart jolts, and I'm not sure if it's because I feel bad or like the fact that she's jealous. It's a little of both. Only, surely, she's joking.

"You heard what I said. Does that surprise you?"

"Yes. You have nothing to be jealous about. Camilla and I have been over for a decade."

"Doesn't mean you don't still have feelings for her."

"You're right. Time doesn't change that. Finding someone else does."

"I was kidding. It's okay. It's just a lot of history to compete with."

"There's no competition. And kidding or not, I want to make something *very* clear. I thought I'd always love Camilla. Our relationship ended before I was ready for it to end, and we have children together. I see her in Paige's eyes almost every single day. I also thought I was done with love and relationships after her. I was wrong. On both counts. I will always care about Camilla as the mother of my children, but that love faded the second I developed feelings for you."

Keeley gasps and I curse internally. We should be having this conversation in person.

"I hate that you're so far away, Keeley. And that alone is proof that my feelings for you are real. My business is in an actual crisis, and I'm thinking about *you*. Actually, not just thinking about you—seriously contemplating forcing you to come here."

"Forcing me?"

"Yes. Would it work?"

"I'm not sure. But you have my interest piqued. What would forcing me sound like? I bet it's hot."

"*Keel-ley*," I warn. "That's not helping."

"You started it."

"I know. Sorry. I'm being selfish. I want you here because I want to talk, and for the first time in my life, I actually want to be distracted from work. But that's not exactly fair."

"We can talk now. Although, something tells me you're the kind of guy that wants to do that in person."

I almost laugh. My thoughts exactly. "I am. But only because I want to make sure we're both honest and open with one another. It's easier to pretend over the phone."

"I agree. So let me help with the distraction then. That I can definitely do over the phone."

"Oh, yeah?" I chuckle to myself. "I'd like that. So, tell me, how was your day?"

Keeley laughs out loud, and it's a good thirty seconds before she stops. "Mr. D'Angelo. Sir. Please tell me you did *not* think I meant I was going to distract you with boring talk about my day?"

Fuck, when she calls me Sir, I want to throw her over my knees. She knows exactly what she's doing. "How are you going to distract me then?"

"Phone sex."

"What?" I choke on the word as my cock instantly hardens. How did I not see that coming? Oh, that's right, I haven't had sex in years. "Ahh..." I scratch my neck as I try not to picture Keeley naked. Though, naked or not, I want her here. Now.

"Ahh, what?"

"How about I arrange for Jeffrey to pick you up? You could be here by early morning. You won't even miss work. You can call into your meetings from my office tomorrow."

Keeley giggles softly, and the sounds don't help my cause as my cock twitches. "That's too long. It's too late for that."

"Too late?"

"The idea's already in my head. It's happening."

Fuuck. "Okay."

"Okay?"

Jesus. I don't even know what I'm saying.

"Have you ever had phone sex before?"

"I can't say I have." I suck in a breath as I laugh. Not only have I not had it, I've never even thought about it.

"Why not?" Keeley asks, her voice inquisitive while seemingly free of judgment.

"I don't know. I guess it just never came up."

"Is it up now?"

I snort and choke at the same time, while Keeley's voice remains even. I can imagine the smile on her face, and it brings about my own.

"It's getting there. What are you doing?"

"I think we should try it. What better way to take your mind off what's happening?"

"You might be right. I don't know... Maybe we should wait until I'm home in a few days."

"Why?"

Because the idea of not being there when you come is not sitting well with me. I want to taste you, tease you, fuck you for the first time. "I'd just prefer to be there with you."

"You are here. You'll be talking me through it. Let me try, and if you don't like it, we'll stop."

If I don't like it? I doubt that's going to be an issue. I'd still rather be with her in person.

"I—" A thought hits me and I pause, an irrational jealousy coursing through me. "Have *you* had phone sex before?"

My chest burns as I wait for a response.

"No."

"No?" *Thank God.*

"I want you to be my first."

Fuuuck. My cock swells even more, pressing against the zipper of my dress pants, making me unbearably uncomfortable. I wish I'd been all her goddamn firsts. But I never considered this.

"Please," she whispers after I've been silent for too long and I blurt, "Yes," so quickly her laughter fills the air.

"Thank you. Are you sitting somewhere comfortable? Or lying down?" she asks before I hear a muffled sound over the line.

"Are you? Where are you?" Is that what's happening? Is she getting comfortable now?

"Where do you want me?"

Holy fuck. "I don't know."

"You don't? Come on, where?"

"Not the bed," I rush out, the request sounding more demanding than I mean for it to sound. I want to be there the first time she comes with me on a bed. I want my cock buried deep inside her. I want to be staring into her eyes.

"Okay. No bed." Keeley's breath picks up speed, her words coming out a little frantic, and the sound is like a switch going off for me. I want to hear more. "Where—"

"In your armchair," I tell her. "Feet planted on the edge with your legs spread." The visual hits my mind as I say the words, and I have to fight not to palm my cock over my pants as it begs for action.

"Okay." Keeley hisses under her breath and it doesn't help my situation. "I want you on the couch, pants off, briefs around your ankles."

Jesus Christ. Instead of doing as she asked, I finally pour myself a drink, watching the brown liquid swirl around my glass.

"Are you ready?" Keeley asks, amusement in her tone.

"Yep." My eyes flash to the couch as the lie leaves my lips. I'm not sure I'll ever be ready.

"Liar." Keeley calls me out. "You have to be able to follow instructions for this to work."

"I've never been good at following instructions. I'm better at giving them."

"Well, okay then. Let's hear it."

"What?"

"I want you to take the lead, *Sir*. It's what you're good at."

Goddammit. I walked right into that one. "How about I delegate? I'll be good. Tell me again. What do you want me to do?"

"I want you sitting on the couch, pants off, with your briefs around your ankles."

"Okay." This time I at least walk in the direction of the couch and sit down. My pants, however, stay firmly in place.

"Done."

"Good. Now close your eyes."

"Done," I lie again.

"Sal."

"Yes, Keeley." My voice is even, in control, and I'm thankful for that.

"Close your eyes. No more bullshitting me. For this to work, you have to be in the moment."

Fuck. I chuckle lightly. "How did you know?"

"I know *you*. You have me where you want me. I have you where I want you. It's time to relax and forget we're on the other side of the country from one another."

That gets my attention. "I have you where I want you?"

"You do. Hang on."

She falls silent, and a few seconds later my phone buzzes with a text. "Fuck, Keels. Was that you?"

"Was what me?"

"Oh. Never mind."

I check the screen and cough when I find an image from Keeley.

"Wait," she rushes out, her whispered voice holding an edge. "Before you click on it, I want you to know. I've never done that before either." Her voice wavers and my stomach knots.

"You don't have to do anything you don't want to do, Keels. Not with me."

"I know. I've never once doubted that. Which is why I want to. You can open it."

God, now it's my turn to get nervous. I open her text, waiting as the image loads and—

"Holy fuuuck, Keels." The image is taken in the mirror, with Keeley positioned exactly as I asked her to be—in her armchair, feet on the edge, legs spread. And while I'm only just realizing I never specified what I wanted her to wear, she's in see-through lace panties and a matching lace bra. "God, you're beautiful."

"Beautiful isn't what I was going for but thank you."

"You're goddamn sexy too, if that's what you were hoping I'd notice."

"It was. And now that you know I'm not lying, are you ready?"

"I am." *At least, I'm ready to hear you screaming my name.*

"Good. I want you to unzip your pants."

Fuck. I chuckle under my breath and do as she asked, finally unzipping my pants to ease the tension, while leaving my briefs on. This is about her. Not me. "Done."

"Good, now imagine me kneeling in front of you."

"No." *I have a better idea.*

"No?"

"I'm the one on my knees, Keeley. With my palms spread across your thighs, I'm gliding a path toward your center, pushing your knees into the arms of the chair."

"Oh *God*."

"*Sal*," I remind her, and her breath hitches before she whispers my name, the sound traveling from my ears to my cock.

"*Sal*."

I bite back a groan as my eyes lock on Keeley's photo, imagining myself kneeling in front of her.

"Can you feel my thumbs brushing against your panties? Running circles over the soaked material, while your hips buck? Tell me, are you wet for me, Keels?"

"So. Fucking. Wet."

Her punctuated words are like tugs on my length. I feel her as if she's here with me, and my head spins.

"I need more, Sal. Please."

I let myself relax, lying back with my head against the backrest, my eyes drifting shut with the visual of Keeley still in my mind, my fingers wrapped around her legs, my thumbs working her core.

"I want you to move your panties to the side, Keels. Give me the access I need to run my thick fingers through your slit, working you from your clit to your entrance, back and forth. Slowly teasing."

"Yes. More. Yes." Her voice comes out breathy, and my cock jolts as pre cum pools on my tip, making me wriggle uncomfortably.

"I want to massage your clit; I want to feel that little bud harden for me while I dip a finger inside you."

"Yes. Fuck. I need to touch you. I need your cock in my hand."

Dammit. The visual attacks my mind and I release my cock, wrapping my palm around my shaft as it thickens in my hand, my restraint out the fucking window.

"Your fingers feel so good inside me, Sal. But I want another. I need three."

Fuuck. My grip around my length tightens but I don't pump. Not yet. I need more from Keeley.

"God, you feel good, Keels. The way your pussy is sucking me in, taking my fingers with ease."

"Yes," she moans, her breathing ragged, and I can't hold back any longer. I run my cock through my hand, brushing my palm over the tip in time with her breaths.

"Can you feel me pumping into you?" I ask as I pump myself harder. "Feel my thumb rubbing your clit, faster." *Fuck*. "Harder." *Fuck. Oh God*.

"Don't stop, Sal. I'm so close. I want you to curl your fingers, please."

"Do it. Now." I barely get the words out before my balls tighten.

"Jesus. Yes. God. Thank you. I'm… *Jesus*." Unlike me, Keeley is able to give a play-by-play, and with each visual, she puts me closer to the edge. "Your cock is throbbing in my hand, Sal. I wish I could taste you. Are you close?"

"Mm-hmm," I grate with my teeth clenched, no longer able to speak at all. Keeley's soft frantic mewls have me in a choke hold, and I'm about to come all over my goddamn clothes.

"Yes. I'm…" Keeley cries out in ecstasy and I allow myself to follow, my release shooting onto my shirt, coating me as I shudder.

"Fuuck. Keeley." I sigh as I come back down to earth, listening intently to her breathing. "You're making me act like a fucking teenager again." I groan, covering my face with my hand. "You know that, right?"

"Well, they do say that age is merely a number."

"So I've heard." Keeley giggles and I huff out a laugh, well and truly distracted.

"Thanks for the help."

"Anytime. But next time, I want to be able to see you. Maybe we can FaceTime." Her voice holds a lightness to it that wasn't there before. Too bad I can't agree with her.

"Next time we're going to be in bed." It's a demand, not a request, and the tone of my voice reflects that. Not that it affects Keeley.

"We'll see." I picture her shrugging, and laugh until I see the state I'm in, groaning again.

"I need to clean up."

"Me too. Have a good sleep, Sal."

"You too, Keeley. Sleep tight."

I'm going to fucking miss you if you decide to walk away.

Chapter Forty-One

KEELEY

After going to bed with a smile on my face, I woke up with a goddamn conscience and a small amount of guilt. As much as I loved the phone sex with Sal last night, I'm pretty sure I was once again deflecting from having to talk about my feelings.

Sal may have said he wanted to be face-to-face to talk about us, but there was a chance that general chitchat would lead to deeper conversations about feelings, and while I know I'm developing feelings for Sal, something keeps stopping me from admitting to it.

All that aside, I do *not* regret where I took things instead. I almost lost my mind. The way he took over, I could feel him there, as though it were his fingers inside me.

And when he lost control. My God.

I could tell he was restraining himself and refusing to play along. Which only made it that much hotter when he did.

His sounds alone almost sent me over the edge.

A soft pang settles around my middle and I sigh. *Dammit.* I fucking miss him. He's been gone less than twenty-four hours and I want him back.

My day drags as though time is standing still, and by the time dinner comes around, I'm feeling even more guilty and nervous, now that I have to face Paige. What do I even tell her if she asks me what's going on?

Since Second Chapter is a short walk from Paige and Easton's and my mom's apartment building, I stop by her place before I go, needing to confirm she's still okay, despite her telling me several times that she is.

I would have stopped by earlier, only I was in "avoid Addie" mode, and like a chicken, I waited until I knew she'd gone home.

I'm a few minutes late by the time I make it to the restaurant and I'm shocked to find Paige already waiting for me.

"You're never on time," I tease her as I sit down, my nose practically inside my bag as I look for the invitation Mom gave me to pass along.

"And you're never late." She laughs.

"I know, sorry. Mom wanted me to give you this." My fingers curl around the end of the envelope and I pull it out, cringing at the crinkled state it's in. "Sorry."

"Ahh, the invitation to Addie's Thanksgiving party."

"You knew about it?"

"I did. We ran into her in the lobby this morning."

Then why the freaking written invitation? "Most people just call their family members, but Addie's a different breed. It's August, for God's sake."

"She's getting organized."

"*I'm* organized. Addie's making sure no one has a chance to find an excuse not to attend."

"Easton already said no."

"At least his excuse is legitimate. I'm not sure 'I've got a meeting' is going to cut it for me. I wish I could play professional football."

"You haven't checked the date, have you?"

"It's Thanksgiving, right?" I haven't even opened my invitation; I was pissed that she didn't mention it to me the many times we talked, instead of making Mom do her dirty work.

"She's hosting the party on the Monday before. Easton has no excuse."

"What?" I bark out a laugh, picturing Easton's face when he found out. "God, she's sneaky. I love her."

"Lucky you do because Easton's not a fan right now."

"I'll bet. But lucky for *her*, he's more pissed off at me."

"Yeah. About that..." She trails off and I frown, preparing to defend myself again.

"I can't—"

"He's here," Paige cuts me off.

"He's what?" I spin around in time to catch the moment Easton spots me across the room, and a little part of me takes pleasure in his discomfort. I know I made a scene at his wedding, but he was a jerk. He should feel like shit.

"He didn't know I'd be here, did he?"

"God, no. He never would have come."

"What does he think he's here for?"

"Date night."

I choke, as something between a snort and a laugh gets caught in my throat. "You two have date nights?"

"That's what you're thinking about right now?"

"Absolutely. I just can't picture it." I smile as Paige huffs under her breath. I guess that explains why she said she'd meet me here instead of her apartment.

Paige glances over my shoulder before she sighs. "God, he's hopeless. Wait here." She jumps up and walks in Easton's direction, leaving me alone, wondering *where am I going to go?*

It's a good five minutes before Easton slumps in the chair next to me, and I bite back a smile at his childish behavior.

"So I fucked your boss. Please tell me how that affects you?" I launch straight into it, and Easton's on his feet so fast that I almost feel bad.

"Sit down," Paige scolds him, pointing to the seat before she adds, "Please."

"I don't have to listen to this. She—"

"Stop. The two of you are sorting your shit out now. Like adults." Her glare shifts my way, and I visibly cringe as I mouth an apology.

"*Paige*," Easton pleads with her and she grabs his hand, visibly calming him when she smiles. I shift uncomfortably in my seat, feeling like a voyeur in their moment.

"*Please*."

Easton nods before Paige turns my way.

"I haven't done anything wrong." She raises her eyebrows and I concede, blowing out a breath. "Fine. I can be an adult."

"Good. Thank you. Do you want to talk alone or—"

"Stay." Easton squeezes her hand. "Please."

"Alrighty."

Easton finally sits down, and silence follows until I can't take it any longer. "I'm sorry I lied."

"That's what you think this is about?"

"It isn't?"

"No. Fuck, no. I'm the last person that can ever call you out for sneaking around."

"Then what?"

"I'm pissed off because you shut me down when I tried to talk to you about it."

"What?" His response pulls me up short. He's upset? I thought he was pissed. I guess I shouldn't be surprised since most of Easton's emotions present themselves the same way. Grumpy. It's his default. Only, I can't for the life of me figure out when he's talking about. "Easton, you walked away at the wedding. Did you think I was going to chase after you?"

"Not then. At the hospital."

"The hospital?" I replay our conversation from yesterday and curse under my breath. "Goddammit, East. You have to be clearer about things. I thought you were talking about Mom."

"Mom?"

"Yes."

"But I said we should talk about what..." Easton trails off as he huffs softly. "Okay. Yep, I can see why you would think that when we were standing right outside of her room."

Paige sinks her hands into her hair and shakes slightly, undoubtedly with laughter.

"So you don't care?" I smile in relief until Easton's eyes widen in surprise.

"Of course I care, Keeley. He's twenty years older than you."

"Not to mention your father-in-law and boss." I throw it all out there. May as well since we're here.

Easton balks. "What? You think *that's* my issue?"

"Isn't it?"

"No. I can't exactly argue with you about off-limits relationships. Like you said, he's my father-in-law *and* boss. And the boss part came first."

"Right. So it's the age difference that bothers you?"

"It doesn't bother me, Keeley. You have it all wrong. Have you thought about how a relationship with Sal would work?"

"No." I roll my eyes to go with my sarcastic tone. Easton doesn't notice, since he's already prepped ready to argue.

"Exactly." He throws his hands into his response as though feeling triumphant for being right. “He’s had kids, and he’s been married. Does he even want those things again?”

“Wait. That’s not... What?” *He’s worried about my future?*

“I don’t want you to get into something that might break your heart, Keeley. Or affect your career. What happens down the line when you realize you want different things and it forces you apart? Are you going to be able to work together? Will you have to leave? Will he?”

Jesus. “We haven’t talked about that yet because things between us are—”

“Casual?”

“Yes.” At least, they were.

My eyes flash to Paige and she glances away awkwardly, clearly wishing she hadn’t stayed.

“It’s not casual, Keeley. At least not to Sal,” Easton says, drawing my attention, my brows furrowed in confusion.

“What do you mean?”

“He didn’t tell you?”

“Tell me what?”

Easton blows out a breath. “I asked him the same questions.”

“You what?” Paige’s eyes widen as though she wasn’t privy to that piece of information, while my chest fills with rage.

“What the fuck, Easton? My future has *nothing* to do with you. We are nowhere near the stage of talking about that stuff. We haven’t even had sex, for God’s sake.”

“Fuck, Keels. I don’t need to hear that.”

Paige cringes and I turn her way to apologize. “Sorry, you didn’t need to hear that either.”

“Definitely not, but I’m working hard to separate it all in my mind. There’s my dad, who’s your boss. Then there’s Sal, your...whatever he is.”

“Thanks.” I smile sympathetically. “I appreciate that.”

“I wish I could say the same,” Easton grumbles. “Only I can’t. And I think you’ll find that Sal agrees with me.”

“What? He didn’t seem that worried when he came to see me on his way to New York.”

Paige and Easton exchange a concerned expression. “That’s good.” She forces a smile.

"What's going on?"

"Nothing—"

"Paige?"

"Okay. The Mikklesons' court case begins next week, and Mom mentioned that she thinks she's being followed because of it."

Jesus. A sharp pang hits me in the stomach.

"And your dad went to protect her?" *Did he lie?*

"God, no." Paige shakes her head, answering my unspoken question. "He's gone to make sure nothing happens to his business. He's already had a few strange occurrences."

"What? He never mentioned that." I frown, confused, until I remember the building fire he rushed back to New York for.

"The fire?"

"Yep. God, I hope nothing else happened."

My chest tightens for Sal as I recall what he said before he left. *"I have a little problem to take care of but I won't be long."*

"Jesus. Poor Sal."

Easton blows out a breath, drawing attention, and my anger at Sal's situation makes me turn on him. "So while all this is going on, you thought it would be a smart idea to add more stress to his plate by telling him I want marriage and kids?"

"I didn't know about the other stuff until after I spoke to him. And that's not exactly what I said."

"What did you say?"

"That he should look at things from an outsider's perspective before taking things further. To ask himself what he'd do if a friend told him she was dating someone much older."

"For fuck's sake, Easton. I don't want marriage *or* kids."

"You don't?"

"No. I never have."

"Okay. That may be true now, but things change."

"Do they?"

"Yes, Paige didn't want marriage or kids either."

"I'm sorry, I wasn't aware that had changed. The kids part, anyway," I snap, and Paige looks my way, her gaze softening. "God, I'm sorry." I physically deflate. "It's the fiery redhead in me."

Paige laughs while Easton groans. I used that many times growing up.

"You have nothing to be sorry about, Keeley. That hasn't changed for me. Nor will it. But I have Isaac. I'm not sure how I would have felt if I didn't have him in my life."

"I'm in a similar situation; I'll have stepkids as well. Two of them. Paige and Marc."

Paige snorts out a laugh while Easton's eyes flash to mine, his expression full of disgust. "It's not the same, Keeley."

"Why not?"

"She's messing with you, Easton."

"I know. It's still wrong."

I blow out a breath and sink back into my chair, putting some distance between us as I prepare to get real. Something Easton and I rarely do with each other. "I don't want my own kids, Easton. I love Isaac, more than I love you, and I couldn't imagine *not* having him in my life. But I don't want that for myself. I never have."

"What if you change your mind? You're still young."

"You're right. I'm young. But that doesn't change my feelings. You don't have to worry about that."

"You can't predict the future, Keeley."

"This isn't a case of me never having given it a thought or suddenly changing my mind. I *know*. With absolute certainty. I was forced to face that reality when I was younger."

"What?" Both Easton and Paige freeze with matching shocked expressions.

"I got pregnant when I was twenty-four. I had a miscarriage at thirteen weeks."

"Fuck, Keeley." Easton's voice breaks a little while Paige's eyes go wide, and I somehow read her mind, shaking my head. It wasn't Vance. But it was another athlete, a guy that decided he was too young for a kid and threw the blame my way.

I was too young for a kid too, only I couldn't walk away like he could. It wasn't an option for me.

"How the hell didn't I know about that?" Easton asks, his tone softer than I think I've ever heard it.

"You were just starting your last year of college. I moved home to stay with Mom and—"

"That's why you moved home?"

"Yep."

"Jesus. Keels. I'm so sorry."

"Don't be. I never told you because it's not something I like talking about. I just needed you to know that I spent months thinking about the prospect of being a mother, and years blaming myself for the loss. I don't want kids. But whether I want them or not, it doesn't change things between me and Sal. We haven't had that conversation because that side of things is new to us. That's like asking someone to talk about their future on the first date."

"I think you should talk to him about it." Paige draws my attention, her voice soft, her expression contemplative.

"About what? Not wanting kids?"

"No. I mean, yes, at some point. If it gets to that. But for now, I think you should talk to him about how serious it is. Because I don't remember ever seeing my dad look at my mom the way he looks at you."

Her words crack my heart wide open, and yet deep down, I think I knew that. I feel it every time his eyes meet mine.

"I—"

"Keeley Reynolds. Is that you?" A deep voice booms from behind me, and I recognize it instantly, making my throat tighten as I try to swallow.

Paige's and Easton's eyes flash to Vance, while I take a second to compose myself and slowly turn around. "Vance. Hi."

"I can't believe you're here. I had a feeling I'd run into you at the stadium, but not before."

What? "The stadium?" I squeeze my fingers around the empty glass in front of me and put on a smile.

"Oh, nothing official. I'm sure you'll find out when the deal's done."

Deal? *Oh, God.*

Vance walks to the empty chair beside me and curls his fingers around the back, huffing out an incredulous laugh. "It's so good to see you. It's been too long."

"A lifetime."

"Yeah. Anyway, I'll leave you to it." He taps the chair a couple of times before stepping back. "I'll be seeing you."

"Bye."

He walks away and I hold my breath, waiting for the calm to set back in. Only it doesn't. My heart races so fast, I feel dizzy.

"Keeley, what's going on?" Easton asks, his brows furrowed with concern.

"Nothing. That was Vance." I replay what he said about a deal, confusion undoubtedly playing on my face. Vance was injured during a preseason game. He was forced to retire. Why... *Shit.* "I think Wes is going to hire him as the new QB coach."

Paige's face pales as her eyes go wide. Easton, on the other hand, nods in understanding. Though he really has no idea.

"I can see that. He was a great QB. It's a shame he had to retire."

Goddammit. I knew he'd retired, but at no point did I ever think Wes would approach him for the coaching position. Although, I should have considered it.

Paige leans forward, and I shake off her concern. I don't need sympathy right now. I need normality.

I can't let him get to me.

I'm better than that.

Chapter Forty-Two

SALVATORE

Fucking Mikklesons. It's them. I know it. They're probably hoping that if they scare me and Camilla enough, she'll pull out of testifying.

But that's never going to happen.

On the outside, Camilla comes across as a well-to-do housewife that couldn't fend for herself if her life depended on it. That's what she likes people to believe. It makes her feel special. As though she's above everyone because she has others to take care of her.

But if someone messes with her kids, she can do more than just fend for herself. Her claws come out and she's taking them down, even if she goes down along with them.

If they think that attacking my business is going to make me put my foot down and demand she retreats, they're sorely mistaken. For one, she wouldn't listen to me. And two, I'm looking forward to the day those fuckers are sentenced to prison. I only wish it was the wives as well as the husbands.

If it was Paige that was testifying, though, it would be a completely different story.

Camilla and I brought this on ourselves. We're the ones that orchestrated their arrest. It makes sense to throw it all our way. Paige had nothing to do with it. All she did was overhear a conversation that set the wheels in motion.

If it was up to me, I would have kept Paige in the dark about all of this until we knew it for sure. The only thing *I* told her is that I have a security detail on her whenever she leaves the house, just in case the media come after her again now that the Mikklesons are back in the spotlight. She didn't need to know they were up to their old tricks, fucking with people's lives in the hope of silencing them.

But of course, Camilla had to play the sympathy card, first with Marc, getting him to move back in with her temporarily—which I'm not entirely opposed to after hearing he was high at Paige's rehearsal. And maybe the wedding. Then she had to include Paige.

She told Paige about the fire, the stalking, *everything*. She clearly has no idea her daughter is as strong-willed as she is, because if anything, that's likely to propel Paige into taking action and offering to testify herself.

Daniel knocks on my office door, his expression weary as I glance up to meet his eyes through the glass. And it's my fault. He doesn't need this right now. None of them do.

"Come in," I call out, waving him in at the same time. "How did it go?" He's just finished a meeting with one of the clients on the Chamberland project, and I could hear the occasional swear word from across the hall. I should have been there, but he insisted I stay away.

"I calmed them down, but we have to cover the costs of the delay and guarantee we'll meet the revised deadline."

"Okay. Good."

"Not really. How can we guarantee that?"

"We can't. But this is my fault, so if for some reason we're delayed again, I'll personally cover the costs to keep them happy."

Daniel rakes a hand through his short, curly hair and sighs. "This isn't on you."

"Actually, it is."

"No, it's on the Mikkleson fuckers. My brother had invested with them. If it wasn't for you and your family, he could have lost everything."

His words pull me short as my shoulders drop. "I didn't know that."

"Yeah, well. I didn't want you to feel like a hero." His lips pull into a smirk, making me laugh. Daniel's been with D'Angelo Construction for as long as I have. He started as a project manager and worked his way up to chief operating officer the year before I abandoned ship. If I had time for friends, he would be one of them. "You're already far enough above me," he adds, shaking his head with a laugh. He's joking around, but I can't laugh along with him.

"That's where you're wrong. You're a better man than I'll ever be. That's what matters most. Not money, or cars—"

"Though you do have a few very nice cars."

"I do, but that's not the point."

"I know. And thank you."

"No, thank you. If I didn't have you here, I wouldn't be able to play ball on the other side of the country. I wouldn't have left if I didn't know my company was in good hands. This place is as much yours as it is mine."

"Thanks, Sal. I love this company like it's my own, so I appreciate the sentiment. What do we do now?"

"We keep putting out fires until those assholes are behind bars."

Daniel comically cringes and I frown until he speaks. "That was probably the wrong choice of words."

What is he... Oh. *The fire.* "Fuck, you're right. This is a goddamn mess." I huff out a chuckle and Daniel groans.

"How long until it's over?"

"Who knows. Camilla has been called for day two of the trial. It starts in just under two weeks. Hopefully they leave us alone after that."

"At least they're not getting personal. It's just property. It may hurt you financially, but it won't kill you."

"I almost wish you hadn't said that."

"I thought the same as soon as I finished. But you have nothing to worry about. If I know you, you already have security on Camilla and Paige."

"Let's not forget Marc."

"I knew it! You probably had security on them before this all started."

"I'm kidding. Camilla has security, but that's her team. I have one guy on Paige and I'm lucky she let me. Marc would kill me if I tried. But he's with Camilla at the moment anyway."

"What about you?"

"What about me?"

"Have you upped your security?"

"I... ah..." I scratch the back of my neck, preferring not to say this out loud. "I don't have security."

"You don't? You're worth millions. Maybe you need something. Just in case." My eyes drop to the photos of the fire damage and the workplace safety report, and I sigh dramatically.

"You might be right. But God, I hope you're wrong."

"Me too."

I stay back at the D'Angelo Construction office until the early hours of the morning, and because of that, it's a struggle to get up when my alarm goes off. Which is not at all like me.

I could work right up until an hour before my alarm, have a short power nap, then do it all again, providing I get a decent sleep the following night. The problem is that I'm not sleeping well in general. I haven't been sleeping well since before Paige's wedding.

Since the moment I first laid it all on the line with Keeley and she told me we'd talk about it. Now we're having goddamn phone sex and still haven't addressed any of the issues between us.

All I know is that I want more. As complicated as that might be.

As complicated as that is.

Keeley is only thirty-three. She's beginning her life while I'm a few years past my midlife crisis. I own a fucking football team to prove that.

She's going to want kids and a wedding. A wedding I could probably come around to, but kids? I'm well past that and— *What am I even thinking?*

We haven't discussed any of that, and until we do, I'm spiraling for nothing. Again. While I have a company that's literally burning to the ground.

I could have demanded we talk last night, but I didn't. Instead, I let her talk me into phone sex, and fuck, was that an experience and a half.

My hand has never felt so good.

And I hate that it feels so wrong.

Like I'm using her without declaring my intentions, as old-school as that sounds. I am fucking old-school and I'm going to own it.

Why the fuck am I in New York when I could be home with Keeley in my arms right now?

Fucking Mikklesons. Yet another reason I need to put a stop to their bullshit.

I groan into my pillow, and I'm about to say fuck the world and roll over to go back to sleep, when my phone rings and I huff out a laugh. Of course someone would call the first time I ever decide to sleep in.

I blindly reach for my phone, only sitting up when I see that it's Wes.

Since we're three hours ahead it must be important. It's only six a.m. there.

"Morning, Wes. I'm hoping the early call means you have some news?"

"I do. I'm meeting Vance for breakfast this morning, but wanted to speak to you first."

"I appreciate that, but you know you don't have to."

"I know that."

"Good. So what are your thoughts?"

"We still have the same issue that Thomas was worried about—with Vance and Beckett being similar in age—but they never actually played against each other. At least, not during the regular season. They've never been considered rivals and have only been mentioned in the same articles when the best quarterbacks have been discussed." I nod even though he can't see me, waiting for more. "He's a solid choice."

"You're right. He could be the exact guy we need to build strong backups so we don't face another situation like this year." *Thank God for Beckett.*

"I agree."

"Good. And after talking to him on the phone yesterday, you still think he's going to fit our culture?"

"Seems that way. He's committed and says he'll work hard to fit in with our team. He's just started a foundation of his own, proving he likes to give back like the rest of us."

"Sounds promising. Have we dug up any skeletons yet?" He has to have them. I know it.

"I found one. He was suspended for a game in his senior year of college."

"Grades or a fight?"

"The reason wasn't listed. I could call his college—"

"That's not necessary. It was college. We all did crazy shit back then."

Wes laughs, and yet, I imagine the two of us are probably the only two people who didn't do crazy shit in college. But we can't fault Vance for that.

"Let me know how breakfast goes. I should be back tomorrow if he's around."

"Perfect. See you then."

"Bye, Wes."

I hang up and fall back onto the bed, releasing a slow drawn-out breath. At least things are falling into place for one of my businesses. Why I thought I could run them both is beyond me.

Is it possible I'm spreading myself too thin? It sure feels like it.

I need to fix that. Fast.

Chapter Forty-Three

KEELEY

After getting home late from my dinner last night, I didn't call or text Sal. Now I wish I had. Maybe then I wouldn't be feeling so anxious, knowing he has this ability to calm me, even via text.

I park in the outdoor lot on Thursday morning, and walk around to the front of the stadium, needing a moment in the fresh air to gather my strength. I should have spoken to Wes when Vance's name was first being thrown around as Thomas's replacement as our starting quarterback, because now that he's here to meet with the Storm, it's going to be a hell of a lot harder.

The warm wind blows around my face as I take in a breath, tilting my head to enjoy the sunlight before I spend the rest of my day locked inside with meetings.

Lightning Stadium's water fountain feature comes into view, and I smile at the statue of Zeus. The eyesore never ceases to make me laugh—a structure of a god in front of a building full of men who think that they're superhuman.

Although today, it could come in handy. I pause before sitting down on the ledge, angling my body to the glistening water, rummaging around in my bag, searching for a dime.

I'm about to give up when a shiny silver coin appears in front of me, making me giddy until I glance up and find Vance smirking my way.

"Do you make fountain wishes every day, or just the days you know you're going to run into me?"

Fuck. I take a subtle breath, ignoring his outstretched hand and the quarter he's offering me, opting to tell him to get fucked in person, rather than wishing it would happen.

"Why are you here, Vance?"

"The coaching gig." He shrugs, his expression neutral, pissing me off.

"No, why are you *here*? In front of me. Acting like things are civil between us. Do you actually believe that I'm going to joke with you? That enough time has passed for me to forget what you did?"

"Come on, Keeley. We were both so young back then. It's been years. I've moved on. Don't you think it's time you did the same?"

"Are you serious right now? You..." I trail off when my voice gets too loud and try again, my heart pounding so hard that it hurts me. "You..." The words catch in my throat while Vance stares at me in question, his eyes full of boredom, as though I'm wasting his time.

Luke's truck comes into view and my feet itch to run to him, to get away from Vance, but he's too far away.

"I what?" Vance questions, taking a step closer, forcing me back until my knees hit the fountain.

"Vance, Keeley?" Wes calls out from the front door of the stadium, and I release a held breath when Vance turns around.

"I've got to go." I move around him—careful not to make physical contact—and stride confidently toward Wes, projecting a strength I don't feel.

"Good morning." I smile. "Do you have a moment to talk before the chaos of the day?"

Wes frowns, his face twisting apologetically. "Not this morning. What about lunch?"

"Lunch? Sure. Sounds good." My facade slips for the briefest of moments and Wes notices.

"Is everything okay?"

"Of course. I'll see you in a bit."

"Okay." His brows pinch until he glances behind me and a smile appears. "Vance, how are you?"

I smile again before rushing through the doors and turning the corner to avoid hearing Vance's response.

I can't let him get to me. Not now. Not ever. He can be as cocky and certain as he wants for the morning. Come lunchtime, I'm bursting his bubble. I hope.

He's not the man for the coaching job, and Wes deserves to know that.

Despite telling myself I'm going to be fine, I'm a wreck all morning, fumbling pens, missing meetings, and bumping into burly football players as they move through the halls.

I'm lost in my own world when someone grabs my shoulder and I flinch, immediately apologizing when I see that it's Reed.

"Sorry, Reed. Hi."

"What's going on? Are you okay?"

"Yes. Why wouldn't I be?"

"Because you just knocked into Peterson and walked away like a zombie. I've been calling your name for a good thirty seconds."

"You have?" I frown, trying to recall that. "Why?"

"To ask if you're okay."

"Oh. Sorry. I'm good. Just having a morning. You know the ones. Nothing goes right. It's like I don't have my head screwed on properly. Maybe I got up on the wrong side of the bed or..." I trail off when Reed raises a brow.

"Run out of clichés to convince me?"

A laugh bursts out of me, and a little of the tension leaves my body as I stand taller. "No. I'm pretty sure I could think of a few more. Honestly, though, I'm okay. Or I will be after lunch."

"Okay. So it's a lack of food that's the issue."

"Food is definitely going to help. For now, I have another meeting to get to. Wish me luck."

"Maybe you should stop at a vending machine on the way, or I could bring you something to your office."

"I appreciate the offer, but it's not necessary. I'll be okay." I turn and run straight into Luke. This time because I wasn't looking and not because I was stuck in my head.

Luke chuckles as he steadies me. "Easy, now. In those heels you're likely to fall and break something if you bump into solid rock like that."

I glance back at Reed to see a hint of concern in his features before he rolls his eyes. "Solid rock? Really?"

"You know it." Luke pats his stomach and I snort out a laugh, feeling ten times better than I did a few minutes ago. These guys are like family. If Wes doesn't hear me out, I've got to believe that they'll have my back. Not that I think Wes will ignore me, but you never know. I didn't think my boss in college would ignore me either. I guess it depends on how desperate he is.

"I really have to go. Thank you, Reed, and thank you, Luke, for saving me."

"What did Reed do?"

"He offered me food."

"Oh-kay." Luke raises a brow and I wave him off, power walking away, careful to watch where I'm going this time, pausing when I'm around the corner.

My phone buzzes, alerting me to my meeting in ten minutes, and I see Sal's name on the attendee list.

My heart skips and I quietly curse myself. If he hears about Vance from Wes, he's not going to be happy about it.

Taking a deep breath, I dial his number and bounce on my toes, silently asking him to pick up.

Come on. Come on. Come on.

When he doesn't answer, I lean against the wall near the stairwell and send him a text before throwing my phone in my bag, determined to salvage this day.

KEELEY: Can you please call me as soon as you get this? After the meeting is fine

One forward planning meeting to go, then I can speak to Wes. I'm almost there.

"We meet again." Vance's voice echoes through the quiet halls, and my stomach twists as I glance up. I *was* almost there.

"What do you want, Vance?"

"I just thought you should know I had a great meeting with Wes." He walks toward me, and my eyes flash down the hall, nausea filling me when I see that we're very much alone. "It's not official yet, but they're preparing me an offer," he gloats, his smirk so big I want to punch it right off his devastatingly gorgeous face. A face that makes my skin crawl. "I have no doubt it's going to meet my expectations. Which means... we're going to be working together again." He settles in front of me, way too close for comfort, and I step back as far as I can.

"I can't have you looking at me like you're looking at me now, Keeley. People are going to ask questions. For no good reason. It's been over ten years since our disagreement and—"

"Our disagreement?" I scoff. "Is that what it was to you?"

"Of course. What else would it be?"

Anger takes over me, and my confidence grows momentarily. Anger is good. Much better than fear. "You attacked me, Vance. You—"

"Keeley." Vance cuts me off, invading my personal space, stepping closer than anyone should for an innocent talk.

A shiver runs down my spine, but I don't let it get to me. "Move back, Vance," I warn.

"I just want to talk."

"I said, *move back*."

"You're being ridiculous." He reaches out, curling his palm around my waist, and I recoil so violently that I stumble backward, losing my footing as I reach the stairs. I call out but it's too late. My heel misses the edge, and a sharp sting shoots through my leg as I roll my ankle, crying out in pain as I fall.

I slam my eyes shut just as my shoulder hits the railing and my knee connects with the concrete, seconds before I land with a jolt at the bottom.

My head spins, and I blink a few times as I try to sit up.

Flames lick at my ankle, as nausea rolls through me, and I buckle over again, flinching when someone stops me from hitting the ground.

The words "I've got you" flit through my mind, and when I don't recognize the voice as Vance's, I relax, glancing up to find Beckett beside me, with Luke rushing down the stairs.

"Fuck, Keeley. Are you okay?" Luke asks, slipping in beside Beckett.

"Thank you, Beckett," I whisper, unable to answer Luke with pain so excruciating, it steals my words for a moment. Tears prick my eyes, and I try to bite my cheek to stave them off, but it's no use. I'm too far gone.

"I think I've done some damage." I point to my bare foot, drawing both Beckett's and Luke's eyes as I search around for my stiletto.

"Jesus. Fuck, Keeley. Luckily it was only a few steps." Luke shivers while Beckett stays silent, not so subtly reaching for his phone.

"Can you stand?" Beckett asks after a beat, and I nod as I wipe my eyes.

"I think so," I lie, hoping I'm not about to collapse again when I give it a try.

More players must be exiting the locker rooms because the sound increases in the halls as a few of them walk past. Luke's attention shifts before he calls out to Easton, making me cringe. "Ugh, I don't need my little brother to help."

"I know. But if you were Lainey, I'd want to be here."

I blow out a breath because I can't fault him for that. He'd definitely want to be here if it was his sister. Though Luke and Easton are very different people.

Easton chooses today to actually listen when Luke talks to him, and the next thing you know, he's by my side while Reed and Zane hover above him.

Maybe *this* is why their group chat's called Keeley's support group. They manifested this fall.

"I'm fine. Can you all please move so I can stand up?"

Beckett does as I ask, immediately stepping back, and I move him up the ranks to being my favorite player. Reed shifts back too, but the other three don't move.

"Fine." I flick the stiletto off my other foot and throw my hands in the air, allowing two of the guys to lift me to stand. I don't bother seeing who. I close my eyes and focus on not crying more than I already am. I can do this. I can.

"Oh, Jesus." The pain's worse than before and bile rises in my throat as I fight not to vomit. "I can't put weight on it."

"Fuck, that's not good." Luke's always helpful responses make me laugh, and I shake my head.

"I think I need Robin," I say, referring to our team doctor, and within seconds he's standing in front of me. "Wow, that was fast."

"I was in the locker room. Wyatt came to get me."

"Thanks, Wyatt," I call out over my shoulder before turning back to Robin.

"What's happened?"

"I can't put weight on my foot."

"Okay. Sit down. I'm going to take a look."

Easton and Zane lower me back to the steps and once again hover above me, making me anxious. "Would you please go home? I'm fine. Robin's looking after me."

No one moves until Coach Pierce's booming voice echoes through the space. "Home now. You're not helping standing around like fucking vultures."

I wave my thanks when the crowd starts to disperse, momentarily distracted until Robin grabs my foot. "Holy mother of—"

"We're going to need an X-ray; I think you may have broken your ankle."

I follow his line of sight to find my ankle the size of a goddamn football and cry out again. "God, what does that mean?"

"It means we need to get you to the hospital."

"Hospital? Don't be ridiculous. I just need a minute."

"I'm sorry, Keeley. But you don't. You need an X-ray and you're likely going to need surgery."

"Surgery?"

"Stop repeating everything he says," Easton grumbles, and I wish he was close enough for me to slap him.

Robin pulls his radio from his pants and buzzes the nurse, saying four little words that make me sink my head into my hands. "We need a wheelchair."

We don't need anything. *I* do. I need a fucking wheelchair and I don't have time for this.

"Easton, can you help me get your sister upstairs?" Robin speaks to Easton next and my head whips around so fast, my neck hurts.

"Touch me and I'll murder you in your sleep."

Someone snorts and when I glance up, my eyes lock on the top step, making me lose my train of thought as a full-body shiver runs through me.

I suck in a breath as I replay what happened, *my heart racing as Vance stepped closer, my throat clogging as he reached for my waist.* I gulp back another breath, and another, each one more frantic as the air fails to fill my lungs.

The world around me spins, and I vaguely hear Easton's voice begging me to answer. All I can do is shake my head over and over.

I need Sal. I have never needed a man for anything. But I need him now.

Chapter Forty-Four

SALVATORE

I call Keeley for the fourth time in as many minutes and pace as I wait for her to pick up. She called me and asked me to call her after the meeting, then our meeting got canceled, and no one can tell me what the hell is going on.

When Keeley doesn't answer again, I try calling Wes, since he was also set to attend the meeting. But I'm once again forwarded to voicemail, making me throw my pen across the room.

As if I don't have enough to worry about here in New York, now there's something going on back home.

After blowing out a breath, I scroll through my recent call list until I find Coach Pierce, and I'm just about to try him next when my phone rings, and my stomach drops.

Easton Wilder.

The one guy I never expected to call me. Ever.

Nausea fills me as I answer. "Easton? Is everything okay with Paige and Isaac?"

"Yes, they're both fine." He pauses as I sigh, but my relief is short-lived. "It's Keeley."

"Keeley? What happened?"

"I don't know exactly. She fell down some stairs and broke her ankle. They're taking her to the hospital, and she needs you to come home."

"Fuck, is she okay?"

"Physically, yes. Broken ankle aside."

"Physically?" *What the fuck does that mean?*

"There's more going on but she won't talk to anyone. She had a full-blown panic attack. She *needs* you here. I...I need you here." His voice comes out strained, making way for his panic to shine through.

"I'm on my way. Which hospital?"

"San Francisco General. She's not happy about it, but I think her annoyance is a front."

Fuck. My heart beats chaotically as I rush around my office, grabbing my keys and wallet. "Is anyone with her?" I ask, praying she's not alone.

"Paige is on her way with my mom. I'm heading home to pick up Isaac from school. How quickly can you get here?"

I breathe a sigh of relief as I close my door, not even bothering to lock my office like I usually would. "I'm already walking to my car; I'll be there as soon as I can."

"Thank you."

He's thanking me? *Jesus.* "I appreciate you calling me. I know I'm not your favorite person at the moment."

"Yeah, well, I'm pretty sure you're hers. So that has to count for something. I'll see you soon."

My jaw drops and I'm silent for a beat before finally answering, "Thank you." I choke back the emotion lodged in my throat. "Bye, Easton."

"Bye."

After hanging up, I call my car service while pressing the button for the elevator at least ten times. It's like I'm a kid that thinks that will make the thing move faster.

"Mr. D'Angelo?" My car service answers and I pause.

"I need a car to take me to the airport. Right away." I'm not usually so blunt, but I don't have time for niceties.

"I'm sending someone now. ETA is three minutes."

"Thank you."

My next call is Tabitha, urging her to book me on the next flight to San Francisco, no matter the cost or seat. Now would be the perfect time to own a private jet, and I'm almost considering it.

If Tabitha can't get me a decent flight, it'll be my next big purchase.

Jeffrey's waiting at the airport in San Francisco, his weary eyes meeting mine as he grabs my bag. "Any news?" he asks when he's settled in the front seat, pulling out into the line of cars leaving the airport.

"Not yet. Easton texted to say she was having surgery but that she should be out of recovery and awake by the time I get there. What's the traffic like?"

"Hectic. I'll be as quick as I can be."

"I have no doubt, thank you." I sigh loudly, letting my head fall back until someone blares their horn and our car swerves out of the way.

"What the hell was that?"

"I'm sorry. Someone decided to stop suddenly, and the guy in front of us almost slammed into the back of him."

"Jesus. Thanks for swerving. I want to get to the hospital fast, but not *ambulance* fast."

Jeffrey smiles as his eyes meet mine in the rearview mirror. "Permission to speak frankly?"

"I thought you always did that."

"True." He chuckles, his gaze meeting mine in the rearview mirror. "I like her. I'm happy you found someone you care about."

I huff out a laugh. "More than work?"

"I didn't say that."

"You didn't have to."

Jeffrey's been with me since before my divorce with Camilla. He's the only person I asked to follow me here, and I'm grateful on a daily basis that he said yes. Sometimes I think he knows more about my life than I do. He certainly sees a lot of it.

"You deserve to be happy, Sal. And the nights I've driven you and Keeley home are the nights you've looked the happiest, your time with Paige and Isaac aside."

"Fuck, I know. But she's..." I trail off. I'm not talking about this with Jeffrey, even if he is a friend as much as a driver.

"Great for you," he finishes for me. "That's all that matters."

"Just drive." I jokingly roll my eyes, and he laughs again.

"Yes, *sir*."

"Jeffrey," I warn, and yet I'm smiling after being so worried when I first got into the car. "Thank you."

"You're welcome. We're not too far away now."

Thank God.

"I'm not sure how long I'll be. Feel free to go home. I can book an Uber later."

"I'll be around. Call me when you're done."

"Okay. I will."

Jeffrey pulls up in front of San Francisco General, and I'm out of the car so fast, I almost trip up the curb. I rush through the front doors, beelining for the reception desk until Paige calls out from behind me.

"Dad. She's this way."

I spin around, finding Paige's soft gaze staring back at me, and when she smiles, I return it, striding her way.

"Thanks, Kid. How is she?"

"Almost as grumpy as Easton usually is."

"I can see that." A laugh escapes me but I know there's more coming, and when Paige's face drops, I briefly close my eyes.

"How is she really?"

"I don't know. She won't talk to me either. Easton said she wouldn't tell him anything after her fall, but I wasn't too concerned. Only now, *I've* tried, and so has her mom. The thing is..." she trails off, glancing nervously over her shoulder, eliciting a heaviness in my chest.

"What thing?"

"She told me something that I promised I'd never tell you."

"What? When?"

"A while ago."

"Paige, honey. I love you, but you need to tell me what the hell is going on. Now." My voice rises a little and I rein it back in. "Please."

Paige closes her eyes and I immediately feel bad.

"I'm sorry, Paige. I just—"

"Love her?"

"Care. I care. A lot. And I know you. If the secret you're keeping wasn't important to the present situation, you wouldn't have brought it up."

"You're right. Only it's not really my place to say. I just care a lot too." I smile and let her off the hook.

"How about I talk to Keeley and see what she says? But if she gives me nothing, you're going to have to come clean."

"I think that sounds fair. Come on. I'll take you to her."

She gestures down a hallway to the left and I walk beside her, my mind reeling with what the hell Paige was trying to say. I'm running through a million possibilities until one sticks and I lose my breath. "Is she sick?" I feel the blood drain from my face as I turn toward Paige.

Is ALS hereditary? "What?" Paige's eyes widen as she takes in my expression, rushing to grab my arm, her head shaking almost violently. "No. God. I'm sorry. I shouldn't have said anything. She's not sick." She pauses for a moment before her face drops. "I don't think so. Jesus. She fell. What if?"

Fuck. "Let me talk to her before we both panic."

"That sounds like a good idea. We're almost to her room."

She points down the hall just as Rochelle walks out, a smile reaching her eyes when she sees me. Meanwhile, I stiffen uncomfortably. It's the first time I've seen her since everyone found out I had a thing for her daughter.

"I'm going to let the two of you talk," Paige announces as if there's awkwardness oozing from my pores and she wants out. Too bad I'm not going to let her.

"You don't have to—"

"I'm going. I was on my way to get something to eat anyway."

"Paige." I try to grab her hand but she dodges me, smiling as she walks away, and when I turn back around, Rochelle's grin is showing her matching amusement. Great. All I need now is Keeley's sister.

"Rochelle. How are you? How's Keeley?"

"She's been better. Though I have no doubt her mood's about to improve. Thank you for coming." She grabs ahold of a walker lying abandoned by the wall, and her smile turns awkward.

"I didn't want Keeley to feel sorry for me. This is my life now."

"Fuck. I'm sorry."

"Don't be. I'm alive."

"And thriving. No one can take away your positivity."

"Exactly. Now, back to my daughter."

I cringe but nod. One day I'll get to actually see her.

"I'm not going to keep you for long, because Keeley needs you. But did Paige tell you she's being particularly stubborn and refusing to tell any of us what's going on?" She laughs, but there's an edge to it, giving away her true feelings. She's worried. As am I. Especially after what Paige said.

"She mentioned it, and I'm going to try my best to get her to talk to me."

"Thank you. If anyone can do it, it's you. And on that note, protect her with your life and we won't have a problem." Her expression turns serious, and I swallow a lump in my throat, waiting for more. Because I have no doubt there's more. "Keeley's in denial about a lot of things, with one of those things being her ability to let others in. Particularly men. If she tries to push you away and you let her, over something as minor as age, we're going to have words. We've all had a feeling something was going on. Well, most of us anyway, my oblivious son being the exception. No one has any issues with the two of you dating. Least of all me. All I ask is that you protect her heart, and don't ever tell her we had this conversation."

"You want me to lie to your daughter?" I raise a brow, hoping my response will hide the fact that I'm not my usual confident self right now.

Rochelle throws her head back and laughs. "Normally, no. In this case, yes. Otherwise, she'll disown me."

"You don't have to worry about me saying anything, or she'd likely disown me too."

"She's a darling, isn't she?" Rochelle's joking, but the thing is...

"She's perfect." I chuckle lightly, avoiding eye contact as I shake my head. I'm so fucking gone for that woman, it's scary. "On that note, I'm going to go."

I foolishly glance back at Rochelle to find her eyes lit up and a little bit watery, making me smile uneasily.

"I don't think I have to worry."

"I'm going to try to make sure that's true."

I squeeze her arm as I walk past, only pausing again when I reach Keeley's room, half expecting someone else to jump out to delay me even more. *I just need to see her smiling face.*

With a soft knock, I push open the door, my heart racing as my beautiful girl comes into view. She pouts when she sees me, putting her whole face into it, and I have to fight to hide a grin.

"It's nice to see you too," I joke, walking closer.

"I broke my ankle, Sal. My goddamn ankle. The doctor said I have to stay off it for weeks. No, not just off it. He wants me to keep it elevated for at least the first two weeks to make sure the swelling settles, and... You're here?"

She throws her head back, letting out a fake cry and I move toward the bed. "Keels."

"No." She raises a hand to stop me. "Please go outside and come back in."

"What?" I half chuckle, half scoff.

"Please."

"As you wish." With my smile trapped between my teeth, I turn around and head back out the door, pausing for long enough to compose myself, then I'm back inside again.

I open my mouth to speak until Keeley's eyes widen with an excited gasp, hitting me with the smile I pictured when I first walked in. "You're here." She holds her hands out and I walk forward, taking them in mine as I stare down at her, my heart pounding in my chest.

I'd laugh at her change in demeanor if I wasn't so worried about the whys.

"Of course I'm here." I press a kiss to her knuckles before releasing her hands and brushing my fingers across her cheek. "I'm sorry it took me so long."

I want to ask her what happened, but if no one else has had any luck getting answers, I need to ease into it. So instead, I cup her face and lean in, taking her lips in a chaste kiss. "You had me worried."

"It's just an ankle."

"Just an ankle?" I raise an eyebrow, and she laughs. "I may have committed to your re-do of my arrival, but I haven't forgotten the first one."

"Ugh. It's just so frustrating. I did not need this right now."

"When would have been convenient for you?" I ask, my lips pulled into a grin, making her giggle lightly.

"Okay, fine. I'll try to be less *Easton*." I open my mouth to speak until she cuts me off. "*Try* being the operative word."

"Trying is good. How are you feeling after surgery?"

"The pain's starting to come back now that the anesthesia's wearing off. It's a dull ache at the moment. And my back's sore too. And my shoulder."

"From the fall?"

"Yep. It was a good one."

"Easton didn't exactly fill me in on what happened. Did you trip?"

Keeley winces before she turns away, no longer able to meet my eyes. I reach for her hand again and she squeezes me tightly. "There's something I should have told you."

"Okay."

"You're not going to like it."

What? She turns back to face me, and her anxious expression guts me.

"Please don't be mad. And please stay. I need you here."

Please stay? Jesus. What is she about to tell me?

"I'm not going anywhere, Keeley. I can promise you that." *I hope.*

She gestures for me to sit down, and I do so with trepidation, my heart lodged in my throat. "You know you can tell me anything, right?"

She nods before letting go of my hands, and my muscles tense.

"I've known Vance for a long time. He's one of the reasons I'll never date an athlete."

Chapter Forty-Five

SALVATORE

Vance. The guy we're about to hire to fucking work with us? If my muscles weren't already wound so tightly, I have no doubt they'd be coiling like a spring at her words.

Vance Fucking McMillan.

And it all comes back. "Fuck, Keeley. Did he do this to you?" As the question leaves my mouth, the thought of that notion has me springing to my feet. "What the fuck did he do?"

"Nothing. Not really."

"Not really? That doesn't exactly ease my mind."

"All he did was grab my waist, and I overreacted. It's my fault. I stumbled backward, not remembering the stairs were behind me." She laughs, her cheeks flushing, as though she's ashamed of her clumsiness. While I can't even smile. I'm caught on the beginning of her explanation. *All he did was grab my waist.*

First, why the fuck is he grabbing her waist?

Second, why the hell is his touch making her move away from him so quickly that she falls down the fucking stairs?

My fists clench but I try to stay calm.

"This wasn't your fault, Keeley."

"It kind of was..." She trails off when I shoot her a glare, and her lips pull into a smile. "Okay. It was an accident."

"No, it wasn't. If you 'overreacted' as you said, it's because he was touching you without your permission. Am I right?"

She nods, and I briefly close my eyes, breathing in through my nose to calm myself. Only it doesn't work.

"Fuuuck."

"Sal."

"I should have been there."

"What? Don't be ridiculous. Why would you have been there?"

"To protect you. I've been so focused on the reasons I should stay away from you, when I should have been worrying about keeping you safe."

"Sal. Come on. We've both been focused on other things, and you could hardly have stopped this."

"Yes, I could have."

"How? Rolled me up in bubble wrap and never let me out?"

"No. But I should have been there. I should have seen the signs."

"Seen the signs? You're not being fair to yourself. And maybe if I'd told you, you would have been."

Her words wound me like a stab to the chest, but I don't show it. She didn't mean the *maybe* as if she's questioning whether or not I'd actually stay to protect her. Though she has every right to. Camilla wouldn't have questioned it at all. She would have assumed I wouldn't be there and hired someone else to help her. I don't want Keeley to ever have to question that. And I know with absolute certainty that I would have made sure Vance never got close enough to even talk to her, let alone touch her.

"I would have been here. For you, I would have come."

"I know. I'm not doubting that. I'll never doubt that." She holds out a hand again and I hesitate taking it. My palms are sweaty from how worked up I am, and I don't want her to know that just yet. Instead, I brush the tips of my fingers from her open palm to her hair, leaning down to press a kiss to her forehead.

"Will you tell me about it now?" I whisper as I pull away, sitting down beside her.

"That depends." Her face twists.

"On what?"

"On whether or not you promise to stay calm."

Since no part of me is calm right now, I can't exactly promise that, so instead I nod.

"Thank you." She accepts my answer before a sigh escapes her.

"I think we need to start talking more, Keeley. I said I didn't want a casual relationship, and yet, that's exactly how we're acting. I need to know what's going on in your life. And your head. It's the only way we're ever going to make this work."

"Likewise."

"I know."

"I'm usually an open book, Sal. You know that."

"Keels, you—"

"Wait. I'm not finished. I'm an open book, but in some cases, I've ripped out the pages, preferring to pretend they never existed."

A thought hits me and I speak before thinking. "You told Paige?" I wince, trying to hide my pain and jealousy, but Keeley sees right through my façade, like she always does.

"Please don't be upset with her," I beg. "She wouldn't tell me what. Just that there was more to the story."

"I'm not upset. I completely understand. I'd have done the same. The thing is, I told Paige because she wasn't likely to go after him."

"What do you mean?"

"If I'd told you or Easton, within twenty-four hours he'd probably end up on the back of a milk carton."

"You think we'd make him disappear?"

"I think you'd want to hurt him, sure. In fact, I *know* it. I can see it in your eyes as we speak."

"You're right. I want to hurt that fucker more than I've ever wanted to hurt anyone. But you told me to stay, so that's what I'm going to do."

"Didn't Paige tell you to leave it too? With the Mikklesons?"

"Not exactly, but..." I trail off, unable to lie to her. "I can't guarantee that if an opportunity presents itself, I'll be able to walk away."

"So if Vance walked in here a week from now, you'd..."

"Have words."

"Words?"

"With my fist."

"He's a recently retired football star. I think he can take you." Keeley laughs, making me sit back. "You don't even know what he did."

"It doesn't matter what he did. He hurt you. And that's what counts. That's enough."

"Aren't you my hero."

"Keeley. Please. You have to talk to me. No more deflecting."

"Okay." She takes a deep breath before glancing at the door, only speaking when I've turned around to follow her gaze.

"Vance and I attended the same college close to where I grew up. He was a year above me, and while he was one of the most popular guys on campus, he was also considered one of the good guys. He was focused on the game. He wasn't a player like the other guys on his team." My stomach knots as speaks, and it's hard not to let my imagination run away from me.

"I'll save you the details, but after a little while he asked me out. Took me to some fancy restaurant away from the college. He was nice enough, and I had a good time, but we didn't click. At least I felt that way. He didn't agree. He'd convinced himself I was a sure thing, so when we pulled up to my off-campus apartment, he wouldn't let me get out of the car."

She pauses to glance away while my hands ball into fists again, and I force myself to release them, flexing once before curling them around my thighs. *He wouldn't let her out of the car?*

"I wasn't the badass I am now." She fakes a smile, making my chest ache as she sucks in a breath. "If I was, I would have kneed him in the balls, or screamed my lungs out. But back then, I let him kiss me. I figured he'd notice we didn't have a connection and pull away. I was wrong."

Jesus, fuck. I stiffen, reaching for Keeley's hand only to have her shake me off as she turns away again, unable to meet my eye.

"He didn't go all the way, but he..." she trails off and I stupidly answer for her.

"He assaulted you? In the car?" My fingers dig into my legs, inflicting an ounce of the pain I want to inflict on Vance.

"He did."

"Fuck." I stand, running a hand through my hair as I pace. "Did you report him?" I glance back her way, as Wes's words flit back to mind, my anger growing. *Was that why he got a one-game suspension? One fucking game?*

Keeley nods, and bile rises in my throat. I'm going to kill him. I've never been one to solve problems with violence, but what the fucker did deserves—

"Sit down. Please. It was a long time ago and—"

"The 'when' doesn't matter. How the hell is he still playing football? Why isn't it on his record?"

"They covered it up and fired me from my athletic department internship."

"They what? Are you kidding me? Who's they?"

Keeley smiles but I don't see what's funny. "Thank you for caring. We can't do anything about Vance or the entire athletics department now. I'm sure they've all moved on."

"They may have, but you haven't. How is that fair?"

"I have moved on. At least, I thought I had until Vance was standing in front of me."

"Then let me do something to help."

"You can't. Hurting him is not going to take the memories away. And he's the reason I'm stronger now. I wanted to ensure that never happened again. That I was never that vulnerable."

"You're allowed to be vulnerable, Keeley. And you can be strong without enduring trauma. He deserves to pay for what he did."

Keeley plays with the edge of her sheet, as she smiles. "I don't disagree, only that ship has sailed. I want to move on. For real this time. Can you help me with that?"

I pause, staring into her uncertain eyes, and drop back into the seat beside her. "Of course. What do you need me to do?"

"Do you think you could ask Wes not to hire him? I know it's been hard to find someone and a QB coach is more essential than a media liaison but—"

"What? No. Keeley..." Fuck, she's worried about history repeating itself. "There is no way in hell we would choose that fucker over you. Or anyone else. Is that what you think?"

"No. Maybe. I don't know. I didn't think my boss in college would do it either, but he's more important and—"

"Keeley, stop. *You* are important. If anyone on that team hurt you, they'd be gone the second I found out. It wouldn't matter who they were. And I have no doubt, Wes would feel the same."

Keeley's eyes water, and I silently curse myself for never taking the time to ask her what she was thinking the few times I noticed her hiding something.

"I promise you, that asshole will be sent packing as soon as we've finished talking. I'm sorry you ever doubted that."

"No, I'm sorry. I—"

"You have nothing to be sorry about. How else can I help?"

"I need you to let me be the one that confronts him. I thought I was okay. I'm not. And-"

"You want to confront him?"

"I do. *Alone.* I want to remind him of what he did to me and make sure he knows how messed up it was. I'm not even sure he realizes the damage he did."

"Fuck, Keeley. I can't. Not alone. I understand you wanting to talk to him, but please let me be there."

I reach for her hand again, and this time she lets me take it, curling her fingers through mine as she contemplates my request. "You'd have to promise to give us space, and you can't say a word."

Fuck. Fuck. Fuck. *How am I supposed to do that?*

"Sal?" she pleads as her eyes grow round.

"Okay."

"Okay?"

"Yes." *Dammit.*

"You can be there."

"Thank you." A breath rushes from my mouth. It's not exactly what I want to do, but at least she won't be alone with him again. If I can help it, that will be the last time she ever has to see his face. "We might need to stall him to keep him in San Francisco. You're not seeing him while the pain is still fresh."

"I know. Maybe we can go after they release me."

"I'll set it up."

"Thank you."

She squeezes my hand, and a little part of me wishes she didn't have such a big hold over me. I want to kill him. I also want to do everything she asks of me. And she will always win. Though, I can use it to my advantage.

"Since I agreed to your plan over my own, I have a request for you."

"Oh-kay." Keeley frowns, making me laugh.

"I want you to stay with me after they discharge you."

"That's not necessary. It's not like he's going to track me down at home and attack me after I confront him."

"Jesus, Keels." My stomach knots as if that's now a possibility. "I wasn't thinking that at all." Until you put it in my head. "I want you to stay with me because I don't want you to be alone. In fact, my guess is that the doctors will insist on it anyway."

"You don't want me to be alone?" she asks, her tone suspicious.

"Yes. The doctor will likely say you need someone with you, so it makes sense." *And I want to be the one to take care of you.*

Always. From here on out.

Chapter Forty-Six

KEELEY

After relenting on me staying at my place instead of his, Sal helps me up to my apartment when I'm discharged a couple of days later, a bag in his hand as proof he's following through with his insistence on staying with me until I feel better. As the doctor ordered.

If I wasn't so pissed off at being told I have to stay home for the next two weeks, I'd probably consider overexaggerating my pain so he stays longer, but I need to play it down if I want to get back to work anytime soon.

I smile as I crutch my way inside, ignoring the ache caused by the blood rushing to my foot.

"I know what you're thinking." Sal gives me a side-eye as he walks around me, making his way into the kitchen. "You can hide your pain as much as you want. It doesn't change anything."

"I don't know what you're talking about."

"You don't even realize you winced just now, do you?"

"Goddammit."

"Come here." He holds his arms out as I slowly move toward him, smiling when he meets me halfway. Actually, more like four-fifths of the way since he's that much faster than I am. He puts his phone and keys down on the counter before taking my crutches from my hand and resting them against the wall, pulling me into a hug, supporting my weight as he holds me.

We stay like that for a minute before he pulls back, his gaze bouncing between my eyes. I'm about to ask him what's going on when he maneuvers me around until I'm balanced against the wall, and cups my cheek with one hand, his other still holding my weight.

"I should have done this in the hospital." He presses his mouth to mine, his touch like a whisper, eliciting a soft mewl from within me. He groans in response, deepening the kiss, and I quiver at the feel of him, bringing me back to the last time he kissed me, with the promise of what was to come.

After devouring my mouth, he drops his head to my shoulder before peppering my neck with slow, shivery kisses. And just when I think it's going to lead to more, he pulls away. All too soon.

"Sorry, I couldn't help myself."

"No apology needed. I'm up for more of that." I shift slightly and cringe when my cast hits the floor.

Sal lifts me higher, the lust gone from his eyes, now replaced with concern. "Maybe later."

"Ugh. What else am I going to do?"

"I know I'm the last person that should be allowed to say this, but it's only a week off of work. After that, they said you can work from home providing you keep your feet elevated. You can get through this. It's a nanna week instead of a nanna night."

"You'd think that would sound appealing..." I trail off as I pout, thinking about how much I have to do between now and the beginning of the season. I'm going to miss the first game, the opening night function...

"I'm not sure if this is going to be helpful, or if I just signed my own death certificate, but I asked Wes to find someone to... Ahh, how do I word it?"

"You had me replaced?" I push him backward and grab the wall behind me for support.

"I definitely didn't have you replaced." Sal chuckles. "We're getting someone in to help in your absence, so you don't return with more work than you can handle."

"I can handle anything you throw at me, thank you very much."

"I know you can. This is a good thing, Keeley."

"Doesn't feel that way."

Sal smiles, and I wish it didn't give me a buzz when I want to be pissed off.

"Has anyone ever told you that you're cute when you're angry?" he asks, bopping me on the nose.

"No. I don't want to be *cute*. I want to be better."

"I know. Come on. Let's get you off your feet so we can get that recovery moving."

With a nod, I hold out my hand to take the crutches, but Sal surprises me by scooping me into his arms and carrying me over to the couch. He positions me lengthways and props my foot up on some pillows, his eyes on my face to gauge my reaction.

"How's that?"

"Good. But where are you going to sit? I can't see you if you sit on the armchair."

"Easy fix." He lifts the coffee table out of the way and moves my armchair in front of the couch, close to my head. "See?"

"Guess we won't be watching a movie." I gesture to the TV behind him.

Sal shakes his head, his beautiful dark eyes fixated on my lips until he snaps himself out of it.

"We can figure that out later. First, we're going to talk."

I visibly wince, not even bothering to hide it. I knew that was coming, and I'm still not ready. "I said a lot the other day."

"You did. And I'm grateful for that. Now it's time to talk about *us*. The future, not the past."

And that's what I'm nervous about. "Where do you want to start?"

"I have no idea. But before we do, I want you to know that I'm only pushing for this because I want a future with you. I want to do this right. I want us both to begin this relationship with our eyes wide open. And that's where it gets hard."

"I want the same, Sal. I do. The problem is, I'm actually more guarded than I ever realized. My darling mother pointed it out. I don't want to be that way with you, only I can't help it. It's ingrained in me. A protective measure to look after my heart." My heart pounds at the thought, and I wish I could tuck my knees up to my chest to protect myself now.

"Do you need protection from me?" Sal asks, his voice gravelly, his eyes locked on mine.

"No. Never. Only it seems to be my default setting."

"Are you sure?"

"Yes. Why would I ever need protection from you? You're the most genuine person I've ever met."

"Thanks, but I don't mean me personally. I mean *us*. Maybe you're subconsciously protecting yourself against getting hurt by the things you'll miss out on in the future. Because of who I am."

"What?" I shake my head aggressively until his meaning sinks in. "Fucking Easton."

Sal laughs. "He told you we spoke then?"

"He did. And he shouldn't have done that."

"He raised valid questions, Keels."

My pulse spikes as my frustrations rise, until it hits me that I might have it all backward. "Do you want marriage and kids?"

Sal's shoulders drop as his eyes soften with sadness. "At this stage in my life, I don't. I can't. It's not a reflection on you at all; it's just not something I want to go through again. I'm not saying never, for the marriage at least, because I didn't think I'd ever want another relationship either. Especially not one with someone closer to my daughter's age than mine. Only, I don't think I'll change my mind again. As for kids. I... ahh." He scratches the back of his neck, clearly uncomfortable. "I've had a vasectomy. I know they can be reversed, but I'm already a grandfather and..." He trails off with an incredulous laugh. "I'm painting a lovely picture of myself, aren't I?"

It's probably the nerves mixed with relief, but a laugh bursts out of me. He doesn't want marriage or kids. It's not just me.

"I don't want either of those things, Sal," I finally admit, making him frown.

"You don't know that. You're focused on work right now and—"

"I'm going to stop you before you say something that forces me to throw something at your balls. The gentleman I know and love would never try to tell me how I feel and..." *Jesus*. I subtly clutch at my chest. Why did my heart jump when I said love? Do I love him? I know I'm falling, but am I already there? We haven't even had sex yet.

"Keeley." Sal stands up and drags his chair forward before sitting back down and reaching for my hand, seemingly oblivious to my minor freak-out. His touch sets me on fire, and I almost flinch away from the burn.

"You know I didn't mean to speak for you," he begins, and I squeeze his hand to stop him again, because I do know that. He's looking out for me. Only he doesn't have all the facts.

"I'm not saying I won't change my mind about getting married either, because like you, I don't know what the future will bring. But I can say with absolute certainty that I don't want kids."

"How? You said so yourself—you're a mother."

"A mother *type*. A protective hen. A carer of lost souls. There's a big difference. The people I mother go home at night. They're not dependent on me."

"That's debatable at times." Sal smirks and a laugh bubbles out of me.

"You're not wrong. Especially with some of the rookies. What I mean to say is that I don't want kids of my own."

My body heats, making my hands clammy. My mind takes me back to when I was twenty-four, and try as I might, I can't stop the emotion welling in my chest. I was able to tell Easton and Paige with a clear head. Now I want to cry?

"Fuck, Keeley. What happened?"

"How do you know something happened?" I laugh softly, hoping it will help ease the pain.

"I can see it in your eyes."

I nod as I find the right words. It was much easier to yell it in anger at dinner the other night than it is to speak the truth now. But with Sal looking at me with his penetrating gaze, his eyes holding so much warmth, I know that I'm safe.

"I got pregnant when I was twenty-four. The asshole dad abandoned me the second he found out. But it wouldn't have mattered. With or without a loving partner, I knew I didn't want to be a mom. And I hated myself for it. I cried nonstop for almost a week. Then I threw myself into work and started looking into adoption agencies." A lump catches in my throat, and I swallow it down as tears fill the backs of my eyes.

Sal jumps up from his chair and lifts me again, this time pulling me onto his lap while keeping my ankle on the pillows.

"You don't have to talk about it anymore, Keeley. I'm sorry I pushed you. I'm sorry I didn't believe you when you said you didn't want kids. I—"

I press a finger to his lips to stop him from saying more, needing to get it all off my chest. "I lost the baby at thirteen weeks. And I blamed myself for that loss. I didn't want a baby. I thought I was doing all the right things, but maybe I wasn't because I didn't care for it like I should have."

I frantically wipe my eyes until Sal removes my hands, replacing them with his own as he softly swipes his thumbs across my cheeks.

"No, Keeley. That's not on you. A miscarriage isn't your fault. None of it's your fault." He pulls me tighter into his hold and kisses my forehead, bringing about more tears. I thought I'd shed the last of them years ago. I was wrong. Like everything else, I'd bottled it up, waiting for the right person to share it with.

I curl into him, letting myself be vulnerable until my emotions subside.

"I'm sorry that happened to you, Keeley," Sal whispers softly before falling quiet, waiting for me, giving me all the space that I need.

I'm not sure how much time passes before I finally pull away, sniffling with a smile. "Thank you. For letting me break a little."

"You don't need to thank me for that. I'm here for anything you need. Always. I hope you know that?"

"I do. I promise. And the same goes to you."

"Good."

"Do we have any other hurdles to jump over?"

"You mean besides the fact that I'm your brother's father-in-law and you're my daughter's best friend?"

"Yes, besides that."

"No, I think we're good."

I snort out a laugh when he delivers his words with a straight face, and Sal cracks a smile. His first since I started telling him about my past.

"Anything you need to get off your chest?"

"Ahhh. Yeah. I might be in a little trouble with the Mikklesons. They're not happy about Camilla testifying against them."

"Yeah, Paige mentioned that." I frown momentarily and silently curse Paige. She needs to tell him she's testifying too. It's going to kill him to know she's been hiding that fact. "What are you going to do?"

"I'm not sure yet. My girlfriend kind of threw my plans into disarray when she broke her ankle."

"Your girlfriend?"

"Yeah. It sounds strange saying that at my age. But it's what I want. If you do."

"I do. I actually like the sound of it."

"Good." He presses a chaste kiss to my lips then glances down at me, his expression serious.

"Anything else you want to tell me about?"

"No, you pretty much... Oh, actually." I grimace as I remember the only other thing I hid from him.

Sal stiffens, quickly trying to hide it. "I'm listening."

"Remember the first GM you fired? Tray."

"I do..." Sal draws out the words, his voice hesitant.

"I told you I agreed with your plan to fire him because he was a sleaze. He hit on me and pretty much every other girl who worked for him."

"Motherfucker." Sal jolts and I have no doubt that if I wasn't sitting in his lap, he'd be up out of the chair. "I knew he was a piece of shit; I just couldn't work out why."

"Yeah, well, you're the only man who noticed that. Most of the guys thought he was amazing. One of the boys."

"Fucker. I wish I could fire him again with that knowledge. I wouldn't have given him such a nice send-off."

"Has anyone ever told you you're cute when you're angry?" I throw his words back at him and he laughs incredulously.

"*Funny*. Is that it?"

"I think so. What about you?"

"Nothing," he rushes out, his pitch rising, making it seem like a lie. Only when I study his features, he seems calm.

"Good." I give him the benefit of the doubt. "So...are you going to take me to bed now?"

Sal half coughs, half laughs, and I hope I never lose the ability to fluster him like that.

"Not a chance," he rasps, shaking his head. "You heard the doctor. Limited movement for at least another twenty-four to forty-eight hours."

"You're joking, right? Please tell me you're joking."

"I'm not. You need to rest, and I need to work for a couple of hours." He stands with me in his arms and positions me back on the couch. "I promise I won't be long."

At the mention of work, excitement builds in my chest. "Can you bring me my laptop?" I hit Sal with a wide smile while he raises a brow, his gaze questioning, giving me my answer.

"Ugh. You suck."

"I'm not actually going in. I have my laptop in my bag."

"What? And you didn't get mine?"

"Nope. But you love me." He smirks and I laugh like he's joking, even though I think I do. At least I would if he'd take me to work, instead of leaving me here to suffer.

"Fine." I roll my eyes, making him chuckle until his expression turns serious again.

"Thank you for sharing your story. I promise to never question your feelings, but at the same time, if those feelings change, I want you to know you can talk to me about it. I don't want you to feel like you're trapped, if you ever change your mind."

"I can promise you that's not going to happen. But also... I'm not the kind of girl that would ever allow myself to feel trapped. You don't have to worry."

"I will always worry."

"I know. Thank you."

"Want me to put on one of those crime shows you like?"

"Nah, that's okay. I'll find something." I stretch to reach the remote, and Sal rushes to grab it, passing it over.

"If you need anything, call out. Please. I'll be at the kitchen table."

"I will."

"Thank you." He kisses me again before turning around to leave, and I smile until he's gone, already feeling the boredom set in. *What the hell am I going to do for a few hours?*

And why the hell didn't I ask Sal to bring me my phone?

Chapter Forty-Seven

KEELEY

I stare at the patterned wallpaper in my apartment, my eyes blurring as the lines all swirl together. Anger consumes me. I thought I loved this apartment, but everything about it is driving me crazy.

It's like a prison in here.

It's been two days since I got home, and as predicted, I'm bored out of my mind. Nothing on TV is holding my interest. I don't want to read any of my books.

For an hour, I had free rein over my phone until Sal realized what I was doing and confiscated it. "For your own good," he claimed, getting a big fuck you in return.

When it hits hour forty-nine, Sal comes in from the kitchen, handing me a salad and a bottle of water, doing all that he can to ensure I stay still.

And I love him for it. Even if I do want to punch him in the face.

"Don't hate me," he begins and I stiffen, knowing exactly what's coming.

"You're going to the office."

"I am."

"I won't hate you if you take me with you."

"You know I can't."

"Didn't your teacher ever tell you there's no such thing as 'can't'? It's 'won't try.'" I stare at him deadpan and he chuckles wholeheartedly.

"Keeley, you have so many things here to keep you entertained."

"Oh, yeah. What would you be doing if you were me?"

Sal glances longingly at his laptop bag, and it's my turn to laugh.

"Okay," he concedes. "Point taken."

"So I can come?"

"No. I promised the doctor I'd look after you. I wouldn't go into work if I didn't have to, but it's important."

"What is it?"

"A meeting."

"What's the meeting about?" I sound like a jealous girlfriend, when in reality, I'm trying to gauge if it's something I can help with, and Sal sees right through my plan.

"Do you need anything before I go?" he asks, ignoring my question, making me pout.

"No. I'm fine here, all by myself, in this tiny apartment."

Sal grins and I shake my head, trying not to smile back. I'm being a brat, but I'm going insane here. Other than my sister's wedding years ago, when I was busy every day, this is the longest I've been off work, and I don't like it. I'm anxious and uncomfortable and...*one hundred percent addicted to working.*

"I might need to see a psychiatrist. I have a problem."

"You and me both." Sal chuckles. "I think you're currently in the detox stage. It will pass."

"Easy for you to say. Off you go."

"Are you sure you don't need anything?"

"Are you sure you won't tell me what your meeting is about?"

"I'm sure."

"Me too."

As though me becoming his girlfriend meant he can't walk away without kissing me, Sal presses his lips to my forehead, and I take comfort in his warmth.

He's trying, and I'm making his life difficult.

He turns to leave, walking straight past his laptop, and a thought hits me.

"Wait. You're not going after Vance, are you?"

"What? No." Sal turns, surprised. "If I was going to do that, I would have done it already, probably while you were still in the hospital. I promised I'd let you confront him, and I'm keeping that promise. It's all set for tomorrow. Though I will say, you're killing me by asking me not to do it myself."

"Good, now you know how I feel."

"It's definitely not the same. I want to hurt someone that hurt you. You're recovering from an injury."

"Neither of us get to do what we want to do. That feels the same to me."

Sal chuckles again, this time under his breath, before he walks back and grabs his laptop, waving before he heads to the door. "I'll be back before you know it."

"Have fun." The sarcasm drips from my tone, and Sal shakes his head with the suppressed smile.

"I'm going to be just as bored as you are. I promise."

"Good." I throw him a smile of my own, this one full of sass.

"God, I… I'll see you soon." Sal's smile turns awkward for the briefest of moments, and a warm glow runs through me. He was going to say I love you. I know it. Only like me, he knew it wasn't the right time.

From the outside looking in, I'm sure people would call us hopeless, but they're wrong. Sal gets me more than anyone else ever has.

And I think I'm finally ready to show him how I feel.

When the time is right.

It's just ticked over to two hours and thirty-seven minutes since Sal left —yes, I've been counting—when someone knocks on my door. I immediately call out for them to come in, not even bothering to ask who it is. I gave my concierge a list of people they could let up unannounced, at Sal's request, so I didn't have to try and get to the intercom. Which means it's either Sal returning, because he still insists on knocking despite practically living here, Paige, or my mom. I figured Easton wasn't going to come on his own, so I didn't bother putting his name down. And I'm not good enough company for anyone else.

Paige walks in, and I hate that I'm a little disappointed.

A part of me was hoping Sal was home with a surprise laptop in hand. *Wishful thinking.*

"Good afternoon, sunshine," Paige jokes and I roll my eyes. "Why is it so gloomy here?" She points to my closed curtains and I point to my ankle.

I'm not going to admit I'm the one that got up and closed them after Sal left. I don't want to sound too tragic.

"You're allowed to move around, Keeley. You just have to stay off your feet for most of the day." She walks over to the curtains, her eyes dropping to my cast.

"I want to heal as fast as possible. The more I laze around, the quicker I recover." I fold my arms over my chest.

"You sound grumpier than when I came by the other day. I will never question if you and Easton are related again. I don't need proof. This personality right here is doing the trick."

"Wrong."

"Wrong?"

"Yes. I have a reason to be grumpy. He's just an ass."

"Wrong." She laughs as she opens my curtains, momentarily blinding me.

"How is that wrong?"

"Because you should be happy about having some time off. You've been working your ass to the bone. Don't look at your injury as though it's taking something away from you. Look at it as though it's giving something back. Time."

I blow out a breath and lay my head back on the couch. "I wish you were right. But time can be dangerous. I can't stop thinking. About everything. I'm replaying my fall, the assault, the various assholes that made me despise athletes—apart from the Storm guys—and my pregnancy. Every damn thing. And on top of that, I'm supposed to be confronting Vance tomorrow."

"Have you told my dad any of this?"

"Some. Though I haven't mentioned that I'm continuing to relive it. And I can't exactly tell him that if he's not here."

Paige's nose scrunches, and I swear I see the hint of a grin before she turns away.

"What was that?"

"What was what?" She looks back toward me, her expression now the picture of calm.

"Never mind. I'm sorry I'm so grouchy. I just—"

"Hate not being able to work? You sound like someone else I know, and think about how well that turned out."

"I'd say it turned out great. Sal's work obsession was the beginning of everything that led you to San Francisco. Without that, you wouldn't have met Easton and Isaac."

"And you wouldn't have met my dad." She raises an eyebrow and I huff out a laugh. "Though, that's not what I'm talking about. Yes, he's happy now; you both are. But for a while there, he wasn't in a good place. He lost his wife and his kids."

"I know. And I promise I'm not making light of your pain. I'm sorry you went through that. All of it."

"Thank you. That's not the reason I'm scolding you."

"I know. I suck at being bored."

"Why don't you watch TV or read a book?"

"I tried that, but I can't get into anything, I just want to work."

"Oh my God." She face-palms before groaning. "The two of you were made for each other. I'm calling Dad. He needs to come home so he can entertain you."

I bite my lip to suppress a laugh just as Paige's eyes widen. "Wait. That came out wrong."

"Did it? I thought it was perfect. We could—"

"Do *not* finish that sentence or so help me God."

"I love you, Paige."

"Yeah, yeah. Anyway, I come bearing gifts." She rummages around in her bag and pulls out a bar of dark chocolate from Hamilton's. My favorite. "This is from Isaac. If you're feeling up to it, I'll bring him over this weekend, before I head to New York."

"You're still going?" I frown. I'd been secretly hoping she'd changed her mind. "Aren't you worried about what they've been doing to D'Angelo Construction and your mom?"

"A little. But I have to go. What if I don't and they somehow get a lighter sentence? I'll always blame myself."

"I understand that. I do. But you need to tell your dad. I'm sure he'll want to set up a security detail and—"

"That's why I haven't told him yet. He already has one guy following me around."

"He does?"

"Yep. I was annoyed at first, but we're actually friends now. He's nice."

I laugh, until the seriousness of the matter comes back to mind. "I don't want to have to do this, Paige, but if you don't tell him, I might have to."

"I figured. And if I'm honest, maybe it's better coming from you."

"Whatever you need. I'm here for you."

"Likewise. Now let's eat this chocolate and forget about our worries for a few minutes." She produces a second bar and waves it around like it's the most wonderful gift in the world, and right now, it is.

"That sounds perfect to me. Thank you, Isaac."

Chapter Forty-Eight

SALVATORE

I pace the floor of my office, my eyes on the field as the guys practice, my mind in New York while I chat with Austin, my private investigator.

"I don't know how we get around this without doing anything illegal, Sal," he tells me, sighing into the phone.

We've been trying to come up with ways of proving the Mikklesons are behind the attacks on D'Angelo Construction, but so far, we haven't come up with anything concrete.

"You know my answer to that, Austin. If we break the law, that gives them more leverage."

"Only if we get caught." I imagine him shrugging and groan. "I'll keep thinking, but for now, I've got a tail on the two of them, and I've reached out to a contact of mine that knows a few of their friends. I'll see if he can get someone into their inner circle. I can't guarantee it though, because they're keeping that circle tight now that the trial is set to begin."

"Thanks, Austin. I appreciate your help. Let's talk soon."

"Yep. I'll be in touch."

With my eyes closed, I lean back in my chair and count to ten. I shouldn't have to worry about the Mikklesons right now. I've got Keeley to focus on. I should be there. I hadn't even planned on coming into the office at all today. I only left Keeley alone to plan a surprise for her, until Camilla called. She's convinced that Marc's being followed now too, and wants me to do something about it before their focus shifts to Paige.

"Marc and I can handle ourselves," she'd told me. "But if they come after Paige, I'm going to break your balls."

And I have no doubt she'd do just that.

It's a fun time to be me at the moment. I've got my ex blowing up my phone and my new girlfriend threatening me with violence because she's bored out of her mind.

I know how to fix the latter. As for Camilla, I'm struggling.

Though I'm not worried about Paige. She's protected here.

After stopping past Wes's office to make sure Vance is still locked in for our "meeting" tomorrow, I head back to Keeley's around four p.m. prepared for another attack.

Only when I get there, the apartment is quiet, and Keeley's nowhere to be seen.

My heart races as I push through the bedroom door, checking to see if she's napping. She's not.

"Keels. Where are you?"

"In here," she calls out from the bathroom and I relax, laughing at myself. It's not like she can go far.

"I'll be in the living room if you need anything."

"Actually, can you come in?"

"Of course." I stride toward the door and hesitate before stepping inside, my heart jolting when I find her. *Fuck.*

She's in the bath, her cast resting up on the edge, her head dropped back, her face pinched in what I assume to be frustration.

My gaze drops to her nipples floating on the top of the water, and I swallow a lump in my throat, ignoring my cock as it twitches. "Are you okay?" I rasp before coughing to clear my throat. "Do you need help?"

"I do. And I really hate that. I thought I had everything close by, but I grabbed two conditioners instead of the shampoo." She huffs as she points toward the shower and the lone bottle sitting on the ledge.

"How did you even get in there?"

"It wasn't easy. But I couldn't go another day without a shower and since I can't do that without getting my cast wet, this is the alternative."

"You should have told me; I could have wrapped your cast in a bag or something."

"Believe it or not, I wanted to do something on my own. I wanted my boyfriend to come home to a clean girl."

"I don't mind you being dirty." I hide my smile until Keeley's eyes flash to mine, and she stifles a laugh.

"You're the one holding back, Sir. That's not on me."

"I've been doing that for *you*, Miss."

"I know. I know. Anyway, can you pass me the shampoo so I can wash my hair? I'd love to feel somewhat normal today."

"Of course." The water sloshes as I turn toward the shower, and my mind conjures images of Keeley's naked body lifting from the water, making me internally curse myself. Now is not the time for my dick to get hard.

I grab the shampoo, and when I look back at Keeley, she's under the water, giving me a full view of her body since she's now lying down.

And my God, is she glorious.

It's not the first time I've seen her naked, though it is the first time I've felt like it's not forbidden.

After a beat, she sits up and wipes her face, holding her hand out for the bottle, but I can't seem to hand it over. I'm not sure why I'm hesitating until I realize I don't want to leave.

"Let me," I tell her.

"What?" Keeley's eyes widen in surprise.

"Let me wash your hair." I put the bottle down and take off my jacket, rolling up the sleeves of my shirt while Keeley watches my every move in the mirror. Her tongue peeks out of her mouth, brushing along her parted lips before she traps a lip between her teeth, forcing me to look away.

"Can you move down slightly?" I ask as I sit on the edge of the bath behind her head, pouring shampoo into my hand.

"You're serious?" she probes as she shuffles forward, giving me some space.

"Deadly. Only, I've never washed someone else's hair."

"Never?"

"Never."

"Not even..." She trails off, laughing to herself. "Never mind. My question would have made things weird."

"Paige?" I wager a guess.

"Yep." Her nose scrunches and I chuckle.

"Not even Paige. We had nannies to do that."

"Right. Okay. Well, feel free to give it a go."

I chuckle softly at the uncertainty in her tone before rubbing the shampoo into her hair, gathering her thick strands into my hands to make sure it's all covered. I try to focus on the task at hand, until Keeley's head falls back and I find myself watching her, my fingers massaging her head. With her eyes closed, she lets out a soft moan, and my breath picks up speed.

When too much time has passed, I force my hands to gently let go, then fill up the cup she had on the counter, covering her eyes as I rinse out the foam.

"Look at you making sure I don't get soap in my eyes."

"What can I say? I'm a gentleman."

Keeley's lips pull into a sassy smile, and I smile right back even though she can't see me.

I begin the conditioning process next, and she moans softly. "This feels so good. If you're not careful, I'm going to force you to wash my hair for the rest of our lives."

A breath catches in my throat, and it takes me a second to respond. "You make it sound like a punishment."

"Isn't it?"

"Absolutely not." *Especially if it means you're planning a lifetime together.*

We both fall silent as I rake my fingers through her hair, spreading the conditioner to the ends, and when I'm done, I straighten, shifting around to relieve some of the tension in my pants. Who would have thought this would make me hard?

"How long do you leave it in?" I ask, remembering Camilla used to take a ridiculously long time on her hair-washing days. The days before she started going to the salon twice a week so they could do it all for her.

Keeley giggles softly. "I'm impressed. A few minutes will be fine."

"Okay." I grab the loofah and squirt some body wash onto the burgundy sponge, before dipping it into the water and gliding it over Keeley's back. She jolts before turning around with a smirk.

"Are you going to wash *me* now?"

"I am. If that's okay?"

"It's more than okay. Thank you."

With a smile, I lather her back before sliding forward on the ledge, ignoring when water soaks through my pants.

I curve the sponge over her shoulder, then wrap an arm around her neck and lean forward to whisper in her ear, "Lie back. I've got you."

She shivers but does as I ask, closing her eyes and trusting me to hold her.

I hold my breath as I glide the loofah across her collarbone, dipping between her breasts that are peeking out of the water.

My heart races as I lower my hand under the bubbles, reaching her belly button before stopping just above her center.

She parts her legs and I pull back quickly, stifling a groan. I want more. I want everything. And I want it now.

"Can you hold yourself up for a second? I'm going to finish your hair," I rasp, filling the cup with water to rinse off the conditioner, standing the second I'm done. "Do you need to do anything else before I help you out?"

Keeley frowns but shakes her head. "No, I'm good. I actually washed myself before you arrived." The hint of a smile tugs at her lips, and I can't stop myself from returning it.

"Well, I appreciate you letting me do it again."

"The pleasure was all mine."

Ignoring her insinuating tone, I grab her towel before standing close to the ledge. "Out of curiosity, how were you planning on getting out if I wasn't here?"

"I have no idea. I hadn't planned that far in advance."

"Give me your hands." I chuckle before lifting her out of the water, waiting until she has her good leg over the side then helping her to stand, keeping my eyes on her face.

"What's wrong?" she asks, raising a single manicured eyebrow as she grabs my shoulders for balance, her lips quirked into a grin. "Are you worried you're going to lose your willpower if you see my dripping body?"

"Keeley, I lost my willpower the second I walked into the bathroom." I dry her shoulders, smiling when her jaw drops.

"You did?'

"Yep."

"Then why the hell are you taking so long?" She grabs the towel from my hand and wraps it around her hair, almost falling as she does. And when she's finished, she reaches for a second towel, quickly wiping herself down. "All done." She smiles brightly, making me laugh.

"What about your back?" I take the towel from her hand and turn her around to face the mirror, holding her waist as I pat her back dry. When I'm done, I drop the towel and hold her with both hands as I lean down, pressing my lips to her shoulder, finally giving in to my burning desire.

Curling my hands farther around her from behind, I splay them over her stomach, brushing a thumb against her breast as I press my body against hers, letting her feel how much I want this. How much I want her.

She gasps softly, and I meet her gaze in the mirror, kissing a path down her neck as she melts into me.

Her hands cover mine and she curls her fingers, running the tips back and forth over my skin, her touch soft and caressing. I let out a soft groan against her neck, and her pulse races against my lips, sending a spark right through me.

"I think it's time I took you to bed," I whisper when her head falls back onto my shoulder and her breath hitches.

"Please."

Without another word, I lift her into my arms and carry her into the bedroom, only pausing when I get to the bed.

I gently ease her onto the mattress, positioning her on the pillow before grabbing the spare and arranging it under her foot.

She opens her mouth to speak until I press a kiss to the skin above the cast, pushing her other leg farther away, spreading her for me.

With my eyes locked on her core, I swallow a lump in my throat, clearing it before I speak. "I know we've both been waiting for this, but I'm going to take my time. I want us to always remember this moment."

Keeley nods as she lifts to her elbows, her wild gaze meeting mine. "Good thing I have nowhere else to be."

Chapter Forty-Nine

SALVATORE

Keeley lays her head back down to the pillow, and I'm about to kiss a path up her leg when she stops me.

"Wait. Come here." She curls her finger, gesturing for me to move closer, and I walk around the bed, standing near her head. "Keep coming."

I climb onto the bed, straddling myself over her, and smile when she bites her lip. Leaning down, I nibble a trail down her neck, and she lets out a delicious moan before pushing me backward. "That's not what I wanted. I'm naked. I need to level the playing field." She lies back again, pulling me down with her so she can unbutton my shirt, her eyes raking over my chest when the shirt falls open.

"Mmm. Much better, thank you."

"You're welcome. Now, can I get back to it? Since you've had your fix."

"Please do. I think you were about to kiss my knee."

"Thank you for the reminder." I chuckle but change my plan, kissing a path from her shoulder to her breasts instead, smiling as she quivers beneath me.

"That feels nice."

"How about this?" I swirl my tongue over her right nipple, then gently bite down when it pebbles, my hand on her stomach as her hips buck.

"So good," she rushes out, curling her fingers into my hair, her delicate touch making me shiver.

I lave her swollen bud, alternating between licking and sucking, teasing until she's writhing beneath me. Her breathing picks up as I release my hold and move across her chest, giving the same attention to the other side, caressing her nipple until it's marble hard.

She moans and reaches for my pants, but I push her hand away, taking that as my cue to move down her body, my hands gliding across her skin as I kiss a path toward her center.

I pause when my chin hits the apex of her thighs, breathing her in as I stare up at her, taking in her wanton expression.

"Please," she begs, rolling her hips as though I need guidance, and I almost laugh until she begs me again, her pitch rising, her voice full of the desperation I feel.

Spreading her pussy, I run my tongue through her slick heat and groan at finally getting to taste her again.

Her clit swells as I circle it, and I feel her getting wetter as I slowly run my thumbs along her folds, spreading her until I reach her entrance.

She moves her uninjured leg wider, bending her knee to open herself farther for me, and I reward her with a finger, curling it inside her as her body flushes, a pink hue coating her perfect skin.

Her arousal coats my finger, making it easy to slip a second inside her, scissoring them both as she moans. Her passionate cries drive me wild, and my length grows, the tip pushing against the waistband of my briefs.

I can't remember ever being this hung up on a woman, this obsessed with her pleasure, while desperate for my own. It's new. It's *her*.

I curl my fingers again, and she moans as her eyes close, her lips parting in ecstasy. She palms her breasts, rolling her fingers over her taut nipples, and my hips buck against the bed. A growl releases low in my throat as Keeley's eyes flash open, a carnal urge reflected in her gaze.

After watching her for a few more seconds, I lower my face to her pussy and flatten my tongue against her clit, teasing as I continue to pump my fingers.

She writhes beneath me, panting as her chest heaves, and her pussy tightens around me.

She's close. So close I can feel her body preparing for release.

I bite down on her clit, giving her more, until she tugs at my hair, begging me to stop. "I want you inside me. Please. I want to feel you when I come."

Jesus. Christ.

A groan rips from my throat as I force myself to pull away, my breaths ragged as I stand, staring down at her flushed skin before our eyes meet with the same intense fire burning in the center.

She blinks, breaking my trance, and I snap into action, throwing the shirt off my shoulders and reaching for the button on my pants.

Her body arches off the bed, begging for my touch as I slowly lower my pants and briefs, only pausing when I'm completely naked, panic hitting me out of nowhere. "Fuck. I don't have a condom."

"We don't need it," Keeley rushes out. "Unless you want to. I've been tested and haven't been with anyone for over a year."

"Christ. Same. And I want that. If you're sure."

"I am. Please."

With a nod, I climb back onto the bed, hovering above her as our eyes lock. She's so goddamn beautiful that I'm momentarily struck still.

She blinks rapidly, and I can't stop myself from cupping her cheek, the pad of my thumb brushing her lips.

I lower slightly until our bodies touch, warm flesh on flesh, an inferno of desire burning between us.

Keeley sighs, and it fills me with a spark I haven't felt before, a love I didn't know was possible.

And it hits me. This isn't just sex. It's so much more than that. It will always be more than that. Only with her.

Reaching between us, I line my cock up with her center, pressing my lips to hers as I slowly push inside her.

My body shakes, and on top of the intense pleasure I expected to feel, a deep sense of peace washes over me. I pause to pull back, meeting her gaze, and when her eyes widen, I know she feels the same. She's with me.

This is it, for both of us.

After a deep breath, I inch deeper inside her, stretching her walls as she bites her lip, her gaze never leaving mine.

When I'm buried to the hilt, I pause, giving us both a second to adjust before I roll my hips. Her lips quiver and I can't stop myself from stealing another kiss, my heart pounding as I lower my body to hers, the connection electrifying from her mouth to her core.

Her pussy squeezes around my cock, and my hips jolt as I lift to watch our connection, to see myself moving inside her.

"Fuck, Keeley. You feel so good. Like you were made for me."

With our bodies molded as one, we take our time until we're both teetering on the edge and I can't hold back anymore. "Jesus." I pump harder, my arms shaking as I hold myself up, rocking my hips, pounding her pussy as a pressure builds low in my stomach.

Keeley cries out as she matches my urgency, her eyes ablaze with a passionate intensity as her hips rock to keep up with me. "More, please. Don't stop."

"Not a chance," I rush out, my voice husky as I grit my teeth, working hard to delay my gratification.

Her walls tighten again, and I feel her impending orgasm as her pussy throbs against my bare cock.

I pump harder until she's gasping for release, her hands curling into the sheets, her fingers holding on for dear life as her body spasms in ecstasy. "Sal. God, yes." She stifles a high-pitched scream as my body jolts, my orgasm hitting me with full force, and I grunt as I empty into her, waves of pleasure rolling through me.

"Ah. Fuck. Keeley."

I shake uncontrollably, my muscles weak as heat ripples under my skin, my release so intense that I'm caught off guard.

"*Fuck.*" My balls tingle as we both slow our rhythm, and when she glances up at me, I'm hypnotized by the brightness of her gaze, my chest tight as she peers into my soul.

I want to tell her I love her, but I am not going to be the guy that throws it out in the heat of passion.

I'm almost certain she knows anyway. Just like I know she feels the same.

When her breathing slows to a less frantic pace, I pull out of her and drop down on the bed beside her, throwing a hand over my face as I chuckle.

"Why the hell didn't we do that sooner?"

Keeley giggles, the sound of it eliciting a sigh of content. I could stay in the moment forever.

"That's on you, Mr. D'Angelo. You were too caught up waiting for a bed."

"Maybe so, but I have no regrets about the location."

Keeley laughs again before twisting to face me, her face pinched as she shifts her foot.

"Careful. Can I help?"

"No. I'm good now. I just wanted to do this." She curls into me, and the peace I felt earlier deepens into a state of blissful happiness.

"How soon before you can go again?" she asks into my chest, the vibrations of her lips sending a jolt of electricity through to my cock, making it twitch for round two.

"Give me a minute and I'll be good. I don't plan on leaving this bedroom for the rest of the night."

I lift Keeley onto the bed after our third intense session, and she groans. "Don't be mad. But I was wrong. That hurt my ankle. A little."

"I told you," I lightly scold her.

"Still worth it."

Despite my arguments, Keeley wanted to mix things up. So instead of having sex on the bed, I sat on the armchair in her room and she sat on top of me, her back to my chest as she faced the mirrored doors of her closet.

It stressed me out, worrying about her ankle, until the second she lowered onto my cock, her legs spread to give me the most glorious visual in her reflection. I'm ashamed to say, I lost my mind so fast that I forgot about her cast until after I was coming back down to earth.

"Maybe we should use the bed again next time?"

"Why? You didn't enjoy it?"

"Fuck, Keeley. I've never enjoyed anything more. But I don't want to delay your healing."

"I'm beginning to think that's not such a bad thing, if this is how we get to pass the time." She bites her lip, and I growl before burying my face in her neck, sucking the flesh until she moans my name. "First, I need a breather. Not long. Just a few minutes. And maybe something to eat." She smiles and I chuckle lightly.

"That can be arranged. You stay here, and I'll make us something."

"That's three times now that you've made me food. I would have thought you'd have people to do that. Hell, I would have thought you'd have people to ask other people to do that."

"I did when I lived with Camilla. But when it was just me, I learned to fend for myself."

"Takeout?" Keeley questions with a Cheshire-cat grin and she's spot-on.

"Almost every night, though I can cook. I just don't have time anymore."

"Maybe we should write a list of things we'd do if we weren't workaholics."

"Oh, yeah? And what would we do with those lists?"

"Toss them in the garbage, because let's face it—we're never going to change." She laughs to herself while my stomach knots. I'm anxious about work, there's no doubt about it, but at the same time, I don't want to go back. Not while she's at home.

And definitely not while she's begging me to stay.

Only, I'm hoping my surprise will help with that.

I just have to wait until tomorrow.

Chapter Fifty

KEELEY

I have a vague memory of someone kissing my head, and when I wake, I find Sal's side of the bed empty. With a smile, I stretch my body, groaning as it aches in all the right places.

I have never had sex that many times in one night, and I have to say, for a man twenty years older, Sal has incredible stamina. If I hadn't said I needed sleep, I have no doubt he would have gone again.

With a deep breath to prepare for more muscle soreness, I lift my head and check the time to see it's already nine a.m. Considering how early I fell asleep, I thought I'd be up before the sun.

After taking a moment to half twist, half crawl out of bed, I slip into my summer robe, sans clothes, and wrap it around myself, hiding the goods, hoping to tease Sal enough that he carries me back in here for round five this morning.

Since Sal set me up with my crutches close by, I quietly thank him and walk out toward the kitchen, assuming he's making breakfast. "God. You must have fucked me into a coma last night because I slept like— Oh, Jesus."

I tighten the robe around myself and secure the tie, smiling awkwardly at the three huge football players standing around my kitchen counter.

"Hi." I wave hesitantly as Luke cracks up laughing, with Reed and Zane standing awkwardly beside him.

"Well, well, well. I'm not sure that's what the doctor meant when he said you need to be taken care of," Luke muses, making Sal groan as he turns away and walks out of the room, mumbling something about making a phone call.

"Nice to see you all. To what do we owe the pleasure?"

"We heard through the grapevine that you were struggling with boredom," Reed fills me in, his lips pulled into a smile.

"But it looks like you found something to pass the time." Luke winks and I roll my eyes.

"You caught me."

"Yeah, we did." Luke bounces his eyebrows, and Zane elbows him in the stomach.

"Now you're just being creepy. Jokes aside, we came to check on you. How are you feeling?" Zane asks, his gaze dropping to my ankle.

"I'm okay. As long as I keep my foot elevated, the pain's relatively manageable."

"I'd imagine lying on your back helps with that." Luke laughs at his own joke before covering his mouth and mumbling an apology. "Last one, I promise. Though I was going to ask about you and D'Angelo. I guess I don't have to now."

"I guess you don't and that's all I'm going to say. Moving on. How's practice going? Are you all set for the opening game this weekend? Please tell me my replacement spoke to at least one of you about doing an interview with—"

Luke puts his finger to my lips, shushing me loudly. "No talking shop or you'll get us in trouble with the boss." He glances over his shoulder.

"He told you not to talk about work?" My jaw drops as my eyes flash to Sal pacing in the living room. If he wasn't on the phone, I'd be calling his ass in here.

"He did." Reed pats me on the shoulder. "But I agree with his logic. You need to be focused on your recovery."

"On that note," Zane cuts in. "What happened?"

"What do you mean?"

"People don't just fall down stairs, Keeley."

"Sure, they do. Especially when they wear heels as tall as I do."

Luke and Reed chuckle while Zane shakes his head. "I'm not buying it. You're always in heels. High ones. You'd probably be able to run a marathon if you had to."

I internally wince because he's not wrong. "What can I say? I didn't see the step."

"Who were you talking to?"

"What?"

"Jesus, Zane. What's with the third degree?" Luke asks, his expression pulled into a frown.

"I'm just asking a question." Zane's eyes bore into mine, silently reiterating what he asked. He knows something. He's always been the quietly observant type. I noticed it when he first started at the Storm, before the drama between him and Easton even began.

I sigh subtly before sitting down on the stool, only for the guys to all panic and insist we move to the couch.

"I'm fine. I plan on kicking you out in a few minutes anyway." I laugh at my humor until Luke's eyes light up and I know what's coming. He's going to tease me about Sal again. "Don't. You said that was the last time."

"Dammit. Back to the guy you were talking to."

I should have let him tease me about Sal; it would have changed the subject.

"It was Vance, right?" Luke asks, scratching his head. "I saw him as I was running over. Jesus, fuck. That asshole left the second you fell."

"Vance?" Zane frowns. "As in Vance McMillan?"

"Yep."

"Did something happen between you?"

"You don't have to answer that," Reed cuts in, his gaze bouncing pointedly between Zane and Luke. "As long as you've spoken to someone about what happened?" His eyes flash toward Sal, and I wait for him to look back before I nod.

"I have. Thank you all for caring. But I promise I'm okay. You can remove me from your group chat name."

"Not yet. I want to annoy East for a little while longer."

I snort out a laugh, shaking my head at Luke. "I'm surprised he's never decked you."

"Me too, if I'm being honest."

The guys stay for another hour until they're due for a group workout session, waving to Sal as they walk by. It's another ten minutes before he ends his call, and his weary eyes have me worried. Especially when he notices me watching him and instantly schools his features.

"What's going on?"

"That was Paige."

Oh. I smile like I normally would if she'd called, despite having a fair idea what she was calling about. "How is she?"

"She's testifying."

"What?" I fake a gasp and Sal rolls his eyes.

"She told me you knew."

"Ugh, I'm sorry. I wanted to tell you so many times, but I'm still trying to work out how this whole best friend versus boyfriend thing is going to work."

"It's okay." Sal stalks closer and wraps me in his arms. "She also told me you begged her to mention it."

"I did."

"Thank you. She's not at all happy about my response."

"What did you say?"

"That I was disappointed."

I grimace. "Damn. You pulled that card."

"Yep. What is she thinking, Keeley? She knows about the fire, and about someone stalking her mom. So, what? Does she think they're going to let her fly into New York and testify without consequence?"

"I don't think she's worried about that. She's more concerned with making sure she does her bit to ensure they go to prison for a very long time."

"That's exactly what she said."

"Why don't you go with her to New York?"

"I don't want her to go."

"I'm not sure you can stop her."

"Fuck, I know. Instead, I'll just add her to the list of people I'm worried about."

"Come on. We both know you were worried about her before you found out she was testifying."

Sal tries to fight it, but his lips lift into a smile and he reluctantly agrees. "I can't process that now anyway. I have something important to do."

"More important than Paige?"

"Jesus, that's a trick question. No, but also yes."

"Call me intrigued."

"I'm taking you out."

"Out?" My eyes widen before excitement fills me. "Are you taking me to the stadium?"

"Definitely not." Sal chuckles while I frown. We're not meeting Vance until four this afternoon, so I was secretly hoping he was going to let me get a few hours of work in beforehand. It would certainly help to take my mind off whatever I'm going to say to Vance. "Sorry." Sal smiles sympathetically. "But—"

"You're just looking after me. I know. Only, where were you when the guys were grilling me about our love life?"

"As far away as I could possibly be." Sal visibly winces.

"And wasn't that so nice of you?"

I raise an eyebrow and Sal chuckles, pressing a kiss to my head. "Sorry. I won't do it again. Now, we're going out because you need some air."

"Then open a window."

"Okay, I'll rephrase... You need a change of scenery."

"I'm fine. A change of scenery is not going to stop me from thinking about work." *Or Vance.*

"We're going out," he tells me, walking into the bedroom without letting me argue. I watch him with a smile until he stops suddenly and rushes back into the kitchen.

"Are you naked under that robe?"

"I sure am." I beam up at him and he groans, dropping his face into his hand. "Are we still going out?"

"Yes. Come on. I'll help you get dressed."

The sun beams through the trees, appearing like flashes of light as we drive toward the beach and away from the chaos. I put down my window to feel the breeze on my face, breathing in the salty air as the ocean comes into view.

"Where are we going?"

We've been driving for about twenty minutes without Sal saying a word, and as we turn toward the water, my interest piques.

"Are you taking me to the beach? I'm not sure my crutches will be that easy to use on sand."

"I could carry you." His eyes flash my way before they're back on the road, so he doesn't see me poking my tongue out.

"I can walk, Sal. I'm not—" I cut myself off when he smirks, and roll my eyes as I bite back a smile. "We're not going to the beach, are we?"

He shakes his head.

"How about I wait and see?"

"I think that's a great idea." Sal smiles as he turns his attention back to the road, while reaching out to curl his hand around my thigh, giving it a squeeze.

I bask in the warmth of his palm on my skin until the car slows, and he turns into the driveway of a huge mansion. A beachfront property that I stare at longingly like it's love at first sight.

"Are we visiting someone?" I ask, turning his way to gauge his reaction.

"No," he answers without emotion, coming to a stop near the front of the circular driveway.

"Trespassing?" I ask next, and this time Sal laughs.

"No."

I stare at him for a beat until an idea hits me and I gasp. "You bought a house, didn't you?" I don't know why that thought popped into my head, but the second it's there, I know it's the truth.

"I did. A year ago."

"What? Why?"

"Because I thought there would come a time when I'd want to grow up and become a homeowner."

"Sal, you own your apartment. Two apartments, in fact—one here and one in New York."

"And a house in..." My eyes widen and he trails off. "It doesn't matter. The point is that I wanted something bigger. What do you think?"

Without giving him a response, I turn toward the house and take it all in, breathless at its beauty.

I've never pictured the type of house I'd want if I ever moved, and yet, one look at this place has me thinking this would be it. If I had unlimited funds like Sal does. It's a modern beachy structure with lots of windows, and what looks to be high ceilings based on the size.

There are manicured hedges running around the grounds, and a huge entry with an angled roofline covering the porch, highlighting the water features on both sides.

"It's beautiful, Sal."

"I'm glad you think so. Here's hoping you like the inside too, because I'm moving you in here."

"You're what?" I huff out an incredulous laugh.

"You heard me."

I what? My jaw drops before I shake my head. "You're moving me in?"

"Yep. And you're not going to argue. You're going to smile, say thank you, and make this as painless as possible."

"I am?"

"Definitely. Come on, I'll show you around."

He jumps out of the car and jogs around the front to open my door while I stare at him in awe, my heart pounding. I could get used to this version of Sal. Protective yet demanding.

I think I just fell for him a little bit more.

Chapter Fifty-One

SALVATORE

Keeley crutches her way through the door, only pausing when we pass over the threshold, her eyes wide, lips parted in awe.

To our left there's a sweeping staircase, leading up to the bright landing of the second floor. To our right, there's a sunken living room with plush lounges and a huge TV. But neither of those things grab her attention. Her eyes are focused directly in front of us. To the open kitchen and dining area and the wall of glass doors leading out onto a deck overlooking the ocean.

"You're asking me to move in?" she whispers, her voice hesitant as she slowly moves forward.

"Did I ask?" I wait for her gaze to snap to mine, and it does, right on cue.

"No. You didn't. You all but demanded I do. And as sexy as that is, don't you think it's a little too soon?"

"Do you want to spend the next week stuck in your apartment? Or would you prefer to be here, with ocean views and a pizza oven?"

"A pizza oven?"

"Yep." I nod, thankful I was able to get one added so quickly.

Keeley laughs, and the relaxed sound makes my heart race. "Obviously the latter but..." She trails off and I'm quick to reassure her. The demanding Sal is gone.

"You can move out again when your ankle gets better. For now, I'm going to be staying here, and I want you here with me. I want to continue looking after you. In this house."

Keeley eyes me suspiciously, and I can't for the life of me figure out why until she laughs. "You spoke to my mom, didn't you?"

"About what?" I'm genuinely confused while Keeley appears to have figured out the answer to the meaning of life.

"Don't mess with me. There are only two things in the world that ever work to still my mind. Well, three..." she muses, shaking her head with a laugh. "The point is that you know yoga is one of my escapes, and the second is the ocean. But I don't just mean the sounds from the water crashing against the shore or the smell of salt in the air. It has to be all of it, hitting my senses in one go. Like a wave washing over me, blinding me from whatever's going on in the world, taking me out of reality."

I watch her as she speaks, her eyes alight with happiness, the calm she's talking about washing over her from the thought alone.

She raises an eyebrow in question when she's done, her expression confident.

"I haven't spoken to your mom. At least not about that."

Keeley's excited appearance morphs into one of confusion, and for the first time since I've known her, she blushes.

"Silly me."

"Wait. It's not silly at all. I may not have known any of that, but I had the house prepared so I could bring you here, hoping for the same result. Hoping to take your mind off things. To calm you."

"You had the house prepared?"

"Yes. That was the meeting I wouldn't tell you about. Until a few days ago, this place was unfurnished."

"Unfurnished? You got a whole house furnished in a few days?"

"I did." I bounce my eyebrows, and Keeley laughs before her gaze sweeps around the house.

"Can we look around?" she asks softly, her voice holding an element of awe.

"Of course. Let me know if there's anything you don't like because we can change whatever we want. I didn't pick any of it, so you won't offend me if something isn't to your taste."

"We?"

"We what?"

"You said we can change it."

"Keeley, this place is yours for as long as you want to stay here."

She mumbles something under her breath, and I swear I hear the word forever but I don't let myself get caught up in it. I could have been deluding myself. But...

Forever sounds good to me.

We take our time walking through the house, with Keeley seeing it for the first time and me falling in love with it again as I experience it through her eyes. She stops when we find ourselves back at the stairs leading to the second level, and her face scrunches. "Lucky there's a bedroom downstairs. I might have to stay down here for a while."

"Nonsense."

Before she can question me, I grab her crutches and rest them against the wall, then curl my arms under her legs, lifting her in my hold. I jog up the stairs, laughing as she begs me to put her down.

"You can't carry me up and down the stairs."

"Wanna bet? How about a lazy million?"

"Oh, sure. Because I'm going to agree to that."

"That's how certain I am that I can do this." I put her down and settle her beside the wall, running down to grab her crutches as she watches me. "We should get you two pairs of these, one for each level."

"That's a bit extreme."

"Maybe." I shrug as I angle her toward the landing, and more importantly the primary bedroom with another wall of windows facing the water. Just like downstairs.

"Holy shit." Her jaw drops as she takes herself closer, her crutches making little imprints on the carpeted floor. "That balcony runs the entire length of the house," she says in wonder.

"It does."

"And...is that the en suite?"

"Yes."

"It's bigger than my bedroom. What's that empty space for? It seems like a waste." She points to the other side of the room that remains unfurnished. At least it does now; the interior decorator had put a couch and armchair there. But when I came past yesterday, I asked for them to be removed. "I thought that would be a good place for a yoga mat and TV, to find your zen by the water. There's a studio in New York that does online classes. My New York assistant was raving about it. I thought you could join their online session when you don't have time to visit Aliive."

"You know the name of the studio I go to?"

"*That* I asked your mom about. I told her it's because I wanted to get you a gift voucher. She thought it was sweet."

"Instead, you furnished an entire house so you could give me my own studio?"

"Yeah." I scratch the back of my neck, only now realizing how crazy that sounds. We only just started dating.

Keeley's silent as her eyes wander the empty space, and I hope to God that she's picturing it all in her mind, instead of contemplating how the hell she's going to let me down.

"Yes," she whispers after what feels like a lifetime. "Yes, I'll stay with you."

I almost whisper *forever* but hold back, instead rushing forward to meet her, wrapping my arms around her waist. "Thank you. I was never actually going to move in here alone. It's too big for one person."

"If we're being honest, it's too big for two...and I didn't say I was moving in."

"Not yet."

"Not yet?"

"You heard me."

Keeley snorts out a laugh before her expression softens, and the smallest of frowns lowers her lips. "I wish I could do yoga. Or any kind of exercise. I'm going to lose my stamina."

"It's only about six more weeks. In the meantime, I'm sure we can think of other ways to burn energy." I glance to the bed and Keeley laughs.

"I'm sure we can."

After a quick tour upstairs, with a few more oohs and ahhs from Keeley, I carry her back down and get her settled comfortably on the lounge chair outside, making her promise me she'll stay downstairs for the next few days if I'm not home to help her. Thankfully she agrees.

The early afternoon sun reflects off the glistening water, and with the sound of the waves and the breeze surrounding us, Keeley finally looks happy. Peaceful. At ease. And my body warms because of it.

"You were right," she says after a period of silence. "This is exactly what I needed."

"Thank God." A loud breath expels from my lungs. "I wasn't sure I was going to survive the rest of the week with the way you were glaring my way."

"Stop. I'd never actually hurt you. And I still want to work as soon as I'm allowed. But this is nice in the meantime."

"Good." I smile until Vance comes to mind, and I hate that I have to ruin the moment. "We probably have another hour before we need to leave. Do you want to stay out here? I could bring you a book."

Keeley blows out a breath, smile gone. "I might head in to watch TV. I'm not sure I can concentrate enough to read."

"Sounds good."

I should be working, but instead, I sit down next to her once she's settled on the couch and lift her legs onto my lap, making sure her ankle's supported, wanting to be here if she needs to talk.

We watch one of her true crime shows in silence, my hand on her thigh, my heart pounding harder the closer we get to having to leave.

While I don't want her to go anywhere near that asshole, I'm prepared to suck it up because that's what she wants. *But...*if his hands go near any part of her body, even by accident, I'm going to intervene.

I'm only human after all, and there's only so much I can hold back, so much pain I can endure. And with Keeley, that level is low. She's already been hurt enough. It's her time to have a happily ever after.

CHAPTER FIFTY-TWO

KEELEY

We move slowly through the halls of the stadium, my crutches clacking against the floor as we make our way toward Wes's office. His door comes into view and Sal pauses, carefully pulling me to a stop.

"You are a strong, incredible woman, Keeley, and I know you've got this. But if at any point you want to leave, if he touches you, or you decide you would like me to kick his ass, please don't hesitate to call out for me. I'll be right outside the *open* door." His gaze locks to mine and I laugh softly.

"Thank you. I appreciate that. But I'm going to be fine." *At least that's what I'm telling myself.*

I turn to hobble away again until Sal's palm curls around my waist, prompting me to pause. "What are you doing?" I ask as he comes to stand in front of me, amusement in my eyes.

"I just want to do this." He cups my face and slams his lips to mine, his kiss more urgent than any of our previous kisses, and it fills me with comfort. I meet his fervor, pouring everything I have into the kiss, while taking everything I can from his warmth. And when he finally pulls away, it takes a second to catch my breath, my eyes widening as I do.

We're at work.

My gaze darts from one end of the hall to the other while Sal's eyes remain on me. "It doesn't matter, Keeley," he whispers. "I'm done pretending I'm not falling in love with you."

"What?" My breath hitches as the love in his eyes settles me.

"I'm falling in love with you. And it's about time I said it out loud, even if I am whispering."

My heart gallops in my chest, his words swirling through me like oxygen. I attempt to suck in a shaky breath before clasping his hands and smiling. "I'm falling in love with you too, Sal." *More than I thought was possible.*

Sal sighs before kissing me again, and when we part, his eyes fill with apprehension. "I'm here. Okay?"

"Thank you. I don't plan on being too long."

"Good. I'm not sure I can handle much."

I smile as I pass him, making my way toward Wes's office with Sal close behind me, and I'm surprised to find that smile doesn't fade. I never would have thought it would make a difference, and yet, with Sal's love coursing through me, I feel invincible as I enter the room, coming face-to-face with Vance.

The man I had no idea affected me so much.

"Vance." I nod, hiding my joy when his face contorts with confusion. He's quick to recover and hides his shock as a smug expression takes its place.

"Keeley. I'm surprised they have you involved in my negotiations."

"They don't."

"They don't?"

"No. There are no negotiations, Vance. Wes was nice enough to give me the honor of telling you we *won't* be offering you the coaching position. We've decided to go with someone who isn't a piece of shit."

"You're hilarious. My reputation is squeaky clean."

"That doesn't mean you're a decent human being. It just means you have friends in high places that can cover it up."

"Fuck off. You know nothing about me."

"Nothing?"

"No. We knew each other...what? Over ten years ago? I think it's time for you to get over whatever infatuation you have and move the fuck on."

"Infatuation? You sexually assaulted me, Vance. You didn't listen when I said no, and forced yourself on me. And as if that wasn't enough, you played the victim and got away with it, making me lose my job."

"Is that what you think happened? Because I remember it a lot—"

"I don't need to hear what you think you remember. I know what happened. I have the mental scars to prove it. I'm no longer playing the part of your victim. You deserve to pay for what you did, but it's too late for that. Instead, I'm going to ensure that no one falls victim to you again. I wanted you to be the first to know, I'm going to make a statement as part of the Women in Sports fundraiser this year. You know, the one that's always covered by media outlets from around the world. And I'm not afraid to name names. I hope you've enjoyed your fame up until now, because it's all about to change."

He steps forward, his eyes dropping to my ankle as he invades my personal space. "That's a big threat for someone that can't run away."

"I'm not scared of you. Try your worst. It'll only make me fight harder."

Vance's nostrils flare, and for the first time since I walked into the room, fear takes over me, but I refuse to show it. Instead, I stand tall, holding his gaze.

"Fucking bitch," he snarls, throwing a chair across the room before storming off, and a sense of relief and pride takes over me.

I did it. I faced a fear that had been unknowingly haunting me for years. I feel amazing.

Sal's through the door before Vance is fully out of the room, his eyes wide as he rakes them all over my body, his fists clenched, undoubtedly searching for damage. His eyes lock on the chair against the wall, and a growl vibrates from the back of his throat before he turns to chase after Vance.

"Stop. It's okay. He didn't hurt me."

Sal closes his eyes as his head falls back, his expression pinched with torment. He sucks in a breath and jogs toward me, pulling me into his arms. He holds me in silence, his rapid breathing the only sound between us until I pull away.

"God, you're so pale." I brush my thumbs across his cheek, and he shakes his head.

"What do you expect when the women in my life are trying to kill me? I'm so proud of you, Keeley, but fuck, it was hard to stand outside and listen to what was going on without being able to see you. At one point, I thought I was going to have to physically restrain myself."

"If it helps, I appreciate it. I feel better now that I've done that. It's as though I not only closed that door, but locked it for good and threw away the key."

Sal smiles, the curve of his lips twisting until the creases meet his eyes. "That helps a little." He kisses my head while his heart pounds against me. "But if that door ever gets unlocked, I'm going to have to kill him."

"I know." I giggle. "Thank you for helping me find closure."

"You're welcome."

We stay like that for a beat, until a throat clears and we break apart to find Wes.

"Wes." Sal nods, unperturbed at being caught in an intimate embrace.

"Sorry to interrupt. I thought you'd like to know that he's gone, and I've let him know he's not welcome here at the Storm."

"Thank you, Wes." I smile softly and he nods in return.

"Are you okay?"

"I am. I needed that to move on."

A somber expression passes over Wes's face before he schools his features. "I can't imagine how hard that must have been. If you ever need to talk to anyone, let me know."

"Wow. Ah..." I would never have pictured Wes as someone to offer an ear but—

"Jesus, sorry. I meant Lucy. Not me. I wouldn't know what the hell to say." His wife, of course.

"Oh, right. Yes. Actually, I'd love to catch up with Lucy. Even without needing to talk."

"Great." His expression brightens and I have to wonder if there's a story there. "I'll let her know."

"Thank you."

"I'll give you two a moment. I'm going to head out to make sure he's left the premises." Wes waves before leaving us alone in his office, and while I'm feeling significantly lighter, Sal still has a shadow hanging over his head.

"Is everything okay?"

"You mean, other than standing by while my girlfriend confronted the man that attacked her?"

"Yes. Other than that."

Sal sighs, cursing softly. "Camilla texted me while you were in there. She agreed that Paige should testify. She *was* on my side until she spoke to Paige. Now she's jumped ship."

He sounds so defeated that my heart aches for him, but at the same time, I feel the need to play devil's advocate. "Maybe Paige's reasons make sense to Camilla since she's also testifying. If she's going anyway, with or without your blessing, wouldn't it be better to help her out?"

"Of course. I've already made arrangements for travel and security, but I'd be more comfortable if your brother was traveling with her."

"He's not?"

"No."

I frown, confused. I didn't think he'd let her go alone. "Maybe you should go with her?"

"Ahh." He scratches the back of his head. "That's the other reason I'm stressed."

"Oh, yeah?" *Why don't I like the sound of this?* "I have to go on Saturday afternoon. I'll be there when Paige arrives, but I can't travel with her."

"Why?"

"I have to meet with the advisory board about the unsafe work practices first thing Monday morning, and I have a few loose ends to tie up before then."

"Loose ends?" *Why does that sound so final?*

"Yeah. I promise I wouldn't be going if it wasn't absolutely necessary."

"I know." I smile while my frantic heart gives away my lie. I believe that he believes that, but I also have to wonder if he considers most things in his business to be absolutely necessary.

God, is that what I'm like?

My mind flashes back to my talk with Paige, and I internally curse myself. Sal and I are one and the same. I've been turning into Mr. Hyde because I'm not allowed to work. Who am I to judge?

Sal closes his eyes, his expression ashen as he talks to Paige on the phone.

"Jeffrey will pick you up around ten a.m. on Monday. Are you sure you won't let Easton go? I'd feel better knowing he was there with you."

Paige responds, and from Sal's expression, I can guess she's sure. It turns out I was right about Easton. He wants to go; Paige won't let him.

"I know I'm there, but I'm not traveling with you, and I'll be at D'Angelo Construction until I meet you—"

Paige must cut him off because he pauses, running a hand through his hair. For a man that likes to be in control, he's been thrown a lot of curveballs over the last twenty-four hours, and he's not coping well. On top of having to watch me with Vance yesterday while standing on the sidelines, he's now being forced to stay back when it comes to Paige. And he has no idea whether or not her life is in danger.

"What's she going to do?" he yells and then scoffs, lowering his voice. "Or your brother? That doesn't give me much confidence."

Sal's head drops back as Paige speaks again, and I almost laugh until his worried expression darts my way.

"Can I speak to her?" I mouth and his eyes light up, probably thinking I'm going to take his side. I'm not. I get it. Paige is strong. She can do this on her own.

"Keeley wants to speak to you." He pauses. "Yeah, I'll put her on."

He hands me the phone, mouthing the word "help" before running his hands down his face. A pang hits me and I'm torn. On one hand, I can understand where Paige is coming from, but on the other, I don't want Sal to spend his time worrying. This girlfriend/friend thing is going to take some time to navigate.

"Hi, Paige."

"Hi, Mom."

I snort out a laugh, shaking my head at the absurdity of our situation. Although, she did just give me an opening to help Sal. "Your dad's worried about you and—" I stifle a laugh. "Sorry. I tried but this is too weird. As your friend, I wanted to see how you were feeling."

"I'm okay. I want that part of my life to be over, and until I testify, it won't be."

"You know you'll probably see Christian?"

"I know. And I'm ninety-nine percent sure that's the main reason Easton wants to come."

"I'm not going to lie and say it's not *one* of his reasons, but I know my brother. He wants to be there for *you*. It turns out, he's actually more caring than we give him credit for."

"You mean you give him credit for? I've known that since we met."

"Okay. Maybe I haven't been the best sister."

"Nah, you're okay." Paige laughs. "And I have the authority to judge that now, with you being my sister-in-law… and my future stepmom."

"Stop. It was funny the first time. Now…"

"I'm kidding."

"I know. But on that note, I'm going to ask you something as your dad's girlfriend."

"So it's official?"

"It is. Which is why I have to ask this. Are you sure you won't let Easton go with you? Mom can come here with Isaac and we could look after him together. With Phil, of course, since we're both physically unstable."

"What would *you* do, Keels? If you were me. I trust you and Rochelle. It's not that. I'm worried about Isaac. He's a smart kid; he can feel the nervous energy surrounding us all. If Easton and I disappear, how do you think that will make him feel?"

I turn to Sal, meeting his eyes as a memory of my childhood rears its ugly head. A memory of my mom going to work when it was clear she didn't want to. It was a sacrifice she made to support us after my dad left. And a realization hits me. Something that has nothing to do with my present conversation. Something I can talk about later.

"I think Easton should stay home," I tell Paige with my eyes still locked on Sal's intense gaze. "I'll talk to your dad."

"Thanks, Keeley. As far as step—"

"Don't even start." I laugh under my breath.

"Sorry, I promise that was the last one. To you, anyway. I might bring it up to Easton every now and then."

"I'd be disappointed if you didn't."

"I knew you'd say that. On a serious note… I'm really happy for you and Dad. You both deserve so much love, and I'm thrilled you've finally admitted to what we all saw. I couldn't be happier for you. *We* couldn't be happier. He might not show it, but Easton's happy too."

"Thank you, Paige. Have you told Isaac? Is that going to be strange?"

"Not yet. But we will."

"Thanks. I hope he's okay with it."

"He will be. He loves you both."

I smile, picturing my gorgeous little nephew. "I guess now all that's left to do is announce it to those on the team that don't know us outside of work."

"I don't think that's going to be an issue. You know Luke's got your back, so everyone else will follow suit. Either that, or he'll force them to shut the hell up."

"You're right." I smile at Sal and he frowns back at me, making me giggle. "I better go. I don't think your dad's happy about the advice I gave you."

"Just tell him it'll always be chicks before dicks. Wait. Ew. I don't want to think about that."

"You said it. Shall I pass that along?"

"Please don't. *Please.*"

"Okay. Only because you begged."

"Thank you. Talk soon."

Sal's at my side by the time I hang up, his eyes wide with questions. "So that's how it's going to be?" He finally smiles as he curls his arms around my waist and pulls me in close, making me hop slightly.

"Not always, I promise. I just happened to see her side of the story."

"Which was?"

"That she didn't want Isaac here worrying about both his parents instead of just one."

"Shit."

"Yep."

"Sometimes I forget that kids worry about their parents too."

"They do. When Paige was telling me her reason, it made me remember worrying about my mom as a kid. I worry about her now too, of course, but as a kid, there's the element of confusion because you never really know the full picture. I knew Mom hated her job because she was forced to do it to take care of us. She wasn't earning money doing something she loved. She was working out of necessity."

"I can see where you get your strength; that couldn't have been easy on her."

"It wasn't. And the memory of that gave me an epiphany. That's why I work so hard. Because I never want to be in a situation where I have to work to survive. Or be forced to work in a job I don't love. And I've experienced losing a job I loved before."

"That makes sense. It's how my work ethic started too. And now we're both thriving. We could probably afford to take it easy every once in a while." He stares at me pointedly before his eyes drop to my foot.

"You're right. I'm going to enjoy this time off. I'm in a gorgeous house with a stunning view both inside and out. It's time to live in the moment."

"Good."

"Good. Anything *you* want to say?"

"About what?" Sal fakes a frown and I roll my eyes.

"Living in the moment?"

"Nope. I'm good."

A laugh bursts out of me as Sal pulls me close again, burying my face in his hard chest, probably so I won't say anymore. Baby steps for him. He's definitely been here more than the office, taking care of me, so that's something. Maybe one day we'll both learn to go easier on ourselves.

Chapter Fifty-Three

SALVATORE

Keeley's still sleeping when I wake up, so I move her crutches closer to the bed and quietly close our bedroom door behind me. My lips pull into a smile as I stare at the handle.

Our bedroom door.

This is *our* bedroom.

I gave her the option to move back home when she was better, but I'm going to fight hard to ensure that doesn't happen. It's only been a few days, and it already feels like a home.

I've always loved her in my space, and this is no exception. Actually, it has one major difference. It never felt like my space until Keeley walked into it.

When my agent told me this house had come onto the market, I knew I had to have it, even though I couldn't figure out why.

Now I know.

It was for Keeley. For us. For our future. And I can't remember a time where I've felt so at home. Even when I lived with Camilla and my kids, as sad as that sounds.

After making a few calls, I've just started cooking omelets for breakfast when Keeley calls out from the upstairs landing.

"I'm coming down. Don't freak out."

"Wait." I chuckle under my breath. "I can help."

"No," she calls back, her tone curt. "I'm a grown-ass woman. I do *not* need to be carried anymore."

"Your loss."

I'm anxious while I cook, despite laughing at her sassy independence.

The reason she's in a cast in the first place is because she fell down stairs. I'm not nervous about her being incapable of making it down on her own; I'm worried she's carrying trauma she hasn't yet acknowledged.

With a deep breath, I flip the omelet in the pan and smile in relief when I hear Keeley's crutches clacking my way.

"You made it?"

"I did. Only now I wish you'd secretly purchased a single-story home."

"No, you don't. You love the view."

"Okay, fine. Did you make breakfast?"

"I did. Why don't you head outside and I'll bring it out when it's ready. There's a blanket already on the chair for you. It's a little cool."

Keeley smiles to herself as she turns toward the patio, her face free of makeup, her body clad in simple silk pajamas, and my heart races at how beautiful she is. How incredible my life is. If I can start my mornings like this for the rest of my days, I'll be the wealthiest man on the planet, money aside.

I finish plating up our food and meet Keeley outside, where she is basking in the summer sun, despite the cooler temperature, and breathing in the salty air. She's admiring the view with the blanket wrapped around her, her arms resting on our deck railing, her auburn hair blowing in the light breeze. I'm quiet as I lower our plates to the table, my eyes on her as I make my way over and curl my arms around her waist.

"How is it so quiet here?"

"It's a private beach. The only people with access are us and the neighbors on either side. And I have it on good authority that the couple on the left use their place as a vacation home, weekends mainly, while the couple on the right spend their summers in France."

"Lucky them." Keeley smiles at me over her shoulder.

"And lucky us." I press a kiss to the edge of her lips as my hand lowers to the waistband of her pajama shorts.

"Won't our food go cold?"

"We can reheat it."

"That doesn't sound appealing."

"Then I'll make it again when we're done. Who needs food anyway?"

Keeley giggles as she twists to face me, wrapping her arms around my neck. "I guess I can be persuaded to eat later."

"Good, because I want to eat now."

Keeley melts into me as my cock pulses, and my phone chooses that moment to blare in my pocket, making us both jump.

"Jesus. That'll be someone from New York," I say, retrieving my phone, ready to toss it onto the lounge until I see that it's Austin.

"Goddammit. I have to get this." I blow out a breath, squeezing the phone in annoyance.

"Are you allowed to answer a work call when you're dressed like that?" Keeley laughs, her brow raised with sass as she gestures to my black jeans, polo shirt, and bare feet.

"It's not a video call, Keels. I think I'll be fine."

"As long as you're sure. I'm shocked you're not in a suit."

"Get used to it. This is how I dress when I'm home."

"You still wear a polo shirt?"

"I do. So what?"

"So, we're going to change that. When I'm finished with you, you're going to be walking around in athletic shorts and an old T-shirt. Or maybe just a towel. That would be convenient."

A laugh bursts out of me as I shake my head. "I'll be back. This isn't over."

"I'll be waiting."

I leave Keeley in peace and call Austin back, crossing my fingers for good news. "Sal."

"Hi, Austin. Tell me you have something positive?"

"Unfortunately not." My stomach sinks at the gruffness of his tone, my eyes drifting back to Keeley outside.

"I'm ready. Lay it all out."

"You're being tracked. You and Paige. I had one of my guys in San Francisco put a tail on you, and it was the first thing he discovered."

"Fuck. That's not good."

"I know. I suggest you increase Paige's security detail and get some for yourself, because the Mikklesons are not messing around anymore."

"Why? It makes no sense. I've been thinking about this a lot. The DA has plenty of evidence against them. I have no doubt they're going to prison with or without Camilla's and Paige's testimony."

"That's the second piece of news. Remember when I said they've been keeping their inner circle tight?"

"I do."

"Well, it turns out, that inner circle is getting restless. One of my men overheard Mikkleson's nephew acknowledging that he's on a sinking ship. We offered him a hundred grand to tell us everything he knows."

"Meaning, I owe you money."

"You do. But we can settle that at the end. Are you sitting down?"

"Why the fuck would I need to be sitting down?"

"For what I have to say."

"I'm not going to have a heart attack, Austin. Just tell me."

"Fine." He chuckles softly and I almost tell him I'm not in the mood. "Camilla knows more than she told you. More than she initially told the police, and the Mikklesons are worried."

"Jesus Christ. That woman."

"Yep."

"Do you know what it is?"

"No, and neither did he. Though he claims it's going to be explosive. It could be the difference between a shorter sentence for embezzlement and the maximum penalty for their white-collar crimes."

I finally sit down, dropping my head into my hand. "In other words, their threats are about to get worse?"

"I'm afraid so."

"Any grand plans for how we can stop it?"

"Not yet. I'm working on it. I plan to keep Mikkleson's nephew on the payroll in case he comes in handy. Hope that's okay?"

"Yep. Do what you have to do."

"Really?" His pitch rises as if I've changed my tune on illegal activity, and I laugh.

"You're already bribing someone for information. That's illegal enough for me."

"You're the boss."

I am, but that doesn't mean I know what the hell I'm doing. I'm actually at a complete loss.

After trying to get ahold of Camilla—with no luck—I call the security company I use and increase Paige's security team, adding Isaac and Easton to the mix. It's at least thirty minutes before I finally join Keeley again, yet she's still smiling. Until she sees me and her smile melts into a panicked frown.

"What happened?"

"The Mikklesons aren't messing around anymore, Keels. I'm being tailed."

"Shit." She straightens in the lounge chair she's now occupying, and subtly glances toward the beach. "That's bad, I guess, but not exactly unexpected. Right?"

"Probably not. Only it's not me I'm worried about. They're tracking Paige too."

"Oh, fuck, Sal. What are you going to do?"

"I wish I knew. I've added more security to Paige's detail and—"

"She's going to love that." Keeley cringes comically and I huff out a laugh.

"Is it bad that I don't care? I'll do anything to protect her, even if that means pissing her off."

"She'll understand. Though might I suggest including her in the conversation, so she doesn't freak out to find she's suddenly surrounded by strange men."

"I will. I promise."

"Good. Are you still going to New York tomorrow?"

"Fuck, I don't know." I run a hand through my hair, tugging at the strands. "I want to be here for Paige, to convince her to stay, but—"

My phone chimes, cutting me off, and I pause before checking it. "This'll be Tabitha confirming my flights. Maybe I should cancel."

I pull my phone from my pocket, and my blood boils the second I read the texts.

UNKNOWN: Last chance to walk away. It's time to protect your assets.

UKNOWN: And while you're at it, you might want to protect your family too.

"Motherfucker."

"What's wrong?"

I drop down onto the lounge chair by Keeley's legs and curl my palm around her thigh, needing her warmth to ground me before I do something stupid. With a deep breath, I hand her my phone before standing up again and pacing the patio.

"Motherfucker," she repeats my sentiment, making me laugh even though it's far from funny. "Can you trace this?"

"I can send it to Austin, but it's most likely a burner."

"God, you're right."

"I have no idea what to do anymore, Keels. I'm ready for a simpler life."

Keeley frowns, and her eyes dart to my phone once more before widening as she glances my way.

"You have to go to New York."

"I'm not so sure. It's—"

"No," she cuts me off, her voice firm with conviction. "You have to. I've got an idea. You're going to want to sit down."

Why the hell is everyone asking me to do that today? I guess that means I'm not going to like this. "Hit me with it. Because I've got nothing."

Chapter Fifty-Four

SALVATORE

The sun is setting as I land, and the second I'm off the plane, I have my phone in my hand, checking in with Austin. "Please tell me nothing has changed."

"We're good. Jill Mikkleson is going to meet you in Battery Park at nightfall, near the East Coast Memorial. Are you sure you're okay with this plan?"

"No. But they've gone too far. I refuse to let them fuck with my family anymore. On that note, any news on what Camilla has on the Mikklesons? She's always too busy to chat when I call."

"Nothing yet."

"Of course not. Fucking Camilla. I bet she's loving the drama of it all."

"I'm not going to take that bet. A few of the guys from her security detail have said she's been having a bit of fun with them all."

"Having fun? What does that— Never mind." I shake off my impending anger. She can look after herself.

"How's Paige?" Austin asks next and my stomach knots.

"Still being stubborn. I'd love it if you could continue to keep an eye on her if you can. She's not happy about it, but she knows. She said she'll talk to Easton about testifying, and while I'd normally want to kick his ass if he attempted to tell Paige what to do, in this case, I'm hoping he puts his foot down."

"Do you think hc will?"

"God only knows."

I push through the doors at JFK, searching for my driver, and find Austin instead, his casual shrug making me laugh.

"You could have just told me you were here."

"Where's the fun in that?" His delivery holds no humor, and another chuckle escapes me.

"Why are you here, may I ask?"

"Because you keep insisting on not having your own protection. Like you're a goddamn hero."

"I'm not being a hero. I'm pooling my resources to where they're truly needed."

"Your resources? Sal, you're the richest fucker I know. You can buy more resources."

"I can, but it's not necessary."

"If you say so." Austin half laughs, half scoffs and I ignore him.

"Does that mean I'm stuck with you until this whole thing is over?" I stare at him through the rearview mirror as his lips curl.

"Lucky for you, no. Though I'll have one of my men with you at all times."

"Great, I hope they don't mind being bored."

"Boredom is actually preferred. Because it means that their subject is safe."

"If you say so." I repeat his words back to him, only half smiling when he laughs.

Austin changes the subject after that, trying to convince me that his team is going to win the Super Bowl this year, and I roll my eyes as he gives me his reasons.

"You have a new quarterback, while we have the best in the league."

"Are you sure about that? Beckett Myers isn't exactly new. He was ranked as one of the best last season."

"Maybe so, but he's new to *your* team. You know it takes time to get settled."

"Agree to disagree."

My phone vibrates, and when I see that it's Paige, I shelve our conversation, and Austin nods in acknowledgment. "Hey, Kiddo, how are you?"

"I'm good. I thought I'd let you know that I'm on my way to your new place to hang out with Keeley, my posse in tow."

"Good. Embrace it. Consider them your shadows until the Mikklesons are in prison."

"Yay. I can't wait."

"*Paige*."

"I'm kidding; I get it. Are you in New York or still on the flight?"

"I'm almost at the office," I lie, hating the fact that she'd never question that.

"Oh, good. I better leave you to it then."

"You don't have to."

"We just pulled up at your mansion. I want to talk to Keeley before the others arrive."

"No worries. Thank you for calling."

"You're welcome." I move to hang up until she calls out. "And Dad?"

"Yeah. I'm still here."

"I love you. And I promise I'm taking your request seriously."

I breathe a sigh of relief, not even bothering to hide it. "Thank you. That's all I can ask. I love you too."

I hang up and stare out the window, silently willing Paige to make the right call, while at the same time knowing she has to do what's best for her and her sanity.

"We're here." Austin slows when Battery Park comes into view, and I feel bad for lying to Paige. Only she can't know. She'd undoubtedly call Camilla, and I can't let that happen. I need to keep my meeting with Jill quiet if I want this to work.

Austin says something about circling the block until I'm done, but my attention has already shifted toward the park, my mind on my looming conversation.

Jill's waiting when I arrive, so I hold back for a while, letting her sweat. She stands confidently, as though she's a seasoned pro when it comes to blackmail and threats. But the longer I leave her waiting, the more I notice the subtle changes. She tugs her hat low on her head and adjusts her dress. She glances over her shoulder, and then pretends to be reading the sign on the monument.

She's rattled. And that's exactly how I need her.

I approach slowly, while making sure I'm loud enough to draw her attention, and she turns to face me, her confidence back in play.

"I'm not sure why you wanted to meet. I'm not supposed to be talking to anyone in your family while my husband is on trial."

I almost laugh. So that's how she's going to play this? "Why'd you agree to meet with me then?"

"Curiosity." She shrugs. "*And* maybe the chance to get back at my husband for sleeping with your wife."

"Ex-wife." *It's like Camilla seeks out trouble.*

"Either way. What do you want, Mr. D'Angelo?"

"I want to know what it'll take for you to stop harassing me and my family."

"I'm doing nothing of the sort."

"Cut the bullshit. I'm not wearing a wire. There's no one else here, except your men hovering in the treeline." *I noticed them as I was walking closer.* "I'm here to protect my family and nothing more."

"I still don't—"

"I've begged them both not to testify. But believe it or not, I don't control my daughter or my ex-wife. They have their own free will, and they want your husband in prison."

She subtly flinches, but otherwise remains calm so I continue on. "You said so yourself, that you wanted to get back at him. Would a large sum of money help? You can live it up while you let him rot for ruining your life."

I'm aware I could get into a lot of trouble for what I'm proposing, yet I'm beyond caring, and I'm hoping she stays quiet considering what she's been putting my family through.

Jill clears her throat and my pulse spikes. *Is that a goddamn code?* Am I about to be attacked by her men?

I shift slightly so I'm facing the direction I last saw them, and she laughs. "You really did come alone, didn't you?"

"I'm a man of my word."

"And you want to offer me money to let your daughter and wife testify against my husband and brother-in-law?"

"No, I'm offering you money to leave them alone."

"How much?"

"Whatever it takes. Think about it. Sleep on it if you must. I need an answer by early morning."

"Why?"

"Because I want this sorted before my daughter arrives."

Jill stares me in the eyes, her expression inquisitive, and I offer her a rare glimpse into my softer side. "Please," I beg, breaking our connection.

We both pause as a guy runs past us, then Jill shakes her head, waving toward her men, before her eyes meet mine once more. "Goodbye, Mr. D'Angelo. I'll be in touch."

"Good. And Jill, in case you need convincing and your husband hasn't filled you in, my ex has more on your husband than she initially told the police. He's a lost cause. But you could save yourself."

Jill stiffens but doesn't turn around, and without a word, she walks away.

I hold my breath, waiting until she's gone before releasing it loudly, turning away as I bite back a smile. I have no idea if this is going to work, but she didn't tell me to fuck off, so that has to be a good sign.

Austin's waiting for me where he left me, a smile on his lips as I jump into the back seat. "My men said that went well. Were they right?"

"Your men? Fuck. I told her I was there alone."

"And you were. One of my guys just so happened to be jogging past, while another was out walking his dog. Purely coincidental."

"Right. Thank you."

"You're welcome." He chuckles low under his breath. "Where to next?"

"Home." My shoulders sag as I turn toward the window, clutching my phone in my hand. "I need a stiff drink. And I need to talk to Keeley."

After a shitty night's sleep, I head into my New York office, accompanied by one of Austin's men, and dive into work, taking my mind off the shit show going on around me.

When Daniel arrives in the early evening, after spending the day off-site, I call him into my office, ready to put a secondary plan into play. A plan that Keeley doesn't know about. Daniel and I spoke on the phone this morning, with him checking in on my family, but I wanted to chat with him in person.

I'm taking another step back from D'Angelo Construction. A bigger one this time. And I've never felt better about a decision.

Daniel looks a little weary when he walks in, and I don't blame him. We're not completely out of the woods where the unsafe worksite investigation is concerned, but it's definitely looking more positive than it did last week.

"I just got off the phone with our lawyer, and he thinks we'll get the okay to start up again on the Chamberland Project at my meeting tomorrow morning."

Daniel's eyes light up briefly before he schools his features. "Really?"

"Yes, really."

"That's music to my ears."

"The complaint was never going to stand. There's no evidence to support it, except for the bullshit they fabricated."

"You're right. I needed your confidence."

"You're confident enough. You just have to trust that we've done the right thing so it will all work out in the end. And on that note..." I smile and Daniel matches my energy despite having no idea what's coming.

"I wanted to talk to you about something."

"Of course."

"I—" My phone buzzes loudly across my glass desk, pulling me from my thoughts. "Sorry, one minute. This could be an update from the Storm game. It should be halftime by now." *Another thing to add to my guilt. I should be there. It's our first goddamn game.*

I jog over to my desk and grab my phone, my proposal for Daniel burning a hole in my hand. Now that I've made my decision, I want it over and done with.

Daniel nervously taps his foot and I laugh. "You're not getting fired if that's what you think. This is a good thing."

"You couldn't fire me if you tried." He chuckles. "I know too much."

"Very true. Not to mention you're irreplaceable."

"Don't ever forget it."

"Trust me, I won't. I'm relying on that for what I want to talk to you about. How would you feel about taking over for me on a permanent basis?"

"A permanent basis?"

"Yes, I want to name you CEO and step back from running the company. Completely."

"What? You're joking."

"I'm really not. You've been running it without me ninety percent of the time anyway, so you deserve the title and all that goes with it."

"I'm. I… Fuck. I have no words. Are you sure?"

"I've never been surer about anything."

"What's the catch?"

"There isn't one. I'll make sure everything the Mikklesons have done is fixed and the company's back to running smoothly. But while I'll still remain the owner, I want to take on more of a passive role, closer to that of a silent investor. Other than that, D'Angelo Construction would be yours."

Daniel stares at me, unmoving, his eyes wide, his mouth parted as he processes what I'm saying. I understand it coming as a shock, because no one thought I'd ever leave this place. And if I'm honest, neither did I. But it feels right.

"Do you need a minute to think?" I ask, as I pick up my phone, making Daniel laugh.

"I need a minute to wake up."

I head back to the couch and hand over the official offer, before finally checking my alert. Since I expect it to be about the Storm game, I have to read it twice for the words to sink in.

Breaking news: Billionaire and NFL's youngest team owner, Salvatore D'Angelo, is officially off the market. Cue the tears from all the single ladies out there because sources say it's the real deal. His new girlfriend, 33-year-old Keeley Reynolds, was seen returning to her media liaison job today with the San Francisco Storm following a broken ankle. We're yet to see any photos of the two, but there's a good chance they'll make their public debut together at the Storm's charity event next month.

Motherfucker.

"That wasn't supposed to happen." I toss Daniel my phone before rushing to my desk and throwing my laptop into my bag. "I have to go."

"Go? Where?"

"Home. Read the alert."

His eyes drop to my phone before he curses under his breath. "You never told me she was thirty-three."

"That's not the point, Daniel."

"You're right, sorry. The timing isn't great with the Mikkleson threats."

"It's not. At all. What the fuck was I thinking? I should have done more, well before it got to this point."

"What could you have done? Had them killed?"

"Funny." I stare at him deadpan as I hold out my hand for my phone. "I don't know what, but I should have done more. Now, I have to fix it once and for all."

"Let me know if I can help."

"You already are. All you have to do is sign those papers and you're changing my life for the better. I promise this will all be over by the time the company is yours."

"I trust you."

"Thanks, Daniel. I'll call you tomorrow."

I'm about to leave when a thought hits me, and I ask one more favor before rushing out the door.

Let this be the last time I feel helpless on the other side of the country. My home is San Francisco. And I wish I'd never left.

Chapter Fifty-Five

KEELEY

PREVIOUS NIGHT

Hayley gasps as she tours the house, moving slowly so I can keep up. "Daddy D'Angelo did good." She smiles my way, bouncing her eyebrows. "This place feels very Keeley-like."

"That's a coincidence. He bought the house a year ago."

"Right, and when did you two meet?"

"Stop. The romance between us is new. We haven't been sneaking around since he took over the Storm."

"You haven't?"

"No."

"Shame."

"Shame?" Paige and Amelia walk in from outside, and I stifle a smile at the mock disgust on Paige's face.

"Oops. Sorry, Paigey." Hayley giggles. "Though you have to admit it would have been a cute story. With elements of payback. You know, because you were sneaking around with her brother."

"You're hilarious." Paige rolls her eyes.

"I am. But it's the truth and it will never not be funny."

Amelia bites back a smile as she sits down on the couch, shaking her head at Hayley. And I finally take a deep breath.

My girls are here. They're all helping to distract me, despite having no idea that I need a distraction. Except maybe Paige.

Sal left for New York around midday after filling Paige in on the Mikklesons tailing them both, begging her to reconsider testifying. She initially refused, but after speaking to Easton, she's starting to reconsider. For Isaac's sake more than anything.

Blair's the last to arrive, and Hayley declares it a party, announcing she's making cocktails for everyone now that I'm off my pain meds. Which is fine by me. I can't do anything for Sal while he's in New York. I just have to hope that my plan actually works. It's a good one, but it's not flawless.

Two hours and three *way-too-strong* cocktails later, Amelia regales us with Luke's play-by-play of Paige and Easton's wedding, including being front row for my moment with Sal, leading to Paige bringing up her mom.

"If you were ever worried about my mom trying to win Dad back, you can rest assured that won't happen. The first thing she said when she saw the two of you together was, 'Thank God, now I don't have to feel bad anymore for kicking him out. I was certain he'd die alone with a D'Angelo Construction ledger in his hands.'"

Hayley snorts while Amelia's and Blair's jaws drop in shock.

I have no words.

Though, I have a feeling I'd get along well with Camilla, if that didn't add one more awkward connection to our already huge list.

"Are we done with the Keeley and Sal teasing yet?"

"Never," Hayley announces, complete with overexaggerated hand movements. "I'm kidding. I'm done. Jokes aside, I'm happy for you. We all are."

"Thank you. I promise I didn't plan on shaking things up. Actually, I hadn't planned on love at all. But I guess that's life. It's not really something anyone can… Why are you all looking at me like that?"

The girls are all staring at me with the same giddy expression. Their eyes wide, lips parted as though they're about to say "aww" to a cute kitten.

"What's going on?"

"You don't even realize you said it, do you?" Paige asks with a laugh.

"Said what?"

"That you love my dad."

"What? I never said that."

"'I hadn't planned on love at all.'" Hayley puts on an American accent, trying to be me, and I laugh her off.

"That's not what I meant."

"Are you sure about that?" She leans back with her arms crossed and her brows raised, staring at me in challenge. And while I can no longer lie to myself, it's surprisingly easy to lie to my friends.

"I'm not there yet. We're not there yet. But when we are, you'll all be the fifth or sixth to know."

"What? Who the hell is above us?" Hayley scowls while Amelia and Blair laugh, with Paige staring at me with a glint in her eye. Does that mean she wants me to be in love with her dad? Or am I misreading that? Either way, I'm definitely not asking. Not yet.

It takes some convincing, but Hayley eventually moves on, and we continue talking into the night, with the girls not leaving until early hours of the morning.

Since Sal's likely to be getting up for his day, I send him a text before trying to go to sleep.

KEELEY: I miss you. I hope it went well last night and you were able to get some sleep

He replies immediately and I smile with relief.

SAL: I miss you too. Everything is going to plan.

My head aches when I wake up in the downstairs bedroom, and I grumble as I rise, internally thanking the girls for suggesting I sleep here. *And* for raiding my closet and en suite, to ensure I had everything I needed. I couldn't imagine navigating the stairs with my head and ankle both throbbing like they are.

I check the time and relax when it's still relatively early. The Storm has a one p.m. game today and I'm going to be there. While the cats are away, the mice—or mouse in my case—is absolutely going to play.

I take my time, eating breakfast on the patio in my pajamas, and when I'm done, I grab my phone off the charger, ready to start my day.

My hand hovers over the number Sal gave me before he left, and I hit the call button, immediately feeling guilty for what I'm about to do.

"Miss Reynolds?" Jeffrey answers with a question in his tone. "Is everything okay? I was on my way over."

I know that, which is why I'm calling. "Yes. It's fine. And please call me Keeley."

"Thank you, Keeley."

"I know Sal asked you to check in on me, but I'm actually about to have a long bath. I didn't want you to be knocking and panicking when I didn't answer. If you want, I can call and check in later. For now, I'm all good here."

"Are you sure? Do you need anything from the grocery store?"

"No, thank you. I'm good. But just so you don't get fired, I'll tell Sal you stopped by."

"You don't have to do that. I can't lie to him."

"Okay, Jeffrey. I'll see you tomorrow." I don't have to ask to know he's not going to let me get away with the bath excuse two days in a row, so I may as well go along with it. Tomorrow's not the issue, anyway. It's today.

I refuse to miss the guys' first game. Why should I? It doesn't count as work, so it shouldn't delay my progress. I'll watch from the family box. It'll be just like watching it on the TV at home.

And it will help with the plan.

After hanging up with Jeffrey, I get dressed in a power suit, with a skirt instead of pants, and apply my flawless makeup, slipping one of the only dressy flats I own onto my cast-free foot before booking an Uber.

When I'm settled in the car, my crutches in the back, I send off a text to Zane, hoping he checks it at some point before the game begins.

KEELEY: You once said you hated being in debt to me, so I have a favor to ask

I must have timed it right, because I don't even get the chance to put my phone away when he texts me back, and I smile reading his response.

ZANE: I'm always happy to help, Keeley. Debt or no debt

KEELEY: Thank you. I'm on my way to the stadium. I'll send you the details now

I type out a long message before closing my eyes, sending off a silent prayer that this all works out, and only letting myself worry until we pull up in front of the stadium. Then it's go time.

It's time to get the show on the road.

I jump when Zane scores the final touchdown, and momentarily forget I have one foot out of commission, grabbing the window frame quickly for support.

An ache shoots through me as the tip of my toes hit the floor, but I force a smile. Zane put us ahead nearing the end of the game, and that's what's important. I refuse to sit down when we're so close.

Amelia watches me for a few seconds but I wave her off. Like Sal, she and Blair think I should have stayed home for the full two weeks the doctor recommended before coming back to work, and my almost fall didn't do me any favors in convincing them otherwise.

Hayley was all for me coming back, while Paige offered no comment, claiming she's not going to form opinions in any Keeley versus her dad conversations, which is probably wise. Although, I think Sal's going to agree with anything she says for the foreseeable future considering she decided not to testify.

My heart slams in my chest during the final seconds, and when the whistle blows, I scream along with the rest of our loyal supporters. My eyes lock on Beckett as he runs out onto the field, his smile wider than I've ever seen it.

The Colorado Cougars weren't the worst team in the league, but they were close to it, usually winning only a few games a year over the last five plus seasons, and Storm just won the first game of the season.

Sure, they won all three of the preseason games, but this is different, and I have no doubt it's the first of many wins. Beckett's going to be happy here. He was amazing today. It wouldn't be off base to have assumed it was Thomas out there with the way he gelled with his teammates—like they'd been playing together for years.

And I'm so happy I witnessed it live.

When the players walk off the field, I excuse myself and slip away from the girls, hiding the fact that I'm going somewhere I shouldn't be.

While I'm much slower than usual, I thankfully make it to the locker room on time, catching the end of Coach Pierce's speech before the interviews begin.

I smile, taking it all in.

This is my element. It hasn't even been two weeks but I've been having withdrawals. I needed this.

I hover around until the locker room interviews are in full force, spotting Zane chatting with a reporter from the national broadcast. One I know well.

Taking a deep breath, I hobble past just as Zane's cocky persona comes into play, and he waves me over, wrapping an arm around my shoulders. "We had to win for Keeley." He winks, undoubtedly making a million girls swoon, while I pretend to brush him off.

"I wouldn't have missed it. You know me."

"Keeley Reynolds." The reporter shifts the conversation my way, just like I knew she would. "You've been in the spotlight yourself today. I'm happy you're here."

I bet you are.

News of Sal's and my relationship started circling just before halftime, and by the time the second half began, it was all over social media.

"I don't know what you're talking about." I fake a smile, making it appear as though I'm being coy.

"How about I help you out? Can you confirm the reports that you're dating Salvatore D'Angelo?"

"Oh. Ah. I think it's best if we keep the discussion on the game. Zane absolutely killed it out there. Did you see his final leap into the end zone?"

"Yes. Yes, I did. Keeley's right, Zane. You were incredible."

"I'll leave you both to it." I move off camera but stay close by, waiting for what I think is about to happen, and sure enough...

"One last thing before you go, Zane."

"Of course."

"Can you confirm the rumors about Keeley and your team owner?"

"I'm not saying a word, but I'm also *not* denying it. If you know what I mean." He smirks, melting more hearts, and I bite back a smile as I walk away.

Thank you, Zane. Consider us even.

CHAPTER FIFTY-SIX

SALVATORE

With my heart trapped in my throat, I wait until I've boarded my chartered flight before texting Jill. She messaged this morning to say she wants twenty-five million, and I have to say it surprised me. It was less than I thought. Not that I had plans to give her anything.

SALVATORE: No deal. I don't trust you. See you in court.

I don't get a message in return, not that I expected it. I figured I'd have to wait until our plan plays out before finding out if she took the bait.

Considering I only got the alert about Keeley's and my relationship going public at halftime, I'm pleased to note that I'm already on a flight home by the time the Storm game is over, with more alerts coming through.

Storm wins by three points.

A close call but a victory all the same.

I wish I had it in me to celebrate. Especially when one of the alerts shows an ecstatic-looking Beckett—an expression I rarely see on his face. If I'd stayed, I would have been there. I would have been closer to Keeley.

But our plan never would have worked.

A few more alerts ping my phone—more highlights from the game, making me feel worse—and I'm about to put my phone away when Keeley's beautiful face comes onto the screen.

Jesus. Fuck. My pulse spikes.

She went to the game.

She's speeding up the process.

She leaked the news early.

And now she's making sure the Mikklesons know where she is by joking around with Zane.

Fuuck, she's brilliant. A pain in my ass, but brilliant.

I'll bet she's thinking our relationship status will garner more attention from the Mikklesons if they think I'm still in New York. And I hate that she's not wrong. Austin confirmed they weren't tracking me there. Most likely because they knew the two places I'd be—home or the office. And let's face it, it's not me they want to attack. They want to push me far enough so I'll make their problems all go away.

There's a big difference between ten years and a lifetime, and people will do crazy things when they feel trapped.

I understand what Keeley's attempting to do, but I don't like it.

After blowing out a breath, I bring up her number and press call, tapping my foot as I wait for her to answer. But of course, she doesn't. That was the deal. We agreed not to speak after the article was released, in case we somehow ruined the plan.

The fucking plan.

I'm an idiot. Why the hell did I agree to this? To leave the woman I love without any protection while pissing off the people who want to hurt me.

I drop the phone to the seat beside me and massage my temples, digging my thumbs in deep, while my mind whirs.

What the fuck do I do?

A pit forms in my stomach as I let my thoughts drift back to the plan Keeley proposed, trying to remain calm.

...

"What if you use me as bait?" she states plainly, not an ounce of humor in her tone, and I almost laugh.

"I'd ask what you mean, but I can already tell you the answer is no."

"Wait. Hear me out."

My shoulders sink at her pleading gaze, and like always, I can't say no to her. "I'm listening."

Keeley smiles, before sitting taller, her expression fierce as she speaks. "Our relationship is private, right? Other than our close friends and family at the wedding, no one knows we're together. That is to say, it hasn't hit the gossip columns yet."

"Why would it ever hit the gossip columns?" I ask, my brows furrowed while Keeley laughs.

"You have no idea what an eligible bachelor you are, do you?"

"Okay, so the news isn't public."

"Exactly. The Mikklesons want to hurt you or Camilla, only everyone you love dearly is being guarded by security."

"Not everyone..." I trail off, because while now is not the time to throw the L word around, I can see what she's getting at. "You want us to go public so the Mikklesons will turn their attention to you?"

"Yes." She pauses before adding the kicker, "While you're in New York."

"No fucking way." I stand, running a hand through my hair. "The only way I'd ever agree to that plan is if I'm here in San Francisco."

"Okay. We can brainstorm the details. But I really think it could work."

I stare at her for a beat, my eyes dropping to her beautiful smile as she stares back at me, and I hate that she might be on to something.

"Let me do this to protect Paige and Isaac." Her expression softens. "To protect your business. Camilla and Marc. You. *Please. I want to help."*

She straightens, her eyes never once wavering from mine, and it's hard to argue with the determination set in her gaze.

"If we do this, we have to plan out every single detail.*"*

"I agree. And we have to keep it between us."

"I'll need to tell Austin, but other than that, yes." I swallow a lump in my throat, my chest tight while I question my sanity.

Meanwhile, Keeley giggles. She fucking giggles.

"You don't have to look so worried." She stands up to cup my cheek. "It's going to be fine."

...

Famous last words.

It's *not* fine because none of this was part of the plan. She's gone rogue.

The plan was for me to be on the plane by the time the article leaked. I was supposed to be in San Francisco before Austin's informant casually dropped the news to the Mikklesons.

Instead, I'm hours away.

We had a plan and... No. We *have* a plan. While the goalposts have moved, the plan's still the same. I just have to play my part, and it will all be okay.

Grabbing my phone again, I call Tabitha to keep up my end of the deal, holding my breath as the phone rings.

"Mr. D'Angelo. How's New York?"

"It's great, thank you. All going well. Remember that tentative meeting I asked you to hold off on?"

"Yes. I have it flagged in my emails."

"Great. Can you please book it in? For ten a.m."

"Is that San Francisco or New York time?"

"San Francisco. Thank you." I need Austin to know what time I'm arriving in San Francisco. The meeting tomorrow morning is a cover for my landing time tonight.

"Okay." I hear typing before she tells me it's done, a smile in her voice.

"Thanks, Tabitha. I appreciate it."

"Anything else I can help you with?"

"Not at this time. I'll let you know if that changes. For now, enjoy your Sunday."

"Thank you, I will. Go Storm," she cheers.

"Go Storm." I try to match her enthusiasm, but my heart isn't in it, and I'm not sure that's going to change until I land. I'm completely helpless while I'm up in the air.

You'd think I was moving backward with how slow time passes, and as we touch down at San Francisco International, I'm more anxious than I've ever been in my life, and I've been through a lot.

Since I'm ninety percent sure the Mikklesons have a tail on Jeffrey too, I make my way to the taxi stand for the first time since I was in college and take a cab. I have no idea if the Mikklesons have access to my cards or accounts, and I'm not taking any chances. As it is, I negotiated with the flight charter company to pay double their normal rate if I can wire the money tomorrow.

Am I being overcautious? Maybe. But I'd rather that than ruin it all because of a stupid error. As of right now, Daniel's buying dinner at a fancy restaurant in New York under my name, using my personal credit card.

I didn't get where I am today without paying attention to detail.

Power will only get you so far.

The risks are too high to fuck around anymore.

If our plan fails, Keeley... Fuck. Emotion clogs my throat and I swallow it back down. I can't think about that now.

It's after ten thirty when I'm finally in a cab on the way to our house, the ominous darkness filling my head with doubts.

I'm close to calling Keeley again when Austin accepts my meeting request, and my world stills, with only the sound of my heartbeat pounding in my ears.

The plan worked. Yet, I have no idea if I'm going to make it on time.

"Can you take a left on Anderson? It'll be faster," I ask the driver, bouncing my knee anxiously, as my phone vibrates in my hand.

"I don't know," my driver responds, his words slow as if we have all the time in the world.

"Why?" I grate with a smile, careful not to piss him off.

"There's reports of an accident at the corner of..." His voice trails off as I internally groan, my eyes dropping to my phone to find a message from unknown—a.k.a. Jill or her people.

UNKNOWN: You might want to check on your projects—vandals are rife at this time of night.

For the briefest of seconds, my heart seizes, but I don't have time to worry about that. I can rebuild in New York. It's Keeley that needs me.

SALVATORE: They're just buildings. They're replaceable.

UNKNOWN: Is your girl?

Fuck. A tremor runs through me as I close my eyes. This is what we wanted, but God, I feel nauseous.

"Can you drive any faster?" I try to keep my voice calm, but it wavers slightly and my driver smiles.

"Of course, but it'll cost you."

"Anything. Just go."

He nods before putting his foot down to speed through the back streets, only slowing when we're on a main road. I allow myself one more moment of panic before I blow out a breath and rid myself of useless emotions, preparing to do what I have to do.

"Just here," I tell the driver when we arrive near the beach house, handing over a wad of cash as I jump out of the cab, then dump my carry-on by the side of the road.

I duck into the shadows of the house next door—knowing they're not home—and make my way closer.

The street is eerily quiet as I walk toward our fence, my jaw clenched so tightly it should hurt, only I can't feel a thing. I'm numb to the pain, my focus on ensuring Keeley's okay.

I slip around the garden and hide behind my car, only then letting myself breathe now that I'm close. I made it. I'll be ready for if and when they—

Keeley's scream pierces the air, and the blood rushes from my body as I take off in a run, adrenaline coursing through me. They were faster than we thought.

I throw open the door, my shoulder pounding into the doorframe as I rush through, but again, I don't feel it. I wouldn't have even noticed if it hadn't momentarily slowed me down.

"Get off me," Keeley yells, the strength in her voice coming through loud and clear as I round the corner to the sunken lounge. The first thing I see is a hooded figure hovering above Keeley on the couch, and without checking for weapons, I dive on top of him, both of us crashing into the coffee table seconds before loud voices fill the house.

"SFPD, don't move."

I jolt as relief fills me, silently thanking Austin for coming through.

But it's not until my eyes lock with Keeley's that I finally relax. She's okay. We're all okay. And this is almost over.

After the intruder's taken away, Keeley and I give our statements to police, and as suspected, they're not at all happy that we didn't report our suspicions earlier. They take my phone as evidence, and I prepare myself for whatever consequences I have to face.

Despite having no intention of paying it, I offered Jill money, and I can't exactly tell the police that I only did it to piss her off in the hope that she'd send someone after my girlfriend.

Since we're in a wealthy neighborhood, it's not long before a media van arrives and reporters are crowding our yard, forcing us to hide inside. Not that we were planning on venturing out anytime soon.

Keeley and I are kept mostly apart, so the second the detectives leave, I have her in my arms, assessing her for damage before I walk her back to the couch.

"I'm fine." She giggles. "Like I told you I would be."

My heart races and I wish I could focus on her happiness, only I have way too many questions to let her off the hook. "What if I hadn't come home, Keels? Or what if I'd arrived five minutes later?"

"If you had, the police would have been here. And I knew you would. I'll bet you were on a plane the second you received the gossip notification." She smiles and I shake my head, an incredulous laugh bubbling out of me.

"You are trouble, you know that?"

"Did you or did you not rush to Paige's defense without filling her in on what you were doing?"

"I did."

"And did you or did you not disappear with Blair's dad to help Zane without telling any of us what you were going to do?"

Fuck. "I did that too."

"And do you trust me?"

"Of course. But—"

"There are no buts, Sal."

"Yes, there is. A huge one. You could have been seriously hurt. Or worse."

"I wasn't."

I stifle a groan and Keeley smiles, standing up on her good foot to pull me into her. She presses a kiss to my lips, and a wave of calm washes over me. She's okay. She's okay. That's all that matters.

"Fuck, Keeley. I understand why you did it, but it scared the hell out of me."

"Ooh. You like me." She grins and I have to hand it to her—after all that she's been through, she doesn't appear affected at all.

"How are you so calm? A man broke into our house and tried to attack you."

"He didn't break in. It's a safe neighborhood; our door was unlocked."

"*Keel-ley.*" I groan. That's not the point and she knows it.

"Ugh, fine. I'm calm because I had to be. I had to trust it would work out, and when I saw Austin's meeting request come through, I knew that it would. Clever idea, by the way. It's like communicating without communicating."

"Austin sent you a meeting request?"

"He did. It said call with Mr. D'Angelo and Austin Newman, ten forty-five tomorrow morning. With the subject, 'confirmation of resources.' I took that to mean ten forty-five tonight, and that someone was on their way to help. I'm assuming his contact came through to tell him the Mikklesons had sent someone. The nephew or whoever it was."

"He must have, but... Jesus, Keels. I guess it doesn't matter if you were wrong because it still gave you the confidence you needed."

"It did. That and my faith in you as a protector."

"I still don't like it. I was supposed to get there before they sent someone. That was the plan."

"Yeah, well, they were faster than I expected." She voices my thoughts. "But luckily Austin got word when he did and it all worked out in the end. My plan worked. Feel free to say thank you."

"Thank you." I stare at her deadpan because while she's right, the plan worked, it could have easily gone the other way. Austin's contact could have been double-crossing us. Or the police could have taken longer.

Keeley laughs, undoubtedly at my sour expression, and I'm about to argue when she winces, her eyes flashing back to the couch. "I should sit down."

"Jesus. Yes. Sit. Can I get you anything?"

"No, I'm fine. Please sit with me."

We both sit and silence falls between us. It's then that her confidence wavers. "In all seriousness, I didn't mean to scare you. I just wanted to help." She sighs, her throat bobbing as she grabs my hand.

"You helped. I'll never be able to thank you enough for what you did for my family."

"Our family." She hides a smile and my heart jolts. *Our family.* She's right. And it's not just because her brother married into my family, it's *her*. *She's* my family. And God, I love her.

No, it's more than that. I don't love her. I'm *in* love with her.

It's beyond infatuation, beyond love, beyond anything I've ever felt. The feeling wraps around me, swirling through my veins until it's ingrained into who I am. Plain and simple, like it's the most obvious notion in the world. I'm in love with Keeley Reynolds, and I've never felt this strongly before.

I shift slightly on the couch, angling my body to face her, an overwhelming tightness in my chest. "Keeley." I draw her attention, my voice raspy as emotion clogs my throat. "There's something I have to say."

Her brow furrows, and I itch to massage the crease there, to wipe away her concern, but instead, I reach for her hand, intertwining our fingers as I speak. "I've never believed in happily ever afters, or soulmates and the meant to be. Even while I was married, that all fell into the fairy-tale category, something I'd read about to Paige. Or at least, something her nanny would have read to her. I never understood how anyone could get wrapped up in giddy feelings and what-ifs. I was too practical for that. That's why business always had my heart. It made sense. Ideas are presented, decisions are made, and they either work or they don't. Of course, it's a lot more complicated than that, but it was easier to handle than uncontrollable emotions and ideals."

Keeley's lips part, her burning gaze locked on mine as though she's captivated by my every word. And God, I hope that's true because I'm captivated by her. She's making me question all the beliefs I had in the past.

"With you, I can see a future, I can see past the day-to-day, and I know with absolute certainty that I never want to be without you. Not today, not ten years from now. You understand me in a way no one ever has before. We're in sync, *a team*, two halves of the same whole. And yes, I realize that sounds a hell of a lot like soulmates, and I'm more than happy to have been proven wrong. The point is... *Fuck.*" I run a hand through my hair, my palms clammy. I can talk to a room full of thousands of people, I can argue my point, fire people without so much as a flinch, but telling my girl that I love her makes my stomach fraught with tension.

"Who would have thought this would be so hard? The point is that I'm in love with you, Keeley. And I think it's been building for a really long time. Even before our first kiss."

Keeley's breath hitches as her eyes well with emotion, the hint of tears shining brightly as she stares my way.

"It's scary how alike we are." She giggles, covering her face with her hands. "If someone had asked me two years ago if I believed in all that, I would have laughed in their face, and yet now, with you sitting in front of me, declaring your love, it's safe to say I've changed my mind. I had faith I'd be okay today because I had faith in you. I've always had faith in you." She smiles as my love pounds inside me, the beating so hard it hurts my heart.

"So what you're saying is..." I trail off, my patience paper-thin now that she's close to admitting she feels the same.

"As hard as I tried to fight it, I've fallen in love with you too. And while I have no clue what the future will bring, I know I want you in it. Always."

"Thank fuck." I cup her neck and slam my lips to hers, feeling her pulse spike beneath my fingertips. This is it. She's the reason I threw myself into work, the reason I packed up and moved to San Francisco, the reason for everything.

My life has been leading me here. I just didn't know it.

Chapter Fifty-Seven

KEELEY

Paige rushes in the front door while I'm eating breakfast the next morning, with my brother following closely behind her. I cringe at the murderous look in his eyes, his expression directed toward the patio where Sal's pacing on the phone. *My* phone, since his was confiscated.

I want to jump to his defense and step between them, only with this stupid cast, I'm stuck in place.

"Easton, stop," I call out from the couch. "You don't know the—"

"I know enough, Keeley."

I'd roll my eyes if I didn't think he was about to punch Sal in the face. I almost wish the police were still here. Though I know Sal will be able to handle it. He also has the option of blaming me for changing the plan, so that would help his case, if he uses it.

"Are you okay?" Paige drops down on the couch beside me, her expression more fitting for the occasion.

"Call off your husband and I'll be better."

"I would, if I didn't feel the same. What Dad did..." She trails off, shaking her head, and I laugh. *Does no one actually know Sal?*

"Do you really think he'd leave me alone, without protection, because of a meeting in New York?" I pause, staring at Paige pointedly until she sighs.

"He's done it before, but no, I didn't think that, until it happened."

"It didn't happen, Paige."

I glance out to the patio to find Easton and Sal talking animatedly in hushed tones, and I really wish I was a fly on the wall. "I love Easton for wanting to protect me, but I am going to kick his ass the second I get the all clear from the doctor. Both of you need to hear the full story before jumping to conclusions."

"Then tell me. I'm sure Dad's filling Easton in."

"God, I hope so."

"What happened?"

I blow out a breath, running a hand through my hair. "When Sal discovered the Mikklesons were tracking you, I suggested we shift their attention elsewhere. To an easier target, someone *without* protection, someone no one was supposed to know about."

"You?"

"Me," I confirm. "Of course, your dad wasn't happy about it at first, but I convinced him to let me leak our relationship to the media in the hope that they'd target me instead of you. A way of luring them out."

"Like bait?"

"My words exactly."

"*Keel-ley*."

I laugh at her very Sal-like response and continue explaining what happened, telling Paige about Sal's plan to piss Jill off, and Austin making sure the Mikklesons found out about us, thinking I was home alone. They wanted to hurt Sal, and we gave them the perfect opportunity.

Paige stares at me in shock, her eyes wide and her lips parted. I've just finished telling her about my brief interview with Zane when she stops me.

"Wait? You didn't tell Dad you were hitting the trigger early?"

"I didn't. We agreed not to discuss the plan after he left."

"Jesus. He would have been going insane."

"He was. I wish I'd thought of the idea before he left for New York, but it only came to me when you and the girls were talking about the game. I figured I'd be easier prey if the Mikklesons had proof of where I was."

"And Storm's first game back after a Super Bowl win was definitely going to garner attention."

"Exactly. Zane winning the game for us was a bonus. I'm certain it would have worked either way, but a lot of people shared his interview because of that."

"You're crazy. You know that, right?"

"I do."

"What if Dad didn't see the alert because he was in an important meeting?"

"I wasn't worried about that. I knew he'd be checking his phone and I trusted him."

"So he didn't leave you alone and unprotected?" Her eyes flash to Sal as her face softens.

"No. He didn't. I was in on the plan the entire time. I'm the reason he only just made it home in time. I went rogue."

"Jesus, Keeley." Her eyes dart back to mine. "And you couldn't tell us the plan before we saw it on the news?"

"No, it wouldn't have worked if you knew. If the Mikklesons had any idea I was being looked after, they wouldn't have come."

"You're both insane."

"Yep. And maybe that's why we work. I knew he'd do anything to protect his family, and he knew I'd do the same. No questions asked."

"Maybe next time you should ask questions."

She comically cringes and I laugh out loud, only stopping when my eyes drift to Sal and Easton's intense conversation.

"What happens next?" Paige asks, drawing my attention.

"One of the detectives mentioned that the intruder has been on their radar for a while now. He's suspected of being a gun for hire, so to speak. We told them everything we knew, and they're going to use that to their advantage. I'm hoping they offer him some kind of deal to share his secrets. At least where the Mikklesons are involved."

"Are you sure it was them?"

"Absolut—"

"I fucking love her," Sal's deep voice booms through the open door, and both Paige and I stiffen.

Her wide eyes flash my way as though asking if that's the first time I've heard him say that, and I laugh. "It's true. He told me last night."

"And you?"

"I said it back."

"Oh my God." Her hand lifts to her mouth as Easton walks back inside still looking as grumpy as ever, only now there's a resolve in his eyes. Pair that with Sal's satisfied grin and it's obvious he got his point across.

"Are you okay?" Easton asks me, his voice soft as his eyes flash to Paige now smiling beside me.

Sal settles behind me, his hand on my shoulder as he gives me a squeeze.

"I'm fine, Easton. I'm guessing Sal explained what happened?" I glance up at Sal and he smiles back at me.

"He did. I still don't like it, but it makes sense. And I know you. You wouldn't have let him do it alone."

My eyes flash to Easton's and I nod, surprised. "Exactly."

"Now you're the one on my shit list, instead of him."

He shoots me a glare and I wince. "That's fair."

"Fair? Keeley, what were you thinking?"

Paige stands up and squeezes Easton's arm. "She was protecting me, Easton. They both were. I think we should cut them some slack."

"Fine," he huffs. "So this is the real deal?"

"Yep." I smile to lighten the mood, adding, "You can call me Mom."

Paige snorts while Easton's face pales. "What the actual fuck, Keeley?"

"I'm kidding." I burst out laughing. "I had to say it at least once."

"Once is all you're getting. If you ever say that again, I'm cutting you off."

"Come on. We both know that's not going to happen. You love me too—"

"Knock. Knock." Luke walks in and my gaze snaps to Paige, a brow raised in question.

"I was on the phone with Hayley when we found out."

"Which means—"

"Oh my God, Keeley." Hayley rushes in with the rest of the gang, and I internally groan. This wasn't supposed to end up as big as it did. Though, I can't complain. If all goes to plan, not only will the Mikkleson men be going to prison, but there's a good chance their wives will too. That chapter will be over for the D'Angelos, and I'm happy to have been able to do my part to help.

Luke and Amelia, Reed and Hayley, and Zane and Blair stay for an hour, catching up on our story while Sal talks to his lawyers in New York. And once they're gone, it's just the four of us again.

One big happy family. Cue my eye roll here because Easton does not look happy.

"You have to get over it, East. All of it. I'm happy. Sal's happy. Your wife doesn't have to worry about the Mikklesons anymore. What is there to be grumpy about?"

Easton jumps to his feet. "I'm not fucking grumpy, Keeley. I was worried. Paige told me that Sal was in New York making sure everything was okay with his business and Camilla, and the next thing you know, your house is on the news and they're talking about a young woman lucky to be alive. Excuse me if I need a minute to move on from that."

Easton finishes speaking and we all fall silent. My heart pounds so hard in my chest that I'm surprised no one can hear it. Words elude me, but I know what I want to do. I hold my hand out for Sal to take, and like always he understands what I need, helping me to stand so I can attack Easton with a hug. A hug he definitely wasn't prepared for because he stumbles backward, cursing under his breath.

"Thank you. For always taking on the big brother role even though you're younger. I will forever be grateful. I will. But it's time to hand over the baton. While we all know I will never need a man, I have one. You don't have to be the guy that worries from the sidelines anymore. Sal's here for that now. Sorry, Sal." Paige laughs while Sal shakes his head and I continue on. "You *know* Sal. You know he's a good guy. Think about that as you move on. And if that doesn't help, just remember that I could have ended up with Luke. He's pretty hot and—"

"Okay. Point made. I'll try to be a little less protective from now on."

"Thank you. I—" My phone rings in Sal's hand, cutting me off. And when I turn his way, his expression is pinched. "What's wrong?"

"It's your mom. I'm guessing she saw the news."

"Actually..." I grimace, my teeth clenched in an awkward grin. "I gave her the heads-up."

"What? How?" Sal asks while Easton's jaw drops.

"Why didn't you give *us* a heads-up?" he complains.

"Because Mom and I can speak in code."

"Code?"

I nod while everyone else stares at me like I'm crazy. "After Dad left, we were watching a show about a group of kids that often stayed home alone. They had a secret word they could use to alert their parents if something was wrong. Mom and I jokingly came up with something we could use. And I used it, but in reverse."

"What does that even mean?" Easton frowns while the smallest of smiles pulls at Sal's lips. He gets it.

"Our word, or phrase in our case, was 'yellow flip-flops,' because, for one, I've never really liked the color yellow. And two, I don't wear flip-flops; even back then I never wore them, unless I was at the beach. Anyway, I called Mom and told her I left my yellow flip-flops at her place. And that if she sees them, it's okay; I don't need them. I'll grab them when I see her very soon. She didn't ask any questions, we had a quick chat, and all was good. I knew that if she saw the news, she'd know I was okay."

Paige and Sal nod, their almost matching expressions showing their awe. Easton, on the other hand, stares at me dumbfounded. "Only you and Mom." He shakes his head.

"You should still call her back." Sal passes my phone over, his awe making way for nerves. It's still going to take time for everyone to be completely comfortable with the two of us dating. But my mom isn't one of them. And before long, everyone else will be shocked they ever questioned it. Our relationship will be old news.

"I will. First, I love you both." I look between Easton and Paige. "But I'm tired, my ankle is killing me, and my bed is calling for a nap. It was a long night."

"Of course." Paige stands up to give both me and Sal a hug. "Call me if you need me. Is it okay if I bring Isaac over tomorrow? While Dad's at work?"

"I'm not going to work," Sal answers before I do. "I'd love to see him too."

"Oh. Okay. Great. I'll see you both tomorrow."

Easton offers me a soft smile before shaking Sal's hand and saying goodbye. I hold my breath until the door shuts, then almost collapse back onto the couch, sighing dramatically. "What a crazy twenty-four hours."

Sal sits beside me, pulling me onto his lap. "Understatement of the year. My heart is still a chaotic mess. Easton's not the only one that needs a moment to move on from what happened. I've never been so scared in my life."

"Sorry."

Sal huffs out a chuckle. "I still can't believe you changed the plan on me. Actually, I can believe it, Miss Independent. What I mean is that it kept me up last night. I still can't help wondering what if I hadn't made it? I don't have the best track record for doing the right thing and—"

"I knew you'd make it. I never once doubted you."

"Keels."

"No, Sal. I knew you'd be checking your phone every time it went off. I knew you'd be on the next flight out of there as soon as you got that alert, and I knew you'd be here when I needed you. Even if the detectives arrived first, I knew you wouldn't be too far behind them. I trusted you completely. It's time you start trusting yourself. You're not the same man you used to be. The husband Camilla got is not the boyfriend I have now."

Sal stares at me for a beat before cupping my face and pressing his lips to mine. "Thank you. As corny as this sounds, it's you that makes me want to be a better man."

"And Paige."

"Her too. And she's okay because of you."

"And *you*. Let's face it. If I hadn't come up with that plan, you would have come up with something else. You're Salvatore D'Angelo. Instead, you get to spend that time worshipping your girl."

"Something I plan to do all day, every day." He smirks before his tongue pokes out to wet his bottom lip, making me clench my legs.

"Are you really *not* going to work tomorrow?" I ask with a raised brow, almost certain I'm going to call him on his bullshit to Paige.

"I'm really not." He chuckles lightly. "Not tomorrow, not the next day. Not until the doctor clears you to go back with me."

"Sounds possessive."

"Good. I'm not leaving you alone in this house. Ever again."

"I don't think that's feasible. What about days when you have to fly to New York, or when you're spending time with Isaac? You can't stay with me for the next however long we live here." My heart lurches over the fact that I just invited myself to move in, but Sal doesn't seem to notice.

"I'm selling the house, Keels. We can't live here after that."

"What? No. I love this house. It has everything we need."

"I'll replicate it. Somewhere else. Somewhere that isn't tainted anymore."

"Sal." I offer him a sad smile but he shakes me off.

"Don't Sal me. I've already decided. Some fucker walked into this house with plans to attack you. Or *worse*. We can't live here. I already called the real estate agent while you were chatting with everyone earlier. It's done."

"What if you don't sell this one?"

"It can sit here empty for all I care."

"How can you be so rich that you'll happily leave a beachfront mansion empty, and yet, you still don't have a jet? I think you need your priorities adjusted."

Sal laughs so hard that the shadow of today finally starts to dissipate from over his head, and I can't help but smile in relief.

"I'll tell you what. When we sell this house, I'll buy you a jet."

"I don't want—" He stares at me deadpan and I laugh. "Okay, you can buy me a jet. Deal."

"Thank you. Now, call your mom back. I'm going to get the bed ready so you can rest."

"The bed wasn't calling me for rest, Sal. The bed was calling *us* so we can turn this day around."

"Is that so?"

"It is. It's time to rock my world again, old man. I need a broken back to match my ankle."

Chapter Fifty-Eight

SALVATORE

My phone buzzes on the coffee table in our new home, and I groan at having our peace disturbed. We moved out of the beach house within two days of the intruder incident, and three days later, I'd secured another house, despite Keeley suggesting we could both move into her apartment.

After seeing her so happy at the beach house, I wasn't about to take that away from her. And in the end, this house is even better. Not only is it beachfront, but it also has a pool and an elevator, making it easier for Keeley while she continues to recover.

It wasn't exactly on the market—it was one of those holiday rental places—but it's amazing what a little determination and persuasion can do. Not to mention money.

The buzzing continues, and the incessant sound pulls me from my thoughts, making me blow out a breath as I reach over, switching it off.

My phone has been ringing nonstop since the day I got it back from the police, two days after they took it. I've had calls from real estate agents, my lawyers, Daniel, Austin, Camilla. *Camilla*. That one was a fun one. It turns out she knew nothing about the extra evidence she supposedly had on Gabriel Mikkleson. *Nothing*. Or at least nothing she could remember. In fact, Austin discovered that Gabriel's nephew, the guy Austin had hired as his informant, had lied to him in the hope of lighting a fire under our asses. He wanted his uncles to go to prison for as long as possible so he could inherit his grandfather's fortune, instead of it going to them. Apparently, his grandfather has a clause in his will to say that his fortune had to go to a male heir, meaning his mom was passed over.

He even gave me my hundred grand back, saying he wouldn't be needing it anymore.

The little fucker played us and we fell for it.

Though it all worked out in our favor. Camilla testified against both the Mikkleson brothers in their trials and is counting down the days until the women are tried too. We all are. With Keeley's and my statements, along with Camilla's reports of being followed and the intruder's deal, Jill and her sister-in-law were both found to be tampering with witnesses, leading to their arrests late last night.

Because of that, I only got a slap on the wrist for offering Jill money.

It's over.

Paige didn't have to testify, and she no longer requires security—though I convinced her to keep one of my guys on speed dial just in case she needs it.

Paige is safe. Camilla is safe. Marc is safe. And Keeley is by my side.

"What are you doing?" Keeley asks, her eyes wide as she watches my uncharacteristic action. I can't remember the last time I silenced my phone, let alone switched it off.

"It's the New York office. They don't need me; they're just accustomed to running everything past me. I've already told them to stop."

"You're really handing the company over to Daniel?"

"I really am. I love D'Angelo Construction. It will always be my baby. But I don't want to travel back and forth anymore. I want to spend every spare second building a life here with you, watching my grandchild grow, and seeing my team's success continue. My goals have shifted. I've done all I can with D'Angelo Construction, so it's time for Daniel to make it his own. God knows I'm not getting any younger."

"Major emphasis on the latter," Keeley teases and I flip her onto her back so fast that her jaw drops. Being careful of her ankle, of course.

"How's that for an old man?" I hover above her, staring into the crystal-blue eyes I want to see every day for the rest of my life.

"You were fast, I'll give you that. But...what if you regret it?"

"Flipping you onto your back?" My eyes rake over her, from her face to the hint of pink material peeking out from where her dress has risen.

"No." She laughs as she tries to shove me back, lifting to her elbows to bring our eye level closer. "D'Angelo Construction."

"I knew what you meant, Keels. But you don't have to worry. I'm happy. I'm still the owner of the company, so if down the road I miss being hands-on, or we want a change of scenery for a while, it will be there."

Keeley's gaze softens, and I have no doubt it's because the truth to my words has sunk in. There's been a nervous energy hovering around her since I announced my decision. And while my timing could have been better, her broken ankle and the Mikkleson attacks weren't the catalysts she believes them to be. I wasn't lying when I said the decision had been brewing for years. I'd even mentioned it to my lawyers a few weeks ago. Before any of this happened.

New York may have been my life for the past five decades, but San Francisco is my future, and it's time to give it my full attention. To give Keeley and my family my full attention.

It's time to shake my workaholic persona. I don't have to be that guy anymore. I don't want to be him. I'm not ready to retire. In fact, I'm far from it. But I am ready to focus on the Storm. Ready to give them one hundred percent of my work commitment, even if that's less than I previously thought it would be.

With Wes at the helm, I can work on the bigger picture and step back on all the day-to-day. We finally have a management team we all trust, players that fit our culture—a family we all love being a part of.

It's my time to focus on what really matters—my family.

"What if I revert back to my old self when my ankle's back to normal? Will you resent me for my workaholic ways?"

"Resent you? Keeley, your work ethic is one of the reasons I fell in love with you. If you hadn't dedicated so much time to work, we never would have gotten as close as we did, and I never would have discovered that my perfect match was still out there."

"Yes. However, when I'm back in the office full-time, you'll see me less."

"No, I won't. I work there too. You can't escape me." I press a chaste kiss to her lips before pulling away and helping her sit up.

"I am never going to try to change you, Keeley. Looking back, I'm pretty sure I fell in love with you not long after we first met. In fact, it's obvious to me now. You are you, Keels. And I love you exactly as you are."

"Likewise. No matter how gray you get, you'll always be the man I fell in love with, which was probably around the same time you fell. As hard as it was to admit that."

"We took our time, but we got there in the end, and I think our relationship is stronger because of it."

"I couldn't agree more." She grabs the knitted blanket that fell on the floor when I flipped her over, and twists my way, lifting her leg onto my lap before covering herself with the blanket.

"You know, it kind of feels like we're an old married couple already, without the marriage part."

"Or the old for some." I wink and she laughs.

"If anyone calls you old again, I'm going to tell them what you did to me last night. I can't imagine there are many grandfathers doing that."

I groan at the visual of our session last night, almost wishing we could do it again, if we weren't expecting Keeley's mom to come over any moment.

"I'm looking forward to showing you how young I feel again later tonight."

"Oh, hi, Mom." Keeley waves toward the door, and I choke on thin air until she bursts out laughing. "I'm kidding. She texted to say she's running late."

"She did?"

"Yep. About two minutes before your phone started ringing."

"How long is she going to be?"

"Another hour, why?"

"No reason." I lift her legs off me and stand up, resting them back on the couch. "I'll be back in a minute."

"Oh-kay. What are you up to?"

"Nothing. Don't you worry." I walk away slowly until I'm out of her line of sight, then I jog up the stairs, taking them two at a time, only slowing down when I reach our bedroom.

My lips curl into a smile as I take in all of Keeley's belongings. I lied when I said she could move out when her ankle had healed. After thinking I could lose her the night of our plan, I decided to never waste another second of our lives together. No more taking things slowly. I'm planning to spend the rest of my days with her by my side, and I'm starting those days now.

I walk around to Keeley's side of the bed and open the top drawer, finding her *friend* Leo buried under some paperwork. She claims she's not going to need him much anymore, but I'm about to prove her wrong. I've been jealous of this little fucker since she first mentioned it, and it's time to show him who's boss.

With the vibrator in hand, I rush back downstairs before casually strolling into the living room, pausing when I realize Keeley has moved to the patio, her bare shoulders visible over the back of the lounge chair.

Is she naked?

With quiet steps, I walk toward her, my breath catching when I find her stripped down, only the knitted blanket covering her modesty.

"It was getting hot in there while I waited for you, wondering what the hell you were going to do."

"So you decided to get naked. Out here?"

"Yep."

"Where anyone could see you?"

"Uh-huh."

"You know I don't share, Keels."

"Don't you?" Her eyes flash to the vibrator in my hand, and a chuckle bursts out of me. I'd forgotten I was holding it.

"This is different and you know it."

"Either way, no one can see us. You told me that yourself when we moved here."

I glance around, taking in the privacy screens on each side of our patio and the emptiness in front of us. She's right. For now. It doesn't mean it's going to stay that way. We're higher up in this place, with the house built into the side of the cliffs, but someone could easily walk past and look up.

"You've got to keep up with what the younger adults are doing these days. It's all about public fornication." Keeley bites her lip to stop herself from giggling, and I huff out a laugh in return.

"I know what you're doing, and I wish I had the strength to get you back by walking away without touching you, but I guarantee I want it more than you do."

"Oh, I doubt it. I'm pretty worked up after stripping down and waiting in anticipation. I'm lucky it's a big house or I wouldn't have had enough time. I hate being slow."

"Slow is underrated."

"Maybe. But if you take your time now, I'm going to have to punch you."

"Not a chance. Leo and I are ready." I move to stand in front of her and drop to my knees before burying myself under the blanket, spreading Keeley's pussy.

She lifts the blanket away from her chest and laughs down at me. "Who would have thought such a powerful man would get on his knees for anyone."

"Only you." I chuckle before pulling the blanket back over my head.

"Stop. You won't be able to breathe under there."

"Then I'll die happy. Now shhh, Leo and I have a job to do." I start the vibrator and press it to her clit, groaning when she bucks her hips, crying out to God.

I instantly change my mind on the blanket. It's got to go. I throw it off and stare up at her, a brow raised. "It's Sal. And fuck, you're glorious when you let yourself relax."

"Now you know the third thing that clears my mind."

"A good orgasm?"

"No, *you*. You're my happy place," she rushes out, her breathing picking up speed as I continue to rub her clit with the vibrator. "You're my safe place." She sighs. "My white noise." She wiggles and mewls. "My fierce protector. But most of all, you're the other half of my soul. I love you, Sal."

"God, I love you too."

"You mean Keeley?" she sasses, making me jump up, covering her naked body with my fully clothed one.

"Keeley." I lean in, brushing my lips gently across hers before pouring everything I have into the kiss. "I love you." I pull back, staring into her eyes. "You've changed me for the better, and I'm ready for whatever life may throw our way. Whatever storm we have to weather. We're in this together."

"No matter what."

We've been a team from the start; we'll be a team until the end.

It's Keeley and me. Always.

Epilogue One

KEELEY

NEW YEAR'S EVE THE FOLLOWING YEAR

Jeffrey pulls up in front of Luke and Amelia's house to drop us off, and as always, Sal jumps out on his side, then runs around to open my door. We've now officially been together for around sixteen months, and his gentlemanly ways haven't once wavered.

Except in the bedroom. It's safe to say, Sal is a powerful man in *all* aspects of his life. And I love it.

Once I'm out of the car, Sal pulls me into his arms and presses a kiss to my brow, taking in a deep breath as silence falls around us. He's soaking up my warmth. His words not mine. But something we both do for each other.

No matter what life throws our way, we're in it together, always there to help each other through.

After the Mikkleson men were sentenced to twenty-five years in prison, Sal sat back and reflected on his life, admitting that he'd been pretty reactive over the years, and that he wanted to change. And change he has. He now only works six days a week, taking Tuesday off along with the team, and has dedicated a lot more time to his family. Including Marc. I'm not sure they'll ever have the close relationship he shares with Paige, but they visit each other often, and they've even discovered a shared interest in boating. By boating, I mean expensive yachts.

"Okay, I'm ready." Sal stands tall and I laugh.

"You're never going to get used to this, are you?"

"You mean attending a New Year's Eve rager with a bunch of my players?"

"Rager, huh? Are you trying to keep up with the young kids' slang?"

"I'm kidding. It's getting easier, I promise. I just really like our quiet moments alone."

I smile at the sincerity in his eyes. "Me too. Unfortunately, sometimes we need to be social. It's time to head into the chaos."

Sal laughs as he clasps my hand, intertwining our fingers before we head to the door.

Chaos is an understatement when we walk in, but it all fades away when Isaac's smiling face comes into view.

His eyes light up when he sees us, taking off in a run, and I try to let go of Sal's hand, but he holds firm until the very last second, then sneakily steps in front of me, wrapping Isaac in his arms. "You were running to me, right, Kid?"

Isaac laughs out loud as Sal playfully tickles him. "I love you, Pops, but I wanted Keeley."

"Don't we all," he mumbles under his breath as he puts Isaac down, ruffling his hair. "I love you too, Isaac. I'm going to go and find your mom."

Sal's eyes twinkle when he refers to Paige as Isaac's mom, and I have no doubt he's feeling the same warmth in his chest that I feel every time I say it. It wasn't an easy road, but Isaac's adoption is finally official, and the Wilders couldn't be happier.

Even Isaac's smile grows. He's been calling Paige Mom since she moved into their apartment, but he's old enough to understand what it means now, and knowing it's official really changed things for him too. It brought him further out of his shell, something he'd been working on with his therapist. "Mom is in the kitchen with Dad," he tells Sal, beaming as he points toward the back of Luke's house.

"Thanks, Buddy." Sal squeezes my hand as he walks away, and I immediately turn to Isaac.

"How was your day?" he asks, always so polite, nothing at all like his father.

"I had a wonderful day, thank you. How was *your* day?"

"Good, thanks, Keeley."

Keeley. Not Aunt Keeley, like he used to call me, just Keeley. Without anyone mentioning it, he stopped calling me aunt after the first day he saw Sal and me as a couple. I was worried at first, until he told Paige it was because I was his family on both sides now, and the term aunt didn't sound important enough.

Bless his innocent little soul.

After our greetings, Isaac drags me toward Juliet, his favorite person right now, and I chat with Amelia, spending the next hour mingling with friends, feeling Sal's eyes on me the entire time.

It took him a while to feel comfortable enough to attend one of the guys' events. He'd heard Paige talk about them regularly, but never considered ever being invited. It wasn't until my mom of all people dragged his ass there, telling him he had to suck it up if he wanted to date her daughter. She had an entire speech planned, but all she had to do was remind him that age was just a number, and that if *I* didn't care that I was dating an old man, he shouldn't care that he was dating someone younger. He gave in after that, knowing I've been saying the same since we first kissed.

The thought of my mom makes my chest tight, while gratitude fills me. She may be struggling a lot more these days and spending most of her time in a wheelchair, but she's still with us, and I'll cherish every moment we get to share.

Thomas ventures over when I'm alone by the bar, his sincere smile always bringing about my own.

"Are you attending the Women in Sports fundraiser again this year?" he asks as he leans against the counter, folding his arms over his chest. "Lainey's been invited to talk about movement therapy in the sporting world. Her speech won't be as explosive as yours, but I know she'd love to have a familiar face in the crowd."

I huff out a laugh as my eyes flash to his wife, Lainey, and I smile. "I'll be there. I wouldn't miss it for the world."

My explosive speech, as Thomas called it, still elicits such a strong internal response for me now. It's always a mix of elation and sorrow. Elation because I made a stand against the assholes in the sporting world who thought they could hurt women, whether physically or by other means, and get away with it. I named names, not only Vance and my supervisor back in college, but also our ex-GM Tray, and our ex-owner Gregory for covering up Tray's many cases of sexual harassment during his time with the Storm.

Suffice it to say, Gregory's book was never published, and his accusations about the Storm team quickly went away with the focus being on him instead.

Since my speech, hundreds of women have come forward, and that's where the sorrow comes in. I never could have predicted how many women, and men for that matter, were suffering at the hands of someone that others trusted. I don't think I'll ever get over it.

Thomas thanks me and squeezes my arm before heading back over to the guys, and I smile as they jokingly call him the boss. After rejecting Vance for the quarterback coaching position last season, Wes shelved the restructure idea, opting to wait until the following season. And lo and behold, Thomas accepted the job.

I'll neither confirm nor deny that he may have been gently coerced by several different people, but the point is, he's now a part of the family again, and we couldn't be happier. Even Beckett seems to like having him around.

The night feels long, and by the time midnight strikes, I'm ready to leave.

As though he can read my mind, Sal glances in my direction, nodding his head toward the door.

I laugh, turning to grab my bag until Hayley sidles up next to me. "You and Daddy D are so in sync it's sickening."

"Ahh, like you can talk. Did you and Reed mean to color match?"

We both glance over to Reed in his blue-and-white striped tee and laugh as I gesture to Hayley's dress. "Point taken. I was only teasing in the hope that you would stay longer."

"I would..." I drag out the word, rocking my head from side to side, "but I don't want to. I love you all, but I'm ready to ring in the new year with my man."

I wink, knowing what she's thinking, but in truth, I'm ready to curl up on the couch and enjoy a nice glass of wine.

I'm ready for Sal and me to be alone just like he mentioned when we arrived.

The second we get home, Sal pours us both a drink and gets comfortable on the couch, leaning back with his arms open, silently asking me to sit down. I settle into his hold, my favorite position, and he stretches out to reach for my drink, handing me my wine before grabbing his own.

"To our second New Year's together."

"And to another great drop."

We click glasses before I take a sip, moaning at the taste. I thought I knew what good wine was, and Sal always amused me by keeping his office well stocked with my drink of choice. Only it turns out, I knew *nothing*.

Sal introduced me to a world of different flavors, and now I'm obsessed.

"Where's this one from?" I ask, glancing behind me to see if I recognize the label on the bottle.

Sal smiles, always enjoying it when he finds something I like. "This one's Australian. The Barossa Valley to be exact. It's from a boutique vineyard specializing in Shiraz."

"A boutique that sells in the US?"

"Nope. I had it delivered especially for you to try."

"What?" I swivel in his grasp until I'm facing him, careful not to drop the red on our light gray couch. "That's amazing. How did you find them?"

"A friend vacationed in Australia last year. He did a road trip through a few of their wine regions, and this was his favorite. Since I know you like that fuller flavor, I thought we should try it."

"Just like that?"

"Yep."

"Did you send your private jet to collect it?" Yes, Mr. Salvatore D'Angelo finally bought his own jet. And yet, he rarely uses it.

"Yes, Keeley," he deadpans. "I sent my jet. I also forced Tabitha to go, to ensure we got the correct bottle."

"You're not the comedian that you think you are."

"Sure I am. Anyway, I had it shipped here. It was their first shipment to the US but they were happy to oblige considering..."

"Considering what?" I eye him suspiciously.

"I may have bought a few cases."

"A few?" My eyes widen as he shrugs. "What if I didn't like it?"

"It was a risk I was willing to take. What if you did? Then I'd have to go and order more."

"Heaven forbid." A soft laugh escapes me as I pat his leg. Sal's great with his money, until it comes to pleasing me. I should really tell him to stop...or not.

"It's a moot point anyway," he continues, waving me off. "You loved it."

"How do you know?"

"The moan."

"Oh, right. I loved it," I admit, making Sal smile.

"I'm happy you feel that way because we have enough to last us until we're old and gray."

"Ummm. How do I say this nicely?" I purse my lips, furrowing my brow exaggeratedly as I glance away in thought.

"Don't," Sal warns.

"Don't what?" I innocently bat my eyelids and he huffs.

"Don't say it," he warns again.

"What? That you're already old and gray?"

"Yep, that."

"If you weren't, I'm not sure I'd be as attracted to you. This is the man I fell in love with." I wave a hand in front of him and he chuckles lightly.

"I'm looking forward to the day you get your first gray hair. No more teasing."

"Oh, I am never going gray. Matt and I have a recurring appointment to ensure that doesn't happen."

"Who the fuck is Matt?" Sal stiffens, crossing his arms, and I bask in his jealousy, taking my time to respond. His brows furrow, and I can't help rubbing the crease between his eyes.

"Matt's my hairdresser."

"Oh, right." He groans. "I knew that."

"I like the fact that you still get jealous over me."

"That's lucky because that's not going to change any time soon. I'll never understand why you chose me of all people. You don't have to worry about me ever taking you for granted, that's for sure."

"I've said it once and I'll say it again. You are it for me, Mr. D'Angelo, so you better get used to it."

He cups my face, staring into my eyes. "I wouldn't want it any other way."

"Good. So where were we?"

"You were complimenting me on the wine."

"I'm not sure that's true, but I do love it. Maybe one day we can visit Australia ourselves."

"It's funny you should say that. Check your email."

"What?"

"Check your email."

With my ass still on the couch next to him, I lean forward and gently place my glass down on the coffee table before grabbing my phone and bringing up my emails.

I have to scroll through the emails I received in the short time we've been sitting here, before I find what I'm looking for.

Travel Itinerary—Wineries of the world

"Of the world?"

"Of the world," he says nonchalantly, as though it's no big deal.

I nod as my eyes drift back to the phone, quickly scanning the contents of the email, gasping when I come to the finer details.

Forty-nine nights.

San Francisco > Australia > Europe (France, Italy and Spain) > San Francisco

"Are you insane? Forty-nine nights?"

"Yep. One night for every year of my life before I met you."

My heart jolts. "Really?"

"Really." Sal smiles softly, the crinkled lines of his eyes making me swoon. He's always had a nice smile. I'm not the only one that's noticed that. But when he looks at me like he is now, smiling with his whole face, his heart, and his soul, I feel like the luckiest woman in the world.

I get to keep him.

"It's corny, really, but I figured that just because neither of us wants to get married, doesn't mean we should miss out on a honeymoon. Of sorts."

"A honeymoon?"

"Of sorts. Yes. Surprise." He waves his hands in the air, and I stare at him, speechless.

Excitement courses through me as I think about the things we can do. I've never taken a vacation. Ever. This will be a first for me and it's forty-nine nights. My stomach knots and I clench my teeth as I sheepishly turn to Sal.

"So, I wouldn't be me if I didn't ask this question… What the hell do we do about work?"

"Don't worry." Sal chuckles, clearly knowing that was coming. "It's the offseason and it'll still be there when we get back. But to warm your little workaholic heart, Tina has scheduled in quite a few workdays for us both, just in case."

"Who the fuck is Tina?" I fold my arms over my chest, just like he did when he asked the same question about Matt, and Sal throws his head back to laugh. Whoops.

"Tina is our travel agent."

"Of course. I knew that."

Sal pulls me back into him, once again wrapping me in his arms. "I think we were made for each other, Keels."

"I think you might be right, *Sir.*"

Epilogue Two

THE END GAME SUPPORT GROUP

A YEAR LATER

LUKE

Amelia steps outside with our friends to wave them off while I hover in the doorway. I love them all but it's almost one a.m. and I'm ready for alone time with my wife.

"Thank you for coming. Drive safe." She doesn't move until the last car has driven away before finally turning to face me.

"Another successful New Year's Eve party. I love that we started this tradition."

"Yeah, except that Reed asked if they could host next year. What's that about? This is my thing." I pout and Amelia bursts out laughing, shaking her head as she walks inside.

"What? Am I wrong?" I follow her in, walking closely behind her so when she stops abruptly, I almost bump into her.

She spins to face me, wrapping her arms around my waist. "You're a sweet guy, Luke."

"Sweet? Where did you get that from? I'm complaining about my friend."

"Because you want to be the one that looks after them all. You want to be the one that brings joy into their lives and helps them relax when there's so much going on in the world."

"That doesn't sound like me. I want the attention and credit."

"I don't doubt you want that too. But we all see through the humor and cockiness."

"Who's we?"

"Everyone. You can't hide the fact that you care deeply for your friends. All of them. You say Reed's the protective one and yet, you're always there, ready to help out. You kept the group chat alive all those years when they needed support."

My eyes widen at the mention of the group chat. It's barely alive, but I should change that.

"Uh-oh. What did I say?" Amelia knows me so well.

"What do you mean?"

"Your eyes just lit up like a kid on Christmas."

"I was thinking about the group chat. We barely use it anymore. We're all so busy. But we should. Even if it's just a weekly check-in."

Amelia laughs before giving my arm a squeeze. "Start slowly. You're going to get mixed reviews on that one."

"Maybe. We'll see." I glance away in contemplation until I realize what I'm doing. Now is not the time to be thinking about the guys. "Let's shelve that idea for tomorrow. We're alone. The kids are asleep. Skye has started sleeping through the night, which is actually a miracle I've yet to completely process. What should we do?"

Amelia hums softly before she checks the monitor, smiling at our youngest asleep in her crib. "I'd love to get a few extra hours of sleep. I only have two more days off before I have to go back into the editing suite."

My shoulders drop as Amelia rubs her eyes, but the second she glances up at me again, I put on a smile. "You're right. Let's get you to bed. I'll warm up your heating pad and be there in a minute."

I turn to leave and Amelia grabs my bicep, pulling me to a stop as she laughs. "After all this time, you're still so easy to tease. Let's go to bed. I want a massage before you eat dessert."

Hell fucking yes.

"I love dessert."

"I know." Amelia lifts to her toes, wrapping her arms around my neck before pressing a chaste kiss to my lips. "Happy New Year, Babe. I have a feeling this year is going to be a good one."

"Happy New Year, Ace. You might be right, but every year is a good one with you." Amelia smiles warmly, but I don't let her soak in that comment before moving us along. "Now it's time to get you naked and ready for me. It's going to be a long night."

EASTON

Paige opens the door ahead of me and pulls back Isaac's bedding as I follow behind her, my not so little boy in my arms. He tried so hard to stay awake. "I'm almost eight now," he'd told me. "I can stay up until midnight."

Paige and I had agreed that he could try, both knowing he'd never make it, and we were right. His eyes were heavy by ten, and by ten thirty-five he was asleep on Luke and Amelia's couch.

Now, if all goes to plan, in four more steps we're going to successfully complete the transfer from one place to another.

"Dad?"

Dammit. Why would I think about that?

"Shhh, buddy. It's late." Paige smiles as I place him down gently on his bed and pull the covers up, tucking them tightly around him. "We can talk in the morning."

"Did I miss the fireworks?"

"We all did."

"You did?"

"Yep. We were all so tired we decided to stay at the Bennetts'."

"Okay. Love you, Dad."

"Love you too." I turn to creep away but he calls out again, trying to sit up.

"Mom?"

Like it always does, my heart jolts when Isaac calls Paige Mom. It's been years, and I'm still thankful she walked into our life and refused to leave.

"I'm here, sweetie." Paige nudges me out of the way to get to Isaac's bed, sitting on the edge to brush her hand across his cheek. "Everything okay?"

"Yeah. Ahh. Was Dad lying?"

Paige's infectious laughter fills the room as she turns my way, shaking her head. He caught me on a little white lie once, and now he's always questioning me. In fact, they both do it. It's an inside joke between the two of them. And despite the joke being on me, I secretly love it.

"*I-saac*," I grumble, exactly like he expects me to, and he giggles, pulling the comforter up to cover his face.

"Actually, Isaac, this time he didn't lie. For once." Isaac peeks and Paige exaggeratedly rolls her eyes, making him laugh once more.

"Good. Thanks, Mom."

"Anytime. Now you need to go back to sleep." She ruffles his hair.

"Good night. Love you both."

"We love you too."

I dim the hallway light as we pass by, darkening Isaac's room, and follow Paige downstairs. The second we reach the landing, I pull her into my arms, trapping her in my hold, sighing as I rest my forehead to hers. "Happy New Year, Mrs. Wilder."

"Happy New Year to you too. What time is practice tomorrow?"

"Not until one. They gave us the morning off since it's a Wednesday."

"So we don't have to rush off to bed?"

"Oh, we're going to bed. But I want you naked and waiting for me with your legs spread. We're celebrating."

"What are we celebrating?"

"Surviving another one of Luke's parties. Will that man ever change?"

"Will you?"

"I don't know what you're talking about?"

"Of course not. You're lucky I love you exactly as you are."

"Good. I love you too, Paige. And always will."

REED

I lift Hayley out of the car and she squeals, hanging on for dear life as if I'd ever drop her. "I can get out on my own, Reedy Boy. What are you doing?"

"I'm carrying my wife to the front door. Sue me for being romantic on New Year's Eve."

"Technically, it's New Year's Day and it's four, five steps maximum."

"Well, I'm not taking you farther with Lincoln asleep in the car."

Hayley grabs my face in her hands, silently laughing. "Oh, Reed. I wasn't asking you to. I meant that I can walk. If you're carrying Linc, who's getting his bag?"

Reed glances back at the car. "For a little kid, he sure has a lot of stuff."

"He's *your* kid, Reed. He's not little. Do you remember when Juliet was this age? She was half his size."

"What can I say? We're raising a football star."

"Or a model. Models are tall too."

"Sure. Or both. I've modeled before."

"You've what?" Hayley wriggles out of my hold and crosses her arms over her chest. "How the hell didn't I know about this?"

"Because I didn't tell you." I shrug and turn away, walking back to get Lincoln.

"I know a lot of things you didn't tell me," Hayley teases, following after me. "It's called the Internet."

"Yeah, well. You won't find that."

"Why not?" She pouts and it's so adorable I want to laugh, but I also don't want to wake Linc. "It's impossible to keep things hidden these days," Hayley whispers as I open the door, her expression screaming "so there."

"It was a friend's photography project in college. Trust me—you're not going to find it." I lift our perfect little human into my arms and almost tell Hayley she's wrong about his height. At just over two months old, he still looks tiny to me.

"I have to see these photos," Hayley continues on as she shuts the car door and runs around to grab Lincoln's bag from the trunk.

"Sorry, but *I* have to get Linc inside," I tease, making her huff.

"This conversation isn't over, Reedy Boy."

"Oh, I know. And I'm the fool that brought it up."

"Yeah, you are." Hayley bounces her eyebrows and I roll my eyes, waiting for her to unlock the front door before carrying Linc to his bedroom down the hall from ours.

I'm on edge as I lower him into his crib, mentally crossing my fingers that he'll stay asleep. He stretches his long legs before tucking his perfect little hands up to his chin and scrunching his nose. A few seconds later, he's quiet and I finally release my breath.

After grabbing the monitor, I pull his door softly closed and turn to creep away, jumping when I find Hayley waiting by the door. "Jesus Christ, Hayls. What are you doing?"

"Waiting for you."

"Did you have to wait so close?"

"I did. Where are the photos, Reed?" She taps her foot and I burst out laughing, covering my mouth to stifle the noise.

"Bedroom, Hayls. Now."

"Uh-uh. I'm not giving you anything—"

With one smooth movement, I grab her around the legs and throw her over my shoulder, turning her complaint into a squeal.

"You can't do this every time you want me to go somewhere."

"Sure I can. Did you see how easy that was?"

When we get to our bedroom, I toss her gently onto the bed, staring down at my beautiful wife. "God, you're incredible, Mrs. Coombs."

"It's Ms. Jackman."

"Nope. The people get to call you Ms. Jackman. To me, you're Mrs. Coombs."

She tries unsuccessfully to hide a grin and I chuckle softly. From the moment we said I do, in a much smaller ceremony than we'd originally planned, Hayley announced herself as Mrs. Coombs, before the officiant did. She loves having my name, but has kept Jackman for work.

"Fine, Mr. Coombs. May I pretty please see the photos of your modeling career?" She bats her eyelashes and...

Dammit. The things I do for this woman.

"Anything for you, Hayley Baby. But you have to promise *me* something."

"What's that?"

"You won't laugh."

"Oh, Reed. There is no way I will ever make that promise."

ZANE

Blair's quiet on our way home, but there's an energy buzzing around her that wasn't present earlier in the night, and I'm dying to know what it is.

"Did you have a good night?" she asks, trying to keep her cool.

"I did. I know I give them all a hard time, but they're a good group."

"They are. We're lucky to have them. They're like family. The family you get to choose."

"I assume you're thinking about my shitty parents as you say that? Your parents are amazing."

"They are. But they're not here. It's nice to have family close by." She squeezes my arm as her smile widens.

"I'm surprised your dad hasn't moved here. He always talks about wanting to retire and play golf with D'Angelo."

"I'm ninety-nine percent sure that's why he's coming over in March. Mom's coming to spend more time with Jade while he spends time with Sal."

I turn to look at our daughter in the backseat, and my chest fills with warmth.

"You told him Sal doesn't golf, right?"

"Yep. But his response was 'all rich people play golf.' Who knows, maybe he'll convince him."

"Maybe. Anyway, enough about my boss. I want to talk about you."

"Me?"

"Yep. You were looking a little tired until you disappeared for thirty minutes and came back hiding a huge smile on your face."

"You caught that, huh?"

"Oh, Little B. When are you going to believe me when I tell you I see *everything* when it comes to you? It's been years."

"In fairness, I didn't know you were watching."

"I'm always watching."

"God, Jade is going to hate it if you take that approach with her when she's older."

"Nothing wrong with being a protective dad."

"There's protective and then there's whatever the hell you are." She waves her hand in front of me and I don't even flinch. I'm happy to own it.

"You love it."

"I do. I'm not so sure she will."

"She's not going to have a choice if she grows up around the Storm crew. They're all just as bad as I am."

"God, that's true. Hayley *is* pretty badass."

"Ha ha. In all seriousness. As long as she waits until she's at least twenty to start dating, she'll be fine."

"Oh, like *we* did," she says sarcastically, rolling her eyes.

"Technically you were twenty-five by the time we started dating."

Blair's jaw drops and I can't help but chuckle. She's always the one that says we were casual when we first started sneaking around as teenagers, and I'm the one that says there was more between us. Turns out, she doesn't like it when the tables are turned. "Tell me I'm wrong?"

"Fine, you're wrong. We started dating when we were teenagers. You were my first love."

"Your *only* love. We don't count the four-year error of judgment in between."

"My forever love. How's that?"

"I'll take it. Now, tell me what made you so happy?"

"My agent called me. A publisher wants to acquire my book. Our story is going to be in bookstores all around the world."

"No way! You did it? Pull over. We need to celebrate."

"On the side of the road?"

"This is a big deal. I need to kiss my wife."

"You always need to kiss me."

"You bet your ass I do. And that's never going to change."

"I think I'm okay with that. But you can wait until we get home. It's only around the corner."

I smile, loving my strong wife telling me what to do. She lost herself for a while there, but now she's back, and I never want her to change. Still, I love to tease her.

"Fine, I'll wait."

SALVATORE

My alarm goes off at eight, and Keeley groans in my arms. "Why do you have to get up so early? I was having a nice dream."

"Oh, yeah? What were you dreaming about?"

"Our vacation last year. I think we need another one." She tucks herself into me, running her fingers through the dusting of hair on my chest, making my muscles tense beneath my skin.

I agree with her, one hundred percent. I think about our vacation on a daily basis. I've never seen Keeley so relaxed and carefree, and hell, I've never felt that way either. It was one for the record books, that's for sure.

"Maybe I should retire."

"As if."

"What does that mean?"

"You love it too much."

"You're right. I do. But I love you more. We could spend the rest of our lives traveling."

"What about Isaac?"

"Dammit."

"And Mom, Paige, Easton, Phil, and Marc."

"Okay, plan B. Because I'm a resourceful man. I'll retire them all and bring them with us. I'll even arrange homeschooling for Isaac."

Keeley laughs at my expense, and I pull her face toward mine, kissing her to stop it. "Plan C, we work for another ten years, taking the occasional breaks to have sex in different villas around the world?"

Keeley hums. "I like the sound of that. Where should we go next?"

"How about Greece? I'll have the jet ready for the day after we win the Super Bowl."

"That'll be my busiest time. How about two weeks after, when all of the hype has died down?"

"Done. Prepare to be well and truly relaxed." I lie back, tucking my arm behind my head as my mind starts whirling. Greece sounds perfect.

"Are you going to let me join the mile high club this time?"

"Absolutely not." I shake my head, not even looking her way. "My reasons haven't changed. No one but me gets to hear your screams when you come."

"People hear that all the time. We're not exactly quiet. Hotel rooms aren't soundproof."

"Maybe not. But those people aren't my staff that see us regularly."

"I can be quiet."

I turn her way, leveling her with a stare. "No, you can't. I had to cover your mouth with my hand the weekend we went away with Easton and Paige. Just in case they came back early from their walk."

Keeley's lips quirk, undoubtedly at the memory of that weekend. "You caught me by surprise that day. I wasn't expecting it. It still makes me laugh."

"Laugh? Keeley, I had your legs around your ears while I plowed into you; you were not laughing at the time."

At my description, Keeley giggles. "I don't mean that. I mean that we were worried about Paige coming home, when it would usually be the kid sneaking around and trying not to get caught by the parent."

"Please don't make me think about that."

"Why? They have sex."

"No, they don't. Ever."

"Yeah, okay. Anyway, back to the jet. Why have a private plane if you can't join the mile high club?"

"So we can go where we want whenever we want. I thought that was obvious."

"Fine. You win." She smiles sweetly and I groan.

I may be a powerful man in the business world, but this woman right here has me wrapped around her finger, and she knows it.

Looks like I'm joining the mile high club on the next trip.

My alarm goes off for a second time and Keeley holds me tighter. "Don't go."

"It's eight, Keeley, and you have to get up too."

"It's eight?" She jumps up so fast that I chuckle until her gloriously naked body brushes past me.

"Change of plans." I curl my arms around her waist and pull her back onto the bed, settling on top of her when she spreads her legs. "I'm canceling the nine o'clock meeting. They don't know we were at a party last night. I'll say I double-booked myself."

"Oh, yeah? What's so important that you'd take off work?"

"You. Always you. And I'm going to need a full hour to get the job done."

I grab my phone to email Tabitha just as a strange message comes through.

LUKE BENNETT ADDED YOU TO THE GROUP "STORM FOREVER"

What the fuck? "What's this?" I show Keeley and she bursts out laughing, covering her face with her hands.

"I wondered how long it would take for them to initiate you."

"Initiate?"

"Yep."

LUKE BENNETT: I'm reviving the group chat. I thought I should add D'Angelo since he's one of us now

SALVATORE: Hi. Thanks. I think? What does "one of us" mean exactly?

"I'm not going to have to do any crazy shit, am I?"

"I don't think so." Keeley suppresses her next laugh, but she's practically bursting at the seams.

LUKE BENNETT: The HABS

ZANE FITZPATRICK: What the actual fuck is HABS?

EASTON WILDER: Whatever is it I want out

LUKE BENNETT: Aww don't worry, East, we won't talk about our sex lives on this chat. I imagine that would get awkward

ZANE FITZPATRICK: 😂 Sorry, East, but that was funny

REED COOMBS: You can't invite Mr. D'Angelo into the group and then be a dick about it. Some of us are still his players. My apologies, sir

SALVATORE: You don't have to call me sir, Reed. I was at your bachelor party, remember?

REED COOMBS: Right. We've moved past that. Sorry, I get into work mode during the season

UNKNOWN: I'm just catching up. Salvatore, it's nice to have you here. But back to an earlier question, which I'm almost afraid to ask… What's HABS?

"Who's this?" I ask Keeley, showing her my phone.

"That's probably Dylan. He's on the chat too."

"How do you know all of this? Do you know what HABS means?"

Keeley snorts and I frown.

LUKE BENNETT: I thought it was obvious. Husbands and boyfriends of strong women

What? Keeley's soft laughter gets louder, and I shake my head with a chuckle. I'll endure whatever this is if it makes her *that* happy.

ZANE FITZPATRICK: Wow

EASTON WILDER: How the fuck was that obvious? I'm out, guys

EASTON WILDER LEFT THE GROUP

LUKE BENNETT ADDED EASTON WILDER TO THE GROUP

LUKE BENNETT: After all these years, you're still pulling that stunt and expecting us to just let it happen?

SALVATORE: I'm confused

"Do I really want to be a part of this?"

"Absolutely. You heard Luke. You're one of them now."

REED COOMBS: That feeling never goes away, Sal. When you open this chat, you never know what you're going to get. Welcome

SALVATORE: Okay.

ZANE FITZPATRICK: HABS is growing on me

REED COOMBS: Me too

EASTON WILDER: Why are we friends?

LUKE BENNETT: Because you love us

LUKE BENNETT: It's a new year. Here's to all the new adventures together

REED COOMBS: To a year of fun

ZANE FITZPATRICK: To winning another Super Bowl

SALVATORE: Hear, Hear.

Maybe this won't be so bad.

LUKE BENNETT: To a lifetime of happiness

EASTON WILDER: Fuck my life. When is this going to end?

THE END

Thank you for reading Salvatore and Keeley's story. While the San Francisco End Game series is now complete, a couple of the side characters are getting their own stories—Beckett and Callum. Both their books are currently available for pre order.

Keep reading for a sneak peek of Beckett's story.

Also By Katherine Jay

COMING SOON

Blinding Lights (Beckett and Lily)

Callum's book (details TBA)

SAN FRANCISCO END GAME SERIES

Beautiful Storm (Luke and Amelia)

Delicate Storm (Easton and Paige)

Reckless Storm (Reed and Hayley)

Careless Storm (Zane and Blair)

Fierce Storm (Salvatore and Keeley)

HOLIDAY ROMANCE

Mistletoe Mail (Mason and Jenna)

SYMPHONY OF SOUND DUET

The Sound Of Silence (Jesse and Willow)

The Sound Of Forever (Jesse and Willow)

HEARTSTRINGS SERIES

When Nothing Else Matters (Summer and Dylan)

Still Here Without You (Joel and Delilah)

It Had To Be Us (Logan and Dani)

Truly Madly Deeply Mine (Wes and Lucy)

A Sky Full Of Stars (Thomas and Lainey)

Ain't No Sunshine (Nate and Cory) – novella

ALL KATHERINE'S BOOKS ARE AVAILABLE ON AMAZON AND KINDLE UNLIMITED

Sneak peek of Beckett's story

Note: this excerpt is unedited and subject to change.

The turf springs perfectly under my foot as I pivot right and launch the ball to my teammate Easton. The ball hits its mark and I take a deep breath, letting the salty air fill my lungs before lining up in position again.

It may have taken longer than I expected to feel at home in San Francisco, but moving here last season was the best decision I've ever made.

I don't want to completely shit on the team I left behind, the franchise that supported me from the start of my professional football career, or the coaches and players that have been a huge part of my life over the last ten years. But we never made the Super Bowl, we never even made the playoffs, and while I could handle that when we were a team that gelled... by the end, the Colorado Cougars supported a culture I didn't want to be a part of.

No one cared, they focused more on theatrics, on being the team everyone talked about. From their over the top touch down celebrations to a questionable mascot. We were loved, sure. But my focus has always been on the game and nothing was going to change that. Something my teammates seemed to have lost sight of.

The San Francisco Storm may have had their fair share of the spotlight, more often than not being portrayed in a negative light, but their new owner has worked hard to prove that the media had it wrong. That at the heart of it all, the team was a family. They faced controversy together, they had each other's backs, and they always put the game first. As evidenced by their two Super Bowl wins in the last four years.

While the camaraderie and "family" talk was more like a repellant when it was first mentioned, the idea of a team working together cohesively and getting shit done, was impossible to turn down.

And I've never looked back. We didn't win last season. We didn't even get close. But the team's confidence never once wavered. Now we're back, stronger than ever. Their pure grit and determination is something I can grasp.

With the Storm, my dream of winning a championship at least once in my career is closer than ever before. Nothing is standing in my way.

I'm living that dream.

Apart from one minor hiccup.

DON'T MISS THE REST OF KATHERINE JAY'S

SAN FRANCISCO END GAME SERIES

BEAUTIFUL STORM

An enemies to lovers, accidental pregnancy sports romance

Luke Bennett wasn't supposed to come back into my life... and we weren't supposed to end our night in a hate fueled one night stand.

But we did.

Now, not only do we have to work together, closely, I'm also having his baby.

I don't need his help, but the more he offers, with his genuine smile and caring tone, the more I want it.

The question is, can we move on from our broken past to raise a baby together? Or is it going to end in a beautiful and messy storm?

DELICATE STORM

A single dad, forbidden sports romance

Easton Wilder is a newly single dad fresh off a Super Bowl win. Paige D'Angelo is the team owner's daughter who blew in like a hurricane, turning his carefully guarded world upside down.

With his ex making life difficult and his son counting on him to keep it together, Easton has every reason to stay away from Paige.

But staying away doesn't seem to be an option.

Their connection is fire, and for the first time, Easton's beginning to understand what a true relationship should be.

But is it worth the fallout that could take them all down?

Sometimes you have to take a risk and find out.

AVAILABLE NOW ON AMAZON, KINDLE UNLIMITED AND AUDIBLE

RECKLESS STORM

A fake dating sports romance

Reed Coombs has it all — Super Bowl rings, adoring fans, and a golden boy reputation. But beneath the glamour lies a decade-long unrequited crush he's desperate to move on from. Enter Hayley Jackman: a fierce Hollywood starlet who needs her wild reputation tamed for a coveted role. Their solution? A fake relationship that gives them both exactly what they need.

Or so they think.

What starts as a playful ruse quickly becomes something neither of them bargained for, and suddenly their feelings are anything but fake.

Seems simple enough.

But what happens if falling in love turns out to be the least of their worries?

CARELESS STORM

A right person / wrong time sports romance

Blair Stevens' thought she had it all — until one devastating moment shattered her world.

Seven years ago, Blair shared a secret love and a future with her brother's best friend, Zane Fitzpatrick. But fate sent them spiraling in opposite directions.

Now she's drifting through life, dating Zane's biggest rival, while he's the NFL's infamous bad boy, making headlines for all the wrong reasons.

Just when she begins questioning everything, Zane reappears, looking at her like no time has passed. And despite her efforts to keep her distance, Zane's unwavering support begins to reignite the strength she thought she'd lost forever.

As the undeniable pull brings them closer together, they're forced to face something bigger.

Because it turns out, Blair's not the only one who's broken. And the only way forward is to face the past... together.

About the Author

Katherine writes angsty and emotional, character-driven romance full of banter, steam and the kind of love that's always worth fighting for.

When she's not lost in a fictional world (writing or reading), she's travelling, falling down a binge-worthy television rabbit hole, or letting the perfect song absolutely wreck her.

Katherine lives in Australia with her husband and two boys, which means she's constantly outnumbered, but wouldn't have it any other way.

For more information, visit

https://www.katherinejayauthor.com

If you want to stay up to date with all things Katherine Jay, come and join her Facebook Reader Group – The Angsty Lovers Playlist — for fun, exclusive content and sneak peeks. Or sign up to her newsletter via her website.

Are you following Katherine on social media? If not, you can find her on Instagram, Facebook and TikTok.

www.ingramcontent.com/pod-product-compliance
Lightning Source LLC
LaVergne TN
LVHW012338100826
845148LV00018B/2709